The Lieutenant Must Be Mad

The Lieutenant Must be Mad

Hans Hellmut Kirst

Translated from the German by
Richard and Clara Winston

Mayflower

Granada Publishing Limited
Published in 1974 by Mayflower Books Ltd
Frogmore, St Albans, Herts AL2 2NF

First published in Great Britain by
George G. Harrap and Co Ltd 1951

Made and printed in Great Britain by
Cox & Wyman Ltd, London, Reading and Fakenham
Set in Intertype Plantin

THE LIEUTENANT MUST BE MAD

CHAPTER ONE

IN the sallow lustreless twilight the goods train rolled into the station at Rehhausen and came to a stop. It stood still warily, expectantly, like an animal that had been slogging through mud.

Lieutenant Strick came out of a goods-wagon, dragging his kitbag. He dropped it on the platform, where it tipped over and lay still, like a corpse wrapped in canvas. Strick looked round, but no one paid any attention to him. He might have been non-existent.

The station-office door opened wide. Out of it stalked an Army major, who went up to the engine-driver and casually exchanged papers with him. Then a squad of soldiers trotted across the lines and uncoupled two goods-wagons.

The train rolled on.

Lieutenant Strick slung his kitbag on his back, straightened his belt and pistol-holster, and walked towards the gate. The major threw him a searching look, and waited to be saluted. Strick raised his hand to his cap. The major responded, his salute a shade more off-hand.

'You have been travelling in a goods train,' the major said. 'That is not allowed.' He spoke as if he were reading out the regulations, his tone expressing annoyance.

Strick dropped his kitbag on the bench beside the closed gate, sat down on the bench, and looked at the major. 'I've had to do a lot of things that aren't allowed,' he said. Pulling out a handkerchief whose original colour was by now indeterminate, he blew his nose.

The major thrust his right thumb into his belt and worked it back and forth to smooth out a disturbing wrinkle in his tunic. A gold swastika glittered on the perfectly tailored garment. 'Leave?' he asked sharply.

'No, transfer.'

'Here, to Rehhausen?'

'Rehhausen Garrison Headquarters.'

The major turned away irritably, but with deliberate dignity. His boots gleamed. The back of his neck had the plump pinkness of a young pig. An energetic neck, Strick thought, a stiff neck, stout neck, prettily padded and stuffed neck.

'Are you,' he called out to the neck, 'the station commandant?'

The other continued on his way, answering with an unfriendly 'Yes.'

'May I use your telephone?'

'No,' the station commandant said. 'This is not a post-office.' He slammed the door of the station-office behind him.

Strick looked round. The station was almost deserted. No passengers, no railway men, no cars. Beyond were trees, deserted streets, houses that looked like match-boxes. Round about the hills blinked in the setting sun like hunched-up old women. Hardly anyone in sight except the soldiers lazily working at the uncoupled wagons.

The war is pretty quiet round here, Strick thought. But that was what you would expect in a remote town in Mainfranken. Somewhere in the neighbourhood there would be a few prisoner-of-war camps, a training battalion, a factory making shell casings, and smack in the middle of it all a headquarters to which he had been transferred for rest and recuperation after his service at the front. A fresh-made bed for tired bones. It would be his first bed after three years on the Eastern Front.

He unbuckled a pocket in the side of his kitbag, and took out a towel and a cake of soap. Then he tossed his cap on the bench at his side, unstrapped his belt and holster, and stripped off his shirt. He went up to the water-tank in the middle of the platform, and tried the tap to see whether it worked. Then he took off his vest and began to wash.

The station commandant reappeared, and strolled up to him with a look of intense disgust. 'Are you washing here?' he said reproachfully. He sounded as though he had come upon a telephone-box that was being mistaken for a toilet.

'As you see,' Strick said, soaping himself.

The major looked delicately astonished. 'These are front-line manners, I suppose,' he growled.

'Have people at home given up washing?' Strick snorted. The cold water felt marvellous. A thick layer of dust and sweat was gradually coming off his skin; it was as if all the filth of the front were pouring down the drain. If he opened his eyes now he knew the world would look brighter. He had discovered that in childhood: if you closed your eyes tight and then opened them suddenly the light shot into them as if it were springing to an assault.

The major examined him with silent distrust, as though Strick were a horse that some one was trying to palm off on him. He saw shoulders none too broad, a starved lanky frame, taut skin, a tanned, bony face, heavily lined, unshaven, looking as though it were permanently grimy. The kind of men they made into officers nowadays, the station commandant thought, sincerely amazed. Really embarrassing to see an ersatz like this one. Mere tools for transmitting orders, without any dignity, style, or knowledge of how to behave in public! Outsiders. But you had to put up with them; what else was there to do in time of need?

Shrugging his shoulders, the major stalked over to the uncoupled wagons, which were being unloaded. 'Get a move on, he called out to the fatigue squad. 'Those boxes must be taken to my office at once. No loafing!'

Strick slipped on his vest, rolled the soap up in the towel, and went back to the bench where he had left his kitbag. He began quietly packing up his things.

Under the major's obtrusive supervision the squad moved the packing-cases no more quickly, but with a great deal more noise. The boxes thudded down on the trollies; springs groaned and a booming echo rolled through the deserted station. The major made crowing sounds of encouragement.

Strick looked up. This major squawked like a gramophone with a broken needle, he thought. Those were big, heavy wooden boxes with a large red 'D' painted with a broad brush on each of their six sides. The danger sign grinned impudently at him.

Strick knew the boxes well. They were one link in a chain of events he was not likely to forget. He had been present when they were loaded aboard the train in the rear operations area of the Eastern Front, and he had got in with them because the train was to pass through Rehhausen. The goods-wagons were filled with scrap, empty boxes, defective equipment, the offal of war, the excremental products of war's non-stop ingestion which were to be reconverted into new food for the insatiable maw.

At the time one wagon had been almost empty. It was one of the two now standing here at Rehhausen station. Wounded men had been lying moaning on the dusty platform, their faces yellow, their blankets encrusted with blood, their bandages stinking of pus, foul water, and carbolic. Strick had gone to the officer in charge of the goods train and persuaded him to put the wounded men into the empty wagon. They would be taken off somewhere behind the lines, he pointed out, and that was better than leaving them here to die.

Then along came the commandant of the front-line railway station, and behind him men were rolling trollies loaded with boxes, the big red 'D' smeared boldly on their sides. Those boxes had been placed aboard the train, and the wounded men laid out again on the trampled stretch of ground that was called a railway platform. When Strick protested the station commandant, a captain, coldly told him to go to hell. Strick tried to argue, and the captain threatened to have him arrested. 'Just one more word and I'll give the order. These boxes are full of secret material, mostly documents. They must go; orders from General Headquarters. Priority One A. Here is the invoice.'

Strick could see that under certain circumstances documents might be more significant than human lives. He got into the wagon, and watched in fascination as the boxes were hoisted aboard the train. He no longer dared to look at the wounded men, but he heard them; especially he heard the groaning of one man. It sounded like an unending, insane, suppressed giggle, the laughter of delirium, forced out between parted yellow teeth. That dying wreck from whom the breath bubbled like gurgling water had once been a strong human being. Strick knew him, thought of him as a friend. He had always felt envious of him; at the same time, he had really liked him. Perhaps the man was no longer alive, since these boxes mattered more than the little life that had been left in him. How cheap it was – a hole in the body, from which sticky blood trickled into the dirt, and the entire man was not worth a few pounds of paper.

Secret documents! Priority One A! That was what the captain had said. And now those boxes were being unloaded haphazardly here in Rehhausen, like so many sacks of flour. There was something wrong here. Strick got up, straightened automatically, and put on his belt and his cap. Then he walked slowly towards those boxes with their big, smeary red 'D's' grinning at him.

Corporal Vogel deliberately removed his socks and laid them, one after the other, upon the table. Two feet away Corporal Hoepfner was consuming half a pound of ersatz sausage meat, and, to make sure his supper was well balanced, munching a slice of white bread simultaneously.

Hoepfner chewed. His chewing was the only sound in the

room. It annoyed Vogel that the fellow did not even notice his socks. Vogel pushed them a foot closer to Hoepfner. Hoepfner cut off another bite of sausage-meat and swallowed it. All his senses appeared to be concentrated upon the act of eating.

Vogel began cutting his toe-nails, performing the ceremony with devotion and care. 'There's supposed to be a new officer coming, I hear,' he remarked, as casually as if he were saying that it was time he washed his feet. Hoepfner only nodded.

'What's his name?' Vogel asked.

'Strick. A lieutenant.'

'Are you sure the name is Strick?'

'Sure,' Hoepfner said, his jaws grinding away, his eyes vacant as those of a ruminating cow.

'Have you seen my brief-case?' Vogel asked. He had managed, with some effort, to swing his leg up on the table, but even this made no impression upon Hoepfner.

'What brief-case?' Hoepfner asked.

Vogel opened his locker and took out a light brown leather brief-case. It had a double lock, several inside compartments, two outside pockets. A handsome article, especially in times like these.

'Keep your filthy paws off it,' Vogel said, as Hoepfner reached for it. Hoepfner stopped chewing, moved closer, and inspected the brief-case with an expert's eye. Vogel turned it round, showed all sides of it, then opened the locks and let Hoepfner see the inside. Hoepfner was enthusiastic. 'We can use it,' he said. 'How much?'

Vogel snapped the locks shut. 'What I paid for it,' he replied. 'Twenty-five marks.'

But that was giving the thing away; it was too cheap to be true. Hoepfner immediately became suspicious. 'What else?'

'Nothing else. Twenty-five marks.'

'Do you want leave?'

'No.'

'Food?'

'No.'

'Drink?'

'No.'

'What then?'

'Nothing.'

But finally Vogel came out with it. 'I want to be an orderly.'

Hoepfner was mildly amazed. 'But you are already.'

'I want to be this new officer's orderly – this Strick's.'

'Why?'

'Don't ask such idiotic questions. New beards are easier to shave.'

Hoepfner grinned his understanding. 'Good,' he said, 'I'll talk to the Old Man tomorrow.'

'Why tomorrow? Do it tonight. What are you his orderly for? Run over to the Old Man, dangle this thing in front of his nose, and tell him what to do.'

Hoepfner agreed. He wrapped the brief-case in brown paper, tucked it under his arm, and sauntered off. Business was business – if necessary even after hours.

The Rehhausen headquarters building was inside the barracks area of Training Battalion 434. In addition to this battalion a company of guards for two prisoner-of-war camps and an Army prison were attached to the Rehhausen headquarters. The Commandant of Rehhausen was Colonel Mueller. The chief of the guards company, directly subordinate to Mueller, was Captain Wolf. Corporal Hoepfner was Captain Wolf's orderly. Hoepfner's friend, comrade, and room-mate was Corporal Vogel, who at the moment was orderly, photographer, and typist, depending on which of his talents was most in demand. Sometimes he was all three at once.

The package in his left hand, Hoepfner shuffled down the long corridor, descended a flight of stairs to the ground floor, opened the double doors bearing the inscription: REHHAUSEN HEADQUARTERS, and stopped in front of another door marked: 'Captain Wolf, Chief of Headquarters Personnel'. Hoepfner knocked. A powerful voice grunted, 'Come in.'

Captain Wolf was sitting deep in an arm-chair, his legs stretched out and spread wide apart. Over a glass of beer he was looking at pictures of his wife and child. He was proud of his loved ones, as he called them. At times, Hoepfner knew, the Old Man would fall into reveries, and would drink to them and sit nodding contentedly over their pictures. Such a strong sense of family had to be cultivated, and here there was plenty of time to devote to it. Rehhausen could be a damnably dull little place. Few duties, long evenings, a little drinking, a little fun with the boys, and now and then the female of the species, to forget the War. No more than a soldier deserved. That was all in the tradition. And now and then a glance at a family photo, a glass or two to commemorate old joys, and a few appreciative words. There was always plenty to drink round here – for Wolf, at any rate.

Wolf took a shrewd look at the brief-case that Hoepfner held under his knobby nose. His thick, stubby fingers rubbed the leather. A useful article, excellent quality. He could use it. 'How much?'

'Only fifty marks,' Hoepfner said.

Wolf laid the brief-case down on the table, took a note out of his wallet. Hoepfner pocketed it.

'Anything else?' Wolf asked.

Hoepfner, as if he were requesting orders, said: 'The new officer, sir – are we supposed to be his orderlies too?'

'Who do you mean by "we"?'

'Vogel and me.'

'Not you, Hoepfner; I need you myself. But Vogel can go ahead. Won't do him any harm if he wags his tail a little more, anyhow.'

'That's what I thought, sir.'

'By the way,' Wolf said, 'Lieutenant Strick has already arrived. He's supposed to be down at the station. The station commandant informed me. You can go and fetch his bags. Lieutenant Strick will share Lieutenant Rabe's room for the present. Fix it up, Hoepfner.'

Hoepfner saluted stiffly, and made himself scarce. The longer I hang around here the more things the Old Man will think of, he reflected. Late at night, at that. Absolutely a menace to a soldier's private life.

He shuffled off through the double doors, up the stairs, and down the long corridor. When he reached his room he said to Vogel, 'It's all fixed. Go down to the station right away. Lieutenant Strick is waiting there for you, with his baggage.'

'What about my twenty-five marks?'

'You'll get it tomorrow,' Hoepfner said, remembering in time that Wolf had given him a fifty-mark note. The note would have to be changed first. He'd go over to the canteen now, and perhaps after the second glass of wine he would get a chance to give buxom Barbara a tender pat on her round behind.

Vogel got ready to go to the station. Hoepfner, although his mind was mostly taken up with Barbara's generous curves, observed his room-mate's zeal with some surprise. What was the matter with the boy – was he getting an attack of disciplinitis? In these times, and here in Rehhausen! Well, let him if he wanted to . . . One man's ambition was another man's comfort.

Vogel really seemed to want to put on a good show. He strode out through the door much faster than usual. 'Button your shirt, Vogel,' the sentry said. Instead of stopping to bicker, Vogel simply mumbled, 'Shut your trap,' and descended the hill from the barracks towards Rehhausen and the railway station, where Strick was waiting.

What could have happened to him, Vogel wondered. He'd always been a queer duck, a blank page waiting to be written on. The fact that he'd risen to lieutenant wasn't in itself a bad sign. Even generals could be decent guys, especially when they took off their uniforms, literally or figuratively. All is not brass that glitters. He and Strick had played together in the sand, copied from each other's work at school, thumped waltzes on the organ in the village church, fought over the baker's daughter (what a dull piece she'd turned out to be, with her respectable marriage and her two kids), and nailed the door to the toilet shut when the headmaster was inside. Then the War – five years' interruption to friendships. No meeting all that time.

We'll see what's happened, Vogel thought. We'll see.

There were no documents in those boxes. Lieutenant Strick felt sure of that by now. He lifted one of them. Heavy, but not full of paper.

The station commandant was standing behind him. 'What do you want with those boxes?' he asked.

'I'm wondering what's in them,' Strick said.

'Is that all you have to do?'

'At the monent, yes.'

'I am a major,' the station commandant said. His voice was low and edgy.

'So I see.'

'Then behave accordingly,' the major said.

'I shall try – sir.'

'You seem to have forgotten a good many things up there at the front. No manners at all, no example to the men. You have come from the front, haven't you?' The major permitted a nuance of benevolence to creep into his voice, a touch of sympathy, which might be interpreted as a prelude to full forgiveness.

'Russia,' Strick said. 'Three years in Russia without a break.' After a brief pause he added, 'Sir.'

Well, that was something the major could understand. Good

Lord – Russia, and three whole years of it. Without a break. No wonder the veneer peeled off. No wonder forms were forgotten, and the hand grew accustomed to scratching the head rather than delivering a regulation salute. This poor devil of a front-line soldier would have to acquire the officers'-club tone all over again. The major became more genial. 'Come and have a drop of cognac with me, comrade.'

Strick said no thanks. The major turned away from this hopeless character. He went back to supervising the unloading, and had the boxes deposited in his office. He tossed a steady flow of directions at the fatigue squad.

Strick watched the boxes disappearing. And beyond them he saw the little station near the Eastern Front. And he saw the doomed yellow face of his wounded friend. He could hear nothing; it was a soundless picture that came to his mind, silent as a monument. He tore his eyes away from the boxes, and glanced up at the faded façade of the station to where there was a small arrow marked in irregular letters, 'Military Police Post'. He followed the arrow.

The M.P. sergeant started to his feet as Strick entered the post. Strick gestured 'at ease', and stepped into the circle of light cast by a green-shaded desk-lamp. The sergeant did not see his face; he saw only the chest of the man before him, with the German Cross in gold on the right side, the Iron Cross, First Class, on the left, the wide bar awarded for close-quarters combat, several ribbons, and the red ribbon of the Iron Cross, Second Class. The decorations alone impressed the sergeant. He was at once as receptive as a microphone.

'Is it part of your job to confiscate embezzled Army property?' Strick asked.

'Of course,' the sergeant assured him. He hastily added, 'If there is clear proof of embezzlement. That's regulations.'

'Suppose certain packing-cases have been shipped which are billed as containing secret documents. But suppose something entirely different is in them?'

'What, for example?' the sergeant asked.

'You open the boxes and you'll find out.'

The sergeant began brooding over the regulations book. 'I must have the proof first. Then I can open the boxes.'

'But the only way you can get the proof is by opening the boxes.'

The sergeant had to think that over carefully. He went

through a sheaf of supplementary instructions, supplements to supplementary instructions, and references to special cases. Finally he said, 'It could be done on suspicion if there were any grounds for it.'

'There are grounds for my suspicion,' Strick said.

Strick's decorations glittered in the sergeant's eyes, and hastened his decision. It seemed as if the lieutenant's quiet but increasingly incisive voice were gently poking him in the ribs. He always felt his first reaction to possible unpleasantness in the region of his stomach. 'Very well,' he said. 'Where are the boxes?'

'In the station commandant's office.'

The sergeant sat down again, slowly, as though he were being lowered by a rope. He was a man who had never overstepped any line, and he did not intend to begin now. 'Then it's all right,' he said. 'The case is clear. It's not our business. That's outside my authority.'

Strick became insistent. He spoke sharply, in the tone of an officer issuing orders. The rain of words battered the complacent sergeant from all sides; he shifted about restlessly. For a while he just squirmed. Finally he reached for the telephone and called his superior's office. On the other end of the line an M.P. officer, presumably called away from a pleasurable evening, gave the unfortunate sergeant a real rocket. He bellowed something about fantasies, shell-shock, and the stupid obsessions of certain people who sniff profiteering in every package. Then he hung up. The sergeant felt like a schoolboy who'd been given a dressing down. He was obviously sorry about the whole business, but regulations, superiors – in short, the War. . . . Regulations, regulations – there they were, down in the book. Strick knew the score. He left abruptly.

It was dark now. The square in front of the station looked like a cemetery without the crosses. A dim, blacked-out light burned above the entrance, and threw a wide streak on the pavement, like a scribble made by dirty chalk. A soldier was standing in this light, apparently waiting. Strick went up to him. The shadowy figure removed his cap.

'Vogel!' Strick exclaimed. He held out his hand. Vogel moved his face into the light, and twisted it up in a broad smile, a smile of clownish exaggeration so there could be no mistake about his reaction – and perhaps his idea was also to conceal an entirely different emotion. Masked faces, primitive, non-committal – that was the way people met nowadays.

'The lieutenant still remembers me,' Vogel said, speaking the grateful formula in a somewhat croaking voice.

Strick, as though trying to dispel the dampening effect of surprise by loudness and jollity, boomed, 'How are you? What are you doing here, of all places?' And Vogel, standing stiffly, a skinny caricature of a sculptured hero, likewise boomed into the gathering darkness: 'Corporal Vogel reporting for duty as orderly to Lieutenant Strick.'

Strick laughed heartily. What a sight to come drifting into view out of the dense mists of these times! Vogel, his old chum! Hard-boiled as they came, a cunning dog, of course – that he'd always been – but a bit of home, of boyhood, of the living past. Those narrow, rounded shoulders carried round on them a whole world, a world which had seemed as thoroughly erased as an arithmetic example on the blackboard. 'Vogel,' he said again and again. 'Vogel! How are you, old man? What the devil are you doing here? So you're still alive. ... I'd recognize you anywhere.'

They confronted one another under the dim light, each peering into the other's face as one would examine a successful portrait. The streak of dingy light was now falling full upon them. Theirs were sallow, drained, pinched faces, the wizened faces of old thieves on twenty-five-year-old bodies – faces that looked as though they had been moulded out of paper and glue.

He hasn't changed much, Vogel thought. He hasn't really changed much, Strick thought. In Vogel's mind this thought meant: he's still the same old idiotic dreamer, romantic, and reformer. And in Strick's mind it meant: still the same old sly trickster, mocker, and shamefaced friend of everybody who gets pushed around.

'Where is your baggage?' Vogel asked. 'Permit me to transport the war booty of a tried-and-true hero and much-decorated defender of the Fatherland.' He lightly brushed the back of his hand over Strick's medals and ribbons. 'Don't even tinkle,' he said ruefully. Strick laughed. 'Do I have to commandeer a truck to take your boxes, sir?'

Boxes. That was a reminder. Strick instantly sobered. 'What kind of man is the Commandant?' he asked. Vogel considered briefly, trying to guess the meaning of this abrupt mental leap. Then he answered:

'Your superior and mine, that is one sure thing.'

'Would it be possible to see him now?'

'Now? Absolutely not. By this time our universally respected Commandant is in bed – usually not alone. You're on the home front now – don't forget that.'

'The place sounds like a high-class pigsty.'

'All the more reason to give you a hearty welcome to it!' Strick drew Vogel along towards the bench where his kitbag was lying. 'Vogel,' he said, 'you're better acquainted with conditions here than I am. Who round here would be willing to fix the station commandant's wagon?'

'How long have you been here?' Vogel demanded incredulously.

'An hour.'

'You've got a lot of ideas in sixty minutes.'

Vogel tested the weight of the kitbag he was supposed to carry. 'You haven't overloaded yourself,' he remarked. 'Or do you have a number of suitcases coming later?'

'This is all.'

'Not much for five years of war.'

'It grew less and less as I went along.'

'Such is life,' Vogel remarked, with an air of being lost in reverie. 'When I travel in my capacity of corporal I always carry a lot of baggage.'

A match flared. Strick held a cigarette between his thin lips. The shadow of his nose threw a line across his forehead. He held out the packet of cigarettes to Vogel, who glanced at the brand and handed it back. 'I don't smoke dried cow-dung,' he said. 'These smoke-generators are good enough for heroes. The home front fights with better equipment.' He snapped open a well-stocked cigarette-case, and offered one of his. They smoked in silence.

'Don't you think there's somebody here in Rehhausen who would be glad to do in the station commandant if he got a chance?' Strick asked.

'They're all glad he's here. They live a lot better because of him.'

'Then the man's a profiteer?'

'I wouldn't go that far. He just makes use of his opportunities. You might call it plain consideration for everybody's belly, including his own. How can you tell these days where consideration ends and profiteering begins?'

The cigarettes were glowing points in the darkness. 'The nearest General Headquarters is in Würzburg, isn't it?'

Vogel nodded, then remarked, 'And they're just dying for you to give them work and make trouble for them. You won't get very far with the Army boys.'

'Then?'

Vogel took a long drag on his cigarette. It glowed briefly, and cast a spot of light into his dark, alert eyes. 'Gestapo methods,' he said in a low voice, stressing each syllable. Strick did not answer. Vogel, as though continuing a muted monologue, said, 'The secret military police in Würzburg have just been assigned a new chief. He was transferred there from the Gestapo, or maybe ordered to take over for the Gestapo – I don't know which. Anyway, he's supposed to light a good hot fire under the Army's tail. The man's name is Gareis. He's your undertaker for inter-Army funerals.'

Still Strick did not answer. He let the butt of his cigarette drop to the ground. It fell in a puddle, and went out with a hiss. So – the man's name was Gareis. How did Vogel know? Who had given him this information? Why did he mention this man's name right off – as though he'd been waiting to do so? Chance, probably. In any case, it didn't matter.

'I have a few things still to do,' Strick said. 'I'll be obliged if you'll take my kitbag back to the barracks.'

'When will you be coming?'

'I don't know how long it will take me here.'

'All right. I'll see that the guard shows you the way when you come. We'll see each other again tomorrow morning.' Vogel shouldered the kitbag. 'Pretty slim for a lieutenant,' he said with disapproval. Then he left, and was swallowed up by the darkness. It was as though a heavy theatre curtain had dropped. But his even, quiet step could be heard for quite a while.

Strick lit another cigarette. He took two hasty puffs, then threw it away and resolutely got to his feet.

Inspector Gareis, on transfer to the secret military police, was a small, quick-moving man with a round, melancholy face, protruding ears, and weary, lustreless eyes. He did not smoke, did not drink, did not care for women. He had only one passion – to catch people who had committed any kind of crime. He was a bloodhound with the ludicrous face of a well-fed rabbit. Once he had been a highly esteemed detective for the missing-persons squad, then one of the shining lights of the Gestapo. But one day in Stettin he had the awkward idea of arresting the gauleiter at a public meeting. The evidence he had on the man was complete and absolutely damning – though most of it had been extorted by torture – but Gareis's lack of tact, his recklessness in proceeding against superiors, and his total disregard for the prestige of the Government and the Party leaders resulted in his transfer to the secret military police. Himmler was supposed to have remarked that if that sharp little bastard wanted to raise a stink he could do it in the Army, where it would do no harm.

At the moment Gareis was highly dissatisfied with himself and his position. There was not a thing going on here in Mainfranken. It was the quietest kind of backwater, deserted by God and all would-be gaolbirds. Not a trace of espionage, sabotage, or organized sedition in the Army. Now and then there was a vulgar escape from a prisoner-of-war camp, nothing more. Gareis caught those clumsy idiots with one hand tied behind his back. His network of road guards was perfect. The system of cordons he had worked out had proved its worth. What else was there? Maybe the new group of captive British officers would provide him with a little chase. They were capable of some sort of foolishness, and a little action would be welcome. But would they try it? He couldn't very well go and ask them to. At any rate it would be nice. But too good to be true. This damned province of Mainfranken was a mattress where you could loaf away the whole War.

Gareis, who spent his days in his office or in his car whenever he was not sleeping in his shabby furnished room, was drafting new control plans. He drew delicate pencil lines like spider-webs across the map. His system hinged on surprise moves that gave the impression of utter confusion, but whose mathematically logical stabs worked out beautifully in the end. What he wanted was an uprising, a large-scale escape, a mass landing of parachute troops. Then he could show the kind of man he was.

The inspector doodled sketches on the margins of the local newspaper, the *Mainfränkischer Beobachter.* His figures had extended necks, broad heads, and long fingers. These were symbols. The long fingers indicated criminal temperament, the breadth of the heads expressed the degree of instinct-impulses, and the longer the neck the easier it was to cut the throat. Whoever died, died guilty, was Gareis's conviction. No one ever lived without guilt. People escaped death only because they'd been overlooked.

The telephone rang. Gareis finished off his last figure, giving its head a backward tilt indicative of intelligence in the criminal. Then he lifted the phone. 'Gareis speaking.' He was drawing in some bristling hair when, abruptly, he stopped doodling and laid the pencil down.

'Who is this? What are you? Give me all the details. Loaded when and where? Declared as what? Where and by whom unloaded? Where stored?'

Gareis pushed the newspaper aside and busily took notes. He framed his questions quickly and precisely. The answers he heard were factual, brief, and illuminating. Together they formed a comprehensive picture, like a good military map. Gareis was pleased with that. He never felt a real liking for anything or anyone; he felt only various degrees of appreciation or of silent contempt. This man on the other end of the line was giving him useful facts. That called for a high degree of appreciation.

'Where are you phoning from? Good. Hang up. I'll call you back at once.'

This was a precaution. Gareis never worked without checking on his position every step of the way. He knew thousands of mistakes that could be made – and were usually made by others. Lifting the receiver again, he spoke to his operator. 'Give me the Army prison in Rehhausen. But keep me plugged in while you're getting the connection.'

The operator placed the call: Würzburg central, Rehhausen central, Rehhausen Army prison, guardroom of Rehhausen Army prison, Lieutenant Strick.

While the call was going through, Gareis, the receiver pressed against his ear, was putting his notes in order. He crossed out several, underlined three words, added a word, connected two ideas within a bracket. 'I want the commander of the guard at the Army prison,' he said. The commander of the guard reported. Gareis said to him: 'There is an officer standing beside you. Will you ask him to show the following papers: his paybook and his travel orders. Do you have them? Good. Read me the first two pages of the paybook. Good. Now read me the travel orders.'

Gareis compared what the guard-commander read with the notes he had made on what Strick had just told him. The dates, figures, and names all agreed. So far so good. He asked to speak with Strick again.

'How is it you are in the Army prison?'

Strick told him that he had been near the Rehhausen railway station and had looked for a telephone. He could not use the station commandant's telephone, nor the one at the military police post. The Army prison was closest. Gareis had a map of the district pinned up above his desk. He glanced at it. Correct.

'Herr Strick,' he said, letting a distinct warmth enter his tone, 'I grant that your suspicions sound justified. But I would much prefer to have actual proof.' He reached out for his pencil, and drew between his notes a long, pipelike neck. Meanwhile he listened attentively to the telephone, like a connoisseur enjoying subtle chamber music.

'I want you to understand me,' he said. 'I want you to be quite clear about this. One piece of actual proof and you'll see the blast I'll set off.' He drew a heavy line cutting straight across the neck. 'Call me at once when you've got the proof. Meanwhile, I'll prepare everything here.'

Slowly, almost caressingly, he placed the receiver back on the hook. Then he pressed a button on his desk, held it down. A huge ox of a fellow loomed in the doorway. Gareis went over to the map and examined it. Then he said, 'Have my car ready. We may take a ride to Rehhausen. I'll want you and one of your comrades to go with me. Have a few cells cleared out in Rehhausen. Three will do for the present.'

The ox nodded and went out without a word. Gareis ran his finger over his special map, tracing the road from Würzburg to Rehhausen. Twenty-eight kilometres. Less than half an hour in his car. A pleasant night drive, with entertainment at the end, and, if things worked out, a pleasant surprise for the commanding general tomorrow morning. Not to mention the howling of the hyenas in Rehhausen.

Of course, he would have to cover his rear, Gareis thought, or there might be a repetition of that embarrassing business in Stettin. He would telephone Kessler, the political officer at General Headquarters. Kessler was a former S.S. leader and section chief in Himmler's Department of Racial Eugenics. He had recently been sent to pump a little life into the Army; his official title was National Socialist Liaison Officer, attached to General Headquarters in Würzburg; he was equipped with extensive special powers.

Gareis's conversation with Kessler was brief. Kessler was all for it. 'Catch them, gaol them! Go right ahead! The Army has to be given a jolt,' Kessler said. Noxious elements must be liquidated, National Socialist ideology hammered in. Rehhausen especially needed a lesson. 'Those fools spend their time drinking or sleeping with women, or talking bullshit. But not a word about National Socialism. Stubborn bastards, too. High time somebody got on their tail.'

Gareis promised to do a thorough job. Kessler roared out a few more phrases about duty, energetic action for the just cause, and National Socialist zeal. And, of course, something about the Fuehrer. Routine rigmarole for police inspectors, Gareis thought, grinning. He assured Kessler he would call him again early in the morning, and hung up.

A few minutes later the telephone call from Rehhausen came through. Gareis was cool and detached, as though he were attacking a simple chess problem. 'Good,' he said.

Then he was in his car, racing towards Rehhausen. The headlights threw a glaring narrow beam which seemed to saw through the trees along the main road. 'Christmas comes but once a year,' Gareis said. His companions, the two oxen, chuckled contentedly. When Gareis got going there was always good fun.

Strick was waiting for Gareis in front of the railway station. Two men from the Army prison detachment were guarding the entrance to the station commandant's office. Brakes screeched, and the car stopped abruptly. A massive figure sprang out of the rear and opened the front door. A short, plumpish man in a loose, light coat got out. He said, 'Don't smash any of the furniture. You're not in the Army now!'

The short man went up to Strick and flashed the beam of his torch into Strick's face. 'You are Lieutenant Strick?' Strick identified himself. The beam of light was lowered to the ground. 'I am Inspector Gareis. Where is the station commandant?'

'Probably at home.'

'So much the better,' Gareis said, switching off the torch.

They went through the deserted station to the space before the gate, and then along the building to the station commandant's office. The door was wide open, and the light was on. Wooden boxes stood all round the floor. A few of them had been broken open, and the room was littered with packing and boards. A soldier who was sitting slumped, like a caved-in loaf of Army bread, rose respectfully to his feet as Strick and Gareis entered.

He was the station commandant's orderly. He stood by stiffly, looking as though he were longing for orders, instructions, wishes, or commands.

Gareis surveyed the situation at a glance. He tilted his hat to the back of his neck. That was one of his gestures of satisfaction; his companion noticed it at once. Then he stooped over the opened boxes. Packages of shortening, tins of cooking oil, furs. He took the shipping papers from the station commandant's orderly. They called for documents, maps, plans. Gareis looked up, looked at Strick. Strick looked at Gareis. Gareis nodded amiably.

Strick reported. 'It was simple. I gave your name and borrowed two men from the prison squad. We broke in here, took care of this orderly, and opened the crates. Then I called you. That's all.'

'Marvellous,' Gareis commanded. 'But suppose there'd been nothing in the boxes except—'

'But there was something else.'

'You can never be sure of that in advance.'

'Exactly. That's why I had to open them.'

This man is a bombshell, Gareis thought. A living crowbar. He handles dynamite as though it were flour. Maybe he's more dangerous than I am. I never close my eyes when the firing starts, but he looks like the type who starts the firing. Comes along, occupies a superior officer's headquarters, breaks open secret boxes like so many walnuts. Not bad. I ought to have him working for me. But only if I could be sure he wouldn't plant any of his dynamite under my chair.

He issued a few curt instructions, and the men began taking the station commandant's office apart. Gareis himself looked over the desk, pulled open drawers, leafed through papers. Some of them he laid aside in a separate pile and later pocketed. Strick used a hatchet to open the rest of the boxes. The commandant's orderly made himself busy helping. They made as much noise as a whole company of men splitting firewood.

Gareis was obviously satisfied with the results. In addition to the boxes from Russia there were other goods which had no business being stored in a station commandant's office. 'There's a whole warehouse here,' one of Gareis's companions remarked with keen appreciation. But the inspector, who was calmly going through the papers, commented, 'Put that bottle back where you found it.' The hulking giant took a bottle of whisky out of one of his big pockets and replaced it in a cupboard, muttering something under his breath. 'You ought to know me by now,' Gareis said.

'Where is the station commandant's apartment?' Gareis asked at last.

The orderly smartly stepped forward, and began to splutter an explanation. 'Come on,' the inspector said, 'you lead the way.' He asked Strick to accompany him. 'You should be in on the fun, after your work.'

The station commandant lived about eight minutes' walk from the station. On the way the orderly blurted out that the major had two rooms reached by a separate entrance. The separate entrance pleased Gareis. 'A separate entrance is absolutely indispensable,' he exclaimed. 'Privacy above all. Especially when the world is going to pieces.'

At a gesture from Gareis one of his oxen tore the door off its hinges as though he were peeling wall-paper. The other ox turned on the light. The room was empty. It was a living-room. There was a table, a sofa with a uniform and cap thrown on it. Gareis crossed the room, opened the door to the adjoining one, and turned on the light. A bed creaked. A gruff voice said something; immediately afterwards a nervous female soprano hit a high note. 'The gal's voice is changing,' one of Gareis's companions remarked cheerfully.

The inspector stood in the bedroom doorway, Strick directly behind him. Two people, half covered by the sheet, were lying in bed. They were quite obviously naked. The bright hanging bulb illuminated every corner of the room. The man, striving to maintain his dignity without his uniform, called, 'Get the devil out of here. What do you want?' The girl brushed her tousled hair away from her forehead in a gesture between anger and shame.

'I hope,' Gareis said, dripping geniality, 'that I am not troubling the major too much. I trust the major has had a good rest.'

The man in bed sat up. 'How dare you!' he said sharply.

'Easy, easy there, my dear Major,' Gareis said soothingly. 'I'm afraid this is the wrong tone. Can it be that you mistake me for your orderly?'

The naked major's mind began to function. He looked searchingly at Gareis, saw Strick behind him, and behind Strick the shadows of two massive men. And he was overcome by a vague premonition. It was as though some one were presenting him with a bill. 'What do you want of me?' he said more softly, and rather hesitantly.

The air was filled with the mixed odour of alcohol, perfume, and sweat. The bed was rumpled; clothing lay on the floor. On the bedside table Strick saw a brandy glass that had tipped over. A yellowish-green liquid was flowing viscously out of it on to the table-top, and dripping down to the floor. Strick thought he could hear the impact of each drop. Somehow it was the most repellent part of the scene. He turned away, went into the other room, and lit a cigarette.

Gareis's voice was still dripping calm benevolence. He spoke to the major like a father trying to quiet an excited child. 'Keep calm and put on warm underwear, Herr Major. And then your most comfortable, not necessarily your most fancy uniform. And a warm woollen waistcoat and coat. We don't want you catching cold on us.'

'What does this mean?' the major demanded. His voice was hoarse, and no longer sounded curt or commanding.

'What does this mean?' Gareis pretended astonishment. 'But, my dear sir. You are being arrested. That's all – arrested. Put on your shirt. Otherwise you may catch cold. That would be too bad – considering all we have to do with you.'

Strick left. Shutting the door behind him, he went out into the night. He shivered. The street was deserted; the sky above was clear. Only his footsteps echoed in the darkness. All else was silence.

Corporal Hoepfner, officially orderly and semi-officially confidant of Captain Wolf, usually got up at seven o'clock in the morning. In a series of tortuous movements, which he grandiosely called his morning callisthenics, he crawled slowly out of bed. He reached first for his trousers, second for his penknife, in order to cut off a section of sausage-meat. Then he ruminated upon that for three to three and a half minutes.

Afterwards he gulped down some coffee and read the advertising section of yesterday's *Mainfränkischer Beobachter*. This process lasted exactly twenty-five minutes. Upon the expiration of this period Hoepfner reached into the cupboard for his shoe-brushes. With an emphatic '— it,' which expressed among other things his opinion of the *Mainfränkischer Beobachter*, he left the room. This sortie took place every morning at 7.25 a.m.

He went down the long corridor, lumbered down the stairs, and passed through the double doors. Exactly at 7.30 a.m. he would stand before Captain Wolf's door. Just as he did every morning. And, as he did every morning, he would slowly open the door – it was well oiled and did not creak – cautiously reach into the corner, fish out Wolf's boots, and, working in the corridor, bring them to a mirrorlike gloss. This was the unvarying routine.

This morning Hoepfner pressed the latch and opened the door. An unexpected sight met his eyes and temporarily paralysed his not-too-agile mind. In amazement he saw that the room was bright; the blinds had been raised and the window opened. In the middle of the room stood Captain Wolf, fully dressed. He was parting his hair, taking bearings like a surveyor to see that the parting ran absolutely straight. And his boots were on his feet, unpolished though they were. At seven-thirty in the morning!

Hoepfner, overcoming his surprise after a manly struggle, thrust his big body in through the half-open door. 'Come in, you monster,' Wolf said, carefully combing several stray hairs to the left side. His head gleamed; the sparse hair looked glued to his skull. As though he used spit on it, Hoepfner thought, pulling his whole body into the room. Incredible, but the Old Man was up and about already. Either he was going courting or he was going to see the colonel with the hope of tickling the colonel's arse early in the morning when he was in a good mood.

'I have to see the colonel,' Wolf said, confirming Hoepfner's second guess. 'I'll have my coffee later. Goddamn mess.'

'Yes, sir,' Hoepfner agreed, 'goddamn mess.' Wolf poured himself a glass of brandy and drained it at a gulp. He's washing down his vexation or he's scared stiff, Hoepfner thought.

'What is this fellow Lieutenant Strick doing?' Wolf asked.

Hoepfner did not know. 'He's probably sleeping, sir. What else would he be doing? He didn't come until late yesterday. I imagine he needs a rest.'

'Yes,' Wolf said, 'he needs a rest all right!' He took another glass of brandy, then shivered from the pleasurable shock of it. He went up to the tall mirror, and examined himself with silent appreciation. 'My belt,' he said. Hoepfner handed it to him. Wolf buckled it on, carefully avoiding wrinkling his trousers. 'Cap.' Hoepfner brought it to him. Wolf put it on with both hands, as though he were the chief personage at a coronation. He gave himself another look of satisfaction.

Stiffly, Wolf walked down the corridor. His boots creaked pleasantly. He carefully responded to all salutes. Leaving headquarters, he went to the so-called guest-house, which lay between the headquarters building and the officers' club. The colonel occupied two rooms in the guest-house.

Wolf knocked, discreetly but distinctly. He waited respectfully for forty seconds, clearing his throat slightly in a manner that indicated both his presence and his lack of impatience. Then he knocked again. 'What's the matter?' a voice called.

'Captain Wolf. May I see you, sir?'

'Come in.'

The colonel was probably still in bed. Wolf entered the living-room, and paused at the bedroom door.

'What in the world do you want, Wolf? To see your colonel in his nightshirt?' The voice was powerful, with an oily overtone. Wolf said he did not. He replied to the colonel's joke with a brief, bleating laugh.

'What, then? Has headquarters burned down? Or have the inmates of a P.O.W. camp made a break? Are you having woman trouble? Go on, tell me. But hurry up about it. I want to snooze for another hour at least.'

'The station commandant has been arrested.' Wolf blurted it out. It was a relief to have said it; he felt as though he had thrown off a tremendous burden. Eagerly he listened for Colonel Mueller's answer. At first the colonel said nothing. But the bed creaked violently; evidently the colonel had sat up. 'You're dreaming, Wolf,' the colonel said. There was no sharpness in his voice, but there was also no trace of his early-morning good humour.

'No, sir. Unfortunately it's true.' Wolf sounded extremely regretful that he was not dreaming. But the fact was the fact. The colonel jumped out of bed. The springs sighed. Wolf heard bare feet speeding a heavy body across the room. A tap was turned on. Water rumbled through the pipes and gurgled into the basin. Hands dipped into it. Some heavy object was plunged in the water. The water overflowed the basin, and splashed on to the floor. The colonel puffed and swore in a low voice.

Then the strong, oily voice called out to Wolf again. It was more distinct now than it had been. 'Did you say arrested?'

'Yes, sir.'

'When?'

'Last night.'

'And why?'

'Presumably for misappropriating Army property.'

'Idiot!' the colonel said sharply. Wolf tactfully forbore to think the word applied to himself. 'The man's an idiot,' the colonel called irritably through the door to Wolf. 'He kept hoarding crates down there instead of delivering them to the troops. It was bound to lead to trouble sooner or later.' Wolf was always fundamentally in agreement with the colonel; still, he attempted to put in a cautious, 'But.' After all, the station commandant was one of his best sources of supply.

The colonel entered the room. Wolf saluted. The colonel waved the salute aside. He was wearing large slippers on his feet. His unfastened riding-breeches hung loosely over his plump calves. A nightshirt embroidered in red protruded out of the back of his breeches. A large Turkish towel was wound round his neck. 'This is a damnable mess, Wolf,' the colonel declared. 'A hell of a big mess. The affair could put us to a good deal of embarrassment.'

That was just what Wolf had come about. 'The arrest must be cancelled,' he said. 'It will be the best thing for all of us.'

The colonel's massive frame towered directly in front of Wolf. 'What does that mean – the best thing for all of us? Are you trying to insinuate something?'

Wolf hastily denied that he meant anything by it. He had not expressed himself very clearly, he admitted. 'But we must try to help the station commandant. He always helped us out when he could.'

'When a comrade is in distress,' the colonel said grandly, 'we will all get behind him. That is natural.' He rubbed his bald pate with the towel. 'But it's not going to be easy. Calling off an arrest – there are a lot of things easier than that. Who put him behind bars, anyway?'

Wolf had been waiting for this question, waiting eagerly for it from the moment he had decided to visit the colonel. 'That's just it, sir,' he said. 'He was arrested by this Lieutenant Strick.' He spoke as though he were the bearer of a revelation. But the colonel did not grasp at once what Wolf meant.

'Lieutenant Strick? Who is Strick?'

'Strick is the new officer who was transferred to us from the front. It would be us, of course. He arrived last night.'

The colonel was surprised. 'You're joking, Wolf. You say he arrived last night, and a few hours later he arrests a major?'

'That's just what happened, sir.'

'I call that moving!' The colonel sat down and looked at Wolf as though the captain were trying to put over a highly entertaining fable. Damnation, there was something appealing about the affair. The man arrived, and a couple of hours later he had the station commandant behind bars. There was an example of military verve for you.

'Let's have it, Wolf. Tell me the whole story.'

Wolf did not know much more about it. This morning the station commandant's orderly had telephoned him and told him simply that the major was locked up. Had been taken right out of bed. And a certain Lieutenant Strick was responsible for it.

The colonel felt the need for a stiff drink. He asked Wolf to get one. Wolf looked over the excellent supply in the book-case, and finally placed a bottle of Cointreau on the table. The colonel disapproved. 'You're a philistine, Wolf. Nobody who knows anything about drinking would have this sticky stuff early in the morning. Bring some cognac.'

Colonel Mueller sipped the cognac appreciatively. 'The devil of a fellow,' he said. 'So he went and arrested the station commandant.' He wagged his large head, poured himself a little more cognac, and swallowed it. What a business! Then he pushed the glass aside. 'Of course, it won't do. After all, I'm in command here. He should have asked me.'

'That's just it,' Wolf said. 'That's just it.'

'It's the devil of a situation. A major allowing a lieutenant to arrest him. A lieutenant going over his commander's head. And besides, the affair will raise a terrible stink if it isn't settled at once, and then those bloodhounds in Würzburg will get a whiff of it. The man's a blockhead, coming along and starting trouble. The fellow is a threat to our peace.'

Wolf was all agreement. He rose, since the colonel had stood up. The colonel ordered: 'Get me all the facts you can lay your hands on. Inform the provost officer. Strick is to report to me at ten o'clock.' The colonel straightened up, so that his broad, hairy chest threatened to burst through the opening of his nightshirt. 'I'll give it to him strong!'

He waved dismissal. Wolf stiffened, saluted, left. The colonel shuffled in his slippers back to the basin. He dipped his big head deep into the water once, then again. He puffed. That lieutenant seemed to be an energetic sort. Arresting a major. Making trouble for Mueller himself, a colonel! Breaking into his well-earned rest. He'd show the fellow who was master here in Rehhausen!

CHAPTER TWO

THE small alarm-clock, muffled in a towel, purred gently but distinctly, like a chorus of cats close to his ear. The morning sun shone through cracks between the curtains. Strick was instantly wide awake, but he lay still and observed the man whose room he was sharing, Lieutenant Rabe. Rabe, he had already learned, was a guards officer, who also functioned as provost officer of Rehhausen headquarters.

Last night Strick had spoken no more than a few words with the man. When he came in Rabe was already sleeping, but he had wakened, greeted Strick, and indicated the bed Strick was to use. He had been polite, but reserved; had sat up in bed and made just the hint of a bow. Then he had gone back to sleep. A highly punctilious person, Strick guessed, even in his sleep.

Now Rabe reached for the alarm-clock, which stood beside his bed, and turned it off with one sure movement of his fingers. He got up at once, took off his pyjamas, and put on a pair of bathing-drawers. Then he did fifty stiff, vigorous knee-bends. After the knee-bends he pranced round on tiptoe for a moment, then reached for a towel and slipped almost noiselessly out of the room. A few minutes later he was back, his hair dripping, his bathing-drawers soaked from his shower. He took up his boots and several brushes which lay at hand near the door, and went out into the corridor. Strick could hear him vigorously brushing the boots. He came back, brushed out his uniform, took his shaving kit and tooth-brush, and again went out to the washroom.

When he returned Vogel was with him. Vogel glanced at the polished boots with cheerful approval. 'You'll do us out of our job, Lieutenant,' he said. 'Or is polishing boots one of your pastimes? If that's so I'll be pleased to leave my own clodhoppers in front of your door every night. We men are always glad to keep the officers happy.'

'To my mind orderlies in wartime are altogether unnecessary,' Rabe said.

Vogel did not appear to mind the sharp tone. Evidently he was used to such early-morning conversations. He raised the lieutenant's boots to the bright sunlight that poured in from the window. 'If you were not an officer, sir,' he said pleasantly, 'you could be an orderly. I won't deny that you're man enough to make a good one. You get to be a lieutenant by going to school, but nobody can teach you to polish boots. That's an inborn talent.'

'An unnecessary business, Vogel, a totally unnecessary business, this orderly and boot-polisher system.'

Vogel laid the boots aside. 'Can't you say the same for the War?'

Rabe was taken aback for a moment. The thought seemed quite novel to him. Then he waved the remark aside. 'Wars are inevitable; there's nothing we can do about them.'

Vogel looked him square in the face. 'Death is inevitable,' he said stoutly. 'So let the murderers kill. People must die anyway.'

Rabe was obviously nonplussed. He studied Vogel as though seeing him for the first time. Then he said thoughtfully, 'Don't you think, Vogel, that there are just causes? Causes which are worth fighting for?'

'And dying for?' Vogel added.

'Yes,' Rabe said earnestly, 'worth dying for.'

Vogel did not reply. 'Where are Lieutenant Strick's boots?' he asked. Rabe showed him. Vogel picked them up. 'Filth was invented so it could be cleaned away,' he said casually, and began cleaning them.

Lieutenant Strick sat up. 'Good morning,' he said. Rabe nodded acknowledgment. Vogel grinned at him. 'Debates are a fine way to start the day off,' Strick said, 'although they don't get my boots cleaned. However, if I may butt into your discussion, I'd say that I too believe dying has its points. Though it's usually more convenient to let others do it. But the big question is what you're pegging out for.'

Vogel listened closely. Rabe thought it over, and apparently had no answer. At last he said, 'It's easier to live when you know what you are living for. And when you also know what you would die for.'

'And you know that?' Strick flashed.

'I think I do.'

'Blessed are the poor in spirit: for theirs is the kingdom of heaven,' Vogel pronounced. He added instantly, 'Present company excepted, of course.'

Strick laughed heartily. 'Just disregard him, Rabe,' he apologized. 'He never takes himself seriously, so why should we?'

Rabe smiled with some constraint, but in a sincere effort to be friendly. Vogel was clever, he knew, but never before had he seemed so downright impertinent. Impudence was suddenly bursting out of him like water from a broken main.

Vogel swung Lieutenant Strick's dusty boots back and forth like a railway worker signalling with his lantern. 'One man's dirt is another man's destiny,' he declared.

'Enough wisecracks for this hour of the morning,' Strick said. 'I want my breakfast.'

There was a knock at the door. Corporal Hoepfner shuffled into the room. He went through the vague suggestion of a regulation salute, and then announced that Captain Wolf, confidentially and in all secrecy, wished Lieutenant Rabe to go to the railway station at once in his capacity of provost officer, and find out exactly what had taken place there last night. Another clumsy salute, and Hoepfner left.

Vogel, already at the door, put down the boots and came up to them. Rabe finished dressing quickly. 'I wonder what's wrong over there?' he said.

Strick obligingly informed him. 'I can tell you. The station commandant has been arrested.'

'Last night?'

'Taken right out of bed.'

Rabe paused in his preparations and looked at Strick. 'How do you know about it?'

'I was responsible for it,' Strick said.

Rabe looked somewhat confused. He had not expected any such reply. The arrest of the station commandant was a serious matter, likely to stir up a lot of muck. It was the sort of thing that needed thinking over. A sensation in a quiet place like Rehhausen; impossible to say what it might lead to. Obviously the first thing was to keep the matter as quiet as possible, to make no unnecessary fuss. And here was this man Vogel standing with his mouth, eyes, and ears wide open.

'Vogel,' Rabe said significantly, 'I assume you have heard none of our conversation.'

Vogel nodded agreement. 'I haven't heard that the station commandant has been put in jug,' he said at the top of his voice.

Rabe was annoyed. 'Very well, Vogel. Go and polish boots.'

Vogel smiled. 'Polishing boots for other people is unnecessary,' he quoted.

Rabe was taken aback. This was not at all like Vogel. The fellow was smart as a whip, no doubt about that. He always saw more than the others, but ordinarily he kept his mouth shut. Not exactly a model soldier, but certainly not a discipline problem. This was unprecedented.

Strick was enjoying himself. 'Corporal Vogel!' he bellowed in a drill-sergeant's tones.

Vogel, sensing a farce, immediately played up. He stiffened like a tin soldier. 'Your orders, sir?'

'Dismissed.'

Vogel swung his arm like a windmill in a salute to end all salutes. 'Dismissed. *Jawohl! Heil Hitler, Herr Leutnant!*' He dashed out as though dodging a stream from a fire-hose, slamming the door behind him so forcibly that plaster trickled from the ceiling.

Rabe was speechless. He could think of no explanation for this strange behaviour. Strick apologized. 'Don't be annoyed with Vogel,' he said to Rabe. 'We're childhood friends. Same school, same girls. This is our first meeting in years. You know, emotion gets the better of you at such times. The veneer of training peels off, and all you've had in common breaks through. You understand – it's kind of gone to his head.'

Rabe understood.

'You wouldn't expect us to behave like superior and subordinate, would you?' Strick went on. 'We were close friends. That explains it, doesn't it?'

Of course, Rabe agreed, that explained everything, but how could he possibly have known? He begged pardon. No, Strick said, if there were any pardons to be asked it was his turn. They both laughed.

'Now, what about the station commander?' Rabe asked.

Strick told him, in detail – his departure from Russia, the packing-cases, his arrival, suspicions, proof, arrest. Rabe listened with silent attentiveness, his candid young face wearing an expression of composure, his large eyes fixed steadily on Strick's face.

'Do you understand my action?' Strick asked in conclusion.

Yes, Rabe understood. He would probably have acted somewhat along the same lincs himself.

'Somewhat?'

'Yes, I would have handled it quite differently,' Rabe said.

'Would you explain what you mean?'

Rabe tried. 'In a war like this,' he said, feeling his way slowly, 'there are all sorts of great events, and inevitably there are side issues. The main thing is not to compromise the big things by laying stress on the unimportant little things, the minor blemishes that come up.'

Strick shifted about, angry and upset. He pushed back his chair and crossed his legs. It was as if he were being addressed in a foreign language. They were getting into deep water, and he felt that he must find the simplest language to make his attitude clear. 'In other words, let's leave the stable as filthy as we find it,' he said.

Rabe thought that this was an unjust interpretation of what he had said. 'No, you have to clean out the stable,' he said. 'But there's no point advertising to the world how dirty it was.'

Strick shook his head vehemently. 'What is there ought to be recognized clearly, and by every one. We have no business holding handkerchiefs in front of our faces so we won't smell the manure. Only by facing up to the facts do we become aware of the distinctions. Only that way do we see what is valuable and what isn't – what's worth fighting for and what we have to fight against, right in our midst.'

Rabe did not agree. 'What we need above all else is the trust of our soldiers. We officers have to go out of our way to see that their confidence is not shaken.'

'That's rot, Rabe.'

'That is what I believe.'

Strick stood up and went over to the window. The barracks was coming to life. Soldiers were hurrying to their duties; a truck drove over to the mess shed; women auxiliaries were chatting together as gaily as though they were meeting for their morning stroll through a park. The vineyards along the river sprawled lazily in the morning sun.

'Then you want to cover up,' Strick declared. 'You want to dress the swine in silk, and hope that others will see the silk and not the swine. Any uniform is a mockery if the man who wears it is a crook. Do you want to go by clothing or men?'

'I want to do what I consider to be my duty.'

'And what do you consider to be your duty?'

Rabe went to the door. 'I see a lot of things, and much of what I see I don't understand yet,' he said. 'A certain amount of criminality is probably inevitable. We can't do anything about that. But what we can do is to avoid creating gossip about it, which can only harm the prestige of the Army. If we want to win this war we've got to have unshaken morale.'

Strick turned brusquely on his heel. 'Look here,' he said, 'you're quoting the official propaganda. Can't you do without the slogans?'

Rabe shook his head. 'Perhaps you take the wrong view of it,' he said. 'Can't you imagine that the ideas which many people think are empty phrases can be the meaning of life to others?'

'Do you really believe those things?'

'I live by them.'

Rabe bowed slightly and went out. Strick looked after him in amazement. He lived by them! What a strange, what a remarkable young man. Rabe must be an idealist. But would he be allowed to live by his ideals?

Regularly, on the dot of eight o'clock, Captain Kessler strode into his office. The office staff rose silently, at the precise moment that he appeared in the doorway, and all extended their arms in the National Socialist salute. It had to be done snappily, smartly, all together.

Captain Kessler lingered at the door and inspected his office personnel. For about ten seconds he scanned their appearance and their bearing. Then he said, 'Heil Hitler!' and they replied, 'Heil Hitler!' A gesture of his hand, and they began to work at once.

The door to his private office stood wide open. Kessler went in and shut the door behind him. He smiled with satisfaction. There was something to this Army discipline. Every morning he experienced anew this warming sensation of receiving unconditional obedience. It was like entering a well-heated room after a long walk in the cold.

For Kessler this war had been the great turning-point in his career. Before that he had gone out skirmishing with the vigilante bands of the Free Corps, had been a student and one of the innumerable unemployed, had fought his way up through the ranks of the Party. Then, always a man who preferred a select group, he had entered the S.S. There he attracted the attention of his superiors, was promoted with unusual swiftness, and became a member of the *Reichsfuehrung* of the S.S., which meant that he was one of the top S.S. police leaders. Now he had been sent into the Army on a special mission, empowered with special authority.

This general headquarters in Würzburg was a modest beginning. Here at G.H.Q. he would acclimatize himself for a few weeks, get his bearings, and study the local conditions. Once that was done he would have more important missions to perform. Presumably he would be assigned to indoctrinating whole sections of the front with National Socialist ideology and methods. A watch-dog to keep an eye on questionable generals and their lower-ranking henchmen. Here in Würzburg he would be smelling out the trail.

His principles were clear and simple – and effective. He was striking at the Army with its own weapons. Discipline was his watchword. He was being an officer among officers, a soldier of soldiers. And to the Army higher-ups he was the man who carried the powers of a commanding general at the very least in his pocket. He insisted on iron obedience.

Kessler, a tall, burly man with rough-hewn, energetic features, sat behind his desk. That evening he was going to deliver an address to the officers of Würzburg, setting forth his programme. He would impress upon them the fact that the Army and National Socialism were one and the same. Indivisible. And unshakable when they were indivisible. He would prepare them psychologically for his plan to instal National Socialist Guidance Officers among them. Those officers would be his bloodhounds; he would set them on the heels of the swine who could not work to the Party line. No one would raise objections, of course. Objection would be treason, and you could be shot for treason.

He went over the outline of his speech. The middle section was unsatisfactory, he thought. He must elaborate on the idea that a bad soldier was a bad National Socialist, and vice versa. And he must get as many officers as possible to attend his lecture, get them from the near-by garrisons as well. If there were some who did not feel the inner urge to come he would have to apply pressure.

The telephone rang. Gareis was here to see him. Gareis, good! 'Send him in.' He closed the folder over his speech, and went to the door to greet Gareis. Gareis saluted with the disarming sloppiness of the untrained civilian. Kessler generously overlooked that. He would not overlook it with anyone else, but he permitted Gareis a certain laxity. He needed Gareis. The man solved difficult cases as though they were examples in elementary arithmetic.

'Drop of brandy? Cigar? Cigarette?' Gareis said no thanks. 'All right, let's have it, Gareis. What happened last night?'

Gareis reported. Kessler was an old acquaintance; Gareis knew the sort of thing the captain liked to hear. He described the scene of the arrest at length. Kessler bubbled with laughter. The two of them in bed – he could picture it. 'And you say, Gareis, they were both stark naked.'

Gareis readily elaborated.

'What else?' Kessler liked such piquant tales, but he needed grist for his mill, and now he suddenly sobered. It was as though a switch had been turned. His body, leaning forward slightly, reminded Gareis of a tiger preparing to spring. Very well, Gareis thought, he would toss a tit-bit into the tiger's maw that would stay his hunger for a while.

He handed Kessler a long list of material that had been confiscated. Kessler whistled between his teeth. A handsome assortment. He began considering which of the details of this startling case he could incorporate into his speech. Naturally he was going to exploit it fully, really rub it in, when he lectured to those Army officers. He would point out to them that there were some smart operators in their ranks. Then they wouldn't be surprised when later on he arrested one or two of them.

Gareis began talking about Strick. A man who went right to it, struck out right and left, and stopped at nothing and for no-one, he said. Kessler pricked up his ears. If he went about it right, Gareis thought, he could talk Kessler into requisitioning Strick. And Strick was likely to prove more than a handful for Kessler, which would be just fine. The busier Kessler was with Strick the less Kessler would interfere with him, Gareis – and all Gareis wanted was a free hand. Of course, you couldn't be sure of how it would work out, but there was no harm in trying. If Kessler and Strick got on famously together, which was another possibility, then they would make things hot here in Würzburg and in the whole district. In either case, Gareis would be right in his element.

Gareis could sense that Kessler was intrigued by the account of Strick's behaviour. He saw Kessler take a separate sheet of notepaper and write down Strick's name.

'At any rate, I'm highly pleased with what you've done so far,' Kessler said.

Kessler always required for his office use a copy of every interrogation and report. Gareis was prepared for that. He took a sheaf of papers from his brief-case and watched with satisfaction as Kessler placed them in a new folder. This was excellent bait, Gareis thought. Kessler was, as usual, gobbling it down. The whole point was to dangle bait skilfully, so that he did not recognize it for what it was.

Kessler was thinking that this was just the kind of material he needed. He would not only incorporate the story into his speech, he decided; he would reorganize his speech round it, show the whole thing through a magnifying glass, make those Army officers sit up and take notice. If it proved worth while - and it looked as though it would - he would turn the affair into the pretext for a major clean-up.

Eagerly he began looking through the reports. Gareis, who suddenly seemed to be in a hurry, asked permission to leave. Kessler granted it, adding a few words of appreciation. Gareis dimly heard him gurgle something about sense of duty, discharge of duty, duty and obligation to the great ideals of the age, final victory, and so on. Apparently this was the inevitable formula of farewell. And then Gareis was outside and glad of it. He would have to keep busy somewhere where he could not be reached for the next few hours, he decided. For, when Kessler went through the report carefully, as he undoubtedly would do, he would notice that the station commandant was the holder of a Gold Party Badge and had, in general, been a highly active Party member. He could scarcely expect Kessler to find these details edifying.

And Kessler did not find them edifying. He came across the item, stumbled, read it again, and then cursed softly between his teeth. He was somewhat mollified to see that the man had been only a member of the S.A. Those storm troopers had never been anything but a pack of loud-mouthed blockheads anyway. As a matter of fact, Kessler thought, when you looked closely, there were a good many things about the Party that simply stank. The organization was full of tired bureaucrats and opportunists who had joined up after the Party took power. Whole sections of it were made up of fat-arsed riff-raff and pensioners without a drop of revolutionary spirit.

At any rate, Kessler decided, he needed this case. As far as he was concerned the station commandant would be simply an Army major and nothing more. The man's Party connections were beside the point; what he had done would be charged to the Army's account, and that was all there was to it.

Now, who was this fellow Strick? A man like that, a man prepared to go the whole hog, could be useful to him. He needed men who could really kick up the dust when given the necessary powers and strong backing. But, before he turned the man loose on his potential victims, everything had to be straightened out officially. He needed a cat to catch his mice, but he was not going to buy the cat blind.

Kessler pressed all the buttons on his desk in a general alarm signal. His office assistants flocked into the room. Kessler sat upright at his desk, the portrait of Hitler on the wall behind him, and waited silently until they were all lined up in front of him, each doing his best to look alert. Then he glanced at his watch. It said 9.18.

'It is now exactly nine o'clock,' he said. 'You have two hours. I want all your reports on my desk by eleven o'clock at the latest. The order I am giving you now takes priority over everything else.'

His assistants put on expressions of keen interest. That was advisable, for a while back Kessler had told them bluntly: 'It is a high honour for all of you to belong to this office. I hope you will know how to live up to it. Devotion to the just cause is more important than anything else, and the name of that just cause is National Socialism. Anyone in this office who does not cooperate is committing sabotage. Saboteurs belong in gaol or on the front lines, and I'll see that they get there. Long live the Fuehrer!'

When Kessler made official speeches he spoke in unadulterated slogans, a highly concentrated hash of the phrases Nazis used to great effect at public meetings. His impromptu remarks, however, would not bear copying down: they were not exactly printable. But his present instructions were exact and to the point – the words gushed out of him like water from an open hydrant. 'I need all possible information on a certain Lieutenant Strick. Lieutenant Strick was previously – write this down – attached to the headquarters at Army Post Office No. 17,830, Eastern Front, Central Sector. He has been transferred to Rehhausen for rest and recuperation in home-front duties. Now get going. I want those telephone wires to smoke.'

Kessler rose from his seat, went over to his first assistant, and planted himself in front of the man. 'You will get me all documents on Lieutenant Strick relating to his Army service. Duplicates of all the personal papers should be at the local draft board office.' To the second assistant: 'You take over Lieutenant

Strick's home town. Get information from the police and the Party. Who is the man, who are his parents, what is their political standing, what did Lieutenant Strick do for a living, what do people say about him? All the usual stuff. The more you fish up the better.'

The third assistant was busily taking notes. Kessler threw a few directives at him. 'Every transferred soldier is given papers to take with him, or the papers are sent on in advance. Check up on the q.t. with the headquarters company at Rehhausen. Get me everything you can on this Strick.'

He lumbered back to his chair, 'As I said, you have two hours. At eleven I want to see what you've found. Also, I want my car here at eleven. Any questions?' He nodded dismissal.

Now what had this Strick been sent home for? Kessler decided to look up the regulations governing shifts of officers from the battle front to the home front. What he read was instructive. 'Special consideration is to be given to meritorious officers who have had many years on active duty.' Then Strick was a meritorious officer. But, when you got down to facts, were really meritorious officers ever allowed to leave the front? In these times? There was a strong chance that this bird had been an undesirable element out there. Not exactly popular with the reactionary gold-braid boys, Kessler imagined, which was a recommendation.

Dr. Friedrich, the District Leader of the National Socialist Party in Rehhausen, was a peaceable body, a willing vessel for other people's ideas. Rumour had it that Colonel Mueller had once said that the Friedrich had the soul of a camel.

Dr. Friedrich would have liked nothing better than for the whole world to consist only of Party members – or for there to be no Party at all. He would no doubt have been happiest if he had been able to stay a dentist – and he had been a fairly good dentist in his time.

He was on his way to the barracks at the moment. He had just been through a prolonged inner struggle over the problem of whether or not to wear his uniform. In the end he had settled on the more painful course: since he was going to meet men in uniform, he had better be in full uniform himself. The prospect was not at all to his liking, for uniforms looked a lot better on his friend Colonel Mueller than they did on him. Besides which, Mueller had a handsome collection of decorations, while Friedrich had only the Iron Cross, Second Class, from the First

World War, and the War Merit Cross, Second Class, without swords, from the present war.

Slowly Dr. Friedrich climbed the winding road up to the barracks. He was walking he always either walked or took the train nowadays, because he had read an order that petrol must be saved, and he was bent on saving it. The exertion was making him hot, and he wanted to take off his cap and carry it in his hand. But then, he reminded himself, he would no longer be fully uniformed as the regulations prescribed. His leather belt bothered him too, and the pistol was a leaden weight. But he bore his burden resignedly; this was the way things had to be, since the regulations stipulated the details of full uniform point by point.

His passion – and he wished to God he had never had any passions at all – was speech-making. He had always liked to talk, even though he was not especially eloquent. In former times he had stunned his patients, defenceless under the drill, with heavy doses of German philosophy and Nazi ideology. And then he had begun to speak in public whenever the chance came his way. He was allowed to speak often, whenever, wherever, and however he pleased. Since Rehhausen had never been a focus for political tension, he had neither to overcome obstacles nor to create them. When the Nazis took power in 1933 Rehhausen lost a fairly competent dentist and acquired instead a totally harmless, loquacious district leader, who showed a certain peasant cunning in skirting the reefs of inter-Party politics.

Dr. Friedrich often wished he had never become district leader of Rehhausen. But he held his office, and even had a reputation for reliability, because he promptly carried out every order that reached him. He himself was absolutely convinced that he lived only to dispose of difficulties. Wherever he looked there were difficulties; whatever he touched turned out to have difficulties; the only things that ever came his way were difficulties.

Now here he was involved in difficulties on account of this station commandant. There were between six and eight hundred district leaders in Greater Germany, and which one of them *would* have direct ties with his station commandant? Himself, Dr. Friedrich, of course. And which one *would* get into difficulties because of a station commandant? Only himself! This major had once been an S.A. storm leader, and a wearer of the Gold Party Badge – and then this same major had become his brother-in-law. Dr. Friedrich had to admit to himself that it was a good idea when Elise, his wife's sister, had finally found herself a husband. That was one less mouth to feed, and one less producer of difficulties in the family. But all morning long Elise had been on his neck, demanding that he protect her beloved husband.

Beloved husband! Whatever love there was in that marriage was all on one side. His brother-in-law was always having to work late and spent nights 'out'. A disgrace, that's what it was. But what could Friedrich do about the man's mistresses? He had already spoken to him, more than once, but without effect. After all, he couldn't very well knock his head off. The major had a whole storm troop behind him, besides which he often went out hunting with Friedrich's superior, the group leader. So there you had it again – nothing but difficulties!

Dr. Friedrich approached the gate to the barracks. His forehead was beaded with perspiration from the strenuous climb. His short, brushy moustache was damp with sweat, and his shirt was clinging to him like a wet rag. Dr. Friedrich looked round to make sure nobody was watching him while he engaged in a most private act. Then he took out a large, lily-white handkerchief, removed his cap, and ran the handkerchief with swift, short, jerky movements over his forehead, cheeks, chin, and neck.

The guard, informed by telephone of the arrival of the district leader, opened the gate with a flourish. Dr. Friedrich walked faster so that the guard would not have to wait for him. As soon as the man saluted he would return the salute; regulations said that a district leader must wait until he was saluted. He would make his own salute disciplined, but also cordial. The guard must be made to feel that an important personage had arrived, but one who also had a friendly, comradely attitude towards every soldier.

Saluting, the district leader strode past the guard. For a brief moment he was content with himself. Carefully he surveyed the area ahead, prepared to respond with precision to any salutes. Since the Commandant, Colonel Mueller, was his friend, the garrison soldiers put themselves out for him. Even officers saluted snappily, and since they vied with one another to see who would salute first, they began the upward fling of arm while they were still five or more yards away.

There stood his good friend Colonel Mueller, the morning sunlight full upon his corpulent figure. His Knight's Cross sparkled as though the additional oak leaf, diamond-studded, were already there. The broad face beamed in his direction, glistened as though oiled with friendliness and fellow-feeling. Above the colonel's head, in clear Gothic letters, were the words: 'Rehhausen Headquarters'.

Colonel Mueller, as if the sunlight had blinded him, pretended that he had just seen Friedrich. He went towards him, his arm outstretched, and greeted him with a cordial, 'Heil Hitler!' Then he swung in on the district leader's left, and walked with him towards his offices. District Leader Freidrich, D.D.S., always felt safe and sheltered with Colonel Mueller. Mueller radiated calm and assurance: he unfailingly offered comradely consolation and understanding for Friedrich's difficulties. In fact, Mueller's transfer to Rehhausen had been for Friedrich the one piece of good luck in a war otherwise beset with difficulties. Since the colonel had been here, the Army and the Party in Rehhausen had worked hand in hand. More than one district ordinance of the National Socialist Party bore Friedrich's signature, but had been conceived in Mueller's brain.

With every sign of appreciation and courtesy Mueller led his guest through the outer offices. There was another door, and he might have taken him directly into his private office, but he seldom let slip the opportunity for the ceremony that now ensued.

In the large main office the clerks rose, and a corporal reported to Colonel Mueller. Mueller waved the report aside; District Leader Friedrich nodded acknowledgment. In the next room the well-padded operations clerk, Sergeant Demuth, shot to his feet. He too reported, and gave a brief summary of late dispatches. Mueller and Dr. Friedrich thanked him.

In the next room they encountered Captain Geiger, the adjutant. Geiger was disciplined, correct, his manners as irreproachable as his uniform. He made his report, and asked permission to show the colonel a confidential message, which had just arrived. 'Later,' the colonel said. 'There's time for that. First I have an important conference with our district leader.' The adjutant clicked his heels obediently. Dr. Friedrich held out his hand, and Captain Geiger shook it warmly and respectfully.

The next room was the colonel's waiting-room. The furnishings had an air of solidity, almost of elegance. The floor was covered with a red carpet, the air filled with a faint fragrance of perfume. The colonel's secretary, Erika Blaustrom, was seated at her desk. The district leader strode up to her, shook her hand,

and declared that he was very happy to see her. Erika's painted lips smiled, revealing two rows of shapely teeth which, as Dr. Friedrich had repeatedly told her, were an absolute delight to him from the dentistry angle.

Now they entered the colonel's private office. There was a huge desk, several soft club arm-chairs, a couch, two rugs, a book-case, and a carved cupboard. It was very elegant, an office suited to the colonel's position. Every time he entered the room Dr. Friedrich felt the truth of this, with an admiration unmarred by envy. And when you sat facing the colonel you saw on the wall behind him an oil painting of Adolf Hitler.

'My dear Doctor,' the colonel said jovially, 'we seem to be having the same difficulties at the same time once more.' Dr. Friedrich nodded. 'But, after all, what are difficulties for?' the colonel asked rhetorically. 'Only to be conquered.' Dr. Friedrich nodded earnestly. How lucky he was to have Mueller in command here. Mueller would, of course, save him immense trouble.

'I take it, then,' the colonel stated, 'that the district leadership of the Party takes the same view as Rehhausen garrison headquarters.' Dr. Friedrich agreed. 'Then it will be that much easier to take care of the matter,' Mueller went on. 'Of course, it is not that we are trying to cover up anything, or that we have anything to hide. But there is such a thing as the prestige of the Army and the Party. The prestige must be defended!'

Dr. Friedrich sat up straighter in his chair, far more satisfied than he had dared fifteen minutes ago to hope he would be. 'It is quite conceivable,' he said slowly, 'that this new officer, Lieutenant Strick, is the victim of an unfortunate error. He simply made a mistake. To err is human, and quite pardonable, of course. Now, if he realized that he had been wrong that would immediately create a fundamentally different situation.'

Mueller nodded agreement. He saw his face feebly reflected in the mirrorlike surface of the desk. Even in reflection the face showed surprise, kept in check by decorum. By God, Mueller was thinking, this fellow Friedrich is not altogether an idiot. He was not noted for intelligence, but he was always pretty good when it came to the theoretical elimination of difficulties. The man was a rabbit, and his brain a rabbit-warren with two dozen hidden nooks. This suggestion of his certainly sounded like the best solution.

'Do you think it possible,' Dr. Friedrich asked modestly, his eyes fixed on the toes of his boots, 'that this Lieutenant Strick will admit he is in error?'

'He will have no choice,' the colonel said with assurance. The face in the polished desk smiled confidently back at him. 'I will have Eri send for Strick. She will butter him up. She has a very nice way with men. She's softened up more than one tough customer.'

'I hope so,' the district leader said fervently. 'I hope so.'

Erika Blaustrom, the colonel's secretary, whom her friends called Eri, barely glanced up when Lieutenant Strick entered her room, the colonel's waiting-room. She was busy polishing her finger-nails with swift, catlike movements. Her nails already had a satisfactory muted lustre, but she held them up to the sunlight to examine them. 'Please sit down,' she said, without interrupting her manicure.

The nail of her left middle finger seemed to her a little too obtrusively bright. It did not have the proper dull sheen; it looked oily instead, glittering rather than gleaming. Directly above her nose a tiny fold appeared in her ordinarily smooth brow. But the frown was not on account of her finger-nail; it was because Strick had taken a chair close to her, and was looking at her with interest. The action made Erika somewhat nervous. The motions of her brush across the refractory finger-nail became faster and shorter, almost clumsy. Strick shifted his chair a few inches closer to watch the process intently. He bent over her hands as though he was admiring precision work by an expert tool-maker.

Erika dropped her hands, raised her head, and looked sharply at Strick. Strick smiled. He had a fresh smile, Erika thought. No one in Rehhausen would dare to smile at me that way. But perhaps the man did not know who she was, and had no suspicion how important she was here. He probably didn't know what her relationship to the colonel was.

'Are you Lieutenant Strick?' Erika asked. Strick looked at her as though she were a fabulous monster. He pretended to be pleasantly surprised. 'Aha,' he said, 'then you are the colonel!' Erika was at a loss. Really, what impudence!

'If you are the colonel,' Strick went on in a tone of dead earnest, 'as you seem to be, then I must say you are the most charming colonel I have ever met.' Erika made a gesture of annoyance. Strick was generously willing to accept correction. 'At any rate,' he assured her, 'you have the most beautiful hands it has been my privilege to see in many months. Works of art, no more nor less.'

Erika took these remarks for a covert attack upon the right of a modern woman to practise beauty culture. 'What do you expect?' she demanded, faintly irritated. 'Do you want us to go round the way you do? Must we wear ersatz underwear and keep our finger-nails filthy just because you men at the front are doing without beauty shops or barbers? Are we supposed to bathe once a week just because you don't have time or are too lazy to wash for weeks at a time – as I hear?'

Strick protested. As far as he was concerned she could bathe in mare's milk every day. He had no objection – quite the contrary, quite the contrary.

Eri looked at him suspiciously, but with slightly more friendliness. Then she glanced at her hands, the hands he had said were the most beautiful he had seen in many months. However, she decided to keep on her guard. Though she had not learned very much in this war, she had learned that not everyone could do well for himself; many people went on living only because others died for them. If you didn't stay on top you went under. Erika was – and in periods of melancholy she found herself very proud of the fact – the child of poor but honest parents. Her father, a book-keeper, used to say again and again that, though he was poor, he had kept his honour. She would remember this with a suppressed pride, but only in her melancholy moods, and these did not occur often.

On the other hand, her normal belief was that her father had stayed poor only because he was honest. Well, he had been a good fellow who went to church regularly, said grace before every meal, and snored so loudly and complacently at night that he could be heard throughout the house. She had been overjoyed to get away from home. She had the war to thank for that, for it had made her free, had liberated her from the stupidity of the poor. For in her eyes - very pretty dark eyes they were - everybody who was honest like her father was stupid. She herself was not stupid, and it was perfectly obvious to her that cleverness was more rewarding.

Whatever Erika looked at became a mirror. Strick's face, too, reflected the fact that she was beautiful. Certainly this was nothing new to her, but confirmation of such a fact is always pleasant. Contentedly she stretched, and she could see by Strick's expression that he thought the rest of her was as well worth looking at as her eyes and hands. She got up, and ran her hands carefully, almost tenderly, down her waist, as though she wanted to smooth out her flimsy summer dress – which needed no smoothing. Then she sat down on top of her desk, and let her legs dangle.

Strick moved his chair an inch or two backward. He had a suspicion that the temperature in the room must be very high – possibly the window, or it might be even the door, should be opened.

He thinks I'm a shrewd customer, Erika guessed. So much the better. If he doesn't think I'm an innocent little lamb he won't try to treat me like one.

Strick spoke up. In a slow drawl he said that the colonel had sent for him. It was a great pleasure to chat with her, and he hoped there would be many other occasions to do so, but he assumed that the colonel was waiting for him.

Erika assured him that the colonel was not waiting. 'The colonel is in conference with the district leader, the adjutant, Captain Wolf, and the provost officer. You will have to wait until the conference is over.'

'How long is that likely to be?' Strick asked. 'I might drop in at the canteen in the meanwhile.'

Erika gently corrected him. 'Here, Herr Strick, officers go to the club, not the canteen. We have a club for officers and their ladies.'

As Erika said the word 'ladies' her voice had a shade of disgust, as though she were quoting the kind of word found scribbled on lavatory doors. As a matter of fact, she had something against those ladies who enjoyed special privileges because they were 'officers' ladies'. Erika was not one of them, and that infuriated her. Her view of the matter was perfectly logical. In the first place, she was far better-looking than all the other specimens of official femininity in the garrison; in the second place, she had more influence than any of these one-time dance-hall girls; and finally, her relationship to Colonel Mueller was just as clear and public as any of the teetering marriages among the officers. Everybody round headquarters – with the probable sole exception of this Lieutenant Strick – knew that very well, and they all subtly indicated to her that they did know; but none of them ever attempted to do anything for her, as far as getting her into the club was concerned. It hurt Erika. She refused to show that she was hurt, and she never said anything to anyone, not even to the colonel, but still, she brooded about it. The whole thing was a rotten deal.

'Why, that's splendid,' Strick said.

Erika looked up. 'What's splendid?'

'That there is a club here. I hope I will see you there frequently.'

Erika, touched at her sorest point, answered curtly, with palpable bitterness, 'Not me.'

'Don't you go to the club?' Strick asked in amazement.

'Only ladies of the officers' corps are permitted to go there.'

'And aren't you a lady of the officers' corps?'

'No.'

Strick had a distinct feeling that a weapon was being placed in his hands which might prove useful. He deliberately added several degrees to his conspicuous astonishment. 'Don't tell me,' he exclaimed, 'that in the whole corps there isn't one officer to take you to the club as his lady?'

The conversation had rather confused Erika, and confusion was something new to her. 'Will you take me there?' she asked.

'With the greatest pleasure,' Strick declared, and he meant this.

Erika tried to disentangle herself. Either Strick was naïve or he knew nothing at all about conditions in Rehhausen. Naturally she would never be allowed inside the club; that was unfortunate, but there was nothing to do about it. Privately she shared bed and board with the colonel, according to whichever function was in demand; but officially she was his secretary, and had no business in the officers' club. Rules and regulations were sacred, even the rules and regulations of a club. And there were certain social obligations, as the colonel frequently remarked, which nobody could escape. The officers' corps represented a tradition which had evolved slowly over the years, and which must be protected.

And so Erika abruptly switched the conversation to another track. She had gathered a number of hints, and now she had to act on them. Without further detours she headed straight for her goal. 'You seem to know very little about Rehhausen,' she said.

'What makes you think that?'

'The station commandant is a deserving officer.'

'I agree – and he's going to get what he deserves.'

Erika could sense the hard core of stubbornness in this lean, middle-sized man before her. And now Strick asked, grinning, 'Are you a member of the Party too?'

Erika was mildly indignant. 'Do I look like one?'

Strick amiably agreed that she did not especially look like it. He took in her shapely hands with their rosy finger-nails, the carefully drawn curves of her lips, the thin, skilfully pencilled eyebrows, and he added emphatically, 'No, you don't look like one of our athletes of the League of German Girls.'

Erika tried again to bring Strick back to the subject, as she had been instructed to do. But Strick dodged. When she began talking about internal conditions in Rehhausen Strick shifted the conversation adroitly to the war communiqués and their effect upon the female civilian populace. When Erika tried to explain the relationship among Army headquarters, the station commandant's office, and the Party district Strick spoke of his urgent desire to know more about swimming facilities in Rehhausen and the vicinity.

Meanwhile it was getting late. The somewhat insipid air in the room grew heavy and stale. It was harder to breathe, harder to think. The late morning sunlight fell full upon the tightly shut windows. Erika stretched herself in the increasing heat as though she had entered a warm bath. Strick looked at her with open appreciation; he felt as if he were drifting into a pleasant dream with his eyes wide open. Erika was well aware of the impression she was making upon him.

Lieutenant Rabe, the provost officer, entered the room from the colonel's private office. He stopped abruptly, his face frozen in a look of intense displeasure. Then he went to the window, opened it wide, and took a deep breath. 'It's like a hot-house in here,' he declared. 'Suffocating.'

Erika threw him a mocking glance. 'How lucky we have you here to protect us from suffocation, Herr Rabe. In fact, you're the born protector.'

Rabe ignored her. 'The colonel will see you now, Herr Strick,' he said in his most formal tone.

Strick rose and turned to Erika. 'About the club – think it over. As I said, I'd love to take you there.' He went out, followed by Rabe.

Erika sauntered over to the window. The sunlight fell upon her thin dress. Deliberately, she raised her right hand and studied her finger-nails. So they were the most charming hands he had seen in many months, even though the gloss on her nails was not perfect. Be that as it may, those hands would in all likelihood never hold a wine-glass in the officers' club – for all that they deserved to.

Strick walked into an atmosphere sticky with amiability. The colonel, filling the chair behind his desk, looked at him with well-tempered cordiality, as though he were expecting a prodigal son, but was not quite convinced that this was really his own progeny. The Party district leader was sitting up straight, trying to make his bearing as impressive as possible. His arms were resting on the wide arms of his chair, so that he looked a little like a sphinx with an absurd uniform. Captain Wolf sat close to the colonel, trying to look strained and graceful at the same time. The adjutant, Captain Geiger, was standing, looking through some documents, and seeming in a vague way extremely zealous. Rabe stood in the background with an air of composure.

Broad stripes of sunlight fell into the room, mercilessly revealing a diaphanous layer of dust wherever it struck the smooth parquet flooring, but disappearing, totally absorbed, into the thick pile of the carpet.

Strick briefly reported – his rank, name, reason for transfer, former assignment. Mueller nodded, and stretched his fleshy hand across the desk. Strick took it. It was a soft, well-manicured hand, but it nevertheless squeezed his strongly.

The colonel introduced those of the other officers whom Strick did not already know. Captain Geiger was polite but distant. Captain Wolf grinned with artificial friendliness; he behaved as though he were entering upon a business deal whose outcome was highly dubious. And then, with a flourish, Mueller said: 'And this is Dr. Friedrich, District Leader of the National Socialist German Workers Party in Rehhausen.' The district leader rose in a demonstration of open-hearted cordiality. 'Welcome to the home front,' he pronounced. Strick bowed slightly. 'Very happy to meet you, Doctor.'

'This, gentlemen,' the colonel declared jovially, 'this, gentlemen, is the man who spends his leisure time arresting Staff officers.' He opened one of the side drawers of his desk and took out a box of cigars. 'Smoke?' He held out to Strick a selection of plump dark brown cigars with blunt ends and brightly coloured paper bands. Strick examined the contents, and picked out a particularly well-shaped Brazilian cigar. The colonel observed this careful choice with a certain approval. The box was passed round. All the men with the exception of Rabe took a cigar. The colonel took out a small pocket-knife, and began the careful ceremony of clipping the end. Then three matches flared and were held out to the colonel. He took one, held it politely under Dr. Friedrich's cigar, and said to the others, 'Please, gentlemen, light up your own.'

An aromatic fragrance began to fill the room. The clouds of smoke hovered in the broad rays of sunlight, flowed together, united, and moved towards the window. The colonel took an appreciative moment to enjoy the first puff. Then he leaned back and looked lovingly at his cigar. He spoke as though he were addressing it. 'With the frankness we always practise here, I must ask you, my dear Strick, was it necessary?'

Strick matched his tone of friendliness. 'To have put off taking action would have been equivalent to becoming party to a crime.'

'Here on the home front such actions have a habit of producing reverberations.' The colonel interrupted himself for a moment to puff at his cigar. 'Have you considered that you are endangering the prestige of the officers' corps?'

Strick made an effort to sound obliging, but he said: 'I should think, sir, that such a remark should have been directed to the station commandant some time ago.'

Colonel Mueller lowered the cigar abruptly, as though it were under attack. What did the man mean by that? Was this insolence? He glanced at Dr. Friedrich. The district leader had, if possible, stiffened his posture even more. His face expressed sincere indignation. 'We shall have to – as the Fuehrer once expressed himself – talk straight from the shoulder,' Dr. Friedrich said.

Captain Wolf's look expressed pure Aryan agreement with this sentiment. Geiger was obviously waiting for the colonel to say some decisive word, so that he could jump in and second it. Rabe appeared to be wholly impartial. Strick seemed in no way conscious that he had said something which might give offence.

Mueller had the feeling that the clumsy slash and thrust would not do in this case. 'My dear Strick,' he said in his most paternal tone, 'naturally you cannot have a clear view of local conditions. We alone understand the situation fully. The arrest of the major is more than a mere unpleasantness. It is – I am speaking with our home-front situation in mind, of course – an extremely unwise step.'

Strick looked as though he were terribly pained at being unable to enter into the colonel's complicated considerations. 'I admit that I was not thinking of either the local situation or what was best for the home front,' he said.

Dr. Friedrich was eager to slaughter the pig before it squealed. 'There you are,' he burst in with impetuous satisfaction, 'now we have made you understand. Now you see what you must do in the interests of the Party and the Army.'

Strick was offended. This was really a little too crude. For them to put things so grossly in such a situation seemed to indicate that they thought him an idiot. He turned directly to Dr. Friedrich, and puffed out a cloud of smoke, as though he needed to take a deep breath. 'I do feel,' he said, putting the matter somewhat more grossly himself, 'that I now understand, though I am not sure you are the one who has instructed me, Dr. Friedrich. But, even if I wanted to carry out your wishes, the wishes of the Party and the Army, I can no longer do so. The arrest has already been made.'

The colonel raised his hand. The long cone of ashes fell like a huge snow-flake from his cigar, hit the polished surface of the desk, and shattered into soft white flakes which lay unheeded. 'I wish to protect an officer under my command from embarrassment,' he said soothingly. 'Understanding the situation as I do, I consider an error perfectly human.' The district leader instantly added in a conciliatory manner, 'And therefore forgivable.'

'I really am sorry that it was not an error,' Strick said very pleasantly.

Mueller made himself go on. 'You ought to think it over carefully. I consider it highly likely that you were in error.'

'I do not.'

Colonel Mueller gave a muffled snort, then took a deep breath. His glance fell upon the desk-top, and with annoyance he noticed the scattered ashes. Bending his head, he puffed powerfully at them. The ashes flew up in a short arc, and wafted down upon Captain Wolf's trousers. The colonel paid no attention. Wolf chuckled softly, as though he had overheard a whimsical remark, and genially brushed his trousers.

The district leader was burning with indignation at the way his friendly and comradely approach had been received. Now he spoke in tones of deepest reproach. 'We are being tolerant in assuming that you are not in a position to understand. Let me put it clearly. The interests of the Party and the Army demand that you do everything you can to undo this arrest.'

Strick shook his head regretfully, as though he could not follow the district leader's train of thought. 'You will probably not believe me, Herr Doktor, but I thought that the interests of the Party and the Army demanded that I send this crook in a major's uniform to the place where he ought to have been sent some time ago.'

That was too strong for Colonel Mueller. He was not going to swallow 'crook in a major's uniform'. He pounded his fist on the desk, so that his cigar ashes rained upon it like a shower of meteors. Colonel Mueller loved such gestures. They demonstrated, he thought, a passionate temperament and firm resolution. Dr. Friedrich was sitting up straight, as though he had become numbed with indignation at the very moment when he was getting to his feet. Wolf stood like a bull that has seen a red flag. Geiger was as usual biding his chance to agree with the colonel's opinion. Rabe stood silent and attentive.

The colonel laughed harshly. 'Do you still not see? I want to save you a court-martial for actions damaging to the officers' corps.'

Strick said tensely, 'That is very considerate of you, sir, but you needn't bother.'

'You will not co-operate?' The tone was low, threatening, challenging, the question being the judge's final word before he passed sentence.

Strick set his teeth. He was outwardly calm, but all his muscles were taut; he felt surrounded by unknown dangers, and he was uncertain of his course; it was as if he were exposed, helpless, with his courage ebbing away. A terrible urge to sleep, to forget, rose up in him. To forget everything that lay behind him: three horrible years in Russia among bugs, filth, blood, and corpses. To forget everything connected with this war, everything. Here was where he could find it, the forgetfulness he needed. Here was the remotest corner of the home front; few duties, long free evenings, a friend, perhaps even a girl. Ample wine grew on all the hills round about, and somewhere there was a room with a bed and cool white sheets waiting for him. If only he could rest, close his eyes, and sink down into forgetfulness as into a feather-bed.

What had the colonel asked? 'You will not co-operate?' He looked around at the questioning faces, broad planes of cheeks and jutting noses, which seemed to be floating towards him.

Faces like carnival masks staggering through a crowd. He saw smoke, ashes, and fine dust mercilessly illuminated by the broad stripes of glaring sunlight. And he saw Lieutenant Rabe's intelligent young face, the only face in the room that was not turned towards him. But he felt that Rabe, more than any of the others, was demanding an answer to the question: 'You will not co-operate?'

'No,' he said.

As he spoke Captain Kessler entered the room, slamming the door behind him.

It had been a few minutes after eleven o'clock when Kessler got into his car at Würzburg and told the chauffeur to drive to Rehhausen. His driver drove fast. He had permanent instructions to get every mile of speed he could out of the car, unless otherwise ordered. Kessler adored speeding. He always took the right of way; signals and traffic-regulations existed only for others to obey. What some people called 'ruthless' he called 'getting my way'. Legalities did not mean anything to him; he considered them so much paper.

While the driver turned sharply to the left at the railway station, wound his way through several narrow streets, and artfully frightened an old woman as he emerged into the main road that followed the bank of the river Main, Kessler examined a number of documents. They contained the material that had been gathered about Strick. Excellent reports. And this fellow Strick seemed a rare bird. He would have to see him and sound him out, of course, before he could decide for certain whether the lieutenant was the man he needed. And then he would have to play the bogeyman at Colonel Mueller – 'fat-arse', as Kessler called him privately.

Kessler glanced at the speedometer. The needle was hovering just over fifty; the car whined through the warm air. 'Can't you get more than fifty out of her?' he asked.

'We're climbing the mountain,' the driver said. 'I've got my foot on the floor.'

'We'll have to get another car,' Kessler said. 'After all, I can't waste time riding in a pram.'

The driver began talking about a new car, an eight-cylinder, which had been assigned to the General Headquarters. 'Who is it for?' Kessler asked.

'The Chief of Staff, I suppose.'

'I doubt if he'll get it,' Kessler said. 'We can put it to better use.' And the driver knew that Kessler would soon have the car. Kessler never ran into difficulties, because he refused to recognize their existence.

Tyres screaming, the car braked sharply in front of the gate to the barracks at Rehhausen. The moment the car came to a halt the driver leaned on the horn button. A guard came forward to check. Kessler jumped out of the car; he stood, a tall, massive, imposing figure, towering in front of the guard, and bellowed at him. The guard, taken by surprise, fell back a couple of steps, and hurried to open the gate. Kessler got into the car again. He saluted curtly, a smirk of satisfaction in the corners of his mouth.

This was his method of imposing discipline, breaking resistance, establishing once and for all who did and did not have any say. He might consistently go through the same scene four or five times if necessary, knowing that when he came the sixth or seventh time the gate would fly open the moment he was sighted from a distance. And that was how he wanted things to be.

The car stopped in front of headquarters. Kessler instructed the driver to wait. He stuffed his papers into his brief-case, tucked the brief-case under his arm, and walked with springy step into the building. He crossed through the large outer office without paying attention to anyone. The fat operations clerk in the next room, Sergeant Demuth, looked up at him with dismayed vexation. This was no way to approach Colonel Mueller's office. His uneasiness was plain to see on his face.

This was another case for Kessler's technique. 'Have you forgotten how to salute an officer, you idiot?' he snarled. Demuth, who had never encountered anything of the sort in his office, thought he had not heard aright. 'Lift your fat haunches off that chair, you parasite.' Kessler heard the Other Ranks in the adjoining room succumbing to an attack of sniggers. This was music to his ears. His powerful frame towered menacingly over the short, fat sergeant. He put Demuth through a drill, forcing the man to bob 'up' and 'down' at command. The Other Ranks peered curiously in through the open door. Kessler skillfully improved on his show. Beads of sweat appeared on Demuth's lardy face. Kessler studied the man with satisfaction.

'If you think, Sergeant, that you are here at home in order to fill your belly you're very much mistaken. You're here to work, get me? To keep discipline. You're supposed to be an example to the men, but not at filling your belly.' Demuth stood rigidly at attention. He wanted to strangle the man before him, to kick him in the groin, to spit in his face. Kessler knew just what was going on inside the other man, and he grinned complacently. Demuth stood numbed, filled to the brim with helpless, furious submissiveness.

'Do you understand that now?' Kessler demanded. And Demuth snapped back in a loud, oily voice: 'Jawohl!'

'Very well,' Kessler said, and started towards the colonel's room. Demuth rushed ahead of him, and zealously opened the door. Kessler smiled contentedly. He knew these men. In the future this fat sergeant would scurry like a weasel in his presence.

Kessler overlooked Erika completely. He behaved as though he were striding through an empty room. It was one of his basic principles not to see such phenomena as Erika. Before Erika had caught more than a glimpse of him he had crossed the waiting-room and entered the colonel's office without knocking.

He greeted the men gathered in the room with an all-embracing gesture, as though they had assembled there solely for his visit. 'Heil Hitler, Colonel,' Kessler said, waving his right arm upward and backward with a certain easy elegance that implied reserves of power. That was the Fuehrer's gesture when thanking the people for ovations. He repeated the salute once more: 'Heil Hitler, gentlemen.'

With deep satisfaction he observed that the colonel was plainly disconcerted by this visit. The other home-front heroes in the room looked positively dismayed and dumbfounded. Then he noticed, of all people, the district leader. 'Heil Hitler, Dr. Friedrich!' Delightedly he poured oily mockery upon the gaping countenances of the men in the room. 'The Army and the Party of Rehhausen united, arm in arm!' he exclaimed. 'What an edifying sight. A symbol of our time!'

Still grinning complacently, Kessler shook hands all round. He paused for a moment when he came to Strick, and looked him over as though trying to judge him at a glance. Then he shook hands vigorously.

The colonel considered. He had to ignore Kessler's behaviour, which certainly did not comply with the ordinary rules of politeness. The question was, did Kessler know about the station commandant's arrest? And, if so, what should his, the colonel's, course be? This man Kessler was no joke; he had to be treated with deadly earnest. His powers were broad enough to imperil even a colonel and garrison commander.

Kessler deliberately drew up a chair and sat down in a comfortable position. He looked round grinning, as though to say, Well, here I am, here you have me, and you'd better be glad about it. He drank in the silence of the others with enjoyment, like a first glass of burgundy. Then as though expecting still more reason for enjoyment, he crossed his legs. 'It's very embarrassing, Colonel, very embarrassing – this station commandant affair. Very embarrassing indeed.' He nodded his head slowly from side to side. 'You know, Colonel, if the situation forced me to report on this matter to the highest authorities I'm afraid things would look very black for all of you.' He looked happily round the group. 'Very black indeed.'

Colonel Mueller had by now regained his composure. So Kessler knew! Then at least the fundamental situation was clear; the rest would take care of itself. 'It is very good of you to have come, Herr Kessler,' he said, and succeeded in imparting a sonorous note of gratification to his voice. 'Your coming spares me the necessity of making lengthy reports. How fortunate that my telephone call reached you in time.'

For a brief moment Kessler was discountenanced. He felt as though a bucket of cold water had been poured over his head. Abruptly he uncrossed his legs and sat up straight. 'I know of no telephone call.'

Mueller rose. 'Well, you came, and that is the main thing. May I ask you to be my guest for luncheon at the officers' club? We dine at twelve sharp, and it is almost that now. I make a point of not making my officers wait for me. . . .'

The others who were still sitting rose with one accord, except for Kessler. 'Gentlemen,' the colonel said with an air both gracious and firm, 'we will meet at twelve in the club. Punctually at one o'clock we can continue our discussion here.'

Kessler had the feeling that he had been outmanoeuvred. But in any case this break suited him, since he could use it to do a little investigating into Strick. And so he said no thanks to the colonel's invitation to drop in at his apartment 'to have a wash and a nip of brandy'.

The colonel started off with the district leader. Geiger and Wolf followed at a respectful distance. Rabe waited for Strick, but Kessler said, 'If you don't mind, Herr Strick, let us go for a short stroll together.'

They went out. Sergeant Demuth, the moment he caught sight of Kessler, ran ahead of them, and flung open the doors. Kessler coolly took note of this. That was the right way; that was how underlings should act when he was around.

CHAPTER THREE

LUNCH, at which Colonel Mueller presided every day, was taken together by all officers on duty at the Rehhausen barracks. This was an established part of the garrison routine, and had been instituted by a direct order from garrison headquarters.

The large dining-room in the club building was an impressive place. The high walls were panelled in oak. From the heavy, beamed ceiling hung two chandeliers. The well-tended parquet floor was almost entirely covered by a huge green rug. One side of the room consisted of large french windows reaching to the ceiling. When these were open they gave on to a terrace which overlooked the town of Rehhausen, the main river, and the vineyards on the opposite bank.

The officers who forgathered for lunch were in the habit of standing round in small groups and chatting until Colonel Mueller entered the dining-room at the stroke of noon. A few minutes before the hour the adjutant would read out the names of the officers who were to be honoured by sitting at the colonel's table. The roster was changed every day, and Captain Geiger made a point of going through the list of officers in regular rotation and carefully avoiding any favouritism.

Today the colonel appeared to be late, which was rare. Conversation among the officers lagged or became shop-talk. Major Wittkopf, commander of Training Battalion 434, had some sharp things to say concerning the behaviour of the extra club orderly, Vogel. He had seen the man leaning idly against the wall, doing absolutely nothing.

Captain Geiger, the adjutant, entered the room. He shook hands with Major Wittkopf, the highest-ranking officer. Then he announced: 'At the colonel's table today, in addition to Major Wittkopf, there will be: two guests, District Leader Dr. Friedrich and Captain Kessler of Würzburg G.H.Q.; Captain Wolf; myself; Lieutenant Strick, an officer newly transferred to us; and Lieutenant Rabe. The colonel has asked me to apologize for his lateness today. There were some urgent official duties which could not be postponed.'

The colonel was waiting in the ante-room. His powerful, thick-set body was swaying with annoyance. He had thrust his hand deep into his pocket, which was another sign of his bad temper. It was already eight minutes past twelve, and his guest, Captain Kessler, was not yet here. Nor was Lieutenant Strick.

The club chef reported for the second time that the meal was ready. Now he stood in the corner with the expression of an artist who had been slighted. It pained Mueller exceedingly that this had to be so, for the insulted chef was a fine fellow, whose cuisine was uniformly excellent. Punctuality, the colonel felt, was the one courtesy a commander could always show his hard-working men.

Dr. Friedrich was thoroughly in sympathy with his friend, Colonel Mueller. He sincerely admired the colonel's fine sense of tradition and propriety, and always appreciated the smoothness with which Mueller put his ideas into practice. For the district leader had never succeeded in establishing anything like gentlemanly etiquette, not even within his own staff. But then his own underlings in the Party were completely without feeling for the social graces. Those louts scratched up his floor with their riding-boots, and flicked the ashes off their cigarettes against his curtains. All they knew how to do was to make difficulties for him.

'Why go to these lengths for this man Kessler?' Dr. Friedrich whispered to the colonel. 'It's much more than he deserves. We'd do better not to worry about him at all.' Both men paced up and down the ante-room, conversing in low tones. Their entourage discreetly withdrew. Wolf tried to involve Rabe in a conversation; he worked him into a corner and began gesturing in all directions as he talked.

'My dear Dr. Friedrich,' the colonel said, taking the district leader's arm for a moment, 'I certainly don't like Kessler, but we cannot ignore him – unfortunately.'

'I, at any rate, would never permit Kessler to interfere in the area of my authority,' Dr. Friedrich said. 'We are the ones who represent National Socialism, and no one else.'

In passing, the colonel instructed Corporal Vogel to open the top window. It was getting warm, and besides he did not like to see soldiers standing round with nothing to do. Inactivity stimulated the brain, and soldiers had no business thinking.

'Dr. Friedrich,' he said, 'if I had my way I'd tell the fellow to go to the devil. I would forbid him to set foot anywhere within the Rehhausen garrison area. 'But' – the colonel took a deep breath, and the district leader could sense how hard it was for him to make this admission – 'but I cannot. Kessler's authority is very broad. His powers are extensive.'

'It's clear what the fellow is up to,' Dr. Friedrich said. 'He wants to put over his brand of National Socialism. I imagine he intends to introduce a National Socialist Guidance Officer into your command, Colonel. If we don't take the first step and appoint some one satisfactory to us as N.S.G.O. he will find some one else. And very likely his choice will prove a nuisance.'

The colonel agreed. 'But whom should we propose?' he asked.

Dr. Friedrich made his nomination hesitantly, as though apologizing for invading the colonel's sphere of authority by even so much as a suggested name. 'Rabe, perhaps?'

The colonel stopped his pacing.

'I should think Rabe might be just the man,' Dr. Friedrich added.

The colonel looked over at Rabe, to whom Wolf was talking with vigorous gesticulations. Rabe stood quietly, his body leaning slightly backward, as though he were trying to avoid being sprinkled with spittle. His expression betrayed a mild unhappiness; his eyes were looking over Wolf's head and seemed to be fixed upon the folds of the portières. The colonel turned back to Dr. Friedrich and resumed his pacing. 'I don't doubt Lieutenant Rabe's unimpeachable loyalty,' he said, 'but he is, so to speak, obsessed with justice. He has a fox-hole view of life. He's too young, too inexperienced, too filled with fantasies about the meaning of front-line fighting to see the realities of life. And the work of an N.S.G.O. isn't like volunteering for shock-troop duty. If that job is put into unsuitable hands, Dr. Friedrich, we will have more trouble than backing.'

The chef approached them for the third time to report that the meal was ready. 'Oh, well,' the colonel said, 'let's go in and eat.' Followed by his little troop, he entered the dining-room. He greeted the others, and sat down at his place. They all sat down. The colonel waved his spoon as though it were a marshal's baton. 'Good appetite, gentlemen,' he called to his brother officers. Twenty-eight spoons dipped into the chicken broth.

The colonel usually opened the general table conversation after the third spoonful. But today the two empty chairs near him, the chairs meant for Kessler and Strick, were a constant irritation, an outright challenge to his dignity. They represented wanton disregard for the order in his club, which meant disregard of himself. But what particularly disturbed him was that the two were missing at the same time. He could smell trouble. Kessler must be pumping Strick.

It was not until the seventh spoonful – a tardiness that boded no good – that the colonel initiated the general table conversation. 'The prestige of the officers' corps is endangered,' he said. 'It is no light matter when the foremost group in the nation is held up to public ridicule.' His table companions ate silently. The district leader nodded gravely. Wolf, his mouth full, eagerly croaked his agreement, and choked slightly over his food.

'Would you,' Mueller said, turning to Lieutenant Rabe, 'would you, just to take an example, arrest a colonel during a parade?'

Lieutenant Rabe said he would not. 'I would wait until the parade was over.' Wolf choked again. Geiger forgot to put his filled spoon, which he had raised, into his mouth. After a slight pause, Rabe explained, 'I certainly do not approve of Lieutenant Strick's method, but I must—'

The colonel interrupted him excitedly. 'Right! You too disapprove. What we are concerned about here is not the act alone. That may or may not have been justified. The important thing for us is the methods used.' The colonel's voice swelled so that it could be heard above the low conversations at the other tables. 'The prestige of the officers' corps is endangered.' Every one in the dining-room indicated his agreement. 'I hope,' the colonel said into the expectant silence, 'that each officer here will govern himself accordingly.'

And Vogel, who was standing behind the colonel, asked in a low voice which the general silence made audible throughout the room whether he might now serve the 'breast of veal with cream sauce.'

'Of course,' the colonel said.

With Strick at his side Kessler was sauntering down the cement pavement of the barrack square. They turned towards the guardroom building. 'We must get out of here,' Kessler said. 'This place is like an ant-heap. People standing around everywhere, everybody gabbling, all of them saluting like robots. There's no place here where we can talk in peace. Let's go outside.'

The moment the guard caught sight of Kessler he flung the

gate open. Its lower edge screeched across the cement of the road. Then the guard froze into a salute. 'They all obey you after you warm them up a bit,' Kessler said. And Strick replied, 'There are plenty of men whose ultimate motivations are ambition and fear.' Kessler nodded.

In the valley before them lay Rehhausen. It was as though the town had thrown itself at the feet of the barracks, motionless, submissive, awaiting judgment, prepared for condemnation or mercy. The Main, its banks covered by vineyards as it entered Rehhausen, moved on through the city like a sluggish drain. Strick imagined he could see the innumerable sewers from these silent houses carrying their discharge of water, urine, wine, milk, and tears. Thus, fed by a thousand creeping channels, the drainage became a river, carrying everything with it, pouring the debris into the sand for the sand to filter. And the earth sucked it all up, filled itself with the stuff, and from the fertilized earth grew plants, grape-vines, and trees. It was sewage upon which prosperity depended.

Kessler noticed a bench some eighty yards from the barracks, standing in the midst of an open field. He headed towards it. 'This place is fine,' he stated with satisfaction. 'Nobody behind us, nobody in front of us, no shrubs or bushes for any sly bastard to hide in.'

Strick smiled. 'You are very suspicious.'

'I've become so,' Kessler answered laconically.

Strick could almost reach out and touch Kessler's shattered world. He knew its rubble, its blasted wreckage. He felt as if he were breathing in with the very air Kessler's lively distrust and contempt for everything.

'The world is a dung-heap,' Strick said.

Kessler agreed, but not entirely. 'It can still be put to use as a fertilizer,' he said. 'But you have to know the rules when you spread it. Your harvest depends on the manure.'

They reached the bench. Kessler gestured to Strick to sit down; he waved his hand as though the bench were his property, and he were generously permitting some casual passer-by to sit on it. They leaned back, and Strick waited expectantly. But for the moment Kessler said nothing. Their groping thoughts reached out to one another while they looked over the landscape, as if they must discover everything about it. Strick could no longer look at any piece of land without breaking it up into battle positions. He was incapable of seeing what others called the peace and beauty of God's Nature. Instead he saw hollows which could lend themselves to trenching, hills that would make good machine-gun posts. The river down below would form a fine main defence line. And from here, where he sat, a keen-eyed observer would have the whole of the enemy's terrain in his pocket.

'Are you what people call an idealist?' Kessler asked finally.

'I don't think so,' Strick replied slowly. 'Experience has made me into a realist.'

'Lousy experiences?'

'The experiences of our time.'

Kessler unbuttoned his coat. The hot sun flung its weight upon them, as though it existed solely for the purpose of warming them. 'I too am a man of facts, not dreams,' Kessler said. 'There is certainly something magnificent about courage and faith when they make us able to conquer whole sectors of the front. But once the schoolboy enthusiasm is over we must fall back on fear. The naked fear for our lives, for our honour, for pensions – or anything in that line. That's what turns the trick and holds the line.'

On the opposite bank of the river Strick saw three solitary poplars. A splendid target. Firing directions: Straight ahead – 1,200 metres – church steeple – to the right: three trees. Target found? Sight 6.2 Percussion fuse. One round. Fire!

'You mean, when patriotism gives out, only the instinct for self-preservation counts?' Strick said.

That was precisely what Kessler meant. 'You've seen it for yourself. After five years of war all the heroic slogans turn your stomach. Ambition and fear matter a lot more than the best training. The same goes for all the cheers over the Greater Germany.'

Strick added: 'It's up to you to promote heroism by a kick in the arse.'

'We agree,' Kessler said. 'We both have the same slant.'

Strick turned away from the enemy hill, where he had been trying to work out a trench system. He turned towards Kessler, and looked at the man's hard, angular profile, his massive, jutting chin, the open tunic revealing a broad chest. Kessler's feet were set wide apart, braced against the ground. His big, solid hands were toying with a sheaf of papers which he had taken out of a side pocket.

'Do you know,' Kessler said, 'that I have been on the telephone all morning on your account?'

'To pull my chestnuts out of the fire?'

'Hell, no. Why should I? You're not especially interested in an easy way out, are you? If it were a soft living you were after you would have asked for your share in the station commandant's loot and kept your mouth shut.'

'Right,' Strick said. 'Right, I could have done that.'

Kessler leaned forward and picked up a hazel switch. Some one must have dropped it here, Strick thought; perhaps a child playing or a young man who let it fall when he met his girl. Such things still seemed to exist in this place – playing children and pairs of lovers.

'But you wouldn't have done that sort of thing,' Kessler said, testing the flexibility of the switch. 'Neither would I. We two just aren't profiteers; we have other ambitions. That's how it always is. Some fill their bellies, some get drunk, but we' – the switch whistled through the air as though it were drawing the dividing line between the two worlds – 'but we – we lead!'

Strick felt the strength and drive of the man. He was a human dynamo; he was made up of nothing but will and muscle; he was a battering-ram of flesh and blood. If he could not shatter other things he would shatter himself. Slowly Strick threaded his way into the maze of the other man's philosophy. 'Then you think the desire to lead is an inborn trait in certain people?' he asked. 'Or a racial trait?'

'Rot,' Kessler said incisively. 'All that racial stuff is hocus-pocus, sham and deception, mythological fog for the mass brain. What really counts is the break-through of the leader-personality. What we're after is to get our way. We can't help ourselves; we just won't truckle to people who have no inner right to give us orders. We – we! – must do the ordering ourselves. From all that I've heard of you, Strick, you're one of our kind.'

It was seductive as the song of the Lorelei. It was more seductive, even, than Kessler knew. But Strick resisted. 'Suppose you're mistaken, Kessler? It's true that they made me an officer for courage under fire, but I have been court-martialled several times.'

Kessler laughed aloud, and struck the switch against his riding-boots, sending up a swirl of dust. He looked through his papers gleefully.

'I'm fairly well informed about that, Strick. In September 1939 you lit into a corporal who was getting ready to rape a girl. Since there was conclusive evidence that rape was what he was after, you were cleared.'

Strick was somewhat taken aback at the accuracy of Kessler's information. He blinked at the harsh noon sun. Down below in Rehhausen a window-pane suddenly flashed. If this was the front, he thought, I would assume that the enemy was signalling. The best way to stop such signalling is to blast away at the source. He wrenched himself away from his obsession and said: 'In December 1941 I faced a court-martial for the second time.'

Kessler laughed again, and tapped his switch against a sheet of paper. 'Don't be so conceited, Strick. I know about that case too. You refused to carry out a general's direct order to protect his retreat. But the Fuehrer personally demoted the general for cowardice, and the charge against you was quashed.'

Strick decided to be astonished at nothing. With a faint smile he protested, 'I assure you I had no hand in that particular turn of events. I was like some one walking on a dark street. There were holes here and there, and I fell in.'

Kessler took another sheet from his sheaf of documents. He tucked the switch under his arm.

'According to the opinion of your superiors, you are everything from self-willed to headstrong. But not one of them has attempted to deny that you have the personality of a leader.' He skimmed through his papers, reread a few items, and then folded up the sheaf. 'You see,' he said, 'we need your kind of man around here. What's more, you come from an exemplary National Socialist family. Your father fought in the First World War and was decorated several times. In addition he has been a section leader of the Party since 1931.' The switch lashed at Kessler's left boot again, making a dark line on the leather where it struck. Strick had a sudden vision of a face being struck by that switch, of blood running downward along the line of the cut, trickling thickly and coagulating.

'You are extremely well informed,' Strick said.

Kessler leaned back. 'I have to be when I pick out a National Socialist Guidance Officer for the Rehhausen garrison.'

Strick felt as though a cannon had gone off right by him. The flame of the explosion dazzled his eyes. In a moment he would hear the detonation, then the hissing withdrawal of the empty barrel as it slid down the oiled bearings of the carriage. The shell would fly with a dying whistle, and land over there in the enemy terrain, precisely beneath the three trees that were the target. In a moment he would see the hit; a mushroom of dust would be thrown up, and four seconds later a feeble report would announce the bursting of the shell.

That had been his daily occupation for the past five years. A glance down a column of figures in the artillery table, a quick calculation, the lightning application of long experience and his gift for this sort of thing – and over there, dead men; on this side, decorations. Five long years. A cog in the wheels of a murder machine. A worker in a factory producing human corpses. He would never escape these things, never again.

He felt Kessler watching him, and he had the impression that his face was damp with perspiration. He wanted to rub his palm over it, but instead he sat up straight and turned his half-closed eyes towards Kessler. Kessler looked straight into his eyes. Finally Strick said, 'You aren't serious?'

Kessler nodded. 'Unusual times require unusual measures,' he said. 'I no longer feel like carrying my special authority around in my pocket for decorative purposes. These people around here are soft as sponges. What they need is a good squeeze. For days I've been insisting that an NSGO be appointed for this headquarters. They've kept shirking it; they keep giving me the slip. I've exhausted my patience with them. I need a man who knows how to get things done in his own way, ruthlessly. You are that man!'

'You forget something,' Strick said. 'By your own information, you see that I don't easily take orders. I've always tried to shake off my superiors. At first that startled them; after a while they got used to the fact that their orders would be carried out only as I interpreted them.'

Kessler slapped his thigh, making a crack like the report of a pistol. 'That's just what I expect from you. I don't want anyone interfering with you, neither the colonel nor the district leader. You have just one job, Strick – to mobilize everything in your area ruthlessly – ruthlessly – for the Final Victory. Crush any opposition to the Fuehrer's orders. Put the screws on everybody who's beginning to soften up. There's nothing to stop you; you won't have to lick anyone's boots. You'll get the fullest authority, unlimited powers.'

The landscape in front of Strick – Rehhausen, the Main, the vineyards – faded from his consciousness. The noise from the barracks intruded. He heard marching footsteps. That marching would allow for no idylls, no diversions, no escape. He had made up his mind to take on the job – but he would not say so until he had made sure of a good jumping-off position. 'Where do you come into this, Kessler?' he asked.

'You will always be able to reach me. We'll keep in touch with one another. But I have a lot of demands on my time. What I am doing here is turning a game-preserve over to you. How and when you hunt in it is your own affair. Only there has to be some shooting – understand that. All doubtful elements must be eradicated. Keep your eye on puppets and charlatans like the district leader and the colonel. They're dangerous because they're reactionary, but we need them. That is why we must train them along our lines. We can mould them like wet clay.'

'I will have full authority?'

'Absolutely.'

Kessler held out his hand to Strick. Strick hesitated, then seized it firmly. In the barracks the men were now singing:

'. . . And what is done
Is done for our dear Fatherla-and.'

The singing was loud, but not hearty. The men were singing on orders. Words could be commandeered, but thoughts could not.

Kessler stood up. He broke the switch, and tossed it away. 'Then it's settled,' he said. He started off, buttoning his tunic as he went. Then he laid his heavy hand on Strick's shoulder. Strick looked into a grinning, self-satisfied face. 'Now we'll take the good news to our little turtle doves,' he said. 'You'll be surprised, Strick, to see the way they fall in line.'

The guard, as soon as he caught sight of Kessler, jerked the compound gate wide open.

Corporal Vogel, who was serving as an auxiliary orderly in the club today, was vastly amused. He was on duty at the club once each week and on all special occasions, and he invariably enjoyed the assignment.

As soon as Vogel turned up at the club, shortly after eleven o'clock, to help with the preparations for the officers' lunch, he would go promptly into the kitchen and announce in a loud cheerful voice that today was another occasion when he could spit into the officers' soup if he wanted to. None of the other club orderlies took that seriously. Vogel had the reputation of being an eccentric; he enjoyed a kind of jester's licence. And he took full advantage of his immunity. Even the chef had a weakness for Vogel. Vogel was a gourmet whose appreciation of food was intellectual as well as physiological. The chef thought highly of Vogel's intellectual attainments, and was dependent on Vogel's judgment. When the chef tasted the food he had Vogel stand by with his own spoon. Vogel would roll his tongue against his palate and close his eyes. Then he would brood over the taste, as though he were meditating upon a problem of world importance. The chef held his breath. Finally Vogel would give his verdict. And the chef swore by that verdict.

This was the real reason why Vogel occupied a favoured position as extra club orderly. The other orderlies waited on the tables; Vogel gave instructions. The others washed dishes; Vogel helped the chef weigh ingredients. All the others waxed or scrubbed the floor; Vogel counted the silver or took an inventory of the wine cellar.

Lunch was now over. The 'veal with cream sauce' had been followed by chocolate mousse. Thereafter most of the officers had withdrawn on the pretext that they had to catch up on work, and were now snoring contentedly in their rooms. Only the colonel and his table companions had gone out to sit on the terrace. There, Lieutenant Rabe abstaining, they were unitedly chopping Lieutenant Strick to firewood. Most of them were using hatchets, but Wolf swung a mighty battle-axe.

Vogel lavished attentions upon the group on the terrace. He dragged over three huge sun-shades, so that the colonel and his entourage would be shielded from the noonday sun. He kept emptying ash-trays and bringing tiny portions of fresh ice to the table. There were moments when the colonel cast long looks of approbation at this super-devoted orderly. If Vogel had nothing to do at the table for a moment he waited by the glass door, ready to spring into action, and listening for all he was worth. Hardly a word of the conversation escaped him. After a while, he noticed, the district leader and the colonel restricted themselves to tossing a few mild remarks into the discussion. They seemed to Vogel like a pair of incendiaries happily watching the fire they had started, and adding now and then a little oil to stimulate the flames. Wolf kept burning up armfuls of firewood, and Geiger assisted eagerly.

Vogel gathered that Strick was a busybody, if not an outright trouble-maker. His not coming to lunch stamped him as a rebel against the sacred order of the club. Vogel also learned that this fellow Kessler, who was incomprehensibly a captain, had the character of a hold-up man, but, unfortunately – the colonel threw in for warning – the powers of a commanding general. Vogel would have heard a good deal more if Rabe, who was an observant sort, had not seen that he was listening. Rabe beckoned to him and said, 'Vogel, I think your hearing is as sharp as your memory is long. We can dispense with both these talents of yours at the moment. Kindly take yourself off. If we need you we'll call you.' The conversation stopped in embarrassment. No one reversed Rabe's order, and there was nothing for Vogel to do but trot off.

He arranged a brief intermezzo in the kitchen, where he advised the enticingly plump kitchen helper, Irene, to eat less or else she would get fat. Outraged, Irene threw her dish-cloth at Vogel. Vogel ducked, and the cloth, heavy with water, flew into a pile of dishes and knocked them off the table. Vogel applauded as though he were watching a vaudeville show. Irene, secure in the knowledge of her desirability, threatened to report him to the chef for breaking dishes. Vogel waved his hand nonchalantly. Irene spluttered that the chef always listened to her.

'You won't say a word to him, pet,' Vogel said with assurance. 'You'll keep the remark I made to yourself. Otherwise your dear chef will start noticing how you've put on weight – even though it's just beginning around your behind. And you know that the chef is an æsthete, which is something you ain't. Besides, the chef respects my taste. You can't afford to have me calling you fat.'

Irene scraped the left-over cream sauce on top of the potatoes into the slop-bucket and, instead of finishing it off as she had intended, tossed in the chocolate mousse. 'Does anybody except Vogel want some chicken broth?' she called. The orderlies were sated. One of them said, 'Eat it yourself till you burst.'

'You're just mad because you can't have me,' Irene screamed at him. And Vogel added, 'Get to be a chef, man. Then you can have Irene and her sort.'

The orderlies laughed. That was Vogel all over. He was the only one who didn't hanker after Irene. But Vogel had no time to enjoy the applause. Through the glass doors he caught sight of Kessler and Strick. They looked like a pair of horse-dealers who had just struck a good bargain. Vogel went up to them as though expecting an order. Kessler said, 'Show me where there's a telephone here, and then clear out.' Vogel showed him, and before he cleared out he heard Kessler ask for General Headquarters in Würzburg – 'and make it snappy.'

Vogel trotted back into the kitchen. There Irene was pouring the chicken broth in with the mousse, the cream sauce, and the potatoes. The smell from the resulting slops was heavy and sweetish. 'If our dear Fuehrer ever heard about this!' Vogel said, with a look of concern. But Irene pushed him energetically aside. She knew that the Fuehrer would have nothing to blame her for. Food was a precious commodity, and had to be used to the full in these times. Whatever was left over, and there always was a good deal left over, went to the club pigs.

These club pigs were one of Captain Wolf's most brilliant inspirations. He was, as Colonel Mueller had whimsically remarked, their father – their spiritual father at least. Left-overs had to be put to use, Wolf had reasoned. Then, the left-overs of officers must be used for officers. *Ergo*: feed pigs on them, and in due time these pigs could be served to the officers again. This would produce new left-overs, which meant food for more pigs. It was an auspicious circle, which uncommonly enriched the officers' table.

Vogel noticed that Kessler and Strick had left the telephone. He sauntered towards them. Kessler was saying: 'Since it's all right with the commanding general, the colonel will have to like it or lump it.' He looked up and noticed Vogel, not without a certain annoyance. Vogel reported, 'The colonel is out on the terrace.' He led the way.

Kessler went straight up to the colonel and blandly asked him whether he had enjoyed his lunch. At the sight of Kessler the conversation had stopped dead; the impression was that they all had been sitting in silence. Then the colonel said in tones of undisguised coldness: 'Please forgive us for not waiting more than fifteen minutes for you to put in your appearance.'

With a sure instinct Vogel sensed the general need for a good supply of cognac. He arranged a tray with large glasses, and placed the bottle within reach – cooling fluid for political motors. The terrace was shimmering with sunlight. The figures under the sun-shades looked to Vogel like washed-out, contourless silhouettes. He could not see the firm outlines of solid bodies, but the voices he heard were not the voices of phantoms. Captain Kessler's voice was loud, booming, penetrating. It echoed across the terrace, thudded down like a club, and the words were so solid they were almost tangible. Kessler was saying, 'While you were lunching, Colonel, I was picking out a National Socialist Guidance Officer for Rehhausen headquarters.'

Vogel could sense the moment rapidly approaching when double brandies would be required. He turned the corkscrew in the cork. Colonel Mueller asked hoarsely, 'And who may that be?'

Kessler, as calmly as an experienced poker-player in a game for high stakes, replied, 'Lieutenant Strick.'

Vogel gripped the bottle between his knees. He pulled out the cork. There was a dull pop, as though a shell were exploding far away. The colonel was saying deliberately, 'You don't have the final say on this, Kessler.'

Unruffled, Kessler replied, 'I have just informed the commanding general by telephone, and he approves.'

There was a profound silence on the terrace. Vogel seemed to be alone in the world with his bottle of cognac. And he needed it. He filled a large glass to the brim and drank it at a gulp. Good stuff, that. It seared its way down his throat. Then he heard the colonel's voice again.

'Suppose,' the colonel said, 'that we informed the commanding general of Lieutenant Strick's part in last night's events. You understand what I mean, don't you, Kessler? We could make a test case out of this if we wanted to. If things came to a head I am sure we would be allowed to choose the N.S.G.O. for our area ourselves.'

Kessler snapped out his answer. 'I doubt that,' he said. 'It is possible, quite possible, that Rehhausen might be assigned a different N.S.G.O. from the one I have proposed. But in that case it is equally possible that Rehhausen would be assigned another Commandant.'

With a sense of desperation Vogel swigged another glass of cognac at the expense of the State. This fellow Kessler hit out like a prize-fighter, and he struck mostly below the belt. Vogel listened closely. The terrace had fallen silent again. Abruptly the colonel called, 'Vogel! Cognac!' Vogel responded as fast as an echo: 'Yes, sir.' He began swiftly filling the glasses he had ready. Then he carried the tray across the terrace and placed it carefully on the table. The company reached out eagerly for the glasses, and gulped down the brandy. 'Leave the bottle here,' the colonel said.

Kessler generously presented the alternatives. 'If the commanding general should find out about that stinking mess with the station commandant,' he said casually, 'the whole case will have to go to the supreme authorities. It hardly seems necessary for us to bother them with it, but if that is the way you want it – all right. I assure you the high authorities will certainly be sticking their noses into this scandal if you raise objections to the N.S.G.O. I've picked out. One thing leads to another. You can take your choice.'

Kessler reached out for the bottle and poured himself and Strick a drink. He touched glasses with Strick, and drank to him. Then his eye lit on the ubiquitous orderly. 'Put down the bottles and clear out,' he said. Vogel, feeling Rabe's probing glance upon him, trotted off again. Anyway, the business on the terrace wasn't so exciting any more. He would have enjoyed listening to the rest of the palaver, but now there was nothing to do but go back to the kitchen and get little Irene worked up again.

In the kitchen he found his friend and room-mate, Hoepfner. Corporal Hoepfner was negotiating with Irene. 'What do you want here?' Vogel asked him.

'None of your damned business, Vogel.'

Vogel instantly became the chef's chief deputy. 'Irene,' he said, 'the chef wants you to go up and clean his room. And be snappy about it. He needs you in a hurry.'

Irene tripped off eagerly.

'Well?' Vogel asked.

'I've come for Captain Wolf's lunch,' Hoepfner said.

'No need,' Vogel answered. 'Wolf has already eaten. I saw him eating with my own eyes.'

'That doesn't matter,' Hoepfner declared with profound conviction, as though he were swearing allegiance to the flag.

'No mother's son in this barracks gets double meals,' Vogel declared solemnly. 'Not even your captain.'

Hoepfner could not understand what had come over his room-mate. 'I come every day after lunch for Captain Wolf's portion,' he expostulated.

'I can well believe it. And then you eat it yourself.'

Hoepfner, seeing his extra meal jeopardized, grew tough. 'Hand it over or I'll break every bone in your body.'

In a casual tone, Vogel said, 'You can have it.'

'That's better.'

'You can have it,' Vogel went on, grinning, 'if you sign a chit confirming receipt of an extra portion for Captain Wolf.'

At this Hoepfner began swearing like an army corporal, all the while feverishly searching for a way to get his extra portion. From the terrace someone called Vogel's name. Vogel rushed off.

With an air of relief Hoepfner watched him go; then he poked a fork skilfully into the platter of veal and lifted several large slices to his own plate. 'Crazy bastard,' he said.

When he reached the terrace Vogel was given the order to bring up a second bottle of cognac, on the double. 'My dear Lieutenant Strick,' the colonel was saying, 'after all, we must drink to our close co-operation.' And then he said, 'What are you waiting for, Vogel? Close your mouth and get moving.'

CHAPTER FOUR

THE first action of the newly appointed National Socialist Guidance Officer consisted in taking a lengthy afternoon nap. Strick was knocked out – partly as a result of the seven glasses of cognac he had drunk at the club.

At 3.30 p.m. Lieutenant Rabe went out to the athletic field; Strick was sleeping. At 4.30 Rabe returned; Strick was still sleeping. At 6.00 p.m. Rabe finished his tour of duty; Strick was still sleeping. At 7 p.m. Corporal Vogel came in, and that marked the end of Strick's afternoon nap. Vogel waked him with a wet towel which he folded twice and let dangle in Strick's face. Strick thrashed out with his arms, and sat up cursing.

'It's seven o'clock, Lieutenant. All duties within the barracks area are finished, so it's safe for you to get up.' Vogel left.

Strick felt as though an invisible somebody was sitting on his head. He pulled at his hair. Oh, yes – those damn cognacs after lunch. He was no drinker; he couldn't take it. If that sort of thing was going to be usual he would have to train for it. Stupid business, these drinking bouts. From his weather-beaten face his grey eyes blinked at the austere neatness of the simple officer's room. No one was there. Strick spied a basin of cold water, and dipped his face into it. That felt good, damned good.

He pulled up his braces, and glanced briefly into the mirror. His was an ordinary sort of face – bony, with the skin drawn tight, a mouth like a line, deep-set eyes, creases like those carved by a knife for crude woodcuts. An average face, one of millions forged in the great foundries of the War. Without his uniform he might have been taken for a street-cleaner. Not an altogether likeable face, certainly not. There were things in it he would like to see erased. He buttoned his trousers and, still sitting, reached out for his socks. Straightening up, he bumped his head against a book-shelf. Aha – Rabe's private collection. What did the man read, beside Grimm's fairy-tales? He glanced at the books. Of course: Hitler's *Mein Kampf*, Rosenberg's *Myth of the Twentieth Century*, Houston Stewart Chamberlain. A library of standard blood-and-soil literature. Would it have Darré and Robert Ley's speeches too? Surprise – they were missing.

Nothing else pure Aryan? Why, what could possibly be the matter with Rabe?

Then what were all these other books? Knut Hamsun, the Nordic bard. And St. Thomas Aquinas! No, that had got in by accident. And in that corner? Not Thomas à Kempis, André Gide, Dante, Bernard Shaw, and Charles Dickens? But that was what they were. And then – was he seeing right? – there were Thomas Mann, Hermann Hesse, and Ernst Wiechert. What did it mean? Did Rabe read all these books or was he using some as camouflage for the others? And if so, which camouflaged which? Or was he simply one of the omnivorous readers who read without understanding any of the implications of what he was reading?

Rabe came in from supper at the club. 'You have until eight o'clock, Herr Strick. Supper is served between six and eight. Every one can come and go as he pleases.'

'If you don't come you don't have to go.'

'If you don't care to eat at the club or have some work to do you can have your tray fetched by your orderly.'

Strick was trying to get into his boots. They went on a good deal harder than usual. For a moment he suspected Vogel of playing a practical joke on him by soaking them in water. Rabe silently handed him a pair of boot-hooks.

'I suppose you expect me to congratulate you on your new appointment, Herr Strick?' Rabe said.

'It would be a nice gesture,' Strick said, groaning as he forced on the refractory boots, 'but no more than a gesture. Besides which, I would suspect you of trying to butter me up.'

'Exactly.'

'Maybe you'd prefer to give me your condolences, Rabe?'

Rabe turned the pages of a thick volume: *Three Centuries of German Lyrics*. Off-handedly he said: 'Condolences for you? I rather think it's the cause you supposedly represent that needs condolences.'

Strick had finally got into his boots. That bastard Vogel really had soaked them in water; through his torn socks he could feel that the boots were damp and cold.

He went up to Rabe. 'Do you mean to say,' he said challengingly, 'that I am not a National Socialist?'

Rabe looked up from his book. 'Perhaps you don't even know what one is.'

'Do you know exactly what one is, Rabe?'

'I am making every effort to learn.'

'Are you really? With what results?'

'I see I'll have to try harder.'

'Is that all?'

'Ideals,' said Rabe dreamily, the volume of lyrics lying open on his lap, 'come to life in the men who hold them. Those men must be examples to others.'

Strick ran his hand over his face to decide whether he needed a shave. His beard was sprouting vigorously, but he was not going to shave again. What for? For whom? After all, he was no example and had never had the urge to be one. 'Apropos examples, Rabe – I suppose the station commandant was one, eh?'

'He was an exception.'

'So! Every crook is an exception; every decent guy is a National Socialist. That's a starry-eyed view of things.'

'What's wrong with you, Strick, is that you don't believe in anything any more. I feel that you aren't even capable of understanding thoughts on a higher plane.'

'The devil with that. I don't dream up things, I see what's in front of my eyes. I have my own ideas about National Socialism, and about a number of other things that unfortunately happen to exist in this world.'

Rabe carefully closed his book. 'I intend to watch your work closely,' he said, and it was as if he were gently uttering a threat.

'And I,' Strick said, wriggling into his tunic, 'intend to show you some of these fine examples you admire.'

'You arouse my curiosity,' Rabe replied. He tucked his volume of lyrics tenderly under his arm and started off.

'Where are you going?' Strick asked. 'Do you intend to elevate your soul by reading lyrics out in God's open fields? Don't worry, I'm leaving right away, and will be gone all evening.'

'I have an appointment in town,' Rabe explained amiably. 'I have some friends there, and once a week we arrange a literary soirée. Come along next time if you like that sort of thing. It's a nice group of cultured people. Captain Geiger always comes. He reads poetry aloud very well, by the way. Tonight we're doing Mörike.'

'Heaven help me!' Strick protested. 'Before I listen to Geiger declaiming Mörike I'd rather have our district leader pull out one of my teeth. Go to your literary sewing circle and God be with you. I prefer getting respectably drunk. Long live the Fuehrer, Rabe! And long live German literature – though I'm afraid the two don't go together very well.'

'You have the manners of a bulldog, Strick – the kind that has to wear a muzzle all the time.' Rabe tipped his cap, and with characteristic courtesy closed the door behind him.

'Muzzle, eh!' Strick growled after him. 'He'll find out whether I'm muzzled when I bite him in the seat of his trousers. Muzzle, eh! That's better than wearing blinkers.'

Lieutenant Strick and Corporal Vogel sauntered together down the hill which led from the barracks to Rehhausen. The sun had set; the evening was peaceful and somewhat pallid. Nature looked bleached, like a skeleton that had been lying long on a battlefield.

Vogel led his friend through a densely planted park into the valley. Their route was a narrow, meandering footpath through a world at peace. On the benches sat soldiers with their girls. The gathering summer dusk laid a mercifully dim light upon their faces as they sought to break through the barriers of personality. These faces looked gentler, shallower, and more peaceful than they did in the harsh light of day. No one seemed to pay any attention to the two quiet strollers. As soon as any soldier started to salute Vogel expansively gestured to him not to bother – an act which obviously gave him great pleasure. 'High concentration of happiness around here,' he remarked. 'Too much love, too little room. When you and I were young we had a whole park to ourselves. Here there are four cuddling on every bench, and another half-dozen behind each bush. What is it the Fuehrer always says? "Germany has grown bigger and more beautiful"!'

Strick looked fixedly to the left, because on his right a couple seemed to be completely absorbed in one another. 'Time was,' he said, 'when you talked a lot differently.'

'Oh, then! Then I went to war for Adolf and Greater Germany. But they don't need me any more since Providence is looking out for them – so Adolf tells us. In those days I was an apostle of the future. Now what am I? A wreck.'

Strick walked on thoughtfully, looking into the twilight as though it were a stretched canvas showing misty, strangely distorted images. He could see Vogel as he had been ten years ago, a jolly boy in shorts. He had always had some pet animal – Hermann the dachshund, or Elvira the rabbit, or Lohengrin the cat, or Abraham the pet shrew. He carried Abraham about in his pocket, and usually put him down where the little animal would be sure to create a flurry. In class, in a train, and once – what a sensation that had been! – in church. In his own father's church, moreover, for Vogel's father had been the village pastor.

It was as though Vogel were listening to these memories, as though Strick had been speaking aloud. With suppressed annoyance Vogel said, 'I suppose you mean that because my father was such a first-class pastor I ought to have some religion in me too.'

Pastor Vogel, Strick thought, had been a highly belligerent preacher. His chief stock-in-trade had been patriotism and the enemies of the Fatherland, and his pugnacity increased whenever there was the slightest threat to the nation. In the village church regular and ardent prayers were said for all honourable defenders of the Fatherland – in peacetime at least once a month, in wartime every Sunday morning. And Strick and Vogel, with the enthusiasm of fifteen-year-olds, had energetically worked the organ bellows and pulled the bell rope.

'We were very proud of your father,' Strick said.

Vogel concealed an impulse of pleasure behind a show of annoyance. 'Proud of him! There's not much trick to praying for the blessings of Providence to be showered on heroes. That's a lot easier than being a hero yourself. What does being proud of something mean? At fourteen I was proud of my first long trousers. At eighteen of my first girl. At nineteen they set me to target practice, and told me I ought to be proud of a score of thirty-five bull's eyes. It's all rot. I've never found anyone or anything worth croaking for, and that's all there is to it.'

They had come out of the park on to a broad highway. The first wooden houses appeared. A heavy mortar shell, Strick thought briefly, and they would collapse like so many matchboxes. He turned again to Vogel. 'So you feel yourself cheated. And your whole philosophy now comes down to this: fill your belly; don't give a damn.'

'What else?' Vogel exclaimed. There was disdain in his voice, as though he were speaking to some one whose stupidity was obvious. 'What the devil else is there? Do you want me to be a text-book hero like yourself? Keep busy producing widows and orphans on both sides?'

Yes, Strick thought, he had a pretty high quota of widows and orphans to his credit. Anyone could see that. His chest was plastered with decorations. In his service record-book there were twenty-six entries: battles, skirmishes, preparatory operations, defence of positions. For example, there was the date March 12th, 1942: Repulse of an attempted break-through at Bolkhov. That was all, but that meant: 116 rounds of artillery ammunition, 830 rounds of infantry fire, 74 hand-grenades, 27 flares. Or, put in other terms, it meant: four burning houses, two women and three children killed, five burned-out tanks, an expiring band of 'enemy' infantry, half a dozen human beings screaming like animals in the night, two dead men close beside him, and four critically wounded men who moaned painfully and stared at him while their faces turned yellow and the death rattle rose in their throats. And on his own face it meant watery blood and splashes of brain shot from the skull of a man to whom, a moment before, he had called out encouragingly, 'Keep going, fellow!' And that was just one entry, one of twenty-six.

Strick looked at the clean, well-swept street before him, at the tended gardens with their neat paths and clipped lawns, at the white houses and the polished windows. How would that all look, he thought, if only a single division fell upon Rehhausen for just three hours? The order for the operation would read: Division, after full artillery preparation, to advance at dawn through Rehhausen and occupy a three-kilometre-wide strip along the bank of the Main. The result: a position on the bank of the Main, occupied according to orders; a few dozen more crosses in the graveyard; and a rubbish-heap the size of a town.

Strick said: 'I've become very tired, Vogel. I was out there almost five full years. Poland, France, Russia – Russia for ever. I've had my fill of it. All I want now is to rest up, that's all.'

Vogel looked at him. 'Rest? Of course, the only way to get rest is to be an N.S.G.O. What do you think you're trying to put over on me? The weary warrior, eh, tired and longing for rest. The prodigal bringing new blessings back with him by killing the fattest home-front calf he can find. And he finds it the moment he arrives!'

Vogel came to a halt in the middle of the street, and gave Strick a long, searching look. Strick met his eyes, squinting with one of his own in the faintest hint of a wink. 'Very sorry,' he said, 'really very sorry, but I had no choice.'

'You didn't want any other choice. I know you – a little, anyway. We have a lot in common, outside of your bad taste in women. You know you deliberately fixed the station commandant. I'm not a complete idiot.'

Strick gave a smothered laugh. 'We are living in great times,' he quoted. 'The Fatherland requires sacrifices.'

'Here, here!' Vogel exclaimed fervently. 'We must drink to that. Let's keep up with the times. Drink, and think about corpses.'

When Corporal Vogel went down to Rehhausen in his free time he was usually Mother Tikke's guest. Mother Tikke loved Vogel like a son. She had a deep longing to love somebody like a son, for she had just lost two sons of her own.

Herr Tikke, Herr Oscar Tikke, was mighty proud of that. Of course, fate had dealt him a hard blow. He had been asked to make great sacrifices. But sacrifices were essential, and Herr Tikke knew what was the proper attitude. He was now the father of heroes, and moreover he was the Nazi Party block warden. Nowadays he got drunk almost every evening to celebrate these high honours.

Mother Tikke took a fundamentally different view of the matter, but she knew it was unwise to voice her thoughts. There was only one person to whom she could relieve her heart, and that was Vogel. One evening when he was drunker than usual Vogel had bellowed fearful curses and had said things against the Government which surpassed anything Mother Tikke had ever dared even to think. Since that evening Mother Tikke had loved Vogel like a son. And when they were alone in the restaurant she became outspoken. Then the blunt terms they used with one another became substitutes for the birth pangs, the childhood diseases, and common boyhood follies which mothers and sons go through together. At such times they were of one mind, young Vogel with his old face, and old Mother Tikke with her young heart.

Vogel and Strick entered the almost deserted restaurant. A ceiling of heavy, carved, exposed beams hung low into the room. They felt that they wanted to sit down in this room and stay for a long time. The small, scoured tables were surrounded by crude wooden chairs or benches. Primitive lamps dangled from the ceiling. Mother Tikke, with a face furrowed like a ploughed field, came up to Vogel. She held out her hand. Vogel took it with both hands, drew her close to him, and embraced her. 'All right, all right,' Mother Tikke said, fending him off. 'You'll get your wine anyhow.'

'Not only mine, Mother Tikke. Wine for my friend too.'

Strick took the wrinkled hand and shook it. Vogel introduced him. 'This is Lieutenant Strick, Mother Tikke. A decent bastard. He is – hold tight, Mother Tikke – the National Socialist Guidance Officer for the garrison. Newly imported.'

'Is that so!' Mother Tikke said, wrapping her hand in her apron as though she wanted to wipe off this handshake. 'So he is your friend.'

Vogel pinched Mother Tikke in the side. 'You see,' he said, 'that's the kind of friends I have.'

'My husband will be delighted,' Mother Tikke said with an obvious effort. The worn little woman with the furrowed face under her sparse hair called loudly, 'Oscar, Oscar!' Oscar Tikke came in. Oscar was a human hippopotamus with a belly like a barrel. A moustache bristled on his upper lip; he shambled, but not without certain dignity. When he put on his block warden's uniform, in fact, he resembled Goering.

Oscar Tikke was overjoyed at having not merely an officer in his modest wine-shop, but an officer who was to boot the N.S.G.O. of the garrison. This man and he carried the same flag. The same name inspired them. They knew what they required of others. A hero and the father of heroes, united in the same spirit. 'You will always feel at home here, Lieutenant,' he assured Strick. 'Mother, get out the Rödelseer Schwan, 1933 vintage. You will like that. Heil Hitler!'

Herr Tikke insisted on their sitting at his special table, which was reserved for friends of the household. This table stood in a raised niche, and was half screened off from the rest of the room by trellises hung with artificial grape-vine. On its two walls, which met at an angle, hung swastika banners, and between them was a portait of Adolf Hitler in storm trooper's uniform. The portrait was wreathed with fresh greenery.

Strick and Vogel sat facing each other with their noses close to the perfume that rose from the wine-glasses. They breathed slowly. Strick inhaled the bouquet of the wine as though it would fill him with new courage for living. The two men looked affectionately at one another. After a long silence Vogel raised his glass and said deliberately: 'A swine's goal in life is always the slaughter-house.' Strick mused over his wine, said nothing.

Through a faint haze of smoke they could see Mother Tikke busily washing glasses and polishing them until they shone like crystal. When she held the glasses above her head at a certain angle, to assure herself that they were clean, she could see, distorted by distance and the shape of the glass, Vogel sitting under the swastika flag with that man he called his friend. There they were, not talking. What kind of man was this, Mother Tikke wondered. If he were a friend of Vogel's – and, frivolous as he was, Vogel had never before joked about friendship – Strick would be entering her life also. What would he bring with him, what would he ask of her? Mother Tikke knew that human destinies were as interwoven with one another as the fibres in straw mats. It was only now, since her sons were dead, that those sons were beginning to govern her whole life. She lived for them and with them. Now that they were no longer here they were more closely linked to her than ever before. And more and more Mother Tikke was coming to feel that it was not enough just keeping her sons in her thoughts. She must do something for them. Acts were needed, not thoughts.

They were already on their third bottle, and still they had not spoken. They were looking into each other's faces, but they seemed unable to find their way back to one another. If only it were possible to turn the world back by ten years. Even by five years – five years would be enough. But then they would have their present-day minds anyway, weighed down by the burdens of experience, crammed with bits of knowledge about this and that. And to go back they would need their young bodies, their unmarred faces, and the world of long ago – the country village, the church, the overgrown path in the woods, the shy girl Irmgard, and the arrogant brat Klaerchen; the cigar they had smoked together, dreamy evenings enveloping them like silk. That was over. Past and done with, never to come again!

And what did they have now? They walked on a tight-rope above the points of bayonets, above an abyss filled with blood. Life had been drawn over their heads like a strait-jacket. They ought to fight against it, struggle to get free. Very slowly Strick said: 'You ought to get yourself transferred somewhere else. Wherever I turn up there's bound to be trouble. Every place I've been up to now has had a lot of dying going on. I've seen so many men die, most of the time honourably and bravely, and always meaninglessly. I've got used to that happening, and I sort of think it will go on happening wherever I am.'

Vogel drained his glass. 'The chief activity of this era is digging graves. It's high time the right people were placed in them.'

'Tomorrow morning,' Strick said, 'I shall begin my work. Not till tomorrow morning.' He ran the forefinger of his right hand round the rim of his filled glass. 'If you do that properly the glasses sing. I've seen it done. Every glass has its own tone. It depends on how full they are. Take eight glasses filled to different levels and you can get the scale. The man I heard played *Dawn So Red*. You know the song, Vogel:

Dawn so red,
Soon I'll be dead.'

'You're an ass,' Vogel declared rudely, his voice already a bit thick. 'You've drunk too much.'

'That may be, may very well be. I need it.'

'It's no good going on a blind with children,' Vogel said testily. 'They piddle away their brains too soon.'

'Tomorrow morning!' Strick said. His tongue moved clumsily. Nevertheless, words kept rising to the surface, and Strick had to suppress them. He ordered himself to keep his mouth shut. No argument, Strick! Just one thing ought to be said, and he said it. 'I'll need some reliable assistants for my office, Vogel. I want you to advise me on that. I'm depending on you. Tomorrow morning!'

'Mother Tikke,' Vogel called, 'Let's have another bottle, so that this babe-in-arms gets enough for once.' Mother Tikke placed the bottle on the table – the fifth.

'He can't take too much,' she commented, shaking her head.

'Let him be,' Vogel said. 'He has a lot to learn.'

Strick snorted, drawing in a deep breath. He felt as though his eye sockets were filling with lead. Wherever he looked everything appeared pleasantly hazy. All objects had become soft and elastic. There was nothing hard, nothing angular, anywhere round him. Everything was melting, disappearing, or floating gently towards him. There seemed to be weights hanging from his tongue. Poor tongue, didn't want to move any more, nice tongue, good tongue, sensible tongue. The hard bench on which he was sitting became an upholstered chair. No, he wasn't sitting on it at all, he was sinking down into it. The bench embraced him, put arms gently round his shoulders, like a lover. The world was gone completely; it had sailed away, and nothing remained but himself. And Vogel, of course. Good old dear old corrupt old Vogel, young boy with his animals, old drunk with his wine-bottles.

How long had they known each other? A hundred years by now. A thousand years, a million years. Both of them toothless old men. The marrow of their bones thrown to the dogs, their blood stirred into soup. Besides, they were murderers. 'Who lives by the sword shall die by the sword.'

The ceiling of the room descended on Strick and smashed against the back of his head. His forehead came down on the scoured table-top with a thud, and remained there. He wept. It seemed to him that alcohol was flowing out of his eyes.

'What a stinking life,' Vogel mumbled. 'The whole mess is coming out of you, Strick. Wash it away, Strick; let it drain out, spit it out, and be rid of it. All right, the world is a pigsty. Our world, anyway. But who says it has to be that way? The world is out of joint – all right. Give it a kick and maybe it will right itself. And if not Strick . . . if not . . . if . . .'

Vogel stared into the haze of the tavern as though he were looking at a battlefield wreathed in smoke. He supported his head with the palms of his hands and stared. 'A stinking life,' he said almost inaudibly. Then he shouted so loudly that Strick started up in alarm: 'It's a stinking mess – that's what.'

Mother Tikke came over to them. 'Poor boys, you've drunk too much,' she said. 'You can't take nearly as much as you think. Pull yourselves together. If all the unhappy people in Germany started bawling we could go rowing in the streets. Save it up. Save it all up. Who knows when you'll need it. We're a long way from the end.'

Strick rose heavily, his face wet and glistening from sweat, tears, and slopped wine. 'I want to sleep,' he said, 'just sleep, sleep, sleep.'

'Well, well,' Mother Tikke said.

'Tonight at least,' Strick mumbled. 'At least tonight.'

Together they stumbled back up the path to the barracks. Clinging to one another, they groped their way forward heavy-footed, seeing nothing but the misery inside their own heads. The night seemed to them fat, swollen, bloated, as though it were stuffed with silent suffering. They wanted only sleep. They reeled past couples lying in the bushes, and did not see or hear them. As they staggered through the gate Strick roared loudly, 'Stinkers, miserable stinkers.' Nobody knew whom he meant by that. Then he vomited, leaning stiffly against a wall. He puked up all his wretchedness at once; it bubbled up out of him like a fountain. A sourish stench mounted to his nostrils, and he was seized by an overpowering disgust. Never in his life had he so hated, so despised himself.

He staggered into his room, threw himself across the bed, and fell asleep. And Rabe, awakened, heard his weeping in his sleep. He's crying like a child, Rabe thought. It was depressing, because unexpected. If he had stormed, cursed, brawled in his drunkenness – very well. But crying – this man crying?

CHAPTER FIVE

HE had turned the shower on full force. The ice-cold water attacked him fiercely, as though to force him to his knees. Strick stood under it with his legs wide apart. At first his head throbbed like a big drum. The water beat down upon the top of his head with a monotonous drone. Then he felt waves of clarity and freshness washing through him. The phantasmal nightmare was over, the wine-induced misery gone. Not forgotten, but unimportant. Instead he felt a sense of cold determination. He rubbed his body vigorously, wrapped himself in the dressing-gown that Rabe had lent him, and went back to his room.

Rabe was getting ready to leave. He examined his uniform carefully once more, and appeared satisfied.

'On duty so early, Rabe?'

'From seven to eight o'clock I lecture to the guard company.'

'On what?'

'Current events.'

'Do you have any objection,' Strick asked, making broad swimming movements as he got into his shirt, 'if I take in your lecture?'

'You mean in your capacity of N.S.G.O.?' Rabe asked mockingly.

'As a humble listener in the background.'

'I can't forbid you.'

For all his politeness, it was clear that Rabe did not think Strick was seriously interested. He suspected Strick of wanting simply to kill time, to make fun of Rabe's political views. But Rabe was not going to duck out of it.

'I'll call for you here shortly before seven,' Rabe said, buckling up his wide belt. 'That will give me a chance to check up on the guardroom, and you can get dressed.' He went off with a springy step.

Strick took a number of sheets of paper from the breast pocket of his mess-jacket, which he had thrown carelessly over a chair. These papers contained, Kessler had explained to him, general directives on the immediate aims and ultimate objectives in the work of a National Socialist Guidance Officer. Strick laid these papers mechanically on the table. Then he looked thoughtfully, with an intense, searching air, at his jacket. Suddenly he began removing the decorations and ribbons covering it. He unclasped the large Iron Cross, First Class, and laid it on the bed. With a vigorous jerk he pulled off the red ribbon of the Iron Cross, Second Class. He then loosened the clasp of the German Cross in gold, and tossed it on the bed with the others. When he was done he gathered up all the medals and dropped them into the chest of drawers. The stripped mess-jacket hung naked over the back of the chair.

Then Strick sat down at the table and looked through his directives. A great deal was being asked of him, certainly. He was required to supervise all key positions. In plain words his task was control of everything that went on in the Rehhausen headquarters area. He was to be the political commissar of the garrison. He could do nothing or everything, according to how he went about it. The important thing was to confirm and add to all the basic details which he had at his disposal. If he carried out all these directives – and he was determined to do so – he would have Rehhausen absolutely in the palm of his hand. 'It will take you weeks,' Kessler had told him. But he was not going to wait that long. He did not dare. He had the feeling that he would not have very much time.

Now that he knew precisely what he wanted he intended to do what was necessary as quickly as possible. He would do the job swiftly and thoroughly. No obstacles could stop him; he would ride over them as if he were driving a tank.

He sat at a corner table, which Rabe obviously used for a desk. Except for the volume, *Three Centuries of German Lyrics*, there was nothing on it. This was what they edified themselves with last night, Strick mused, smiling to himself. They read poetry while I got drunk. And a good many kilometres away men died, as usual, by the thousands. They intoxicated themselves with delicate rhymes, I with full-bodied wine. Both of us escaped from the present for a while. And at the same time others, stuffed chock-full of loyalty and faith, went down into the mass graves.

Strick reached out for the volume of lyrics. He opened it to Mörike's poems. A number of typewritten sheets of paper lay between the leaves. More poems. And there was a snapshot of two girls, carefully posed under a tree in a garden. One was an ordinary, pretty sort of girl with an uncomplicated smile. The other girl's face was tart, if not stern. She had smooth hair, intelligent eyes, held herself rather rigidly. Probably some sort of intellectual female.

Strick smiled. Did Rabe do nothing but read poetry with them? Likely enough. And which of the two did he read to most expressively, and what sort of poems? Love poems? More likely ones that dealt with love for the Fatherland – that love which could be so amazingly misused.

Strick shook his head, completely baffled, and pushed the volume of poems aside. He immersed himself in his directives.

Rabe, young, fresh and vigorous, stood at the reading-desk. His notes, in the form of cue phrases, were on a slip of paper before him. To one side Strick sat listening attentively, and looking at Rabe. The young man chose his words carefully; his arguments were considered, and he delivered them not without a certain passion. But Rabe himself remained immobile. He spoke almost entirely without gestures. His cap on his head, his pistol belt buckled on, he stood in perfect posture and talked. He was like a statue wired for sound.

In front of him sat the members of the guard company in rows of ten men each. There were about a hundred altogether, young faces and old, smooth and wrinkled, melancholy and cunning. Some, at least those in the front rows, appeared to be interested. Some, among them Corporal Vogel, put on a look of rapt interest. But a great many weary and indifferent faces floated like detached masks in the room. In the back row two men were fighting hard against the stubborn early morning fatigue. One man was already fast asleep.

The room was painted a sickly green and was without decoration. Most of the paint had been rubbed off the walls, and the floor was scraped by many boots. Through this room Lieutenant Rabe's clear voice rang, cutting through the stale, heavy atmosphere produced by the exhalations of a hundred human bodies. This lecture on current political events was a weekly affair. It was supposed to be attended by all men, and would normally be given by a troop commander personally, that is, by Captain Wolf. But Wolf thought the junior officer of the garrison, Rabe, was good enough for that sort of thing. And Rabe went at his lecture with a good deal of real enthusiasm.

A sizeable section of the garrison, Strick saw at once, made a business of cutting the lecture. Probably they stayed away not because they were against political instruction as such, but because the lecture was something they could get out of. That was a big point in the private soldier's creed – to get out of whatever you could. Some were on guard duty, some had just had guard duty, and others were getting ready for guard duty. Orderlies were polishing boots, clerks were clerking, cooks cooking, the telephone operator was at his switchboard checking connections with the women civilian employees, and so on. Vogel was here because he found such situations farcical. And Corporal Hoepfner was sitting beside him because Vogel had dragged him along – he liked plying his slow-witted room-mate with topsy-turvey versions of what was said.

Rabe talked on. He presented a picture of the general situation – a picture which, it had to be admitted, was quite honest. He did not try to gloss over the situation, but he somehow projected a sense of confidence. He spoke of cautious, well-planned withdrawal movements. Strick saw Vogel whispering excitedly into Hoepfner's ear. Hoepfner listened to him attentively, while with the other ear he followed Rabe's exposition.

'If you examine the map closely,' Rabe said, 'you will see that the distances are getting smaller and smaller.

Hoepfner held his hand high. Rabe, visibly pleased at having stirred the dull, silent mass of men to some reaction, gave him permission to speak. 'Is it true,' Hoepfner asked with naïve self-importance, 'that our troops on the Eastern Front have retreated a hundred and eighty kilometres in the last seven days?'

Strick saw at once that Rabe was taken aback. Either he did not know the answer or he was somewhat alarmed by the blunt figures. He reflected briefly. Before he could reply Vogel raised his hand and stood up. 'That isn't much,' he said with an air of complacent reassurance. While Rabe groped for an answer, Vogel went on merrily: 'A hundred and eighty kilometres isn't anything. The week before our troops did two hundred and ten.'

The whole room seemed suddenly to come to life. There was a low murmuring in one corner. The sleeper in the back row woke up with a start. Vogel sat down with a pious air. Hoepfner, feeling himself the centre of attention, was still standing contentedly. Rabe cast a brief, somewhat nervous glance at Strick, who returned him a friendly smile.

'At the moment,' Rabe declared, a faint undertone of anxiety in his clear voice, 'I do not have the facts at hand.' Some one in the crowd called in a loud voice, 'Too bad!' And some one else added, 'Why don't you?'

'But next time I shall give exact figures,' Rabe continued, trying to regain control of his audience. 'One hundred and eighty, or even, as some one said, two hundred and ten kilometres, per week is, I think, an exaggeration.'

A blond lanky young man shot to his feet. 'Even if those figures are accurate,' he said with conviction, 'they go to show that we are stabilizing the front. Last week two hundred and ten, this week one hundred and eighty. We are making progress.'

'And how!' some one called out. It sounded like Vogel.

Rabe checked the mild uproar. 'I am pleased to see your interest,' he declared. 'That is very good. And, after all, what are two hundred kilometres in a week? I can remember a time when we were driving the enemy back more than three hundred kilometres in a week. That is a good deal more impressive.'

Rabe now turned to the subject of internal politics. He spoke with great earnestness of justice, freedom, and equality of rights. Strick noticed at once that his favourite word was socialism. 'Socialism,' Rabe said, 'is the ultimate goal of the world order. And we must accept everything, co-operate with everything, put up with everything that helps bring us nearer that goal.' The words, although spoken to the audience, were plainly addressed to Strick.

Slowly, the pleasant morning drowsiness began to spread over the room again. Every one made an effort to keep his eyes open, and scarcely anyone was paying attention to the talk. Phrases, the men were thinking, empty phrases, the same ones they'd heard a thousand times before, for years. Always the same tomfoolery – how well they knew it. They heard it every day, from the radio in the canteen to the newspaper in the latrine. Not a mother's son of them could take it seriously any more. It was nothing but Government-issue sleeping-pills. Rest in peace.

Strick alone was wide awake. He could feel Vogel's sharp eyes upon him, but he did not look round. He was watching Rabe in fascination. Was there nobody in this room, he asked himself sadly, who realized that Rabe absolutely meant every word he said? Given a chance to act, he would act on these very principles. This fellow Rabe was phenomenally sincere – or else he was the most successful liar on the face of the earth.

'This goal,' Rabe was saying to the brooding, unresponsive audience, 'is a great and noble one. Measured by it, all imperfections – even the bloodiest mistakes – seem to me petty and inessential. For the sake of this goal good men have died. That must have a meaning.'

There was scarcely anyone in the room who understood what Rabe was saying. All the men felt was relief that he was winding up. Now there would be a peroration about love for the Fuehrer, Reich, and Folk, a pledge of allegiance, and then he would fold up his notes and they could go. One more hour got through.

Damn it all, Strick thought, everything has been spoiled, corrupted. They have slimed up all the great words and great ideas with lies. There are no great words any longer; they've been polluted, adulterated, devalued. Nobility, sacrifice – they've been dragged through the mud and are nothing but lies. Anyone who doesn't understand that is a fool. And therefore Rabe is a fool. The kind of high-minded fool that Parsifal was. Even if he has not been a fool all along he has become a fool now, when all that ever was noble has gone to pot.

The room emptied. Viscously the crowd moved towards the door, and trickled noisily into the corridors. Rabe carefully signed the register. Then, somewhat embarrassed, he turned to Strick. Strick took his arm, and went out into the corridor with him. Their footsteps re-echoed through the now-deserted passage. 'Why do we like so much to dream, Rabe?' Strick asked. 'Do you suppose it's a German national trait?'

Rabe seemed to have no ready reply, nor to be particularly interested in the question. All he said was, 'I'm glad you don't praise my lecture, Strick. It would make me uncomfortable, and it certainly would be unlike you.'

They stood for a moment at an open window, and looked out over the barrack square. The soldiers who had been at the lecture were forming into a column and marching off towards their barracks. The operations clerk, Sergeant Demuth, was trundling his bulk slowly across the square towards the headquarters building. It was precisely eight o'clock. Captain Wolf walked grumpily, but with a certain self-conscious erectness, into the club for breakfast. From a window in the headquarters building Captain Geiger was watching a small group of civilian women assistants who were nearing the gate.

'Socialism,' Strick said pensively, 'is a lovely word. Perhaps the most decent idea left on this battered earth. But where are you going to find it? Here? Take a look at our fellow-fighters in the struggle for socialism – as you call it. Look them over objectively, minus their insignia of rank, their comradely handshake, and their "Heil Hitlers." Give them a good looking over, Rabe, the way a man buys a cow. You will notice amazing differences.'

Rabe said nothing. He leaned against the window-sill and seemed to be looking across the square, the road, and the people in it to where the German war flag streamed from the flag-pole above the gate. The cross and the swastika. Black, white, and red. Was that his emblem? Strick asked himself. Was that an emblem for anyone at all? Could it still be, after all that had taken place under that flag?

Behind them they heard a soft voice, edged with gay mockery. 'Good morning. Are you gentlemen still asleep?' Strick felt that he was being addressed directly. It was as if some one had nudged him gently, almost tenderly, in the side. That must be the cute little piece from the colonel's office. Correct, there was Erika Blaustrom standing by them. He turned round to a picture of neatness and freshness. Erika was highly decorative. Her face was tanned, her curling black hair was brushed to a high gloss. Her dress was bright-coloured, fragrant, and thin, thin as a veil.

Strick drew upon all the cordiality he had left. It was not much, but enough for a friendly greeting. Erika held out her shapely hand like a well-brought-up cat offering its paw. Too bad, Strick thought for the first time in his life, that I never learned fancy manners. Here was a hand it would be a pleasure to kiss – at least, the hand would be a good place to start on. Or did you kiss the hand only of married women? What was the proper etiquette? Oh, well, no matter. He didn't bother with such nonsense – on principle. Once you let yourself get started you would have to wipe your lips on every paw that came your way.

Rabe had visibly stiffened in Erika's presence. He was terribly 'correct', so deliberately withdrawn that he was almost being discourteous. His own hand made the briefest possible contact with hers, and then he stepped back. Erika was amused. 'Afraid I'm going to bite you, teacher?' she said. Rabe became even more embarrassed. He increased the distance between himself and this person who represented the antithesis of his high principles.

Strick simply could not understand why Rabe reacted this way. The girl was a ravishing specimen of vitality. She had, no doubt, some of the characteristics of a bird of prey, but all the same she was good to look at. 'Really,' he exclaimed with good-humoured amazement, 'I don't get it. Doesn't Rabe appreciate your charms?'

Erika's white teeth flashed in a smile. It was pleasant to hear Strick say that. She could feel, almost with her body, that Strick found her attractive. Of course, there was nothing out of the way in that. She knew she quickened the pulses of almost every man who came her way, except Rabe. But which of them was so beautifully frank about it? Strick struck her as incredibly fresh, but she liked that. Besides which, he was the N.S.G.O. here, and would be having a good deal to say. It wouldn't be a bad idea to meet him half-way.

With a half-childish gesture of curiosity, as though she wanted to look out of the window, she approached Strick. To Rabe it seemed that she was thrusting herself upon the other man in a deliberately provocative manner. Strick and Erika stood close together, facing one another, Strick with his back to the open window. The light from the window bathed Erika's smooth face, a face that could still expose itself recklessly to the brightest light. The girl could not be more than nineteen or twenty, Strick thought, and yet she already had the skill of a seductive, experienced woman of twenty-seven. The contradiction attracted him; he felt a charge penetrating his skin and trickling into his blood, then pulsating through his veins until it reached his heart. The devil take these twenty-year-old girls, Strick thought.

'You're exceptionally frank,' she said. 'I like that. Other men hardly let themselves think what you say right off to my face.'

'It's a very pretty face,' Strick said.

Erika accepted this remark as her due. 'You could take some lessons from Herr Strick, Rabe,' she said.

Rabe had always detested the forwardness of the girl, detested her whole personality. 'Go easy, Strick,' he said coolly. 'I hope you realize what this – lady here represents.'

Erika's dark eyes flared with fury, although her face remained as unlined as before, and her voice kept its friendly, mocking note. But her hands clenched tightly. She seemed to know precisely where Rabe's weak spot was. 'It rubs you up the wrong way because I don't go goose-stepping along with the Party, doesn't it?' She smiled brightly at him. 'Are you worried about my political principles? Or my readiness to make sacrifices?'

Rabe, who understood just what she was referring to, spoke very formally, with the hint of a bow, as though it were necessary to make a declaration. 'I would not dream of imagining that there is any – that between the colonel and yourself there could be any . . .'

'Any relationship,' Erika said, helping him out with a dangerous air of friendliness.

Rabe accepted her term for it. 'I consider that quite out of the question. As incompatible with the character of the colonel as it would be with the imperatives of our time.'

Erika turned to Strick. 'Herr Rabe can't bear me,' she said lightly. 'I'm not simple and pure enough for him.'

Rabe continued his attack. 'There is a lot of gossip about yourself and the colonel, and you encourage it. You use it for your own benefit.'

Strick decided that the quarrel was getting too nasty; he had better intervene. 'I admire your courage, Rabe,' he said in a joking tone. 'But you underestimate the power of women. I am more than ever convinced that you're an exceptional person, Rabe. A kind of saint, untemptable. You're like the calf who has decided to visit a celebration of the butchers' union. You absolutely amaze me – that you could have been born in present-day Germany is one of Nature's jest's.'

The gleam of anger in Erika's eyes slowly died down. She felt that Strick was emotionally close to her. Like herself, he must have very few scruples. His frank admiration pleased her, and compensated for Rabe's insults. She smiled at Strick, and switched from pretty venomousness to dangerous beauty. She even forgave Rabe with a smile. 'Our friend, Rabe,' she said mockingly, as though she were tapping his chest with her manicured finger, 'is a hopeless case. He thinks the whole feminine world is named Magda. Poor fellow, that's his weak point. He won't let himself look at anyone else.' She was being openly malicious; but even malice became her, Strick thought. Rabe listened, his face rigid.

She walked off with short, lilting steps. Strick watched her fine legs move across the stone floor of the corridor, across those monotonous, dirty-brown paving-stones over which ordinarily only heavy soldiers' boots tramped. Almost at the end of the corridor she stopped. She turned round once more and said, 'Give me a ring some time, Herr Strick, if your heavy duties as N.S.G.O. leave you any time. I can't say I dislike your type of Party representative.'

Then she vanished round the bend of the corridor which led to headquarters. Strick heard the crisp *tap-tap* of her high-heeled shoes, and it seemed to him that her slim figure was still standing before him, that he was still looking into that pert, self-assured face.

Strick knew that if he turned round he would see Rabe's earnest, probing gaze, tinged with reproach, contempt, perhaps even pity. Poor devil, Rabe would be saying to himself, comes direct from the front, hasn't seen a girl for months, falls instantly for the first hot-house specimen that comes along.

Rabe said as much aloud. 'Why do you let that girl get the upper hand, Strick? You can see right off the kind of bitch she is.'

Strick turned to him. The man walked round on a pair of idealistic stilts. He would have to knock him off the things. Maybe Rabe would understand other things better when he had his feet on the ground. 'So you hold the opinion,' he said, speaking slowly and very distinctly, 'that the colonel is a dirty son of a bitch who thinks the rest of us are easy to fool.'

Rabe was shocked. He looked into a hard, taut face, a face from which all soft emotions had vanished. 'The colonel is a first-class soldier,' he protested. 'Perhaps a little too rough and ready on a high level, but basically a fine man.'

The defence was well-meaning, Strick thought, but not very convincing. He was determined to shake Rabe's naïve faith if it was the last thing he did. 'So you think he is a fine man and a first-class soldier. And such a man keeps as his secretary a girl who I'm supposed to see is a bitch after five minutes' conversation.' He took a step towards Rabe and asked, as though it were a question of conscience, 'Is he sleeping with her or isn't he?'

'Of course not.'

Poor Rabe with his prompt 'of course not.' For his own sake Strick fleetingly wished Rabe were telling the truth. After all, it might be the truth, and the colonel might be honest in every respect, including this one. If he were, Strick might as well give up his plans right away, bury himself pleasantly here and take it easy, drink, sleep in soft beds, and stuff his belly until the fat accumulated round the brain. No – he could not. Rest for him would not begin until he was laid in a coffin. He must go on, and first of all he must knock some sense into Rabe. God knows, it was no great pleasure, but it had to be done. And it was essential for his plans that the colonel should be as corrupt as the station commandant.

'What makes you so sure about that? All you know is that the colonel is a man of honour because you say he is. Does his uniform make him one, or his rank, or his position, or your worship of authority, or his chumminess with the district leader? For heaven's sake, fellow, come down to earth.'

He turned away and walked off angrily. Rabe looked after him in confusion. What kind of person was he anyhow? He spread unrest wherever he went. There was something funny about it. What was he after?

Since the start of the War Vogel had decided he was a universal genius ... There was nothing he had not done by now. He was among many other things, a cook, surveyor, medical aide, observer, quartermaster, boot-polisher and orderly, camp administrator, court attendant, tank mechanic, dentist, frontline bookkeeper, architect for the tombs of heroes, sewage worker, and club waiter. Among many other things.

But the best of all the jobs he had held in the Army of Greater Germany – probably his eighty-third job – was one he had created for himself. He considered it a brilliant inspiration. He was now a photographer for officers, philistines, operations clerks, and their assorted ladies. In addition, he was constantly called upon to take identification photos for the training battalion, the guards company, and the male and female civilian employees of the garrison. One of his specialties was the gallery of photographs – full-face and in profile, each with name and number – of the inmates of the Army prison in Rehhausen. Recently he had been called in to take pictures of a group of captured British officers. He had liked their looks. They had the eyes of active men, of intelligent men, men who were close observers and close questioners, who demanded answers. They had looked at him with the most eloquent silence he had ever encountered. Now, as he gazed at the photographs lying on the table before him, he felt a longing to talk with these men. The photography room, which Vogel called his 'studio', was in the loft of the headquarters building. There Vogel would work without interruption – that is to say, he hung on the door a sign reading: 'Developing! Please do not disturb!' Then, if there was nothing in particular to do, he would lock the door from the inside and take a snooze. For that purpose he had an Army bed in one corner, behind a folding screen. The studio was Vogel's favourite retiring-room.

Today he had no sooner stretched out on the bed than he was

disturbed. There was a violent knocking on his door. Vogel was annoyed. 'I can't let anyone in,' he called indignantly. 'I'm busy developing. Kindly read the sign on the door.'

'Open up at once,' some one shouted back, 'or I'll smash the door and you too.'

That must be Strick. Vogel got up and opened the door. 'What do you want?' he asked coldly.

'To see you,' Strick said.

Vogel scowled. 'It's outrageous. You condescend to have a few drinks with an officer and he starts thinking he can take liberties.'

Strick examined a group of negatives of pass photos which Vogel had strung up on a line like tiny pieces of washing. Vogel hoisted the line higher, removing it from Strick's field of vision. 'I hope you don't count on making this your hang-out. Or did you come to get me to polish your boots? I recommend following Lieutenant Rabe's example. There's a man for you – he polishes his boots without any outside help.' Vogel glanced lazily through his file of negatives, and took out two which he laid on the table.

'I need a room for an office, and two assistants,' Strick said.

Vogel held the negatives against the light. 'Below the Commandant's office,' he remarked casually, as though he were quoting the day's communiqué, 'there are three rooms. The quartermaster's wife has taken them over for the library and the archives. Put her into one room, let the middle one be used for the books and as your waiting-room, and occupy the third room yourself.'

'Are the rooms favourably situated?'

'Very. At least three exits – two doors and one window. You can go and come unseen whenever you like. The window is handy when girls want to visit you. Also hand-grenades can conveniently be tossed out through it. All in all, ideal.'

Vogel switched on the main light, and drew the curtain over the window. He shut the door, switched on the red lamp over his work-table, and put out the main light. The red lamp fell mysteriously upon his sly face. With sure movement Vogel's hands stretched paper over frame. He clipped the negative to it, turned the light on briefly, and slid the paper into the developer.

Strick knew that Vogel had never been a photographer. Like most boys he had played around with a camera and chemicals, but that was all. Things must have been thoroughly muddled up at first when Vogel started experimenting on the garrison. But by now he seemed to know just what a photographer was supposed to do. He rocked the developing fluid back and forth over the two positives. Strick bent over the pictures, which were now slowly appearing. The contours emerged from the paper, and seemed to swell as they took on clarity, filled out, and became pictures of an old man and a young woman. Vogel picked them up with a pair of pincers and slid them into the fixing-bath which stood beside the developer. Then he swiftly pulled aside the black-out curtain, opened the window, and switched off the red light.

Strick looked at the two pictures in the basin. 'Who are they?' he asked.

'They,' Vogel said quietly, 'are the two members of your office staff. The National Socialist Guidance Officer's assistants.'

'What kind of people are they?' Identification pictures give only the roughest impression of living persons; they capture only the outermost surface. The man seemed to be a respectable citizen, good-natured and perhaps simple. The girl looked stern and forbidding, stiff as a marionette on a wire. And yet her picture seemed familiar to him. 'I must have seen this girl somewhere,' he said; but he could not recall where or when.

'The man is Old Tannert,' Vogel said. 'Take a good look at him. He works in the clothing room. Compulsory war duty. By trade he's a tool-maker and draughtsman.' Vogel grinned. 'You'll have a good time with him.'

'How do you know him?'

'From Mother Tikke's,' Vogel said laconically.

'And the girl?'

'She's his daughter. That way you keep everything right in the family.'

'Do you think I'm looking for a family unit to fit into?'

'What I think is this: You need a shorthand typist. It isn't necessary for her to be very good, but she must be reliable and a decent sort. Doesn't hurt if she's good-looking. If headquarters gets the idea that you're immoral that's all to the good. They'll think you're a first-class swine, and therefore take it for granted that you're a straight Party-liner. This set-up is a house of joy anyway. Strength-through-Joy, you know.'

'What is the girl doing now?'

'She's due to be transferred.'

'Where to?'

'Occupied territory, or some such place. Plenty of careers

opening up for half-trained whores in Army uniform, thanks to the generosity of the higher-ups.'

'And why is she being offered this splendid opportunity?'

'Doesn't co-operate willingly enough.'

'Look,' Strick chided, 'do we have to have all this filth?'

'That's what I often ask myself.'

Strick picked the girl's photograph out of the fixing-bath. Where had he seen this face before? The liquid dripped along his fingers and fell to the floor. The girl's face was wet, as though she had been weeping. Poor kid – drafted for Army work, her body evaluated like meat in a butcher shop. They stuck her into some unit, and now she was being transferred because she would not co-operate. 'Who is the man in the case?' Strick asked.

'Wolf,' Vogel said.

'And you're interested in the girl?'

Vogel was struck dumb. 'What the devil!' he said indignantly. 'Do you think I'm trying to get you to protect my women? You of all people! What kind of moron do you think I am?' He took the wet photograph from Strick's hand, and laid it beside the other between two blotters. Then he pressed them hard. 'Anyway,' he said slyly, 'this girl's first name is Magda.'

Of course! This was the girl whose picture Strick had seen tucked into Rabe's volume of lyrics. And it was the same name that Erika had mentioned maliciously. Magda. She was Rabe's weak point.

'And that swine Wolf can get away with transferring the girl because she won't . . . Doesn't Rabe know anything about it?'

Vogel drew back the blankets on his bed. 'What else do you want?' he demanded brusquely. 'Can't you see I'm about to take a well-earned nap? I'm tired out. Last night I had to transport a dead-drunk wreck of a lieutenant back to the barracks. That's enough work for one week.' He patted his pillow. Then he opened the door wide and pressed the still-damp photographs into Strick's hand. 'You're an outstanding mass murderer and war hero,' he said, 'but you don't know the first thing about women. Do you think the girl would ever tell him that somebody made a pass at her? And do you think Rabe would ever find out by himself? That sweet-souled innocent! Now get out of here, you numskull.'

Vogel slammed the door behind him, and turned the key violently in the lock. Strick heard Vogel throw himself loudly down on the bed. The sign over the door rocked furiously back and forth on its nail. It read, as before: 'Developing! Please do not disturb!'

Captain Geiger, the adjutant, was friendly and obliging today. His manner of studied reserve was gone, and he was now all politeness and comradeliness. With his own hand he drew up a chair and struck Strick jovially on the shoulders as if dusting off his tunic.

'Well, now, what can I do for you?'

Strick fished his notebook out of his breast pocket. 'First of all, a few minor matters. Take them down, won't you?'

'Go ahead.'

'I need an office and waiting-room. I'll take the rooms now occupied by the library. Please see that the library is moved out – let's say some time today. Then I will need two assistants, probably civilians. I'll pick them out myself. Please see that I run into no difficulties on that score.'

The adjutant held his pencil suspended. 'Yes, but . . .'

'Must I apply to some one else?'

'Not that, but . . .'

'My dear Captain Geiger,' Strick said, with a glint in his eye and a grin at the corners of his mouth, 'is it possible that our National Socialist Guidance programme is going to be sabotaged?'

'Certainly not.'

'Very well! Then please see to these matters. Show your stuff.'

'I personally am completely in accord with all this, but . . .'

'No "buts", Captain. That is all I'm asking for – at the moment.'

Geiger squirmed slightly in his comfortable office chair. 'It will not be easy,' he said at last, running the middle finger of his right hand under his collar.

'Captain,' Strick said, in a tone that implied surprise at the adjutant's humble opinion of his own powers, 'seeing that these requests are complied with should be no trouble at all for you.'

'Certainly not,' the captain mumbled.

'Very well, then, everything is all right.'

Captain Geiger saw himself forced into a position of granting favours. He had become a kind of promoter. Very well, he would take care of it. After all, he was not some one to make difficulties. Always glad to help, as one comrade to another.

Officers had to stick together, he said, help each other and smooth out the difficulties in each other's paths. A matter of mutual aid.

Strick nodded approvingly. 'Very well, Captain, is there anything I can do for you? Anything you want?'

Geiger looked painfully embarrassed at hearing such a profanely specific offer in answer to his highly generalized remarks. Cautiously, simulating the tone of disinterested inquiry, he asked, 'Do you plan to take direct charge of everything that could come under the heading of N.S.G.O. work?'

What axe did the man have to grind? Strick wondered. 'I'm not that greedy,' Strick replied obligingly. 'If there's any favour I can do for you please ask it.'

Geiger straightened up. This seemed a good time, and Strick sounded reasonable. Geiger spoke jerkily, in short sentences, disguising the soft core of his request behind angular phrases. 'Up to now I've been in charge of all entertainment for the troops. Movies, vaudeville, Strength-through-Joy. Also concerts and serious stuff, of course. I like drawing up programmes, arranging for guest artists, and so on. Were you planning to take that over now?'

Strick had to stop himself from laughing out loud. This was the best sort of horse-dealing. Will swap: one thoroughbred Arabian for one hobby-horse. Or: one signed blank cheque exchanged for a bottle of ink. He knitted his brows, struggling to give his face an expression of sombre dignity. 'Not at all,' he said. 'If that is your pleasure – I'm certainly not going to be a spoilsport.'

Geiger was overjoyed. He rubbed his hands contentedly; his pet avocation was safe. 'I really think culture is of the greatest importance,' he declared animatedly. 'Tremendous entertainment in it, for one thing. And I make a special effort to promote the eternal values, you know – Körner, Anacker, even the Nordic Eddas if it comes to that.'

Strick was amused. The good-natured fool was throwing all the Nazi Party crap at him, as though he expected Strick to eat it up. Poor Geiger – so anxious to please every one. Well, he would look for a chance to take advantage of that streak in the man's character.

'What about Geothe?' Strick asked with spiteful intent.

As he had expected, Geiger took the hook at once. 'Goethe too, of course. Do you know the "Cannonade at Valmy"? Just parts of it? I must recite it to you some time.'

'Some other time.'

'Of course. As a matter of fact Goethe wasn't as unsoldierly as you think. I have a new article from the *Voelkischer Beobachter* on "Goethe and the Generals." Highly informative. I'd like to read it to you – some other time.'

Strick had risen, and was making his way towards the door. Geiger, like a mill-wheel at flood time, was grinding on steadily. 'I'm in the midst of preparation right now for a very unusual programme. Exquisite. For the next evening gathering at the club, ladies invited. Nothing but love-lyrics. The basic theme "Hearts in Harness', or something of the sort. Expressing the Nordic temperament, you know.'

'That sounds very impressive,' Strick murmured, groping for the doorknob.

Geiger's naïve enthusiasm flowed on undiminished. 'I'm really very much obliged to you, Herr Strick. This matter of entertainment for the soldiers is dear to my heart. You will see, you'll be delighted with our next programme. Have you any special requests? Details are still quite open to change, you know. I assure you the recitations will be first-class.'

Strick could imagine Geiger gloating over every choice rhyme. A queer duck. Ordinarily the man was as reserved and shut up as an ice-box, but as soon as you touched his soft spot he thawed out and started to melt like the grease on Captain Wolf's head under this glorious July sun. Queer people altogether. None of them really lived in their uniforms. They had just got into the uniforms as if they were going to a masked ball. Disguised themselves as officers – that was all. If they had been engaged in teaching a class of schoolchildren or in selling stamps they would have been normal, likeable human beings. But in uniform they were all marionettes and fakes.

'Then I can depend upon your arranging the matters we spoke of, Captain?'

Geiger accompanied Strick through all the rooms of the office out to the door. 'Of course. In general, Strick, if you have any other special wishes – I'm not adjutant here for nothing.'

Strick shook hands with him, saying, 'Thank you, I may take you up on that.'

CHAPTER SIX

WHEN you looked closer at Old Tannert he turned out to be not particularly old. He must have been about forty-five. They had not yet succeeded in making him worn out or stooped. It was his excessive reserve which added to his age. Once he had worked as a railway mechanic. The type of work he did was measured with micrometers. He could handle a file with such delicacy that the finest precision machines seemed like steam-rollers by comparison. But now Tannert, called 'Old Tannert' by practically everybody, worked in the clothing room for the Rehhausen garrison. He had been drafted for war work, and was in charge of clothing for prisoners-of-war and for the inmates of the Rehhausen prison. He handed out these clothes when new prisoners-of-war were brought in; he took the clothing in again when, as Captain Wolf put it, the prisoners had been 'scratched'. The used clothing was supposed to be deloused, cleaned, patched, and made ready for use again.

An entire attic was given over to the clothing supplies. A large part of this space was filled with excellent uniforms which were on the inventory as reserve clothing for the front-line troops. The stuff had been shipped here because evacuation of some central storehouses had been ordered. Though the clothing was earmarked for the front-line troops, no one could really object when the members of the garrison headquarters eked out their wardrobes with it. After all, there were such enormous quantities of clothing in dead storage here. As Corporal Vogel had once explained, if they had what they wanted they would not have to steal it.

One small room was stuffed full of rags which had once been trousers, jackets, underwear, and socks. They gave forth a sharp stench, as though they had been soaked in sweat and then baked bone-dry in the full midday sun.

Every morning, before he began his work, Tannert changed his own clothes completely in the small ante-room. This done, he was transformed into a kind of convict in international uniform. Hs jacket was of French origin, his trousers probably Russian, and the inside of his shoes still bore the legible stamp, 'Polski'.

Tannert's principal occupation was rearranging the stored clothing. If he had not shifted the stuff round it probably would have coagulated into a solid mass. More than once he had proposed an airing for the rags in his charge, but he had been refused permission. He hated to distribute the stinking rags. It was bad enough that those poor devils, the prisoners-of-war, were rotting inwardly, without having their clothes rotting on them. But the repeated cleanings that were needed, and disposal of the worst rags, had been strictly forbidden – the quartermaster was afraid of exceeding the budget. And so Tannert kept shifting the stacks, hoping to give the clothing some sort of airing in the process.

The one advantage of the job for Tannert was that he could work by himself and completely undisturbed. He came at eight o'clock, took an hour for lunch at twelve, and was off at five. His instructions required him to stay in the clothing room during working hours. He kept the books, and was responsible for every rag. Once a week the quartermaster dropped in to check the issues and receipts.

Old Tannert oiled shapeless things of leather which were listed in his records as boots. He worked the oil in well, and arranged pair after pair in rows. Feet would be stuck into those boots, and men would be attached to those feet, and those men would be given orders: drag, run, pull, carry, march through sand, wade through puddles. Then the feet in the boots would swell, the softened, sweat-soaked leather would expand to fit, and then it would dry out again and become as stiff as iron, and it would chafe the feet at ankles and heels until the blood ran. And the poor devils would have no oil to soften the tough leather.

The boots and shoes stood in front of him, row upon row. Then suddenly there materialized before him, at floor level, a pair of glossily polished officer's boots, like a top hat that has been thrown out by mistake and lies upon a rubbish-heap. Tannert looked up those boots, up a worn uniform to an officer's collar-tabs and epaulets. Topping it all was the face of an unhappy cowman. The eyes alone were alert and lively. They blinked brightly down at him.

'I am Lieutenant Strick,' the man said. Tannert slowly stood up. Well, what about it? What did this busybody want? Not a new uniform, by any chance? Tannert said nothing. He waited; he had plenty of time. The other man would speak up soon enough. Not likely that he could stand the concentrated smells of clothing and graveyard for very long.

'You are Herr Tannert?'

'Yes,' Tannert said, mildly amazed that anyone should address him as 'Herr'. He was Tannert, Old Tannert, civilian employee Tannert, and nothing more – except on the radio. There, when he happened by mistake to turn on a German station, he learned that he was Folk Comrade Tannert. Formerly he had been just plain Comrade, and he had liked that better.

'I have heard about you,' the officer said. 'I need a reliable permanent assistant. Would you be willing to take the job?'

'What kind of job is it?'

'I am the National Socialist Guidance Officer of this garrison.'

Tannert slowly sat down again. He forgot the stench of the clothing room. Long ago, Tannert had been an active Socialist, a small, unimportant party functionary. Before 1933 he used to go down to the meetings that Dr. Friedrich was wont to address. Friedrich's oratory infallibly made him laugh. Sometimes he had asked questions in the discussion period. When 1933 came he had been slugged like a sack of flour. And he had been as silent as a sack of flour; he had refused to talk.

The leader of the group that administered the beating was the then storm leader of the S.A., the very same station commandant who had just been put in the clink – by some accident, no doubt; it was much like throwing away an empty bottle. The little incident in '33 had resulted in seven months in the hospital for Tannert, and a heavily underlined note on his work papers. He was officially designated by the Nazi Party as unreliable, a potential enemy of the State. That was the end of the draughting, which he had studied night after night until his head slumped down wearily on the drawing-board. For the rest of his life he would be a cripple, and for the thousand years the Third Reich was to endure he would remain an ordinary mechanic. The case was perfectly clear.

'You had better look through my papers,' Tannert said. 'I was a revolutionary Socialist.'

Strick merely squinted slightly, as though a not entirely unexpected headlight was glaring into his face. 'So you were a fighter on the barricades, eh?'

'Yes.'

'Are you still?'

'There aren't any barricades in Germany at the moment.'

'Fine.' Strick looked as though his sole interest in the world were these worn-out boots and shoes which glistened with oil. 'Fine. So you were a radical Socialist. Why not? Since 1933 you haven't been anything. Nothing unusual about that. But you are supposed to be able to do nice lettering and poster painting. That is all that concerns me.'

'You don't expect me to make Nazi posters for you?'

'You will have no choice. Don't forget you're conscripted for duty here. What you do is a matter for whoever is in command to decide. Right now I am in command – until I'm recalled.'

Tannert stood up, and then collapsed again like a rusty pocket-knife with a weak spring. This man was like a battering-ram, and he seemed to know just what he wanted. 'You will have difficulties,' Tannert said, 'since I was after all a Socialist. That makes me unreliable . . .'

Strick took up one boot and tested the thick, tough leather. He pressed on it, as though he were squeezing a dead rubber ball which was no fun to play with. 'I take it for granted,' he said, 'that you will do the work I assign you. That goes without saying. Where others might only lose their jobs, Herr Tannert, you run the risk of losing your head as well.' He tossed the boot over to the others; it thudded to the floor, and tipped over on its side.

Tannert felt as though he were suddenly standing on the deck of a pitching ship which altogether unexpectedly had weighed anchor and was now sailing out on the high seas. The rudder was whirling like a top round its axis. And over everything there lay the dense, seething stench of the clothes, like burned milk turning to steam.

'Finish off your work here. Turn this knacker's shop over to some one better suited for the job.' Strick stalked off towards the door over mountains of leather goods and rags. 'You'll start with me first thing tomorrow morning. By tomorrow noon I want to see sketches for your first placards.' Abruptly he grinned like a mischievous small boy. 'Heil Hitler, Herr Tannert!'

Early that afternoon Captain Wolf thrust his fat face through the crack in the door – the same face of which Vogel had remarked that it ought to wear a pair of trousers. 'If it's all right with you,' Wolf said with the excessive cordiality of a brothel-keeper, 'I'll show you my canteen supplies now.'

Strick invited Rabe to come along. Rabe did not want to. 'Oh, come with us, Rabe,' Strick said. 'Bottles of whisky can be more inspiring than poetry.' Wolf concurred with a bleat of laughter.

'I went with you to your lecture this morning. Now come along with me while Captain Wolf opens up his cellar. And not only his cellar, Rabe – he will open his heart as well.' Wolf beamed expansively at them.

Rabe finally consented to go along on the sightseeing tour since, as Strick had expected, he had never yet seen the garrison's canteen supplies. 'Don't let yourself be inhibited because of Lieutenant Rabe,' Strick remarked to Wolf. 'He's a good friend of mine.'

Captain Wolf was glad to hear that. Fundamentally he thought Rabe pretty much of a simpleton, though a valuable man to have around for daily duties. Always ready, always reliable, never grumbling. Just give him an order, and Rabe would take over duties and perform them precisely according to regulations while he, Wolf, could loaf as much as he pleased, like a fat little hamster hibernating in his hole. And at the same time Rabe was the soul of integrity – or a dumb bunny, depending how you looked at it. Up to now he had never asked for anything – no cigars, no drink, no soap or perfume for his girls. Or did Rabe actually not care for any of those things – not for alcohol, or tobacco, or even women?

This fellow Strick was another sort entirely. Went at things like a pig at the trough. He hadn't been here two days – hadn't been N.S.G.O. much more than twenty-four hours – and what was he up to? Ready to go in and see the canteen supplies. Putting on a pretence of being interested in an official capacity, saying he wanted to gather information. Information? He wanted some drink to guzzle, that's what he wanted.

Wolf unlocked the door, then the safety lock, slid the bolts, and opened the cellar door invitingly. The room was as big as a dance-hall, encircled with well-stocked shelves and jammed full with packing-cases. In one corner were piles of packing, bits of wood and wrapping paper. 'This cellar is bomb-proof,' Wolf declared with the air of a cicerone.

There were cases filled with cartons of cigarettes, boxes of cigars – and there were bottles, plump-bellied bottles, slender, reedlike bottles, and square bottles. There were soaps, combs, perfumes, powder-puffs, rouge, jars of cold cream. And eatables: preserves, smoked meat, sausages, jars and tins and boxes.

'Magnificent, really magnificent,' Strick said. 'You really are a man of parts Captain Wolf. Practically a supplier for the throat, belly, and lungs of the whole Army.'

Wolf was flattered, but modest. 'You exaggerate. My responsibility is only to the garrison area. We could use far more than we can obtain.' Strick studied the serried ranks of whisky bottles, each properly in its place as though on parade. 'This is where you keep the supplies, then, for the soldiers, the canteens, and the officers' clubs?'

'And for the hospitals, guardrooms, and prisoner-of-war camps,' Wolf added readily.

'You don't say! Do you issue drink to the prisoners-of-war too?'

'Not the prisoners, but to the guards.'

'And the administration.'

'The administration too, of course.'

'Of course.'

Rabe ran his fingers fondly over a group of bottles near him. 'Well now, Strick, my boy,' Wolf said patronizingly, 'What would you like?'

So I'm already 'Strick, my boy,' Strick thought, and he replied, 'Well, Wolf my boy, what have you to offer?'

Wolf looked down the row of his bottles, not without a certain pride in possession. Then he glanced somewhat mistrustfully at Rabe. Rabe said, 'I'll be going now.'

Strick protested. Not at all, he said, Rabe could only learn by staying, and he should never miss an opportunity for instruction. Wolf agreed.

'Well, then, my dear Captain Wolf, say away. What can you spare?'

'What do you need? Are you all right on cigars?'

'Oh, I have enough, but nothing very good. What chance of a light Havana?'

Wolf sniffed respectfully. This fellow was a connoisseur. 'Why, you're spoiled,' he exclaimed.

'No doubt about it. Too much easy living at the front. Been spoiled these past five years. Or do you think we're fighting a war with seaweed out there?'

'You can have a box of Brazils. Any time.'

'You don't have any cognac?'

'At the moment only Bisquit Dubouché. And a medium-good Hennessy.'

'Only Dubouché and Hennessy! You're a miracle-worker.'

Oh, Wolf had things pretty well organized. He was aware of that, but appreciation of this kind from a connoisseur such as

Strick seemed to be always made him expansive. 'Well, what shall it be?'

Rabe, Strick was happy to see, was standing stiff as a post. 'Extraordinary, all the things you have to offer here, Captain Wolf. Absolutely extraordinary. I'll pay another visit to your shop at the first opportunity. Tomorrow at the latest. You understand?'

Did Wolf understand! 'Glad to have you any time,' he said. 'We work on a system of proportional distribution. Just let me know beforehand and I'll see you aren't done out of anything which could add to your pleasure.'

'You can depend on me to make things pleasant for myself.'

'Just bring along a brief-case, a large one.'

'Agreed,' Strick said. 'And have your books ready. I'll take a look at them – a good close look.'

Wolf's face was like a large pancake grinning up from the plate. 'We understand one another,' he said, opening the door.

Followed by a silent Rabe, Strick went down the cellar corridor. They climbed the stairs, crossed a short hall, and went out. The sunlight lay like a huge dull platter of flattened silver upon the compound. 'Co-operation between comrades is a wonderful thing, don't you think, Rabe?' Strick said blandly.

Rabe was unbending, inaccessible. 'You seem to be a thoroughgoing crook, Strick,' he said stiffly.

'Don't you think you've got the wrong address?'

'I can't figure you out, Strick. If you wanted to profiteer you could just as well have done it in collusion with the station commandant.'

'Maybe he wouldn't make a deal with me.'

'And why do you have to make your deal with Wolf in my presence?'

Strick laughed heartily. The fellow was really like a schoolboy trying to play the grand inquisitor. 'Keep your eyes and ears open, Rabe. You're on the trail. I want to make a profiteer out of you. That's the whole idea.'

Rabe looked thoughtfully at the man who stood facing him. It seemed to him that he was meeting Strick anew every time he saw him. Each time he was a different person. Hard to understand him, very hard. Obviously Strick had taken him along only because he wanted to. But why had he done it? 'You're a strange person,' Rabe said. 'I really wonder about you.'

'You'll find a lot more to wonder at. Do you know what I'm up to now? I have a rendezvous, Rabe. And guess with whom. I give you three guesses.'

'I'm not interested.'

'I think you are. Do you know who I'm going to meet now, my dear fellow? Magda! Magda Tannert. Don't make a face like a dish-cloth. Shall I give her your best regards? What, you're going, Rabe? I thought you'd be glad to accompany me again. You're not? All right, in that case I'll have her all to myself. So long, Rabe. Or Heil Hitler. Whichever you choose.'

The barrack gate, Strick decided, was the ideal place for molesting every single member of the Armed Forces in the area. Every one who left the barracks went through this gate; almost every one who returned to the barracks would pass through it.

It was a heavy, wrought-iron affair with twisting rails intricately interwoven. In the centre was a sort of eagle, squashed flat, bearing in its flattened claws a gilded swastika. A handsome gate, embellished with the symbol of the times. Right next to it was a smaller gate intended for pedestrians of all ranks. It was comfortably wide; Goering could have passed through it. To the left and right of this gate were globular lights in the form of oversized stable lanterns. They sat on stout columns.

These stout columns caught Strick's eye. They stood there provocatively, like the columns on which advertisements are posted, and they were impudently naked. They obviously should be pasted over on all sides, so that every one who passed by here would read slogans and walk on, edified, strengthened, or cheered. Pithy dictums must be posted there, vigorous catchwords to belch fire and smoke into indifferent faces. Ah, he would work up such a National Socialist campaign that every one's eyes would pop. He could already see it wherever he looked: posters, pictures, banners, show-cases, bulletin boards – all crammed with selected and interpreted reading matter. He would have the men practise Nazi songs, he would make up Nazi slogans – each more hard-hitting than the last.

A sort of washerwoman in the uniform of the Army auxiliary approached him. Her clothes hung loosely over her figure as though she were a rabbit slung into a sack with only the head showing. The light hair looked like the unravelled ends of a hempen rope. The scarecrow carried herself well, however, with an implausible air of dignity.

'You sent for me?' the female scarecrow asked, examining him as if he were a laundry basket full of clothes that needed washing.

Strick felt his stomach turn over. 'What's that?' he asked.

'You are Lieutenant Strick, aren't you?'

'I am.'

'Very well. You sent for me.'

Strick could scarcely believe his eyes. The woman's skirt was wide and wrinkled, swathed round an unrecognizable form. The jacket must have belonged to a fat, hearty female with well-padded shoulders and behind. It was impossible to guess at the figure hidden behind this costume. The woman was a cat in a bag – and he was thinking of buying it.

'Do you always dress like that?' Strick asked.

'You didn't want to see me to discuss fashions, did you?'

'I rather think you could use a few hints.'

The girl smiled faintly. She was not without charm, Strick thought, and she had damnably intelligent eyes. Her smile was attractive, and in fact he had the feeling that there was something to her. But it would take a lot of extracting. Why in the world was she wearing these awful clothes? The sight of her was enough to chill you to the bone, even in this broiling heat.

The girl smiled again, gently and with great reserve, as though she were amused, but trying to conceal it. She explained, 'I've just received my uniform. We always take clothes that are too big for us. Then we can tailor them to fit. By tomorrow' – she swung her ample sleeve – 'this will look different.'

'So you are Magda Tannert?'

'Right. And you are to be the National Socialist Guidance Officer for this garrison?'

'Right.'

'Must you be?'

'I want to be.'

'And what do you want with me?'

Strick was still trying to guess what kind of person she was. The flopping clothes irritated him somewhat, and the cool, searching gaze still more. He felt that he was being weighed, tested, estimated, and categorized. And he did not like it.

Her cool glance wavered, and her eyes became for a moment less defensive. They glistened briefly with friendliness, and the sharpness of her features softened. 'Well,' she said again, 'what do you want with me?' For the first time her voice did not sound brittle and harsh.

'So you have just been given your uniform,' Strick said. 'Up to now you were a civilian employee. Is that right?'

'There was no longer any job for me here. My training period is finished, and so I was enlisted. The normal procedure.'

So – the normal procedure, was it? No longer any job for her. Strick thought of Vogel's explanation, that she had refused to co-operate willingly enough. No longer any job? She probably would never lend herself to certain types of work. Hard to imagine that anyone would even have thought of it, it seemed so absurd. . . . But then, how could you really tell? How could you know what there was under the preposterous clothes? The face was certainly not without charm. Its shape was a pure oval, its expression that of an energetic madonna. The lips were full, but tightly pressed together. No wrinkles in this face, but it looked somehow prepared for them, as if waiting for them to be impressed by force. And now the eyes were growing cool again, shutting themselves off like a lake beginning to freeze. 'Well?' She spoke curtly, harshly, rudely.

'Would you like to work in my office?'

'It will not be possible. As I've told you, I'm being transferred.'

'I can rescind your transfer.'

'Why should you?'

'Because I need you for my office.'

She slid her outspread fingers through her short blonde hair. The movement was graceful, and her breast rose with it. He wished he could see her in a bathing-dress. Then she let her arm drop abruptly, as though recalling an objection. She stiffened and said, 'I know nothing about National Socialism.'

'You don't have to. Your work in my office will be like any other work you might do in this great conflict of the nations. Except that instead of taking down shorthand on Army bread and underwear you will be dealing in – ideology and Final Victory.'

'Tell me, are you the officer who arrested the station commandant the night before last?'

'Certainly.'

'Good. When do I begin work?'

'Tomorrow morning.'

'What about my transfer?'

'I'll see that it's cancelled.'

'Then I'll report to you tomorrow morning.'

Strick watched her go. There was no denying the girl had grace. Her movements were easy and flowing, but underneath there was a vibrancy, a tension, a strength. A graceful, walking sack. It would be interesting to see what was inside. . . .

Well, then, he would paste slogans on the two pillars at the entrance. And why not have the big sides of those stable lanterns lettered also, so that the light would shine through the slogans at night. They would make beautiful Chinese lanterns, ornamental, vivid, and inspiring. What about: 'All out for the Final Victory!' Or: 'Do Not Weaken!' Or, even better: 'The Day Will Come!' He would leave the choice to Vogel. Vogel was like a barometer. He would see what tickled Vogel most. The voice of the people!

In addition, right opposite the barracks, where the road turned sharply left and down towards the valley, a large banner could be stretched. Some striking pronouncement of the Fuehrer's painted in large letters. He would find something useful – or invent it. After all, who knew every word the Fuehrer had said? He could teach them a few things.

Colonel Mueller watched, with mixed feelings, as Strick approached through the officers' club garden. Impossible to tell what kind of person he was or what he was up to. No doubt he was planning some little shock to spoil the evening.

After a day's work, including supper, was done, the colonel liked to sit in the club garden with a good cigar. There, by the rose-bed, was a curved bench on which the colonel rested, puffing at his cigar and gazing thoughtfully into the blue smoke while he considered whether he should telephone Erika or whether he might not prefer a game of cards – his favourite was *Schafskopf*. And, if it were to be *Schafskopf*, with whom, where, and for how long?

It was an unwritten law of the club that the colonel must not be disturbed during this evening meditation. At such times the conversations on the terrace – he noted this with appreciation – were usually conducted in lowered voices. The garden automatically became out of bounds; it was shunned like a minefield.

Strick alone, presumably because he was ignorant of the customs or because he had no sense of tact, was now crunching along the gravel path towards him. The fellow was a riddle. Hitherto the colonel had always been able to choose his own assistants personally, and his choices had been infallibly sound.

But this fellow had been thrust upon him without so much as a by-your-leave.

'Well, my boy,' he called out to Strick, 'how do you feel in your new position?'

Strick took out of his brief-case – the man already had a brief-case! – a number of sheets of paper. 'Here, sir, I have various proposals.' The colonel looked through Strick at the sunset. So the fellow had proposals – already!

Strick handed him one paper. 'Here are my suggestions for special controls within the command area of this headquarters.' A second sheet. 'This is the draft of the headquarters order to be issued to this effect.' A third and fourth sheet. 'Here are the first items in the sphere of propaganda and enlightenment for the Final Victory.'

The colonel balanced the four closely written sheets of paper on his palm, as though estimating the material by weight. 'You work at a remarkable tempo,' he said finally.

'Not I – Kessler is urging speed.'

Four closely written pages on the very first day. It was a little too much for the start.

'Before I read this stuff here, Strick – cut out fifty per cent of it. You may have good ideas, but that is no reason for me to ruin my eyesight.'

'Examine the details, sir. All the proposals are strictly within the limits of my special authority.'

The colonel saw red. 'What? You are getting special authority also?'

'It's on the way. Kessler promised me it.' Behind Strick the blue of the mountains dissolved softly into black. 'But I don't see, Colonel, why I should begin my work here by invoking such authority. Wouldn't it be more to the point for you to assign me my sphere of activity? Wouldn't it be better to have the National Socialist Guidance Programme set in motion by you, rather than enforced by me? The details I have in mind provisionally are listed here.'

This was sheer blackmail, the colonel thought. This man was not an officer and a gentleman, he was a thug in disguise. He probably carried a knife on him somewhere.

'Sit down, won't you?' the colonel said. Strick sat down beside him, and nonchalantly stretched out his legs, as though hoping that some one would trip over them. Reluctantly the colonel read the papers Strick had handed him.

'Controls, good Lord! Control of the kitchens! Which ones?'

'All, sir.'

'The club included?'

'Formally speaking, yes. But since this kitchen is already under your direct control anyway . . .'

The colonel began to think he could tell which way the wind was blowing. So Strick wanted to stuff himself, to eat better than anyone else. His political principles seemed to be on the alimentary level. Maybe the man was not going to make trouble; maybe he just wanted to have a good time. 'All right. You can have it, as far as I'm concerned,' the colonel said.

What else? 'You also want control over the guards? That is what the officer of the day does.'

'All the guards in the garrison, sir, ought to have the feeling at all times that the Commandant or an officer in direct contact with him can hold them responsible.'

'Well, if you don't care to do anything better with your nights than check on the guards – go ahead.'

What else? 'Supervision of the war effort of the civilian employees? That is Captain Wolf's job.' Absolutely shameless, this fellow, the colonel decided. A busybody, sticking his nose into everything. The colonel would have preferred to tear that scrap of paper to bits – if only the whole business weren't so damnably ticklish. He could not afford to be called an enemy of National Socialism.

Strick pointed to the postscript to his proposals. 'Please take note of this, Colonel. This certifies that I am carrying out all my activities directly under your orders, and am responsible to you.'

'That is the least I would expect.'

'My work will be in accordance with your ideas, sir.'

The postscript, the colonel decided, was not so bad. It gave him personally a good deal of leeway, allowed him room to tack comfortably and to decide what he would and would not be responsible for; left something to his discretion, at any rate. As for the whole show Strick intended to put on, or pretended he was going to – whichever it was – he, the colonel, could give or withhold his blessing when he wished, case by case. And it was true that it was much better for him to issue the order at once than for Kessler to intervene. Kessler was certainly one to let the heads roll where they might. So Strick's work would be in line with his ideas? 'I am honestly curious to see how far you will succeed in doing that,' the colonel said.

The lines of writing began fading, as though the oncoming night were gently erasing them. Stupid idiot, the colonel thought, picking out this time and these surroundings for his crazy ideas. The colonel sucked violently on his cigar, which abruptly lit up like an electric-light bulb. 'Now, what's this? Measures for Enlightenment? Goebbels supplies us with enough of that. The men are fed up with it.'

Strick stretched his legs out a few inches farther into the gravel path. 'We don't want to remind the soldiers directly of the War,' he said, 'but rather to impress upon them the greatness of our epoch.'

'By posters?'

'Yes, posters with catchy phrases, sound slogans.'

'But certainly not by this kind of thing, Strick. Look what you've put down here: "We can do anything we wish to do"! That's sheer nonsense. Nobody can do anything he wishes to do. Can I drink a glass of Veuve Cliquot Moselle? Can I become a general?'

'Why not? The only question is, when.'

' "We can do anything we wish to do"! What utter rot!'

The gravel garden path was a dirty grey by now, nature's waste material petrified. 'Such statements are dung,' the colonel said vehemently.

Strick spoke softly, as though he were addressing a sick man. 'That statement was made by the Fuehrer, sir.'

The colonel was overcome for a moment by a sensation of horror. This was damnably embarrassing. What had he just done – rebelled against the Fuehrer? Spoken slightingly of the Fuehrer? True, the man was a clown, a corporal come up in the world, a regular gutter-snipe – but still, that was not the kind of thing you said aloud. You kept such thoughts strictly to yourself. He was annoyed. 'Why didn't you say so right off? Why isn't the author's name written below? I don't want any of these ambiguities in my area, if you please.'

Strick held out an indelible pencil to the colonel with a friendly, resolute air of offering him a dagger. The colonel took it and reflected briefly. Then, reluctantly, he scribbled his initials at the bottom of each sheet. The M was large and impressive. M for Mueller, Colonel and Commandant of Rehhausen. Read, approved, signed – therefore, so ordered.

Strick placed the signed papers carefully into his brief-case, handling them as a collector would his art treasures. 'A lovely evening,' he remarked, gazing with satisfaction at the twilight. The hills round Rehhausen were vanishing as though dark curtains were being draped over them. The Main flowed between them like molten coal, splashed here and there with silver by a broad, unsteady brush. The sky was inverted over it all like a blue-grey bowl. Far away the stars were torches dimmed by silk.

'I want to say something to you, Strick, once and for all. You're a man very much to my liking. That's been so right from the start. Poke around here and there, wherever and however you please – I won't interfere with you.' The colonel took two vigorous puffs on his cigar. It glowed warningly like a traffic light at a cross-roads. 'But don't take the notion of poking into my private affairs. Because if you do things will start to smoke. Well, there's probably no need of my saying this – you're no idiot.' Again the warning light flashed. 'Have you met Eri yet?'

'Briefly, sir.'

Mueller stretched out on the bench as though it were a bed. 'After all, what has our life been like, Strick? Dedicated to Germany from the start. Have we had time to establish families, carry on a tradition, plant our gardens? No, my dear friend – battle has been our element. For decades we have been building the houses in which the next generation will some day live. But what have we had for ourselves? You see, I've always liked children, and I've particularly wanted to have a daughter. So, you see, I've kind of adopted one.'

Strick saw nothing but blackness for a moment, although a broad band of light from the open doors of the club made a path almost all the way to the garden. So Erika stood in the relationship of a daughter to him? What did you know about that! 'I quite understand,' Strick murmured.

'And you see, it would be damnably embarrassing to me to feel as though an absolute idiot of an N.S.G.O. were working in my command.' The colonel left a long pause, and then remarked with obvious satisfaction. 'I suppose you understand that you've already blotted your copybook with the district and therefore with the Party?'

'I don't feel that that is important. Your headquarters comes first, Colonel. I'll take care of other matters gradually.'

The colonel leaned towards him. 'I warn you, Strick – in the most friendly fashion, of course – if you ever try to get me into trouble you're' – the colonel smiled like an operatic hero – 'a dead man.' Then, without transition, he asked, 'Would you care to join me in a game of *Schafskopf*?'

'I'm much obliged, sir, but I still have work to do.'

'Don't overwork yourself.'

Strick did not intend to. He would telephone Eri. Since the colonel was going to play cards, she might have time to go for a walk with him. One thing led to another. And a man should not neglect his emotional life.

CHAPTER SEVEN

SEVEN days had sufficed to turn the life of the garrison inside out. Lieutenant Strick was spreading National Socialist ideology with a vengeance. It was as if he were strewing large quantities of manure over a field he intended to plough. The catch-words had been painted on the big stable lanterns at the entrance to the barracks. The fluted surfaces of the pillars were decorated with impressive phrases, garlanded with indoctrination. And opposite the barrack gate, painted in huge letters upon a canvas banner five feet by fifteen feet, was the slogan: 'We can do anything we wish to do.' This was Strick's favourite saying. It was, as he jovially remarked to Vogel, his special fly-catcher, and he was tremendously interested to see which ones were going to be caught by it.

The 'National Socialist Guidance Programme Special Order No. 1,' initialled by Colonel Mueller and signed by Lieutenant Strick, was an excellent instrument for rapping knuckles. The implications of this order were of the widest possible extent. The N.S.G.O. had the right to check up on kitchens, quarters, and administrative offices. The N.S.G.O. could fix the dispositions of guards and special squads. The N.S.G.O. could attend any and all activities in the line of duty. The N.S.G.O. had the right to examine all secret messages and secret files. The N.S.G.O. was directly subordinate to the Commandant and responsible to him alone. And the N.S.G.O. was Lieutenant Strick.

The situation in regard to general political instruction had taken a sharp turn for the better. The class was to be given not once but twice a week. Attendance was obligatory; there were no excuses. Those who stayed away had to report to the N.S.G.O. and state precisely their reasons for absence. The absentees would report the following day, half an hour after their tour of duty was over, at the N.S.G.O.'s office, in order to make up the class they had missed. 'Enlightenment' was indispensable. It was also ordered that one of these weekly sessions was to be conducted by the troop commander personally – that is, by Captain Wolf, in the presence of all officers of his unit, which included Rabe. Even the N.S.G.O. dutifully attended these instructive hours and took most voluminous notes which irked Wolf immeasurably.

The second hour was taken over by the N.S.G.O. personally The room was literally jammed. Scarcely anyone was absent; and those who were only because they could not help it. For Strick's classes in current events and political instruction were always lively affairs. It was National Socialism all right – from a humourist's point of view.

Another new custom was inaugurated – political instruction for all officers attached to the headquarters. This took place once a week, every Monday evening at six o'clock. Strick had gallantly left it to the colonel to decide whether he himself or Strick would give this class. The colonel thought it would be quite sufficient if Strick undertook it.

Banners hung in the dining-rooms, the canteens, the lecture halls, the guardrooms, the corridors. Every room had a portrait of Hitler. Vogel proposed that brief extracts from Hitler's *Mein Kampf* should be posted in the latrines, but after lengthy consideration this idea was rejected – in spite of Vogel's candid admission that he liked to read certain types of literature in those places.

Kessler was sent a copy of Special Order No. 1 and of Strick's 'provisional report', and was so impressed that he had the commanding general fire a congratulatory telegram to Rehhausen:

SPECIAL PRAISE – HOPE FOR FURTHER EXCELLENT RESULTS – HARD TIMES – EXAMPLES NECESSARY.

(*Signed*)

LIEUTENANT-GENERAL

Lieutenant Rabe was playing the piano. He rapped out heartfelt but well-tempered nostalgia: German romanticism quavered from a varnished wooden box.

They were at the Baers', a respected family long resident in the town of Rehhausen. 'They' were Captain Geiger, Lieutenant Strick, and Lieutenant Rabe, and some other gentlemen who had been considered worthy to attend, drawn from the increasingly sparse civilian populace. In one corner leaned a middle-aged haddock, staring vaguely out of watery blue eyes, his hair like clippings of low-quality fur. He was a doctor at the local hospital. The boy on the chair beside the desk, a herring with a bulbous nose, was a law student.

The so-called fair sex was sitting in a loose circle. There was Irmgard Baer, the daughter of the house, an unpaid office helper in her father's wholesale business, as ready to embrace the Muses as she was their male votaries. There were two other full-grown girls who resembled geese. And there was Magda Tannert, stiff and tense, a wooden madonna.

The room, called the drawing-room, was a well-upholstered museum piece. There was plush everywhere, most of it showing wear, but all of it well brushed. Nothing of the wall, not a single board of the floor, could be seen; everything was covered by plush. It was a world totally draped. The stucco on the ceiling was artfully worked into whorls, arabesques, and flourishes, all merging into and folding over one another, and in all the folds dust slumbered.

Rabe translated his emotions into finger gymnastics. His body swayed like a Balinese dancer in a trance. He breathed music. According to the announcement that had been made beforehand, he was playing Schubert. He pressed keys which released hammers upon strings that quivered pleasantly; air was set in motion, eardrums made to vibrate, brains interpreted the rhythm of the sound-waves as music. Feeling is all, as Goethe so aptly remarked. The dust in the plastered ceiling slept on undisturbed.

Strick rested on a sofa in a corner of the room. He could feel the springs under him thrusting stuffing, muslin, and plush against his body. Beside him lay Rabe's book, *Three Centuries of German Lyrics*. The photograph was no longer in it, but the typewritten poems were still tucked into its pages. Tonight they were doing not Mörike but Hölderlin – so Hölderlin was still to come.

He unfolded the typewritten sheets – the paper was the colour of bleached cheese. They were love poems, the author unnamed: verses that had the taste of sugared lemons. And they sounded oddly familiar to him; he must have read them once upon a time, and a long time ago at that – in his senior year at school, he would guess, when the hidden goal of his night's sleep was to get his trousers pressed by laying them under the mattress. For eight hours he would lie stiff as a board, and his reward the next morning was to receive a glance of approbation lasting two and a half seconds from a girl at a window. That was love life for you.

Sie liebten sich beide, doch keiner
Wollt' es dem andern gestehn;
Sie sahen sich an so feindlich
Und wollten vor Liebe vergehn!

Interesting verses. Remarkable verses. Weren't they by ...? Oh, of course, certainly. They were by Heine, Heinrich Heine. No doubt about it.

Now, who could have copied them? Rabe himself? That would be strange, to say the least - Rabe and Heinrich Heine. Or had some one copied them out for Rabe who, since no author's name was given, had no idea what he was carrying around with him. Hmm. That was probably it. And then what were the poems meant as? A hint, perhaps? From Magda? It was possible.

Strick folded the sheets of paper carefully, and slipped them into his breast pocket. The paper crackled softly. He stretched contentedly, so that the spiral springs groaned, announcing that they were not accustomed to such a posture.

Meanwhile Rabe poured his feelings into the steel wires. The final tone hung in the air for a moment, then roosted in the ceiling decorations. The haddock clapped his fins in approval. The two geese uttered muted quacks. Irmgard's bosom heaved visibly. Magda's eyes were like soft cushions for Rubens angels. Geiger was bursting with eagerness to recite.

In the next half-hour Geiger ran through Hölderlin - ran him through the heart. His voice pitched to noble lamentation, he strode through Hellas as he would the streets of Rehhausen. But the tapestries on the walls absorbed the shock of his words, and the great-grandparents of the house of Baer, wholesalers for Rehhausen and vicinity, beamed complacently from their frames, which hung side by side in a prominent position.

The lamplight brought out the delicate pastels of Magda's face. Rabe, who was now sitting beside Strick, seemed to be melting and flowing in her direction. Their eyes searched hesitantly for one another, or played chess together on the carpet pattern. Whenever they looked at each other directly a slight flush rose to Magda's face, as though she had been dusted with a pink face-powder.

If he ever kisses her, Strick thought, she will flare up and burn out. It would be like fire catching in a heap of straw. With Erika, whom he now called Eri, it was a different matter. Eri was always on fire. No matter where you touched her she was burning, burning to the lobes of her ears. Magda was a breath of air which could abruptly become a hurricane; Erika was an eternal sirocco. It gave you slight headaches and made you dead tired, but it also produced a pleasant feeling of intoxication. She was like live cocaine, palpable alcohol. Magda was sweet and beautiful: Erika was heady and vivid. Magda yielded to you: Erika welded you to her.

And Geiger was reciting Hölderlin. The words boomed out of him like music from an organ with all the stops out. His voice filled the room, thrust itself between Magda and Rabe, pushed violently against the overflowing bosoms of the young ladies, penetrated into the large heads of the two fish, tugged at the dust in the stuccoed ceiling without loosening it. Mellifluous, resounding Hölderlin. And in Strick's breast-pocket, as he shifted about on the squeaking springs covered by plush, muslin and stuffing, the sheets of paper crackled softly – the poems of a man named Heinrich Heine. Strick looked at Rabe and Geiger. The verses would come in handy, would come in very handy.

Strick and Rabe were in the room together. Rabe was reading the *Reich*. He underlined passages, cut out some items, marked certain sentences with additional exclamation marks, and placed his cuttings in his lecture folders. These were arranged according to a great variety of subjects: Theory – Ideological Warfare – Practical Warfare – Internal Politics – Art.

Strick looked up from his reading of De Coster's *Ulenspiegel*. 'You ought to make a chart,' he said. 'Symbols signifying so many thousand men. Figures on sinking of ships. How many drowned? Bombing attacks. How many burned? Rectification of lines. How many blown to bits? War prisoners. How many will survive? And then the deportees, the famine victims, the victims of judicial murders. And then figures for amputees, the blind, the burned, the one-lunged. And then the legion of psychological cripples – men who no longer care what they do, mothers who have lost their children, girls without shame. And then place a large question-mark at the bottom meaning, "What is it all for?"'

'Germany, Strick, Humanity.'

'The remnants of humanity. And what do you mean by Germany? I've taken the liberty to borrow some papers of yours.

They contain copies of poems, remarkable poems. Do these poems also belong to your Germany?'

Rabe squirmed with embarrassment. 'Did you recognize the author?' he asked.

'Why are you afraid to say the name of Heinrich Heine?'

Rabe busied himself with his folder of cuttings.

'Is it all right with you if I keep these poems for a few more days?' Strick asked.

'For my part you can do whatever you like with them,' Rabe answered gruffly.

'Thank you. It won't be what you think.'

The poems were turned over to Vogel.

'What am I supposed to do with them? Improve my mind? I don't need poetry for that.'

'Can you manage to slip these into Captain Geiger's hands at the club?'

'I can if I think it's worth while doing.'

'It is.'

Corporal Vogel read the lyrics, his face expressing deep mistrust, like a backwoodsman being offered a plate of oysters. 'Who wrote these poems anyhow?' he demanded. 'Have you been milking the amorous midnight muse yourself?'

'The author is named Heinrich Heine.'

Vogel gave vent to a wolf whistle. 'Then Geiger will get them.'

'Tomorrow Rabe has guard duty, so he won't be there for lunch at the club. That would be the right time for it.'

'Good.'

The afternoon of the next day Vogel reported success.

'In my capacity as extra officers' club orderly I went in and left the poems in the cloak-room. Waited patiently as a faithful servant of Mein Fuehrer. An orderly comes bustling in. Spies the papers, reads them excitedly. Aryan brainstuff works feverishly, without results. I saunter by casually. "Found some poems, eh? They must belong to Captain Geiger. He's the poetry man around here." Orderly, expecting praise, anticipating benevolent smile, bustles into dining-room. Returns radiant with joy over superior's appreciation. Says Captain Geiger nodded gratefully and took the poems.'

'Not right off,' Strick said. 'I was there in the dining-room. Geiger took the poems with an air of surprise. Read them, then called out, "Do these poems belong to any of you gentlemen?" Rabe was not there, so no one spoke up, and Geiger pocketed them.'

'Well, what will come of it?'

'If we're lucky he will recite them before the entire officers' corps, with ladies present.'

'Oh! And then we'll catch him with his trousers down.'

'Not him; Wolf.'

'How do you make that out?'

'Chain reaction.'

That same afternoon Captain Geiger was flattered to discover that the N.S.G.O. was highly interested in the cultural programme for the forthcoming officers' club entertainment, with ladies invited.

'These days we must stress solemnity,' Strick said. 'We must never lose sight of the grandeur of our times. The reading-desk ought to be covered with a swastika flag. On it candles, the symbol of light. To each side a row of potted laurel-trees arranged in diagonal lines so they form a triangle at the back of the platform. And what do you think we should have at the apex of the triangle, Captain Geiger? Well? A portrait or bust of the Fuehrer, of course.'

'Of course.'

'Now, about the make-up of the programme. Have it printed, not mimeographed. A large national eagle in light colours, dominating the page. Over it, thick and heavy, in patriotic Gothic lettering, of course, the order of selections. Let's say: "Hymn to the Fuehrer", by Baumann; "Ode in Field Gray", by Anacker; String Quartet on Germanic Folk Themes, by Herms Niel. And so on. Expense is no object; as you know, I have a fat budget and the right to draw on certain special funds.'

'That sounds fine.'

'We must cultivate the spirit, Captain Geiger. And you are doing a splendid job of it. Your ideas are often quite original. Rest assured, I'm behind you. I'm always looking for new ideas. The only thing, you know, is that we still need a new touch, new talent. Love-lyrics, say, that really touch the heart and spirit. We want to bring out our men's deepest emotions, you know.'

Geiger fell for it promptly. 'Have already thought over your suggestions. Share your opinion completely. You're absolutely right. Art reinforces militancy on the home front. I have just discovered a new, unknown poet. The fellow has a real knack for poetry, but prefers to remain anonymous. Possibly the bashful author is in our own officers' corps. Pegasus in uniform, you know. I was thinking of including some of his stuff in the programme.'

'But that's wonderful, Captain. We all like surprises. And I'd really be delighted if I could mention some such novelty in my next report "upstairs".'

'You can depend on me.'

And Heinrich Heine was recited.

The wall lights had been covered with paper shades. They illuminated the blue drawing-room of the officers' club softly, like a bedroom. Strick sat in a deep armchair, quiet and alone, and looked at his wine-glass. The liquid was palest yellow, with the aroma of tart apples.

From the adjacent room came vigorous applause. Now, Strick thought, Geiger would be beaming like the full moon and bobbing up and down to express simultaneously proud satisfaction and modest gratitude. Now, according to the programme, came the main interval. Heinrich Heine had already been recited.

The door to the blue drawing-room slammed against the wall as it was wrenched open. Rabe, in the pose of an outraged archangel, stood at the threshold. 'Well, Rabe, was the poetry reading interesting?' Strick picked up his glass and meditatively rocked it, so that the full-bodied wine swirled.

Rabe rushed up to him, as though he meant to trample him underfoot. 'How did my Heine poems fall into Captain Geiger's hands?'

'I've wondered about that myself.'

Rabe was quivering with excitement, fury, and humiliation. Strick regarded him as if he were a trapeze artist whose performance was competent, but not unusual.

'He had the impudence to call him an unknown poet,' Rabe said with honest indignation.

'Berlin publishers have had the same idea before Geiger. Did you notice how enthusiastically the district leader clapped? Either the man is an ignoramus or no National Socialist.'

'No one is going to put up with your methods much longer, Strick.'

'Who is no one?'

The colonel sailed into the room. 'Well, now, I must say, so that's where you are. High-flown tripe those poets write. Makes me want to throw up my lunch and give the proceeds to the Victory fund. Have you any cognac there, Strick?'

'No. Just a rather strong Würzburger.'

'That will do at a pinch. Pour me a glass.' The colonel settled heavily in a chair, reached for the glass, and drank it down at one draught. 'It's easy for you, Strick. You claim work or some such excuse; you can afford to do that. And meanwhile you sit here quietly and guzzle. But I have my public functions to perform. I have to nod approval after every effusion, and when each group is over I give the signal for applause. Unless you've done it you can't imagine how a life like that slowly wears you out. Why haven't you refilled my glass yet?'

Rabe brusquely turned away. He strode hurriedly across the room, and slammed the door behind him. The colonel looked up angrily. 'What's the matter with that fellow? What a way to behave in the club! These young people have no manners any more.'

'Maybe the poems got on his nerves.'

'I doubt it. I don't think he's got that much sense. This wine isn't bad at all, Strick.'

'From Wolf's special corner of the cellar.'

'That Wolf is a wizard.'

'Let's hope he doesn't whiz us all behind lock and key, Colonel.'

'Don't talk nonsense, Strick – fill my glass instead. In a moment I must pay my respects to the ladies in the yellow room. All misbegotten old bags. As many complexes as they have hair on their heads; they all ought to be scalped. Whenever I see them I'm happy I never married. That's the one excuse for being those hags have – to act as a warning. Aren't you coming along? But no, if I know you, you'll get out of it. Here's to you, you coward.'

The district leader trotted into the room with Captain Geiger, who was twining round him like a creeper. 'Cultural indoctrination, Dr. Friedrich, a totally neglected field,' Geiger was saying. The district leader answered by citing the headings from his latest letters of instruction: 'Mobilization of the German soul. Teutonic poetry, selections from the Eddas, and quotations from the Fuehrer.'

'And Goethe, Dr. Friedrich!' Geiger drew up a chair for the honourable Party leader.

'That's the way it is,' the colonel said. 'The twin glories of

Germany: Goethe and Hitler. No other nations could produce them. No bombings could wipe them out. *Prosit!*'

An embarrassed silence followed. It was as though a tell-tale puddle of water had suddenly appeared on the floor and every one present felt somehow to blame for it.

Wolf waddled in through the door. He grinned, a general, humble grin, like a butler sincerely concerned for his employer's comfort, and bellowed like a town crier: 'Colonel Mueller, sir? Wish to announce ice-cream sodas!'

There was a general exclamation: 'Ah!'

'More surprises later,' Wolf proclaimed with the air of a mid-summer Santa Claus.

'What about cigars, Wolf?' The good captain had them, of course. Everything prepared in advance. He stalked over to the window, drew the curtains aside, and carried the boxes stacked there over to the group. One of them, a small box in the loudest colours, he presented to the Commandant. 'For the colonel and the district leader. Genuine Cubas.' He tossed another, larger box over to Captain Geiger. 'I'm sure the other gentlemen smoke Brazils – long, thin, hand-rolled, spicy without being sharp.'

'Much obliged, Wolf,' the colonel grunted, sniffing his handsome Cuban cigar as though it were a meaty bone which promised to make a good meal. 'Men who work hard ought to eat, drink, and smoke well. Not to forget women, of course – nicely graded, according to rank.' The colonel licked his cigar so that it would not unwrap when he clipped it. He glowered at the men round him. He was obviously none too fond of the kind of club entertainment that was being offered this evening.

Geiger was making terrible efforts to warm up the tepid prevailing mood. He functioned instinctively like a thermostatic heating-plant to provide automatically the most comfortable room-temperature. 'How was it good old Goethe put it? Evil times, joyous festivals. If he had lived to see our Party programme . . .'

Strick lashed out sharply, 'You're not trying to say that Faust's Gretchen would have been a member of the League of German Girls, are you?'

The embarrassing imaginary pool on the floor seemed to have enlarged, and along with it the circle of those under suspicion. The colonel cleared his throat loudly. 'Have you read my last headquarters order, Dr. Friedrich? Extension of the National

Socialist instruction programme. Step-up of faith in the Final Victory. Have you seen it yet?'

'I regret to say I haven't, Colonel. You know how the Party values such testimonies of loyalty. All the more surprising that—'

Strick broke in, abruptly changing the subject. It was as though he were picking up a stick in order to whack someone on the head. 'Is that all you have to offer us, Captain Wolf? No genuine French cognac? No Scotch whisky? Not a glass of imported vodka?'

Wolf's honour as a good provider was sorely touched. It was as bad as being denounced as a eunuch when all along he had been boasting of his potency. 'Be patient,' he snapped. 'Each thing in its turn.' He stalked off contemptuously.

The colonel scrutinized Strick thoughtfully. At last he came out with what was on his mind. 'Is it true, Strick, that you have put up a poster reading: "Childbed too is part of the home front"?'

'Quite true, sir. It hangs near the entrance to the women's living quarters.'

Geiger was highly amused. 'Remarkably to the point. I suppose it's an invitation to the dance?'

'I have my directives from above, gentlemen. From the High Command of the Armed Forces. Has anyone any objections?'

The colonel picked up his glass and sniffed it like a dog trying to choose a post. Finally he mumbled into the glass, as though he were entrusting his private opinion to the wine alone, 'A preposterous idea. The men will be laughing so hard they won't be fit to work.'

The district leader turned to Captain Geiger with the hope of guiding the conversation in a more pleasant direction. 'Have you read the latest letter of instructions?' he asked. 'An article by Dr. Ley entitled, "The world will be astounded." I was happy to find that Dr. Ley, the Movement's great idealist, heartily endorses your own type of cultural endeavour.'

Geiger expressed his regret that he had not seen the article. District Leader Friedrich, D.D.S., looked concerned. 'You ought to pass on the instruction sheets as soon as they reach you, Lieutenant Strick,' he said. 'Their contents may be more important than gigantic posters bearing unclear statements.'

'All quotations from the Fuehrer, Doctor.'

Dr. Friedrich became stern. He risked a reprimand. 'I missed you tonight in the hall. I suppose German art means nothing to you.'

'Possibly I stayed away because it does.'

The colonel choked on his wine, laughing in spite of himself. 'Strick seems to be a professional jester,' he said.

Geiger immediately began plucking his second string. 'Strick covers up his essentially kind nature by toughness. Once Goethe swore violently to conceal his emotions. Tremendous personality, he was.'

'I must go to the lavatory,' the colonel said. The district leader had the same urge. Geiger was about to join them.

'I must speak to you right away, Captain Geiger,' Strick said. He spoke in a curt, peremptory tone, making it plain that this was an order. Geiger stayed, outraged. Strick was a boor, to put it mildly, snapping commands at him as though he were an errand boy. No forms, no courtesies, no feeling of tradition. The others went off, but Geiger stood stiff as a forgotten ironing-board leaning against a cellar wall. It was sometimes inconvenient, he thought, being an adjutant, the mainstay of headquarters. No matter what the business was everybody applied to him.

Strick held the wine-glass with the finger-tips of both hands. He looked at it with an expression of distress, as though he found himself obliged to smash it. 'I'm very sorry for you, Captain,' Strick said. 'But after everything that has taken place I am unfortunately forced to make a report.'

Geiger bristled. 'Don't know what you're talking about,' he said.

Strick raised his head slowly, like an artillery piece fixing on its target. 'Then I must speak bluntly, I suppose. You've been carrying on Semitic propaganda.'

Geiger reacted as if he were caught in a revolving saw. He took a deep breath, and words spurted from him like sawdust. 'I strongly resent that.'

Strick gently drove the saw deeper. 'I'm afraid you don't realize how serious the situation is. Semitism is sabotage, and sabotage means court-martial.'

'Sir! I am a soldier who can take a joke, you know, but too much is too much. My anti-Semitism is a matter of deep personel conviction. My father served in South-west Africa. In 1907 in Windhoek the Jews cheated him out of one shilling and twopence per hundred pounds on beef. That kind of thing leaves its mark; it isn't so easily forgotten. Our family makes no pacts with crooks.'

'Then your behaviour is all the more amazing.'

'I request an explanation.'

Strick sat the glass down on the table without having touched the wine. The table top was highly polished varnish, smooth as a new-frozen sheet of ice on a forest pool. The glass slid a little upon it. 'You put certain poems on the programme and alleged that the author was unknown. Are you trying to make me swallow that too?' The glass braked sharply. Strick withdrew his hand, leaned back in his chair, and looked coldly at Geiger. 'You know perfectly well that the author was Heinrich Heine.'

Geiger staggered. 'What's that?'

'Heinrich Heine.'

Geiger felt himself utterly innocent. What was he being accused of? How had he ever deserved it, he, the son of an anti-Semitic father? He, who had always striven to be a good Nazi. He, who had a successful military career behind him and good prospects for the future? Should he of all people have made this fatal mistake? And on top of it all had he had the ill luck to fall into the hands of this unscrupulous bastard Strick, this hangman! It couldn't be true. 'You're trying to pull off a bad joke, Strick,' he said desperately.

The room round Geiger changed colour. The blue faded out. All that was pleasant and soothing vanished. In place of the curtains he saw bars; in place of the carpet he saw a well-worn floor in a prison barracks. The polished table became a barrier, and behind it, sitting calmly like an overseer of slaves, was Strick. And Strick was saying, 'I really wish I could let you off a court-martial. But what moral right have I to do that?'

Geiger squirmed like a dog trying to dodge a blow. 'It was only a mistake, an unfortunate accident.'

'That I happened to be listening?'

'No, no, I didn't mean that. After all, I'm loyal to the Fuehrer, you must believe me.'

Court-martial meant extinction. Geiger knew: interrogations, investigation, trial. A mill: on top men were thrown into it, and below a bloody pulp trickled out. Even at best it meant being thrown aside like a piece of spoiled meat. It meant no longer being an adjutant, no longer having any chance of promotion, being struck off the Army List. It meant the end of a man's career, transfer to a front-line unit, if not to a disciplinary battalion or an

Army prison. Avoided by his comrades, condemned by the Party. No more recitations at private gatherings, no more tastefully arranged evenings at the club under his direction. The object of vulgar barrack gossip, another scandal to be discussed at the officers' ladies' teas. Mockery, shame, and humiliation. That was what lay before him.

'I really want very much to spare you a court-martial, Geiger. Believe me, I do. But then I would have to have some convincing proof of your sincere attachment to the ideals of National Socialism.'

Geiger snapped up the offer like a starving mongrel. 'What proof?'

'Up to now I have searched in vain for Captain Wolf's personal papers. Everything – records, documents, correspondence – is missing. But they must be somewhere. Where are the papers which pertain to his department?'

'In the Commandant's safe.'

'I need those documents, Geiger. Let's say tomorrow morning at eight-thirty at my office.'

'But what about the colonel?'

'The colonel will be up late tonight, Geiger; we have a long evening ahead of us. Tomorrow morning he's going to want to sleep. Realize the strain his public duties impose, and show some consideration for him. Besides which, you know that I have authority to examine all papers, including top-secret governmental matters. So why complicate the business? I need the documents; you will get them for me. A simple process.'

'What about the responsibility?'

'I will take it. Personally I'm very fond of you, Geiger, and I'd really regret seeing you in court.'

'And then I can depend upon your—'

'Look here,' Strick interrupted, 'if anyone has cause to be wary it's me, not you. Do I get those documents tomorrow or don't I?'

'You'll get them.'

'Your word?'

'My word of honour.'

'Then everything is all right.'

Lieutenant Rabe came tearing in, and strode straight up to Captain Geiger. 'Captain Geiger,' he said wrathfully, 'will you kindly explain to me how those poems of Heinrich Heine's came into your possession?'

Geiger, who had felt on the point of touching land, was once more plunged into the wild waves. He drifted submissively, prepared to be drowned instantly. With Rabe on his high horse the outlook for him was bad. The Party idealist would stop at nothing. Probably, Geiger thought fearfully, he felt his lily-white National Socialist conscience had been smirched by exposure to forbidden authors. Was everybody already talking about the Heinrich Heine affair?

'I demand an explanation, Captain,' Rabe repeated.

Strick rose to his feet. 'It was a mistake of mine. Captain Geiger came to my office to have me approve the programme. The poems of Heine were lying on my desk, and by mistake were put back into Captain Geiger's brief-case along with the programme. He was the victim of an oversight.'

The dust, the squalor, the misery of prison, which was all Geiger had been seeing, vanished abruptly, and the bedroom blue of the room glowed vividly again before his eyes. He made each of his movements very formal. 'I'm very much obliged to you, my dear Herr Strick, for this unqualified exoneration. You are a man of honour. Extremely decent of you.' He bowed his gratitude like a puppet. 'You can count on me, Herr Strick. Any time.'

Geiger glided off, anxious to return to the sphere of the Muses. The second half of the programme had already started. He must be on the spot to supervise and to receive the tributes of the audience. In his soul he felt the profound joy of a man who has miraculously escaped ruin.

'Well, Rabe,' Strick said, 'how about a glass of good cognac with me?'

'You seem to be a thorough-going swine, Strick.'

'Wait a while. Your flattery is a little premature.'

CHAPTER EIGHT

THIS was the night when Oscar Tikke had to attend the instruction class for Party leaders. Attendance was obligatory for all block, cell, section, and district leaders. Oscar never waited for the call of duty to be repeated. He changed obediently into his brown Party uniform.

The monthly instruction class obviated the necessity for following the newspapers. Dr. Friedrich read aloud a general situation-report, plus commentary. Then he discussed internal Party questions related to the Rehhausen area. The list of possible difficulties was run through. Then followed special explanations on the methods for recognizing and eliminating difficulties of every species and sub-species, including indirect difficulties. The Hitler salute, all present standing, brought the instruction class to an end. It lasted four hours – officially.

On such evenings Mother Tikke could do as she pleased in the tavern. Not that otherwise Oscar Tikke had much authority over his wife, in spite of his being a prominent specimen of the master race. But still, he was an uncongenial sort, from Vogel's point of view. Instruction class for Party leaders always meant a party with friends for Vogel.

Vogel trundled in, and went up to the counter where Mother Tikke was rinsing glasses in a bowl. He embraced the wrinkled old woman as though she were a young girl. Mother Tikke splashed water, called Vogel 'young scoundrel', and swung the bottle-brush like a battle-axe. 'Don't waste energy,' Vogel said affectionately. 'Save it up. There are plenty of others who need to have their heads broken.'

Carefully, like a pedantic pharmacist going through his shelf of poisons, he selected one of the bottles in the refrigerator. He held it up against the light, uncorked it, and sniffed. 'Much too good for an old proletarian,' he said.

'Is Tannert coming tonight?'

'He's coming. Get the private room ready, Mother Tikke. We don't want to be disturbed tonight.'

'You don't want your drinking disturbed, you mean.'

'And then we want to blaspheme, Mother Tikke. Till the ceiling threatens to fall. And talk about what pigs the others are, and what marvellous fellows we are after all. We are Germany's future, Mother Tikke. That will cost you four suppers and six bottles tonight.'

'First carry this basket of empties out to the yard, my son. And stack them. But do it neatly – none of the sloppy work you do up at the officers' club. When you come back I'll tell you who was here last night.'

'Who?'

'With a lady. As Oscar's guest of honour.'

'With a lady? Holding hands and all that? At the private table – under the swastika?'

'Go on, don't talk so much. I'll tell you when you come back.'

Vogel trudged off. With every step he took the bottles rattled. So some one he was interested in had been here yesterday. And with a woman, besides. Could it have been Strick? He worked faster, piling the bottles as though they were urgently needed shells. Hard to believe that the man would waste his substance on love-making. He should know better than that.

Dragging the basket behind him, Vogel hurried back to the counter. 'Was it my friend who was here last night? The lieutenant?' Mother Tikke nodded. 'With the colonel's miss?' Mother Tikke nodded again. 'And both of them all wrapped up in each other?'

'He more than her.'

'Mother Tikke, he's straying off the straight and narrow. That smart little bitch will eat him up for breakfast. And then what will be left of us? You should have given him a glass of milk and kicked him out after fifteen minutes.'

'They drank two bottles of wine.'

'And then?'

'No "and then". Not in my place.'

Old Tannert stuck his head in through the door from the private room. 'Are you coming or not, Vogel? Do you think I have all night?' He vanished again, closing the door behind him.

'Listen to that, Mother Tikke. Playing the Party-line game with me. A fine old scamp you've thrown my way. He treats me like a screwdriver.'

'You blab to much, Vogel. You ought to do something.'

Vogel did a parody of the disciplined soldier. He stood up very straight and jerked out: 'Will drink up bottles. Thereby producing new bottles to be piled.' Then he about-turned and rushed off into Mother Tikke's private room.

Old Tannert was sitting at the table. 'Well?' he said. 'What's new, Vogel? Why did you send for me?'

'Probably to look upon your charming countenance.'

The face before him was wrinkled like a drying apple. Vogel sat down at the table. 'Before I forget, Heil Hitler, Herr Tannert.' He raised his hand to his mouth and stuck out his tongue.

'Have you drunk much already, Vogel?' Tannert asked.

'If I'm drunk it's because I've been reading your posters, Tannert. Let me see your mitts. You must have worn your fingers down drawing. You're working yourself to death, Tannert.'

Tannert grinned contentedly. 'Nice work, eh? The texts are priceless. I've turned this whole barracks into a comic sheet.'

'But that N.S.G.O. is a regular idiot.'

'I wouldn't say that. There's something likeable about him.'

'Two weeks more of this, Tannert, and you'll be applying for membership in the storm troops.'

'Or Lieutenant Strick will be giving lectures to the soldiers on Marx's *Kapital*.'

Vogel looked like a puffed-up frog about to burst. 'The man's an idiot, I tell you. Another three days of this and the colonel will chase him out of the barracks or put a couple of bullets into his belly. Do you know what he's doing? He's running around with that slut Blaustrom.'

'I know. He calls her up on the telephone several times a day.'

'And calls her honey and darling, I suppose.'

'Nonsense. He just calls her Eri.'

'Just Eri! Oh, you innocent. Do you know what that means, Tannert? The little vampire will suck him out like an oyster, and throw away the shell.'

Old Tannert sat calm and unruffled. 'Maybe you don't know Strick very well, Vogel.'

'I know him like my own waistcoat pocket.'

'You don't wear a waistcost.'

'Don't be silly, Tannert. I thought you were going to help me get this lazy bastard of an N.S.G.O. moving. Instead you pull the indulgent old-fogy act – "boys will be boys".'

Old Tannert pressed his broad chest against the table, and moved closer to Vogel. 'Let's be serious now. Do you think Strick will come in with us?'

They looked at one another searchingly, and Vogel's expression was deadly earnest. It was a strange contrast to his usual grimaces. 'Come in with us?' Vogel repeated. And then, like a judge announcing a carefully considered verdict, he added, 'He must.'

'Then let us ask him frankly.'

'That won't do. He would give you a completely ambiguous answer. I don't know just what his game is, but it's clear that he intends to play it alone.'

'Then the only thing to do, Vogel, is to confront him with an accomplished fact.'

Vogel's face lost its fixity. He wrinkled his forehead. 'And suppose his reaction is entirely different from what we expect? Tannert, the man is either a very heavy bomb or an enormous balloon filled with hot air. But, if he is a bomb, suppose he blows us all up?'

He got up and paced the room restlessly, his head lowered, his shoulders hunched, his arms dangling. He walked past the whitewashed walls and the windows covered with black-out paper, he paced over the floor polished smooth by the feet of Oscar and Mother Tikke in the course of forty years.

'Answer me one question, Tannert, and answer it frankly and honestly. In your opinion is Strick a Nazi?'

Tannert shook his head. 'Yes and no.'

'Is he an anti-Nazi?'

'Yes and no.'

'Then the man is nothing.'

'He is something, Vogel. I'm certain of that. Since this war began I've never seen anyone work so hard. The man is a motor; he runs without stopping, without even refuelling. But where he's going isn't clear. Nevertheless I'm dead certain he has a definite goal.'

Vogel sat down again. 'At any rate, we are not going to wait patiently until he deigns to inform us of his intentions.'

'We must not be reckless.'

'We will seal our lips, stuff cotton-wool into our ears, wear dark glasses, and bury ourselves somewhere. Hibernate Teutonically and wake up strengthened after the Final Victory. . . . Mother Tikke, we want to eat.'

Mother Tikke shuffled in. 'Have you settled all your business?'

'Like hell we have,' Vogel said. 'We have decided that we're a pair of idiots.'

'Did it take you all this time to find that out? You don't get anything to eat until you're through.'

She started out angrily. Those men talked and talked and talked, and nothing ever came of it. Talked their mouths dry, and imagined they'd accomplished the Lord knew what. And never asked her!

'Frau Tikke,' Old Tannert called. Mother Tikke shuffled suspiciously towards him. Tannert took out of his pocket an object, wrapped in paper, which was no bigger than a match-box. 'Put that with the rest,' he said.

Mother Tikke was more annoyed. 'All you ever do is stock up. But the stuff has no practical value at all.'

'What do you have there, Tannert?'

'Another official seal. This time a reproduction of the General Headquarters seal. Seven nights' work.'

Vogel shrugged expressively. 'Well, what of it? What does seven nights' work amount to? Do you expect a medal, Tannert? You may as well be strangled with piano wire, after your bones have been broken and your guts ripped out.'

Tannert winced. 'You talk too much nonsense, Vogel.'

Mother Tikke wanted to slap his face. Not too hard, but hard enough. There was nothing Vogel had any respect for, nothing he would not talk down. He chopped all emotions to bits. If he ever prayed he would no doubt start with a long preamble on his godlessness. 'What was that you gave us last week, Vogel?' she asked.

'Printed paper.'

Tannert moved closer to Vogel. 'Forms?'

'Some blank paybooks, travel passes, marching orders. But Mother Tikke is right. All we do here is stock up. And what for? Some day Oscar will get it into his head to poke around – and what then?'

'Oscar never will,' Mother Tikke said with conviction. 'He's too lazy.'

Tannert waved the matter aside. 'Even if he does do you think he's going to run off to the Gestapo? With stuff found in his own house? They would start working him over right away – even Herr Tikke can figure that out.'

'But what's the use of all this junk?' Vogel said.

'We must be ready. The time may come all of a sudden when we have to help some one.'

'For seven months we've been waiting for it.'

'Do you call that any length of time, Vogel? I've been waiting for eleven years.'

Vogel tapped his pencil against his wine-glass. 'Mine Hostess, a medal for Tannert and a bottle of wine for me.' Abruptly his voice became cold and sharp. 'Listen,' he said, 'we ought to have a dress rehearsal. With a lot of alcohol and a little trust in God much can be accomplished.' He sipped his wine and continued. 'Tomorrow morning I have to take more pictures of the British officers in the prison camp. I said that the others didn't turn out well. While I was taking the first batch of photographs I slipped a note to the English captain. This afternoon I was back at the camp to arrange a date for the rest of the pictures. The captain was standing at the fence picking his left ear. That was the signal that he agreed to my proposal. We will make all the arrangements so that in four days, on Monday, that is, he can go over the hill.'

Mother Tikke silently refilled the glasses. The only sound was the gurgling of the wine in the neck of the bottle. 'Be ready here Monday evening, Tannert. We will see how useful your official seals prove to be. I already have the photo of the captain's face for the pass, and I'll fix it up with a German lieutenant's uniform. So be ready for a visitor Monday evening, Mother Tikke. A lieutenant. And you'd better watch out, because if this kind of thing goes on your tavern will become a hang-out for the goddamn officers' corps.'

Old Tannert pulled a glass towards him with slow, painful movements. 'A lieutenant, eh?' he said quietly, in a tone implying his submission to fate.

'You've got the idea, Tannert. We save the Britisher and we rope Strick in at the same time. Strick will have to show which side he's on.'

'And if he does?'

'Then we're sure of him, and through him we have the whole garrison in our pocket.'

'And if he's on the other side we get blown sky-high.'

'As it is we have a few hundred pounds of dynamite under our backsides. There are plenty of ways to croak in this slaughter-house. At least we'll have made some tests to find out what we're croaking for. Why are you looking at me so foolishly, Mother Tikke? I'm not rotting in the grave yet. Or am I already beginning to stink? If you don't bring something to eat soon I'll die of starvation right here in your arms.'

The War faded, the world was full of pleasure, it was a joy to live. So Strick thought.

The Main lay calmly before him, lush as a mature woman painted by Rubens. They had spread out their blankets on the grass. The sky above them was pale blue and tranquil. Strick breathed heavily, inhaling the tart sweetness of the soil rising up towards the heat. And he inhaled Erika, her flesh and her perfume mingled together by the sun's fire.

The War was as far away as the frozen North. The Main flowed by them with monotonous melody. Erika, in her bathing-dress, on the blanket beside him, breathed deeply, slowly. An aeroplane crossed the sky with an irritating drone, and instantly it seemed to Strick that he could make out the technical details – the cockpit, the machine-gun turrets, the bomb-bays. A cry, 'Air raid!' and a flak battery rushed to its guns. The range-finder groped for the objective. The predictor began to purr. Curves met and released electric currents. At the guns lights flashed on and raced with nervous haste round the gun-mountings. Gun-barrels tilted upward. The jaws of the automatic fuse-setter snapped at the head of the projectile. The mouth of the breech yawned, demanding to be fed with ammunition.

It was over. Strick closed his eyes in order not to see the plane as it glided past. But the noise pierced deeper into his ears, as though the plane were suddenly miles closer to him He covered his ears with his hands. His head roared. The Main was gone. Erika was gone. There was only the War, nothing but the war.

At last he opened his eyes wide and clasped his hands under his head to lift it, so that he could see the target better. He estimated the direction of the flight and the speed. He made out the plane-type. A Heinkel III. Wretched crates those, petrol-eating wrecks.

Erika's hand touched his arm and closed on it gently, sensitively, as though she were testing the quality of his muscles. 'Are you asleep?' she asked.

'Could anyone sleep with you around?'

'Do you sleep well after you leave me?'

'Very well, always.'

Eri turned over on her face, braced her elbows on the blanket, and moved closer to him. 'Is everything going well with your work?' she asked. Strick looked into the face bending over him. Beautiful as statues are beautiful, and living besides. Liveliest were her glistening eyes, woodland pools with varying depths, abysses here, only ankle-deep there. And cold, almost always ice-cold. And, in the moments of ultimate forgetfulness, closed tight.

'Does that interest you, Eri?' He played with her hair, which dangled down into his face.

'I'm not eager to lose you,' Erika said, examining his face. 'You don't have many friends here.'

Strick reached out absent-mindedly for her ear, and ran his finger-tips tenderly round the satiny lobe. 'I know. But it doesn't bother me. That's the way I wanted it.'

With veiled eyes Eri said, 'If you wanted to you could even throw the colonel out of his post.'

Strick gripped the soft neck that was pressing against his. 'You are a woman for whose sake one could commit murder or burn a city to the ground. Compared to you the whole war is a molehill at the foot of Mont Blanc. You even manage to keep me out of my office for an entire afternoon.' He stood up and began dressing. 'You'll leave later?'

Erika gazed above her toes at a point on the opposite bank of the Main. 'There's no other way,' she said, moving the pretty tips of her toes as thought she were trying to write her name upon the air. Then she added, 'Is there any way I can help your work?' Her foot described a large question-mark.

'Your being here at all is a great deal for me.'

'Nothing else?' With her toes she made a series of dots in the shimmering waves of heat.

Strick worked his feet into his boots. 'Go on doing what you always do, keeping your little ears and your big eyes wide open. And if you think anything would particularly interest me you can tell me. Or, even better, show it to me.'

'Perhaps I will do that.'

Fully dressed, Strick dropped down at her side. 'Why will you?'

Eri turned on her back like a kitten playing with a ball of wool. She stretched our her arms and looked at her manicured hands reaching out to the smooth silk of the sky. 'Why should I, I wonder? Perhaps I think I'll get something out of it. Perhaps I think it will be worth my while. Perhaps actually because I love you. It could be anything.'

'And what about the colonel?'

Erika dropped her hands abruptly, laid them on her shoulders, and drew up her legs. 'That is a subject we will not discuss.'

'We shall have to discuss it sooner or later.'

'Don't attach any importance to it.'

'Is it unimportant, Eri?'

'You'd better go now – you'll be late,' she said.

CHAPTER NINE

THE personal papers of Captain Wolf, which Geiger had obtained, were a disappointment. There was nothing of special interest in them. Even Wolf's private credentials were nothing unusual. The Party and the Armed Forces testified to his zeal, devotion to duty, patriotism, loyalty, and reliability. But the papers were obviously doctored. Some documents seemed to be missing, and the table of contents on the inside of the file cover had simply been ripped out, some time ago apparently. Strick hardly thought Geiger would have dared to do it before he delivered the papers.

He could work on fat Sergeant Demuth and get what he could out of him. But Demuth was only the clerk. Not very likely that he had been asked to tamper with documents. All he did was arrange the files. His work was purely routine. And there was no doubt that he would obey regulations to the letter. Even if that poor boob knew about the papers removed from the file he would no longer be able to get hold of them, so he might as well be left in peace.

But in that case the documents Strick had now were not enough to roast Wolf. Strick had four affidavits before him. One of them testified to bribery, another to fraud, the third to blackmail, and the fourth proved damage to the prestige of the Army. But all the evidence was too slight. There was, besides, Strick's own investigation into embezzlement of the canteen supplies. The figures he had were incontestable and considerable, but still, they were not good enough for his purposes. And Strick was not really concerned about Wolf. He wanted to pay Wolf off, all right, but his primary aim was to shock Rabe. The others would come later.

His N.S.G.O.'s office was a large, bright, hospitable room. A centre of Nazism. The bookshelves were filled with Party-line literature. Strick had commandeered from the local library every specimen of Nazi ideology, and assembled the books in his office for purposes of study. The illiterate could recognize these noble works by the fine layer of dust covering them. Strick would not permit them to be cleaned, for cleaning might damage the books, and damage must be avoided at all costs. There were also two shelves devoted to banned literature. The section was marked by a sign in roman letters: 'Slanderous and Trashy Literature'. These books enjoyed great popularity. Strick quoted from them in his lectures and read entire chapters aloud; he discussed them at length in order that specimens of the thing in question might arouse in his audience the proper degree of disgust. He also lent these books to interested students of corruption, and indulged in long and friendly conversations with the borrowers.

There was a huge desk almost in the centre of the room, and in front of it a stiff-backed chair that looked as if it had been carved from stone. No visitor could feel comfortable in it for more than three minutes. In one corner were two easy chairs, with a table between them on which lay banned picture-books. In this way National Socialist ideology was strengthened by exhibition of shameless specimens of cultural bolshevism. The favourite book, which the officers of the garrison requested again and again, was that repulsive example of unpatriotic satire, *Deutschland, Deutschland über alles*, by Kurt Tucholsky.

Old Tannert had been given a kind of cellar studio where he turned out posters by the dozen. Magda Tannert worked in the room adjoining Strick's. Otherwise Strick could not have stood it. He could not have Magda round him all the time. She was dependable as a dictaphone, punctual as an electric clock, discreet as an Egyptian tomb. But she was utterly inaccessible, wholly shut off, a valley without echoes.

But now he needed Magda. With her help he would storm the wall that Rabe had constructed round himself, would break down the solid structure of the man's fanaticism. Wolf was a kind of sacrificial elephant. Strick would kill him, use his corpse to prop up a ladder, and so reach the top of the wall.

In answer to his ring Magda Tannert entered the room, her shorthand notebook in her hand. She stood before him like a lilac-bush in full flower – charming, pale, clean-smelling. 'Sit down please,' Strick said. Magda sat down on the edge of one of the easy-chairs, and placed her notebook on the small table. The beautifully poised face looked up at him, attentive, ready. He could dictate, and her fingers would race across the paper.

'Never mind that,' Strick said. 'I want to discuss something with you.'

Between him and Magda was the big desk, two yards of empty space and two feet of table top. Magda approached no closer. She looked up at him wordlessly, alert for whatever he would say. Her very intelligence was like a barbed-wire fence round her. The girl is the little daughter of the snow, Strick thought. Ice water in her veins and frozen ice round her bones. You'd have to thaw her out with a blowlamp.

'What work did you use to do here?' he asked her.

'I was an assistant to the accountant of the guard company.'

'Then your troop commander was Captain Wolf.'

'Yes.'

Abruptly Strick hurled his shot at Magda. 'Did Wolf want anything from you?'

Magda tensed. 'How am I to understand that?'

Strick became blunter and harsher. 'I mean plainly and simply, did he ever molest you? Did he ever take hold of your chin or any other part of your body? Did he ever follow you round, in the cellar or in the office? Did he invite you to visit him, or did he bother you anywhere outside? Did any such things take place?'

Magda did not flare up nor did she burst into tears. The girl's poise was magnificent. She smiled pleasantly at him. 'What makes you want to know?'

'Maybe that sort of thing amuses me. Filthy stories are one of my passions. I can whisper them to the ladies of the officers' corps and stir them up to a voluptuous indignation.'

'And what is the real reason?'

'Do you see this stuff?' He held the affidavits and papers up in the air. 'These ought to be enough to hang Wolf. But I'm not quite convinced that they're adequate. I need one more bit of evidence to do him in good and proper.'

Magda's peaches-and-cream complexion neither paled nor reddened. 'A sworn affidavit on an attempt at rape?'

Strick felt as though he had been hit on the head with a wooden mallet.

'That would do it,' he mumbled.

Magda rose gracefully to her feet, 'I'd rather not answer questions on this subject. I can guess what would interest you, and will write out a detailed affidavit and sign it. Then all you need is to countersign it and it will be an official document. I think I can have it ready in half an hour.'

She left the room quietly. Strick sat at his desk as though he had seen a mirage.

Twenty-five minutes later Magda came in again. An affidavit, in quadruplicate. 'Informed of the object of the investigation and requested to tell the whole truth and nothing but the truth, I vouch for the following facts.' What followed was the driest possible précis of the plot of a moralistic novel; invitation to private room under pretence of examining documents. . . . Drink offered, refused. . . . Attempt to touch. . . . Sharp reprimand. . . . Brutal manual assault, without preliminaries, upon the seat of female modesty . . . Short struggle. . . . Flight.

Strick's face was the colour of a ripe tomato, Magda's an egg-shell white. Long after he had finished reading the affidavit Strick sat staring at the girl's face. He had imagined that her testimony would run something like this, but he had expected entirely different reactions from Magda. It was obvious that he had never understood her, that he knew nothing at all about her. In that icy cave there slumbered a she-bear. She was capable of tearing to pieces anyone who intruded upon her private affairs. She was ominously quiet, but not dumb. She was reserved, but at the decisive moment she could speak out. And she forgot nothing. She was ready and eager when the chance came to avenge the insult to her. He was a fool. He had mistaken an eagle for a goose.

Strick's coarse-grained sense of superiority left him. He spoke very seriously. 'Believe me, I feel ashamed because of that swine.'

'Why? It had nothing to do with you.'

Strick felt that he had betrayed himself in an attitude totally different from his usual one. He faltered: 'We wear the same uniform.'

Magda gave him a soft look, as a sister will look at her brother when she finds unexpectedly that he understands her. 'You don't have to pretend anything with me. I understand you. You don't have to sham.'

Strick's voice cracked with an emotion he could not suppress. 'What do you think you understand?'

'Everything.'

The bright afternoon sunlight flooded in at the window. Magda continued, as though to herself, 'I too don't like shamming. You know my life, as well as anyone with imagination can know some one's life from his documents. My father was a Socialist. That was why they beat him until the blood ran. They did it with me in the room. I was ten years old. That was the picture I grew up with. I want to live for a time when it will be wiped out.'

Strick sprang to his feet. The chair behind him thudded to the floor. He retreated a step, as though some one were pulling him back. Then he stood motionless, but his hands were quivering. He clenched his fists, trying to control the quivering. Magda looked far away, in a distant valley, beyond reach of his explanations, his apologies. Then the words burst out of him. 'You seem to be overestimating me dreadfully, Magda. I'm not a planner, I'm just a harried man, a driven man with confused instincts, running amok because my sense of justice has been trampled upon. Don't expect much from me, Magda. Don't embarrass me by looking up to me. I'm nothing but a man full of hate, a fanatic out of ambition or out of humiliation. I stumbled into this part I'm playing as a blind man might fall into a well. I'm helpless, Magda, sunk.'

He felt naked before her. She had led him to a recognition of himself clearer than anything he had yet arrived at. And because she expected it he was being forced to take a step which would mean a fearful plunge, a calamitous, endless plunge into nothingness. He tried to move out of range of the mild power of the girl's eyes. He had to fight free of her. He had to set her going in a totally wrong direction. Only that way could he avoid the path that attracted him like a gigantic magnet. When he spoke it was to shout down his own thoughts.

'Don't give me any of that stuff about ethics, justice, resistance movement, and so on. We have had our backs broken and are merely crawling through the muck.'

Magda spoke very softly, with sweet indulgence. 'Why are you so frightened of your own longing for another kind of Germany?'

Strick screamed out at her, as though a bandage had been mercilessly torn off a wound. 'Get out. Get out of here. I can't listen to your stupid nonsense another minute. Why don't you go away? What else do you want?'

Magda smiled quietly, so restrained a smile that it was scarcely visible. It was the smile of some one who has discovered a hidden beauty, a smile of astonishment and half-realized gratitude. She went to the door, and paused there as though she felt herself being called. Then she turned round and said, 'I would like it very much of you will go on calling me Magda.'

'All right,' Strick said weakly. He felt drained, empty, slack, and exhausted. 'Forget what we were talking about.'

'I will keep it to myself.'

'Thank you, Magda.'

Strick was talking on the telephone with Inspector Gareis.

Of course, Gareis told him amiably, Strick could arrest anyone whenever and wherever he pleased. He had ample authority for that in his capacity as N.S.G.O. But it would be better if the colonel himself issued the order for arrest. Nothing without evidence, however. In emergencies strong suspicions would do.

The further procedure was simple, Gareis explained. The arrest would have to be reported to the proper judicial authorities, in this case the court-martial. Report accompanied by a summary of the evidence. However, Gareis warned, at the moment it was not easy to determine which authorites were the competent ones in which cases. In case Strick needed backing on such matters Gareis would gladly give it to him.

'But your authority is restricted to political cases only, isn't it, Inspector?'

'My dear Herr Strick, looked at in the proper light, everything is political nowadays. Isn't this man you want to arrest a Party member also? Well, there you are, I thought so. Just tell me what you want to get out of the fellow. As soon as he reaches me you'll have all the evidence you need within twenty-four hours.'

Strick could sense that Gareis was grinning with anticipatory pleasure. And in fact Gareis was feeling, to the degree that he was capable of it, a certain crabbed cordiality. After all, Strick was the fellow to whom he owed that amusing incident with the station commandant, the one really entertaining bit of business he had had in recent weeks. That sort of thing put you under obligations.

'And then, my dear Herr Strick, one more piece of advice: telephone Kessler beforehand.'

'You think that is necessary?'

'It's better so. If I know Kessler he won't make a fuss about it. But it's advisable not to go over his head. Besides, it's worth considering that with his direct participation your action has a lot more push. And one thing more – when you do call him it's not absolutely necessary to go out of your way to tell him that your latest victim is also a Party member. He might . . .' Gareis cleared his throat, and there was an undertone of good-natured mockery in his voice, 'misunderstand that.'

The second telephone conversation was brief and no less profitable.

'Of course,' Kessler bellowed so that the wires shivered, 'lock the fellow up. Don't worry about the casualties, go on the way you've been going. We'll fix the bastards.'

Strick went out to the athletics field, which was in one corner of the huge drill ground. There, every Friday from six to seven o'clock, the officers engaged in sports. The colonel had introduced this innovation after his doctor had ordered him to take exercise. He preferred to scourge himself in the company of others.

The officers' sports were organized on a generous basis. Every one played whatever he pleased. An officer in charge of equipment, aided by two soldiers who did the actual work, brought out on a hand-cart everything that could possibly be needed. There were hand-balls, footballs, medicine-balls, punch-balls, tennis-balls, punching-bags. And rackets, measuring-tapes, nets, bats and whatnot.

Lieutenant Rabe, stop-watch in hand, was circling the athletics field at a good pace. He wanted to carve off at least two minutes from his time for five kilometres. Captain Wolf was throwing up a medicine-ball and trying to catch it. The quartermaster was still trying, as he had been for the past half-hour, to find a partner for a tug-of-war. Colonel Mueller was playing punch-ball with Captain Geiger. Corporal Hoepfner moved round at a respectful distance behind Colonel Mueller, and caught all the balls which went out of bounds or were missed by the Colonel. But this happened rarely, for Geiger hit every ball very carefully, with long swings of his arms that made it look as though he were playing in slow motion.

Strick walked straight towards the two, a brief-case tucked under his arm. The colonel, in his capacity of athlete, looked at Strick with something of the mixed emotions that a thoroughbred horse must feel at the sight of a tractor. 'Important business? In the middle of the sports hour? Never happened before, Strick.' Mueller punched the ball back.

'Evidence for an arrest, sir,' Strick said pleasantly.

Geiger returned the ball gently. It bounced close to the colonel, was ignored, and went on in shorter and shorter bounces back to Corporal Hoepfner, who fell upon it with enthusiasm. The colonel went up to Strick. 'So you want to arrest some one else now? Good Lord, man, do you think arrests are a pastime? Who is the victim this time?'

'Captain Wolf.'

The colonel took a deep breath. His broad chest expanded under the thin athletics shirt he wore, and his paunch was sucked in. 'Out of the question,' he stated flatly. 'That won't do.' He signed to Hoepfner to throw him the ball, but before he punched it he said, 'You seem to plan putting the whole garrison in gaol one at a time. Kindly put such crazy ideas out of your head.'

Strick swung the brief-case in his hand like a *torero* holding his red cloth ready. 'Colonel, we can't put it off any longer,' he said.

The colonel let his arm, which was holding the raised ball, slowly sink down. 'What's that, "we"?' he said. 'Why "we"? I have nothing to do with your cut-throat practices.'

'If there were just ourselves and our own preferences to consider, sir, there would be no problems.'

'No evasions, please. I will never endorse your proceedings against Wolf. This is a question of my honour as an officer, and in such matters I do not yield.'

Mueller punched the ball vigorously. It flew quivering through the air over the net and fell deep in Geiger's court. Geiger raced after it, but could not reach it, and the ball bounced out of bounds. 'As you command, sir,' Strick said calmly, as if the matter were closed. 'I really regret it. Frankly, I hate to concede Kessler this triumph.'

The colonel turned very sharply away from the court. 'What's that? It's none of Kessler's business what goes on here.'

The colonel walked away from the court, took Strick's arm, and began irritably walking up and down with him. 'Well, tell me? What has Kessler to do with it?'

Strick inserted regret, sincerity, and honest warning into his voice. 'What doesn't Kessler have a hand in, Colonel? You yourself know best what a sharp watch he keeps on everything that happens here. Unfortunately we can do nothing about it. But we can try to put him off the trail.'

'Go on,' the colonel said impatiently, as Strick made a studied pause.

'You know how suspicious that fellow Kessler is, sir. It can't have escaped your notice that he is no friend of the Army. And no friend – to speak quite candidly – of you yourself, Colonel.'

Mueller stiffened, as though he were ready to face a new opponent at punch-ball. 'That doesn't bother me a bit,' he said.

They circled wide of Captain Wolf, who was testing the medicine-balls for weight, obviously trying to find the lightest. The quartermaster had laid out the rope and measured it off. Lieutenant Rabe ran past them, panting and glistening with sweat. Major Wittkopf, the commander of the training battalion, was checking two stop-watches to determine whether they agreed within one-tenth of a second after seven minutes.

'Unfortunately,' Strick said, 'we have to reckon with such types as Kessler. But the thing to do is to beat them to the draw. When we clean up round here in our own fashion he can no longer exploit such actions for his personal triumph. It takes the wind out of his sails.'

'That may be,' the colonel said thoughtfully.

'Kessler suspects you, sir. In every telephone conversation he mentions your name or Wolf's. Just an hour ago I said to him in the bluntest possible terms that I thought his suspicions entirely without foundation. I told him that *you* sir, while *he* was still debating, had already taken the initiative.'

'How have I done that?'

Strick went on with the plausible smoothness of a cattle-dealer: 'Sacrifice Wolf. Admittedly he may have been useful, but he is replaceable. Fundamentally the man does more harm than his services can possibly be worth. In his blind greed he's acted so stupidly that a court caretaker could draw up an indictment against him. You have to get rid of Wolf. He is dangerous to have around, wide open as he is to the most cursory investigation. Take this chance, and the clean administration in your district will become famous. And you can depend upon my making a suitable report to the higher authorities.'

The colonel skirted the long-jump pit, and walked on to the close-clipped turf in the centre of the athletics field. 'It would be unsafe,' he said, as though he were estimating ranges. 'Wolf has seen a great deal, enough to make it risky. He has' – the colonel looked up at some distant point on the other side of the athletics field – 'wormed his way into our confidence.'

'For that reason alone, sir, you ought to proceed personally against him. That will throw out any suspicion against you from the start.'

'It would have to be arranged so that there was no occasion for him to make a statement,' the colonel said.

'I would suggest calling upon Lieutenant Rabe in his capacity as provost officer. We can turn the documents over to him. He has a reputation for the highest integrity. That will make the thing seem all the more a move towards clean administration.'

'What exactly is in these documents, Strick?'

'Neither your name, your person, nor your office is mentioned in any of them, Colonel. I expressly assure you of that.'

'Very well, Strick,' the colonel said. 'It is a hard decision for me, but I suppose it is unavoidable. You see to the rest of the affair, Strick.'

Rabe was rubbing down his sweat-drenched body. 'You seem to be in a great hurry, Strick,' he said. 'What do you want?'

'Put on your shirt before you catch cold.'

Strick handed Rabe several papers from his brief-case. 'Please look through these papers at once. Examine them in your capacity of provost officer. The colonel wants to know whether they are sufficient basis for an arrest.'

Rabe took the papers, and began reading through them. After reading for only a few minutes he looked up. His face, tired and relaxed from his run, bore a look of reproach and of deep regret. 'Can't this be avoided, Strick?'

'No.'

A group of officers laughingly finished a hand-ball game. The quartermaster had begun a tug-of-war with Captain Wolf. They tried three variations of pulling: with the left hand alone, with the right hand alone, and with both hands. The colonel was having his back rubbed down by Corporal Hoepfner. His gaze wandered from Wolf to Strick, from Rabe to the quartermaster, while Hoepfner scrubbed his back as though it were a scrubbing-board.

Rabe went on reading, page after page, silently, without looking up. Strick watched him closely. Since he could detect not the slightest change in Rabe's expression, he opened his brief-case again and took out the last affidavit, which he had not yet shown to Rabe. It was the paper that Magda Tannert had signed in her clear, straightforward handwriting. Should he spare Rabe the pain of reading this or should he be merciless? He could not decide.

The colonel, wearing his athletics shirt and muffled by the ample Turkish towel, sauntered up to them. 'Well, Rabe, what do you say to that?'

Lieutenant Rabe placed the papers carefully together, as if they were unique and priceless documents. He said in clipped, measured tones: 'I have examined the documents. Formally, they are quite sufficient as a basis for arrest.'

Strick stood up at once. 'That's fine. I think, sir, we can let Lieutenant Rabe, as provost officer, take care of the rest of it.'

'I ask to be relieved of this task,' Rabe said, standing very straight.

'I believe the colonel will see no reason to release you from your duties, Rabe.' Strick fixed Rabe with a sharp look.

The colonel was quite calm by now, an impressive mountain of flesh breathing easily in his blue athletics shirt, with the white towel draped picturesquely round his neck. He stated matter-of-factly, 'You take care of it, Rabe. It is in the course of your regular duties.'

Rabe said in a low, incisive tone: 'I don't understand you, Strick. You exploit your position, tempt a man who is easily tempted, and then construct out of it a pattern of embezzlement, cheating, and theft. Let's assume that Wolf had never run into a person like yourself. Assume further that no one had ever dropped broad hints to Wolf, saying he was so and so, held such and such a position, and therefore had so and so much influence, and would like to have a bottle of whisky or a box of cigars – only if it were convenient, of course, not at all necessary, but if convenient. . . . That sort of thing is never made specific. Oh, no, Wolf is simply asked to do it as a favour. And Wolf must decide and take the responsibility. What choice does he have, really? If he doesn't comply somebody else will.'

The colonel was standing rigid. 'What are you getting at?' he demanded tartly.

'We are receiving a lecture on current political questions,' Strick said. 'The subject today is: Integrity in everyday conduct of our duties.'

Rabe paid no attention to the colonel. He fixed his eyes intently upon Strick. 'That is a filthy, stinking swindler's manoeuvre, Strick. Trap the fools, get the little fish, and let the big ones go. Justice begins at the top.'

'Just what do you mean by that, Rabe?' The colonel loosened the noose of the Turkish towel round his neck. 'Your arguments are getting on my nerves a little. Are the documents sufficient for arrest, yes or no?'

'They are sufficient.'

'Well, then?'

Rabe said obstinately, 'But it's still not right.'

Colonel Mueller unwound the towel and hung it over his arm. His face had hardened. It looked as though it were of poured metal. A furrow ran vertically across his forehead. He took a deep breath. But, before he could speak, Strick took the last document out of his brief-case and handed it wordlessly to Rabe.

Rabe took it, stooped, and with his body held rigid, his head down, he began to read – obviously resolved not to make any concessions, not to be swayed in the least from his point of view. Suddenly his whole body jerked almost imperceptibly, as though some one had slapped him sharply on the back. The muscles of the hand holding the sheet of paper twitched convulsively. His arm dropped, and for a brief moment he stood there looking quite helpless, his eyes wandering from Strick to the colonel and back to Strick. Then, with an effort, he pulled himself together and continued reading.

'What's the matter with him?' the colonel asked Strick.

Strick, with no note of triumph in his voice, almost with weariness, replied, 'That is the sworn affidavit of a girl. Wolf ordered her to come to his private room. First he tried blackmailing her. When that failed he called to mind the fighting spirit of our times and tried to rape her. When that too was unsuccessful he decided that the least he could do was to get her an assignment directly behind the front lines.'

Mueller was fascinated by this story. He pulled open the zip-fastener of his shirt and aired his broad, compact chest. 'Incredible,' he exclaimed. 'That old hound! Trying to lay her without preliminaries. And using force, too! I wonder what the man thinks pleasure is. No normal man would try to smoke a cigar non-stop. Who is the girl, anyway? She must be quite a piece to get him worked up like that.'

Strick readily set the colonel straight. 'It was Fräulein Magda Tannert, sir.'

'Oh, no. You don't say! I can't understand it at all. That's absolutely an aberration in taste. But there you are – where love enters in reason goes down the drain. Why are you looking like a fish out of water, Rabe? Haven't you ever heard that sometimes a man wants more of a girl than just to hold her hand? All right, take care of this matter. With as little fuss as possible. Is that clear, Rabe?'

'Perfectly clear, sir.'

Mueller slung the towel round his neck again. His face was crinkled good-humouredly now. Queer how life was all round! He walked off, but turned round again after a few steps. 'Those petty frauds aren't too significant, Rabe. Don't make too much of them. But this erotic funny business is a nasty thing. Make that your main charge.'

He walked away, his hips swaying, his shoulders twitching with laughter. Devil take it if this wasn't an odd life. He never would have expected it of Wolf. In wartime everybody accumulated complexes – that was it. No more healthy sexuality around nowadays. After all, there were plenty of willing females, but no – that old Wolf had to try rape. In this garrison, too, and probably wearing his full uniform.

Rabe stood still, a lost soul surrounded by yawning gulfs and impenetrable mists. He felt incapable of taking a single step. But he was conscious that Strick was looking at him. 'You tried to spare me that, Strick,' he said. 'That was decent of you. Thank you.'

Strick was hard now. Rabe's gratitude rebounded from him at once. He forced himself to be cold and unfriendly. Rabe had reached out towards him; he deliberately repulsed the young man. 'Don't be getting sentimental, Rabe. I haven't the slightest intention of sparing you anything.'

Corporal Hoepfner poked round apathetically at his extra portions. Today the food was tough as a motor-car tyre, it seemed to him, and tasted pretty much like rubber. He chewed his way into it like a cow at pasture, and with much the same expression. Hoepfner felt abandoned, cheated, betrayed.

Vogel, who was spreading his dirty underwear out on the table, looking it over, and making entries on the laundry-list before he rolled it up again, looked sympathetically at his room-mate. 'I guess this will be your last extra portion, Hoepfner,' he said. 'Today they've locked up your Captain Wolf. Tomorrow it will be your turn.'

'But I'm completely innocent,' Hoepfner said, without for a moment interrupting his mastication.

'That's what they all say,' Vogel remarked. 'But when you come before a court-martial they'll pull the guts out of you and string fiddles with them.'

Hoepfner choked on his food, and coughed violently. Vogel slapped him helpfully on the back. Meanwhile he gently took up a slice of meat for himself. 'Look here, Vogel,' Hoepfner said, 'I've never done anything but obey orders. And I've never done anything wrong.'

'I believe that to the letter,' Vogel agreed. 'We ought to have a drink on it. Or aren't you in the mood for drinking?'

'I'm all right. But where will we get the stuff?'

'Why,' Vogel exclaimed in astonishment, 'Wolf must have a private stock somewhere.'

Hoepfner choked down a chunk of meat. 'Oh, he has all right. But suppose he comes back?'

'You have to work it smart,' Vogel explained. 'After all, you're concerned for his welfare. You can't get at the main supplies, so you have to dig into the special stock. You supply your good captain in his cell, and yourself at the same time. Or do you intend to let your noble patron go hungry and thirsty on bread and water? He's used to a different kind of life entirely. You have to keep his strength up. And your own too. Doesn't that sound reasonable?'

It sounded eminently reasonable to Hoepfner.

Wolf felt as though he were inside a closed, empty cigar-box which had lain for a week in sewage water. The walls were rough and painted with a dingy whitewash. The floor was warped. Wolf was sitting on a bed. It was hard as stone and stank of fermented remains of bread, and of sweat and horse-blankets. Through the close-woven mesh over the window chequered light fell into the wretched cell and flooded over Wolf with a gentle, irresistible pressure.

He drew from under the bed the carton that Hoepfner had brought him, and took out a bottle of wine. He tried to loosen the cork with his finger-nails, since his pocket-knife had been taken away. His nails broke, but the cork did not give.

Wolf stared at the bottle. Should he simply smash the neck? But then splinters of glass might fall into the wine, and he remembered hearing that you could die from that – your throat would be torn open, the walls of your intestines cut to ribbons by the glass, or something of the sort. An ugly prospect.

He wrapped a blanket tightly round the bottle and struck the bottom of the bottle against the wall, hoping to loosen the cork by the reaction. There was a dull thud, as though someone were chopping wood in a living-room. Immediately the locks of the connecting door in the corridor rattled and a heavy footstep approached his cell. A slot was lifted, and a harsh voice said: 'Behave yourself in there. No noise allowed.' The slot fell shut, the guard marched off, and the chains of the bolts rattled provocatively.

Wolf sniffed the cork. The fragrance of the full-bodied wine penetrated through the pores of the cork and mounted to his nose. He snuffed it in like a dog. Then he tried to grip the cork between his teeth. That too failed. He was breathing heavily by now. At last he resignedly placed the bottle back in the carton and pushed it under the bed. He stared at the dirty, whitish-grey wall as though expecting some invisible hand to inscribe upon it directions for opening bottles without a corkscrew.

His cell door opened. Strick waved away the guard who had accompanied him, and approached Wolf. 'It's a dirty shame that you are locked up here, Captain,' Strick said.

Wolf thought so too. He expressed his opinion vigorously to Strick. A stinking shame, that's what it was. He, who had always been a hard worker, devoted to duty, always reliable, to be arrested and locked up by a young snot like Lieutenant Rabe. And what for? No definite charge given.

He had been sitting here three hours already. That scoundrel Rabe had taken all his valuables without a word and given him a receipt for them. He had also taken every object in Wolf's possession that could cut or stab, in fact, everything made of metal. Finally, he had even unbuttoned Wolf's suspenders and removed his shoe-laces. In order, Rabe had said, to prevent any attempt at suicide. An absolute boor, that Rabe.

Then, after he had been here for two hours, Hoepfner had come, bringing him two blankets and a pillow. Wolf did not mention the package which had been hidden between the blankets. And those guards, he added, were behaving as though he had never been their superior. He had been refused paper and ink, which he had requested in order to draw up a petition. He had not even seen the warrant for his arrest, and unfortunately he had forgotten to ask for it. Rabe, the tight-lipped bastard, had not thought it necessary to give him any detailed explanations.

Again Strick declared that it was scandalous. He sat down beside Wolf, who readily moved over for him, and vigorously expressed his indignation at such shameless treatment of a fine officer. Wolf agreed heartily. And Strick declared, 'I have been assigned to search this cell, I certainly don't intend to. I've already noticed your package under the bed, but only privately, you understand. Officially I make it a principle not to see such things.'

In his painful predicament such words sounded warm and encouraging to Wolf. Strick was better than most of them, he thought. And then he came out with his special need – a corkscrew. Otherwise he could not open the bottles, and at the moment he was badly in need of a little stimulant.

Strick violently suppressed a convulsive wave of amusement. Wolf sitting here with bottles of drink and no corkscrew. Tantalus in Rehhausen! He took out his pocket-knife, obligingly snapped out the corkscrew, and handed it to Wolf with a brief bow. Wolf took it like a drowning man grasping a straw. He pulled the carton out so fast that it screeched over the gritty floor. Bottles clinked. Wolf grabbed one indiscriminately by the throat and drilled the corkscrew into it with accurate, if somewhat hasty movements. Then he took a long drink and offered the bottle to Strick – if Strick didn't mind drinking from the same bottle with him. Lieutenant Strick did not mind.

'Do you know who signed the warrant for your arrest?' Strick asked, after the liquid in the first bottle was a lot lower.

Wolf said he did not know, he knew nothing at all, had not the slightest idea.

'The warrant bears the signature of Colonel Mueller.'

'No!'

'I assure you it's so.' Wolf began uncorking the second bottle. 'And do you know on what grounds you have been arrested?' Strick went on.

No, Wolf did not know, could not imagine. He was out of his depth.

'For diversion of canteen supplies, misappropriation, and embezzlement.'

'Is that so?' was all Wolf said. 'Is that so? And that has been signed by the colonel. Well then, *Prosit*!'

'You see,' Strick said, 'that is just what surprised me too. I can't figure it out.' He drank from the bottle. Wolf too let another, longer drink slide down his gullet. So that was it. He was supposed to have made away with canteen supplies. And the colonel had signed that! The colonel! What a laugh!

Half-way through the third bottle Strick remarked, 'and at the last social evening in the club he said, "All for one and one for all. Loyalty for loyalty, and to every one his due." '

Yes, he had said that. Wolf remembered it distinctly. That evening the ladies had drunk genuine Chartreuse and the gentlemen Fin Napoléon, from stone mugs. He remembered it perfectly well. And the colonel had smoked a Henry Clay cigar, the kind that came in individual glass tubes.

'And now they say you've misappropriated canteen supplies. That's the limit.' Wolf drained the third bottle to the dregs, and groped for the fourth. The cell had become a crude shelter on an imaginary front. The war was on. This was a rest between battles. The men were relaxing. His own pistol had been cleaned, his troops given their orders, and now Wolf was refreshing himself with a nightcap. How else was a poor devil in the front lines to get some sleep? Just the way it was in Russia, precisely the way it was in Russia.

'So I misappropriated canteen supplies. Me! And what about the case for the colonel in March? And the case for the colonel in May? And where does the quartermaster get his butter? And doesn't Wittkopf have his closet crammed with bottles? And what happened to eighty cartons of cigarettes from the June quota?'

Wolf spluttered away, he bubbled over like a fountain. 'Excuse me for just a moment,' Strick said. And during the next few hours he had to excuse himself several times. In the latrine he feverishly filled pages of his notebook. When Wolf, his face rosy as a stuffed pig, began singing thickly, 'The day of vengeance soon shall come,' Strick took his leave, promising to pay another visit shortly.

CHAPTER TEN

THE political lectures for the officers' corps of the Rehhausen garrison were held in the large dining-room of the officers' club. Chairs were arranged in rows for the officers who could attend. Up in front was an easy-chair for the colonel, and at the head of the room a teaching-desk, at which Strick stood. The audience was keenly attentive. Almost everybody was there: the officers of the garrison itself and of the training battalion, the new station commandant, the commanders of the prison camps and the officers of their guard companies, the warden of the Rehhausen Army prison with his two legal officers, a quartermaster and three administrative officials.

Attendance was obligatory. By order of the colonel – N.S.G.O. Special Order No. 5 – absence suggested political indifference, and could be permitted only upon presentation of a written excuse. Officers having duties at this time should, as far as possible, assign deputies from among the ranks of the non-commissioned officers to do their work. Political instruction had priority.

As a matter of fact there was no officer in the entire Rehhausen area who would have deliberately attempted to get out of the lectures. For those whose duties kept them out of town the ride to Rehhausen was a pleasant change. In addition, Colonel Mueller allowed a little treat after the lecture. He benevolently gave his fellow-officers the happy opportunity of obtaining – of buying, that is – two or three glasses of wine at the club. But the chief attraction was that Lieutenant Strick's lectures were far from uninteresting. Strick was as free-spoken and blunt as a court jester. No subjects were taboo with him. His favourite saying was, 'We don't want to befog our minds, gentlemen.' When he was in a particularly good humour he addressed them as 'Officers of the Fuehrer'.

Today Strick was quoting large sections from Erich Maria Remarque's *All Quiet on the Western Front*. He gave a complete résumé of the book, and the extracts he chose were full of disrespectful mockery towards the officers' corps soldierly honour, patriotism, and allegiance to the flag. 'Here you can see, fellow-officers of the Fuehrer, the disadvantages the German soldier has been working under. What I mean is, this sort of thing has corroded our military strength. This is like poison, and it is still operating today. It is not so easy to stamp out this kind of thing. Is it any different when soldiers right here in Rehhausen say to one another that the majority of the officers' corps are corrupt, that all they care about is filling their bellies, and are glad for the opportunity to shirk the front lines? This same Remarquable - pardon me, Remarquian - spirit is expressed by the men who say that this club is nothing but a fancy brothel. Fellow-officers of the Fuehrer, you know very well that this place is not at all a fancy brothel.'

Strick was on the point of illustrating the Remarquian spirit by further examples that came close to home. But at that moment Sergeant Demuth trundled through the centre door and went up to the colonel. He bent close to the colonel's ear and whispered some hurried message. The colonel stood up, and for a moment posed like a statue. Then he said: 'I am sorry to have to interrupt the extraordinarily illuminating remarks of our N.S.G.O. State of alarm, stage B, for the entire garrison area of Rehhausen! A group of prisoners-of-war have broken out of Camp 709. Geiger, distribute the prepared special orders. Assemble search squads. Bridges, road, and railway stations to be occupied at once according to Plan B. Further orders to follow.'

The meeting dissolved swiftly and chaotically. Outside there was the scream of motors starting, and the cars roared away, breaking the quiet of approaching evening. Rabe alerted the garrison guard company. Geiger telephoned Würzburg and found out that Inspector Gareis was already on the way to Rehhausen, and wanted all the platoon leaders of the search squads to be waiting at the barrack gate. The colonel had returned to his office, and, in high good spirits, was telling Eri about Remarque and *All Quiet on the Western Front*. He was surprised that Erika had never heard of the book, and did his best to enlighten her.

Strick went to the barrack gate to wait for Gareis. He was eager to greet him, and to see him at work again. He felt himself curiously, almost uncannily attracted to Gareis. Somehow he felt that it sharpened his own wits just to observe the little man's cold, lightning-fast reactions. The man emanated power and cunning.

The platoon leaders of the search squads gathered one by one. They had calm, inflexible faces. Their expressions would remain the same whether they were peeling potatoes or, as now, getting ready to hunt down escaped prisoners-of-war. Those faces were shut up tight. They received orders and carried them out with no show of feeling. Like masks – one could never tell what thoughts lurked behind the taut, tanned skin of such faces.

Gareis's car roared up to the barrack gate and came to an abrupt stop. Gareis got out, gave a brief, keen look round, and discovered Strick. They approached one another. 'I suppose making arrests is one of your passions, eh, Strick?' Gareis grinned. 'You love it, don't you? Won't ever miss a chance, eh?' They shook hands.

Then the detection machinery inside Gareis began again to whir. His questions now came fast. 'How many men do you have?'

'Forty.'

'You?'

'Twenty-five.'

'You?'

'Sixty-four.'

After a few more rapid-fire questions Gareis knew that he had two hundred and seventy men at his immediate disposal, and could get another two to four hundred later on. That would suffice, he said. He spread a map of the Rehhausen region over the hood of the car and bent over it. 'Where was the break?'

'From Camp 709.'

Gareis pointed his finger at the barracks marked on the map. 'Out of the camp itself?'

'No, from the prisoners' place of work.'

'Where is that?'

'Three kilometres north-west of the camp. The prisoners had been assigned to road work.'

Gareis instantly found on the map the spot in question. 'Exactly when?'

The exact time was unknown. 'Some time between four and six o'clock. At six, when the squad was to be marched back to the camp, three men were missing.'

Gareis scarcely looked up from his map. 'The guards must have had a good afternoon nap,' he said dryly.

'That section of the road is winding and lined with undergrowth – hard to keep every one in sight.'

'That is no excuse, merely one more reason for increased alertness or more guards. What were the men who got away from you?'

'Two Russian enlisted men and an English captain.'

Gareis ran his finger in a large circle round the prison camp. 'I could raise a howl about your letting a captured officer get out of the camp at all. But I suppose you'll say he was eager to work. Doesn't matter to me, anyway. But we've got to catch those birds.'

Strick bent over the map along with Gareis. 'Child's play,' Gareis said. 'Let's assume for safety's sake that they skipped out at four o'clock. It is now seven-thirty. How far could they have gone in three and a half hours?'

'The average man marches six kilometres in an hour.'

'An escaping prisoner-of-war,' Gareis said matter-of-factly, 'is not the average man. He will not cover twenty kilometres in three and a half hours. He hides out somewhere. He'll do his travelling at night, but now he's crawled into some hole. Where would that be?'

Gareis's finger described another circle. It moved across roads, open fields, and along the Main, and came to rest on a wooded area near the place where the prisoners had made their break. 'They are dressed in convict clothing, so they will not stay out in the open. They cannot cross the Main. Roads and bridges are guarded. All that remains is this stretch of woods. We will comb it thoroughly. Nine square kilometres of woods make fine grounds for beating game. We'll cordon it off on all sides with the men we have. Then, when the other three hundred-odd men are mobilized, we'll beat our way through. Want to bet that we'll have those boys within three or four hours?'

Gareis assigned sectors to the platoon leaders. His instructions were precise and laconic. The man, Strick thought, had the gifts of a first-rate divisional commander. He would control his sector of the front like a virtuoso. As it was, the inspector was an artist, a genius at hunting down his prey.

Gareis jumped back into his car. 'Groups that arrive later are to wait here for further orders. I am going to check up on that cordon. See you later, Strick.'

His car roared away. The platoon leaders scattered in all directions, while Gareis's car raced down the hill towards the setting sun. It's whining purr died out as though swathed by layers of dust. In two hours it would be dark. By then a human fence had to be erected round the wooded area.

Strick stood thoughtfully by the gate, staring at the deserted road. 'This man Gareis knows what he's about,' said a voice at

Strick's side. It was Vogel. 'His calculating that they must be in the woods is a stroke of genius.'

'Possibly,' Strick said. 'But he could be wrong about it.'

'That's just it,' Vogel said in a low, emphatic voice. 'He doesn't happen to be wrong.'

Strick did not at once grasp what Vogel was saying. He thought he had not heard aright. He whirled round and looked into Vogel's drawn face. 'What's that you're saying?' he demanded.

'Yes,' Vogel said, a little heavily. 'An ingenious fellow, without a doubt. Sensed precisely where his game would be hiding. Precision work, that – deserves the highest praise. The man's a genius, I tell you. Too bad he's on the wrong side. The other side could make better use of his sort.'

'You're not trying to say that . . .' Strick did not dare even to think out the rest of his sentence.

'Exactly,' Vogel said, 'that is just what I'm trying to say. Now listen: I've ordered a car. It ought to be here any minute. It will take you to the woods that Gareis is cordoning off.'

'And?'

'You will do me the favour of taking me along. We'll see then what can be done. Is that clear?'

'This is the most awful mess I can imagine, Vogel.'

'Not yet,' Vogel said, 'but it could be that.'

As they raced towards the woods the trees seemed to come towards them. They spread out before them, expanded in height and breadth, and at last lay large and expectant close by.

The platoon leader of the cordon squad hurried up to Lieutenant Strick and reported his name, the number of his squad, his assignment. 'Thanks,' Strick said, touching his hand to his cap. 'Splendid organization,' Vogel boomed appreciatively from behind Strick.

'I'll take a look round in the woods,' Strick said to the squad commander. The man offered to lend him some men to accompany him. 'Won't be necessary,' Strick said, and with Vogel he walked towards the woods which rose in a wall of green before him. The sinking sun was painting the tops of the pines a golden yellow. Shadows lengthened, lost their hardness, and seemed spongy and tangible.

The silent woods swallowed Strick and Vogel. They walked together down a road. Strick said, 'I don't want any explanations from you, Vogel. Not a word. I don't want to see or hear anything. If I can help you by doing nothing, very well. But that is all. Within the limits of my power I will try to save you from the hangman. Nothing else and nothing more. But once this affair is over, Vogel, we part company. When it's over as far as I'm concerned you're through. I'll have nothing more to do with you.'

'I understand you,' Vogel said. 'I understand you only too well. You want to say, the devil with all talk about justice. You want to outlive the war, sit on your conscience, and afterwards put away your uniform, plant cabbage, establish a family, raise children, go to church regularly, and at night sit over beer and cigars and swap stories about your war experiences.'

'Something like that. And you ought to try for the same sort of thing.'

'Exactly, exactly. What have we got to die for? For Adolf? I wouldn't even break wind for him. For Germany? Never met the lady. For freedom? How much food will your blessed freedom buy?'

Strick took long strides. He was shivering slightly. He wanted to get this over with as quickly as possible. The shadows closed in round him, as though to smother him. He had expected almost anything of Vogel, but not this. 'It's senseless,' he said. 'Everything is senseless. We live in filth. Not even a god could harvest wheat from a swamp. If you live in this country you can't keep your hands clean.'

Vogel kicked a pebble that lay in the road. 'Quite right. Let's make our apologies. I've never knocked myself out for Final Victory, but still, in spite of myself, I've made my contribution. And you became an officer. You shelled tanks, including the men who were inside them. Oh, yes, once in a while you were fresh to your superiors. Marvellous accomplishment. And then you explained things to your soldiers so that they would die quietly and proudly. And you wrote inspiring letters of condolence to their parents, wives, and sweethearts.'

'What actually do you want of me?' Strick asked, standing still.

Impatiently, Vogel pushed him to start him moving again. 'I am paying tribute to your work for Folk, Fuehrer, and Reich. I am admiring your achievements as a soldier in the front lines, and your eloquence at telling the widows and orphans to keep up their courage. My friend, you can no longer tell your arse from your elbow. Some people are criminals – they have to be killed. Some people are idiots and morons – they have to be kicked in the behind now and then so that they keep in mind which way is forward.'

They strode on, wading through the dense shadows. Vogel indicated a side-road to Strick, a narrow, trampled path that led to a small clearing where there was a pond.

'Here,' Vogel explained, 'if everything has worked out right you will have the pleasure of meeting a charming fellow-officer. I assume you will enjoy your conversation with him. I also suggest that you get out to the road with him, but then, instead of returning to our starting point, continue on through the woods to the opposite exit. I will go back and send the car round there. In that way we will avoid having the platoon leader, who saw one officer and one corporal enter, notice that two officers are coming back.'

'What about the driver?'

'He won't arrive on the other side until you're already out of the woods. That way he will assume you met the officer there. Get it?'

'And suppose Gareis comes by there and sees us both?'

'Then we can start digging our graves.'

'Nice prospect. And suppose everything goes well that far, Vogel?'

'Then we will drive together back to the town of Rehhausen. There you will drop us off somewhere and consider your duty done. Or else you can come along if you like.'

Vogel went into the clearing and stood still. From the bushes appeared the slender figure of a man wearing the uniform of a German lieutenant. He wore a number of decorations also. Strick, standing behind Vogel, realized instantly that the uniform was his own spare uniform, that the man was wearing the medals he had discarded, as well as his boots and his cap. And undoubtedly that dog Vogel had also borrowed his razor, his one from last pair of socks, and his one usable handkerchief.

Vogel examined the approaching lieutenant. 'Well, fits you like a glove,' he said. Then, grinning, he introduced the two officers. 'Lieutenant Strick, National Socialist Guidance Officer of the Rehhausen garrison. Lieutenant XYZ, at present in transit.'

The stranger had a thin, pale face. His eyes were piercing, extremely alert, his skin like crinkled parchment. His hand, as

Strick shook it, was cold and seemed to be shaking slightly. Behind them the darkening wood was like the menacing, open mouth of a great whale.

'You've taken care of your other things?' Vogel asked.

'The prison clothes and the wrapping paper I weighted with stones and threw into the pool.' The stranger spoke a somewhat compressed German, as though the words were being forced out through a broken loud-speaker.

'Good,' Vogel said. 'Don't take it into your head, Captain, to show off your gramophone-record German. If there's anyone in earshot be silent as a mass grave. Strick will do the talking for you. That's part of a political commissar's job. It's unfortunate, Captain, that two other men broke out along with you.'

The captain knew nothing about this. At a favourable moment he had slipped away and plunged into the woods. He had found the parcel where Vogel had said it would be, had shaved himself, and changed his clothes. In fact, since there was plenty of water he had even had a bit of a bath. If anyone else had escaped it must have been later, after he had made his getaway.

'We must get going now,' Vogel said. 'We can do our talking later.'

It seemed to Strick that the road through the woods was like the last stages of a long march with a heavy pack. His legs moved forward with automatic, dragging motions. The burden pressed down upon his back so that he felt it in the soles of his feet. His brain no longer functioned. It was dead, as though the current had been switched off.

Strick listened for some inward voice. There was nothing. All he could hear was the footsteps of the man beside him, who was wearing his good uniform. The man's face was tense with awareness of the innumerable dangers confronting him.

Now the apparently calm, tight voice spoke, in a forced, artificially casual tone: 'Please do not expect conversation, explanations, or requests from me. I am leaving. I am in a foreign country.'

That was not a question, Strick thought, and therefore it required no answer. Besides, it was not his function here to say anything. And, even if he wanted to, he could not. What he was doing was still an automatic reaction. Something was happening, but he did not know why it was happening.

The road through the woods seemed endless. The twilight

shadows crouched among the trees like huge beasts, silently lurking, waiting with slitted eyes. What they were waiting for was not clear. A sinister silence welled up from the sluggish darkness. The silence was broken only by the echoing footsteps of the two men. The sound of the footsteps struck against that silent wall of shadows, rebounded, and came back to them intensified.

'How is it you speak German?' Strick asked.

'Learned it at school and college. Eight years of it.'

Strick quickened his pace. 'What I am doing for you is very little,' he said curtly. 'Don't overestimate my help. Once we are out of these woods we will separate. Others will take care of you. Others who can do it better.'

The Englishman at his side threw him a brief, meaningful glance, like a searchlight flashing on and as abruptly being shut off. 'The important roads in life are usually short,' he said. 'I have a cottage near Hastings. Three minutes from there to the Channel. If I ever see it again it may very well be only because you are walking with me now.'

The woods surrounded them like a wall. Strick did not know what to say. What could he explain in these few minutes? That his escorting the Britisher was merely a mechanical function, the product of pure chance, a ridiculous trap into which he had stumbled like a bear into a pit? That would not help. 'We do a lot of things without knowing just why,' he said, as if apologizing. 'My contribution to your liberation is insignificant.'

'You Germans are a strange sort,' the Englishman said thoughtfully. 'When you do something decent you apologize. I rather think you're too proud. You all wear a uniform, all the time. You somehow can't believe that certain men are no good even though they're wearing the same uniform as you.'

'Some of the people you've met round here,' Strick said, 'have lived in misery for five years. At least five years. That hardens men, don't forget it.' He hurried on, taking long strides. The Englishman had difficulty keeping up with him. They had come to the end of the road through the woods, and stepped out into a pleasant, muted twilight.

The leader of the cordon squad on this side went up to Strick and reported. Strick touched his cap and thanked him. 'Isn't my car here yet?' he said. The corporal, a man with the rosy face of a ripe apple, said it was not. 'Then we will wait,' Strick said.

'Jawohl!' the corporal snapped, as though he had been asked his opinion.

Strick went off some distance to one side, the Briton in his German uniform following him silently. They sat down on the stump of a tree and waited.

'The fact that there are people like you gives a fellow confidence,' the Englishman said at last. 'Since I have met your kind, I know more about Germany. Wholesale judgments on nations are always foolish.'

Strick was growing nervous. He heard a car approaching, but there was no way of knowing whether it was his or Gareis's. It swerved round the turn in a cloud of dust. In it Vogel sat enthroned.

'Come along,' Strick said. 'If you only knew how much of blind chance and how much of cold calculation it takes to produce such an "honourable" action you would shiver in your boots. Never forget this: you have met the people of a country where justice cannot be established except by killing.'

The Briton smiled, a somewhat twisted, unaccustomed smile.

They sat together in the back of the car. The vehicle, with its crude springs, jolted them violently. The motor howled like a whipped dog. Behind them was a cloud of dust. They stopped in a side-street in Rehhausen. Vogel jumped out. 'Shall I show you the way, Lieutenant?' he asked the British officer.

The Englishman hesitantly climbed out. Then he turned to Strick, who had stayed in his seat. He gave him a long look. Then he held out his hand and shook Strick's. 'Danke, Kamerad,' he said softly. He straightened up, swelling his chest to make himself fit better the uniform of a German lieutenant, and strode off with short, measured steps. Vogel trotted along beside him on the left, obviously pleased with himself.

Strick watched them go. He felt a strong impulse to go along, to ask questions of this man, to be given answers, to find in some one else what he was seeking in himself. He listened to their footsteps moving farther and farther away, fading out in the dusk. And still he heard the words distinctly: Danke, Kamerad.

'Shall we drive to the barracks, sir?' the driver asked.

Strick pulled himself away from the vision and the words. 'Of course,' he said. 'To the barracks.'

Even after midnight everybody was having an uproarious time at the club.

Colonel Mueller was in his most urbane mood. He was celebrating the ignominious defeat of Inspector Gareis. For the third time he raised his glass to toast Gareis.

'My dear Inspector,' the colonel said, 'that's what comes of sticking your nose into our affairs. It's we of the Army who take the prisoners-of-war, and we can look after them. When they break out on us we catch them again. We, Inspector – the Army, not civilian criminal departments. If somebody pinches a silver spoon that's a job for you. But let us handle our own affairs.'

Gareis looked round at the many uniforms in the room, uniforms clothing well-grown, well-fed, physically powerful men. The colonel's assumption was that he was feeling like a schoolboy being browbeaten by a whole team of teachers. The colonel's laughter boomed out, and the other officers quickly seconded each laugh.

'I don't understand why you gave up so quickly,' the colonel said. 'You caught the two Russians promptly enough. Good, that's something at least. But where is the English captain? At ten o'clock you called off the search and said flatly, "It's no use." Surely you could have shown a little more perseverance.' Again the colonel's laughter rumbled out of him as out of a barrel, and the officers round him joined in heartily.

'It's really amazing, Gareis.' It served him right, the colonel thought, this icy, mean little bloodhound who arrested Army officers at the drop of a hat. 'The blame is all yours, Gareis. I never would have thought that an experienced criminal-chaser like yourself would give up the struggle after no more than three hours. I would have combed through that area until no stone was left unturned.'

Gareis made an effort to smile. 'You could have turned over every stone, Colonel, and still you would not have caught the man.'

'And why not?'

'Because he's probably no longer in your area.'

'What makes you think that, Gareis?'

'And if he is here, Colonel, it is probably disguised as a baker, cell leader, railway worker, guard, or lieutenant.'

'You're raving, Gareis. You're not trying to say that . . .' The colonel lowered his glass as if to check himself from throwing it into the man's face.

'Exactly that, Colonel. This wasn't a simple gaol-break. That captain knew just what he was doing. Right here in your command area some person or group of persons is backing such actions.'

The colonel hesitated, unsure whether to throw the glass, laugh, or cut off the conversation. He decided not to take Gareis seriously. 'Once I had a troop commander under me,' he said, 'who let six tanks get away from him. What do you think the fellow said? Six weren't worth his while, he was waiting until the enemy brought up two dozen.' The other officers laughed loudly. The club orderly went down to the cellar with the basket. He had a sure instinct which told him that a good deal more drink would be needed before the night was over.

Gareis peered among the uniforms to a corner where Strick was sitting. 'Would you care to play a game of pool with me, Strick?' Gareis asked.

Strick rose, nodding assent. The colonel called out complacently, 'Watch out, Gareis. Strick will be telling you that the prisoners broke out because they weren't getting political instruction.' There was a gale of laughter. 'And also,' the colonel said, 'Strick will have you believing you need political instruction too, because you seem to be so short-winded.' More laughter. 'Geiger,' the colonel continued, 'send Inspector Gareis the prospectus of our course of lectures. You'll be a very welcome guest, Gareis. We'll keep a comfortable chair ready for you at all times. Dunce cap provided free if you need it.'

'I will seriously consider your kind offer, Colonel,' Gareis said, and he opened the door for Strick, inviting him into the adjoining billiards-room, which was totally deserted.

Gareis placed the first two balls on the table. 'You begin,' he said. 'You make the break.'

Strick had the feeling that he was approaching a mine-field. His soldier's instinct warned him to be cautious, extremely cautious. Gareis's manner was warning enough.

He picked up his cue and sighted. 'You ought to chalk the tip,' Gareis said politely. 'It makes the stroke surer.'

'I'm not a very good player.'

'I know,' Gareis said, 'but then you ought to learn.'

Strick cued violently. The balls crashed into one another, rebounded, raced towards the corners, but jumped the holes. They trembled for a while, then came to rest on the green surface. 'An easy shot,' Gareis said. 'Easy game for me.' He shot a ball after the other two; all three disappeared into the pockets and rolled down the runways with a sound like a wagon thumping across a distant bridge.

'Do you really think I'm an idiot, Strick?' He set up two more balls, sighted briefly, and then stroked the ball gently as though his cue were a butter-knife skimming a thin film of butter. Two more balls vanished into the pockets as though they had been sucked in.

'I'll always be careful not to underestimate you, Gareis.' Strick watched the inspector's small, sinewy hands reaching for the balls.

'And yet the solution is child's play, Strick,' Gareis said. He looked up. 'Or isn't it?'

Strick leaned carefully against the wall. He felt that he had to prop himself up, had to be leaning against something when the blow struck him.

'Then you know the solution, Gareis, and won't say?'

'Do you want to hear it?'

'I would rather not have anything to do with your professional secrets.'

Gareis laughed shortly. 'Very noble of you.'

He shot once more. The balls dropped, rolled back. 'These times are a carnival for killers,' Gareis said. 'Sometimes it's amusing to wander around at the fair and pretend to be an idiot.'

'If you enjoy that sort of thing . . .' Strick felt like a swimmer caught in a powerful undertow and uncertain how to get out of it.

'I do enjoy it,' Gareis replied amiably. He sat down on the billiards table and began gesticulating with the cue as if it were a pointer. 'When do you think a prisoner tries to escape, Strick? When he has some prospect of making it. And when is that prospect best? When he can count on help from outside.'

'Men have been known to escape from prison camps without help,' Strick said.

'Certainly. But hardly without making preparations. And our captain did not come to life until five days ago. I made detailed inquiries about that. He's been a prisoner for eight months. He read books and newspapers, played chess, and wandered about mournfully. Nothing unusual about that. Then five days ago he suddenly decided he wanted to work.'

'What about it?' Strick pretended scepticism. 'Is there anything unusual about that? He was tired of being idle and wanted to do something.'

'In order to escape.'

'Of course.'

'I prefer to assume that his attention was called to an opportunity for escape.'

'By whom, would you think?'

'Perhaps you can answer that question.' Gareis smiled, but, without waiting for a reply, he went on, 'To continue. He runs off. Follows the map, of course, straight into the woods. Child's play. There, at some prearranged spot, he finds clothing waiting for him. He changes.'

'And that, Gareis, is the very wood you surrounded. The only patch of woods anywhere around here. You sealed it off completely. Your fox was in the trap. Why didn't you finish combing through those woods?'

Gareis balanced the billiards cue on the tip of his finger. 'Also quite simple. First he was in there, and afterwards he wasn't.'

'Do you mean he passed through the cordon?'

'Precisely. Right through the centre of it. As if by magic.'

'You'll have to explain that to me.'

'Gladly, Strick. If I'm wrong on any important points you can correct me.'

The cue went off balance and started falling, suddenly, but was caught by Gareis with a swift, sure movement just before it touched the floor. 'How does a man get out of a cordoned area? Very simply – when he is known. And how does he get into it? The same way. Colonel Mueller, for example, is well known. He can go in and out anywhere in his district without showing a pass. There are a number of others who can do the same. In this *battue* of ours there were unquestionably two men whom all the platoon leaders knew – if only because of our conference at the barrack gate. Those two men, who were utterly beyond suspicion, were myself – and you.'

Strick, breathing quietly, looked at Gareis out of narrowed eyes. It was as though he were sighting on a target, locating it precisely on the cross-hairs; but as though, also, he were not yet sure it was an essential target, the kind you have to shoot at if you don't want to be shot yourself. 'You seem to be very sure of yourself, Gareis,' he said.

'It was easy to work out,' the inspector said dreamily, 'that the fugitive would take refuge in the woods. It was still easier to work out the rest. You see, Strick, I have a very bad habit. I always ask a great many questions. I cannot be with a person for as long as a minute without asking him at least five questions. When I checked along the cordon I always began by asking, "Who passed by here or who wanted to pass?" Embarrassing, isn't it?'

Strick did not reply.

'And so,' Gareis went on in a schoolmasterish tone, 'when I hear on one side of the woods that two persons went in and that only one came out, and then when I hear on the other side that two persons came out there that makes three in my arithmetic book. Two went in, and three came out. The case is perfectly clear, isn't it?'

Again Strick did not answer.

'May I borrow your paybook for a moment?' Gareis said. Strick handed it to him. Gareis opened it at the last pages and glanced through them. Then he handed the paybook back. He drew the billiards cue through his hand as though it were a dagger from which he was trying to wipe off blood. 'That really is very clumsy,' he said, in a tone mingling satisfaction and mild criticism. 'The officer who accompanied you wore the very same decorations you have received. The very same ones. That is bad stage-management. Something you want to avoid.'

Strick felt his shoulders bowed beneath a tremendous weight. It was nothing but cotton-wool, but tons of it, gently suffocating him. He said slowly: 'I assume you are not telling me all this to entertain me. You know, but you don't care to make use of your knowledge. Not at the moment, anyway. I take it for granted that you have no need of boasting to me. Therefore you have some definite object in mind.'

Gareis toyed with a billiards ball. He held it up to the lamp-light as though he were examining its sheen and roundness. 'You think slowly,' he said, 'but relatively surely.'

'Everybody says you are a crafty customer, Gareis. Some say you have never yet made a mistake. You're famous for your surehandedness. Now you tell me in so many words that you have me in your palm. One word from you and I'm done for. I'm convinced you know me. Therefore you must know that I would shoot you straight off if I thought your existence endangered my life. Consequently you are counting on my not considering you an enemy.'

'Shall we go on with our game?' Gareis said calmly. 'It's your turn, Strick.'
'How high is the stake?'
'We'll see about that. When the occasion arises I'll ask to be paid off.'

CHAPTER ELEVEN

THERE were moments when Strick thought he had plunged into an enormous pit. He seemed to be surrounded by dense darkness, and he groped his way forward like a blind man who has lost his stick. All along he had assumed that he was out in the open, alone, but apparently there were more obstacles round him than he had ever suspected.

Very well, then, he had stumbled and fallen, and now he expected utter blackness round him. But, instead of the bottom of the chasm, he was at last seeing what he had never seen before in his hesitant meanderings on the upper earth – a patch of sky above him, a rent in the darkness, as though a heap of trash, torn apart, had revealed a naked body.

He saw, without knowing precisely what he was seeing. He was as alert as only a man in mortal danger can be. But for the first time he was aware that he was not alone. The streets swarmed with those who shared his views – and with spies, touts, and opportunists. Moreover, there was darkness everywhere, blackest night. The thing now was to find the right man to go forward with. But how? He could not advertise for that, he couldn't put up a poster, or have his wants cried in the streets. He had to be cunning as a fox, crafty as Gareis, sharp as a sword, if he did not wish to run himself through.

He neglected the case of Wolf entirely. Wolf, he sensed, was but one drop in the river, far too petty to be worth wasting time on when the problem was to dam a torrent. All the testimony which Wolf had supplied so gladly and liberally Strick assembled into a file which he labelled C – the C standing for the Commandant's office. Gareis, like an angler reeling in a fish on the hook, took over the case of Wolf. He pumped every bit of information out of Wolf, and let the empty husk lie in the Army prison. He sent copies of his interrogation – 'with best regards' – to Lieutenant Strick.

Vogel behaved as though nothing at all remarkable had happened. Strick could get nothing out of him. He battered him with insults, with accusations: Vogel was a fool, a criminal, a saboteur, a traitor, a dealer with the enemy. Vogel accepted these charges with the meek indifference of a letter-box. Even when Strick hinted that Inspector Gareis had come dangerously close to the right solution Vogel remained placid. 'If he wanted to,' Vogel said, waving the matter aside, 'he would already have sewn us up. Who could have stopped him? You?'

'And when am I going to get back my spare uniform, my boots and my underwear – to say nothing of my handkerchief?'

'Apply to Gareis. Perhaps he can get them for you.'

What really gave Strick cause to worry was his conviction that a solid cordon was being drawn round him. Powerful groups were already beating the bushes for him. He had received a confidential letter from his home town. The district leader of Rehhausen, so a close friend informed Strick, had asked for detailed information: (*a*) on Strick, (*b*) on Strick's parents, and (*c*) on anything connected with Strick.

'Last night, Vogel, I checked on three telegrams which were sent directly to the Commandant or by him. And all three were concerned exclusively with my personal papers.'

'There, you see,' Vogel replied, 'how the world is full of ingratitude. You're trying to take the shirt off their backs and they suspect you. You're doing your best to get them locked up, and they flatly refuse to give you a parade and beat the drums for you. Can you imagine such unaccommodating people!'

'Where is the English officer, Vogel?'

'What English officer? Do you know any? I don't.'

'You deserve to be arrested.'

'Who's going to do it? Not you, by any chance? Don't make me laugh. Or do you feel a crying need to land yourself in gaol? To quote your favourite phrase: "there's sufficient evidence". And our good friend Rabe would just love doing it. He'd enjoy demonstrating what a tried and true loyal Aryan-Nordic-patriotic German he is.'

'Things can't go on this way, Vogel.'

'My word. Whom are you telling that? Come to Mother Tikke's and hear about the nice people in German officer uniforms who have been showing up there. Oscar Tikke promptly placed him at the special table. What a howl that was. The captain blushed with delight, and the way he saluted! Man, you should have seen that. As if he were at the Party Day in Nuremberg. That alone was worth the whole show.'

Strick knew that he had to take only one more step in order to find himself over the border-line. One step, one word. But he hesitated, turned sharply away, and continued to pace back and forth along the border-line. 'Clear out,' he said to Vogel. 'And don't drag me into any more of your idiotic messes.'

'What I want to know,' Vogel said, 'is how long you're going to go on playing blindman's buff.'

Dr. Friedrich, the district leader of Rehhausen, still possessed the same residence which he had had as a dentist. And the same wife also.

The house was in a side street – a brick box with stucco facing. In front a garden: a perfectly level cemetery for flowers. A green-painted fence. On the door a sign: 'K. Friedrich, D.D.S.' The lower half of the sign was carefully pasted over. Presumably it had read 'Office hours, Monday to Friday, 10 a.m. to 5 p.m.'

The first floor of the house was occupied by a pensioned major, now head of the Rehhausen rations board – a splendid example of total commitment to the war effort. A worn staircase led to the second storey. It had been scrubbed so hard the white of the wood showed through, and the entire staircase smelled of brown soap.

At Strick's knock the door was opened instantly, apparently by the district leader's charwoman. The woman wore an apron and a blue dish-cloth was wrapped turban-wise round her head. But she had a certain presence, and Strick found out in the nick of time that he was speaking with Frau Friedrich.

'The district leader is not in yet,' Frau Friedrich said. 'Perhaps you would like to wait. He will be home any moment.' Strick was glad to wait. He asked Frau Friedrich whether he could help her with anything. Emptying pails, carrying out refuse, perhaps beating rugs?

Frau Friedrich thought she could manage alone. 'What about your maid?' Strick asked.

'We don't have any. What are you thinking of? Imagine our having a servant right in the midst of the War. My husband, the district leader, would never hear of that.'

She led him into Dr. Friedrich's study. It was scarcely a room, it was a billet, assigned quarters, furnished for heavy traffic. There were traces of boots on the worn and trampled carpet, traces of boots on the legs of the chairs and the sides of the desk. Piles of Party bulletins, letters of instruction, newspapers, magazines, pamphlets, circulars, letter files, and folders lay on the desk, the window-sill, and several of the chairs. The man who worked here was swamped with paper.

Frau Friedrich sat down facing Strick. 'When my husband still had his practice,' she said, 'this place looked *very* different.'

Strick could imagine it very well. Undoubtedly things had looked different, and the woman herself as well. She must be about forty, but her face was wrinkled like an elephant's hide, and she had the figure of a herring barrel. Presumably they had been married for twenty years or so. She must have been Friedrich's receptionist or something of the sort. Then she had helped out as nurse, raised children, and scrubbed the stairs. As the dentist's practice increased a servant girl had been added to the household, and possibly a new receptionist as well. Two sturdy sons grew up. And then Dr. Friedrich had discovered politics.

He took politics more seriously than his practice. Patients drifted away, the receptionist had nothing to do but doze and realize how superfluous she was. As Friedrich's passion mounted, his income diminished. First the receptionist went, then the servant girl, and once more Frau Friedrich scrubbed the floor and the family bathroom. But Party Member Friedrich had undoubtedly declared, 'This too is a sacrifice for the coming new age.'

And then the new age had come. Party Member Friedrich became district leader. His prestige increased, and he stopped his practice entirely, functioned solely as district leader. His sons went into the Hitler Youth, and his wife was again assigned a maid. But the house became dirtier than ever; the boots of the Party members tracked up the floors. And so the duster was in her hand all the time, and her sons carried the banners of the Hitler Youth, but would not bother taking rubbish out to the yard.

For the Party was an affair for men. And Friedrich devoted himself to it completely. He had always been an idealist, and would always remain one, even if it killed him, his wife, and his children. Frau Friedrich was a housewife; the fact that she was a district leader's wife scarcely touched her. She did not attend meetings, demonstrations, and celebrations. She was never present at the club or at the receptions in the town hall. She was just a housewife – and a mother.

Her sons exchanged the uniform of the Hitler Youth for the uniform of the nation. One died over England. The other was still bashing his head against the stone walls in Russia. And, as the War became total, the earnestness of the times made total demands upon Frau Friedrich, the housewife. The maid left, but the number of trampling boots increased. And so she had become what she was now, a barge proceeding silently and patiently behind her panting tugboat, Dr. Friedrich.

Dr. Friedrich came in and laid down his stuffed brief-case. Printed matter billowed out of it. Dr. Friedrich looked dead tired. He held out his hand to Strick – a cold, almost lifeless lump of flesh that did not press Strick's hand at all. Then he dropped into the chair behind his desk and slumped in it for a while. 'Shall I bring you your slippers?' his wife asked. The district leader straightened up. 'No,' he said.

He groaned to think of all he had gone through today, all the difficulties. And all day yesterday – difficulties. And tomorrow – difficulties. Difficulties behind him, difficulties before him, and this man Strick was the worst difficulty of all.

'Why are you always making difficulties for me, Herr Strick? Tell me why. After all, we have the same goal. We ought to be working together.' Dr. Friedrich was weary, weary to exhaustion. If Strick had not been there he would have closed his eyes and gone to sleep at once. 'Is it all necessary, Strick? You keep interfering in my province. You have ordered the hospital kitchens to be divorced immediately from the Party welfare organization. You have declared that Army civilian employees must resign at once from the German Labour Front. Why have you done all this?'

'The Party organizations, Dr. Friedrich, are no longer reliable. There's hardly a breath of life left in them, no go to them at all. They're practically corpses, little more. The men in my charge are only being spoiled by the Party, Dr. Friedrich. I cannot put up with that. I am responsible for putting over the Party line in my area. I must oppose all half-way measures.'

More difficulties, in other words! The district leader closed his eyes as though he had been attacked by a terrible spasm of cramp. One of his hands dangled limply down, the other lay on top of the desk, like some lifeless object that had been put aside. 'You are going too far, Herr Strick. That has been clear to me for some time. You drag people in by force. That is not good. In that way you accomplish the exact opposite of what is wanted. The exact opposite. That's it. What you are doing does not bring light to people, it burns them up.'

'I am mobilizing, Dr. Friedrich, mobilizing everything for the Final Victory. Those are our instructions.'

'But certainly not by such methods.' The district leader complained like a sick child. He was weary, all he wanted was to sleep. If only Strick would go, would let him alone. For a few hours at least. If only he could have a couple of hours, one hour, without difficulties. 'This morning,' he said wearily, 'you commandeered all the loud-speaker trucks in my district for Army headquarters.'

'I am entitled to do so. Those loud-speaker trucks are not Party property. They belong to a firm which rents them when the Party needs them. If the Army needs them we have the right to confiscate them. That's perfectly normal in wartime.'

'It's dreadful to see how you misjudge the situation, Herr Strick.' The district leader ran his finger-tips over his forehead and down his temples. His breathing was deep and painful. 'We are tired, Herr Strick. What we need is rest. Our strength is nearly exhausted. Why do you want to stir everybody up by these furious propaganda campaigns? Why are you sowing unrest and uncertainty among the soldiers? Why these arrests, why this eternal pressure?'

'I really am very much surprised, Dr. Friedrich. You know I am doing my best to separate the sheep from the goats. And what do you say about it? Please, no difficulties, leniency, rest, let things slide. That's no way to get anywhere. No, sir, what we must do is apply pressure. We've got to see that the men get off their behinds and start moving.'

The district leader simply could not understand it. This man Strick represented another world, and Dr. Friedrich could not even find the entrance to it. He bumped his nose into a wall of glass. But the glass was probably not bullet-proof.

And Strick could not understand the district leader, could not enter into what Dr. Friedrich called his world. Was he the representative of a movement? The man was soft, rotting, used up, decayed and hollow. Representative of a movement! He was nothing but rotting straw, useful only for fertilizer.

Strick moved on from one lecture to the next. From the guard company to the training battalion, from there to the civilian employees group, from there to the local hospital, the Army prison, and the personnel of the prisoner-of-war camps. He talked and talked. By now scarcely anyone in the entire Rehhausen area knew what National Socialism was supposed to be. Not that they had been too clear about it before; but hitherto they had not questioned their knowledge.

The strange thing was that each separate thing Strick said was precise and immediately understandable. It was only that the overall effect was of startling novelty. Those theories seemed somehow familiar, but where had they heard them before? No one could say. His speeches were like a thunderstorm, lowering the air and threatening to burst at any moment.

To the civilian workers he said: 'You are civilians; the Army cannot give you orders, it can only issue regulations. When an organization is not well regulated it cannot issue regulations. You must keep that in mind.'

To the guards at the prison camps he said: 'Prisoners-of-war are soldiers like yourselves. Treat them as you would like to be treated if you become a prisoner-of-war. For none of you here are perfectly secure, you are here only for the time being. It may be that three days from now you will be transferred to some sector of the front. It may also be that a mere twelve hours afterwards you will be captured. All that is in the realm of possibility. Or it may be that they will come all the way here and lock you up on the spot. We must calmly confront all possibilities, the Fuehrer has said.'

To the officers he said: 'Soldiers do not love their superiors, they only obey them. The exceptional ones are the officers who are clowns or martinets. That kind the men remember for a long time afterwards, and never without a special glee. If their superiors were clowns the men remember them for their idiocy. If they were martinets they remember how lucky they were to get away from them. Now, what is National Socialism? National Socialism is providing examples. Who provides the significant examples? The Fuehrer, the generals, the heads of the Party, and other superiors. Hitler, Guderian, Ley, and Colonel Mueller. It is essential to imitate these examples. Those who do not imitate them are not National Socialists. That is simple arithmetic.'

To the wounded and the sick in the hospitals he said: 'You have been assured that you have earned the gratitude of your Fatherland. And you have earned it. You have no arms, no legs, no eyes, one of you lacks a part of his lungs, another a section of his stomach, another left a bit of his brain in the trench or in the pail under the operating table. Therefore you have earned the gratitude of your Fatherland. And now consider precisely what this gratitude of your Fatherland looks like. Start a balance sheet. Write on top: "Gratitude of the Fatherland". And then make the entries. On the left, "Debit: 117 nights without sleep, 4 colds, 38 bruises, 15 boils, falling hair, flat feet, kidney trouble, beginnings of heart disease, digestive disturbances, trembling hands." All that can be put down as a general contribution. And then come the specific contributions for each individual: "left leg amputated to the middle of the thigh, or, stomach wall ripped open, intestines exposed, artificial feeding." And all the other ills the flesh of the soldiers is heir to. And then, on the right side of the ledger, the credit side, enter the following: "One wound badge. Cost of manufacture twenty-five pfennigs. One handshake from the commander, price included in his pay. One propaganda speech by the N.S.G.O. had for nothing." And all the other good things you can think of.'

That was the way Strick spoke, and he was listened to with genuine astonishment. If that was Nazism, the soldiers told themselves, then everything they had previously claimed to be Nazism was not. Therefore they must learn to distinguish. Furthermore, they must choose. The worst part about this man Strick was that he forced you to think. You had almost forgotten how that was done.

Wherever Strick went there followed in his wake a surge of impassioned integrity and clean administration. Since Wolf's arrest the quartermaster had been losing weight by the day, and his wife spent less time in malicious gossip about other people. Private soldiers, now that Strick had called their attention to their right to do so, began weighing their portions of food. The officers' club piggery was hastily disbanded.

The subject for political instruction this week was the Soviet Union. From his involuntary travels in Russia Strick had brought back an entire brief-case full of pictures, first-class material. On the cover of the folder he had written in red pencil: CAUTION! ENEMY PROPAGANDA! Inside was everything the U.S.S.R. was proud of: Lenin and Stalin hand in hand; workers on Red Square; May Day celebrations among the Kirghiz; Stalin dedicating a dam; *Pravda* pouring out of the rotary presses; a Tschaikovsky ballet at the Opera House; the headquarters of the Communist Party in Leningrad; Stalin addressing metal workers; and so on.

He had these pictures mounted on slides and projected them on a cinema screen. His commentary was non-committal. Mostly he encouraged the audience to guess the proper captions – and was privately amazed at the astonishing knowledge of things Russian the members of the garrison betrayed.

Another pet subject for his lectures was the British Empire. He found it necessary to quote fully from Winston Churchill, and showed numerous pictures of the chubby British leader: Churchill with his dog; Churchill at his easel; Churchill with Westminster Abbey in the background; Churchill with the King.

All the great writers of France, said Strick, had won fame by their pernicious anti-authoritarian works. To illustrate this point he discussed Voltaire, Hugo, Zola, and the Dreyfus case. He used slides to put on a grand fashion show for the female civilian employees, and he pointed out sombrely that it was obvious that a nation which made such dresses couldn't help losing the war. And then he showed Paris – the buildings and the people, the squares, and the places of amusement. What a contrast to the disciplined Great German way of life! Our German women, he stated, preferred the uniform of the Women's Army Auxiliary to flimsy evening dresses!

It was after one of these lectures, when Strick was packing up his materials and getting ready to rush off to another unit, that Rabe came up to him. 'If you don't mind, Strick, I'd like to walk with you a little way.'

'Glad to. But I'm in a hurry.'

They went outside to the paved road between the blocks of the barracks. It was oppressively hot. 'I hope you won't misunderstand me, Strick, but I'm sorry I have been avoiding you these past few days.'

Strick had not the slightest idea what Rabe was getting at. He was already thinking about his coming lecture to the civilian employees, this time to the women alone. He would talk to them about German womanhood. At the end – or should it be at the very beginning? – he would have them sing *Deutschland, Deutschland über alles*. He would make a point of the second stanza: 'German women, German fidelity!' That was a good subject. A great variety of things could be said about it.

'I realize,' Rabe was saying, 'that Fraulein Tannert feels drawn to you, Strick. Of course, I have no say on that matter, but perhaps you would like to know what I think about it.'

Strick stood still. He saw Rabe facing him, struggling to keep his dignity, to make himself clear. Behind Rabe was the close-clipped lawn with its edging of rough-hewn stones.

'Go on, Rabe. I'm very interested.'

'I have kept asking myself why you are doing all this round here, and what the fundamental meaning of it could possibly be. Now I think of it this way: the arrest of the station commandant was just an accident. The fuss you've made about rations, canteen supplies, and your attempts to bring things into line – all that was just to discharge the resentments you built up as a soldier at the front. And the reason for the arrest of Captain Wolf? A woman – Magda.'

Strick had a vision of the misunderstandings burgeoning and swelling all round him. What a strange spectacle – people were certainly racking their brains over him. In a way, it was fun.

'I'm not blaming you, Strick. Certainly not because of Magda. It's perfectly understandable that you should have Captain Wolf arrested on her account. I myself should have taken the initiative. My hesitation was responsible for my losing her, I suppose.'

'What do you mean by "losing her", Rabe? Did Fräulein Tannert tell you that?'

'I have not spoken to her since.'

'Good Lord, Rabe, you *were* born yesterday.'

'You see, up to now I always thought—' Rabe broke off, embarrassed.

'What did you think, Rabe?'

Rabe hesitated, looking as confused as if he had lost his identity papers and was no longer sure who he was. But then he came out with it all in a rush. 'I always thought you had very definite ideas, a definite goal in mind. I fancied that you had theories about the way things should be done, that you were interested in radical changes. I really thought for a while that nothing short of a revolution would satisfy you. But it turned out that all you wanted was a purge – for the sake of some one you loved. Nevertheless, as I said before, I understand you perfectly. Of course, everything you've done has a certain significance. It's only that your motives are different from what I thought.'

'Rabe,' Strick said from the bottom of his heart, 'Rabe, you're an ass.'

Old Tannert and his daughter Magda occupied two rooms and a kitchen in a small, two-storey, ramshackle house right along the shore of the Main. He had moved into this flat in 1923 when he married. Here he had sat in the evenings at his drawing-board, smudging his fingers with ink. Here his daughter had been born, his wife suffering and groaning like a dying animal. He himself attended her at her confinement. There was no money for a doctor or a midwife. His wife did not rise again from her bed. After a few months she died like a fading ember. Here, in 1933, before his child's terrified gaze, he had been beaten and dragged down the steps like a sack of potatoes. Then he lay in the very bed where his wife had died, and a child dabbed the blood from his face and listened to his delirious ravings. That incident had seeped into her like an infection.

Father and daughter had lived together for twenty long years. They knew one another down to the least movement of their finger-tips. They each had one room, and shared the kitchen between them. There they met over the morning coffee. There they sat in the evening after work, usually in silence, making those brief, simple gestures with which love and affection speak to one another. And they never talked about politics. Discussing politics, Tannert seemed to imply, was superfluous among those who shared the same views. Politics was something to be gone through, lived through and suffered through. On hot nights, when he sat in the kitchen with his shirt open, his scarred, slashed chest was political commentary enough.

Old Tannert watched his child attentively. He watched her grow up as he might watch new worlds unfolding under a microscope. His guidance was generally silent. It often took the form of sentences underlined in books, of newspaper items cut out and laid on the kitchen table. And Magda understood him. Some of her decisions, it seemed to Tannert, were made just as if they had thought out and discussed the matter together at length. She was his child to the core. His life had meaning because she existed. And when he thought over the course of the War, when he drew his silent conclusions from it, it seemed to him sometimes that he ought to be grateful to the Nazis for having thrashed his mind into wakefulness and confirmed for good his defiance and rejection of all they stood for.

If that had not happened he might have tried to forget, for the sake of his child, what many people he knew called his pig-headed convictions. Their life would have been pleasanter, easier to endure, more comfortable. But, as things were, it was a life that remained honest and clean. The time was coming now when merciless accounts would have to be drawn up and he felt that he could present his own balance sheet without shame. Magda would be able to live for what he had almost died for.

During these past few weeks of vital decisions what had surprised Magda most was the discovery that her father had a sense of humour. It was bottled-up, ghostly humour, like a series of uncanny flashes of electricity on a quiet summer night. She had encountered it for the first time when Strick and Tannert were discussing in her presence new ideas for posters. They argued over words and turns of phrase with the gravest, most self-contained demeanour, but their eyes sparkled with devilry. She would never forget how the two men's eyes groped for one another, lit up briefly, and then slid aside as though something quite insignificant, inessential, had taken place.

Her father had never said a word to her about Strick. And she felt clearly that here too there was no use asking questions, because her father would not answer her. Not because he was unwilling to answer, but because he could not, could not yet, at any rate. But she was convinced that her father felt as drawn to Strick as she herself. It was inexplicable why this was so, but it was undeniable.

Old Tannert was reading the editorial in the *Mainfränkischer Beobachter*. 'Courage,' it said. But the courage was obviously phony. It reminded Tannert of a rider on a merry-go-round horse. The rider was getting sicker and sicker, but the merry-go-round would no longer stop. It kept circling relentlessly in the same track. And between the lines Tannert could detect quivering terror, bucked up by alcohol and made to sound like firmness. Worth noting, that.

There was a knock on the door. Tannert called, 'Come in,' and Strick entered. 'Is the coast clear?' he asked. Tannert thought instantly of his secret seals and linoleum blocks. But they were well hidden, and in any case he was not worried about Strick.

'I wanted a chance to have a private talk with you,' Strick said. 'But feel free to throw me out if you have something better to do.'

'I'll keep that in mind,' Tannert said, and Magda saw again that rare sparkle of devilry in the eyes of both men. 'Let's go to my room. Or have you come on Magda's account?'

'To be perfectly honest, no. But perhaps your daughter wouldn't mind going out for a stroll while we talk here.'

'Certainly,' Magda said.

'And I would advise you, Fräulein Tannert, to walk down to the lower bridge over the Main. The view there is particularly lovely at this time of day.' Magda tried not to blush under the gaze of those mocking eyes. She realized at once whom she would meet by the bridge, and hurried out.

Old Tannert's room was like a good wood carving – simple, the lines clean and effective, free of contrivance, and yet full of unusual objects. There was a hand-carved picture frame, a hammered ash-tray; there were wrought-iron book-ends. Everywhere was the neat, clear signature of a craftsman.

'Herr Tannert,' Strick said abruptly, without explanation, 'you are a member of a Socialist group!' That was putting it clearly, putting the cards on the table. Tannert rolled up like a hedgehog that has been touched. With eyes squinted, half-closed so that the sparkle in them would not betray him, he said slowly. 'I belong to no organization.'

'But that's what your papers say, Herr Tannert.'

'They wanted me to admit it. That's why they kept beating me. They kept at it until I said yes. But it wasn't so. You see, at that time – it sounds stupid – I bled. What for, I asked myself. Certainly not for the Nazis. Rather for the opposite of the Nazis. And so after that I felt myself a revolutionary Socialist.'

Strick, who was listening with keen attention, asked, 'Felt?'

Tannert squinted a little more. He placed one hand on top of the other, and avoided looking at Strick. 'You are a stickler for words. Yes, "felt". Many things have changed since. Recently I haven't been altogether in sympathy with that movement.'

'But why the devil not?'

Tannert said, 'Because of you.'

Strick made a face as if he had bumped his nose into a lamp-post. 'Am I hearing right?' he said in amazement.

'I've been wanting to tell you this for some time, but I couldn't very well do it at the office. Up to now I've had little contact with Nazis. Perhaps I really never knew what they were like personally. You're the first one I've ever talked with much, and worked together with. And I like what you're doing. If that is National Socialism, your action in regard to the station commandant and Wolf and the audit of accounts and your support for the enlisted men and your personal modesty – if all these things are National Socialism then I'm with it.'

The situation was so crazy, so outrageous, so dumbfounding that Strick broke out in a short, jagged laugh. 'What do you think I am, anyway, Tannert?' he asked.

'A man of honour.'

'I thought I was supposed to be a National Socialist.'

'Very well, a National Socialist man of honour. And if it would give you pleasure, Herr Strick, from today on I will gladly greet you with "Heil Hitler".'

'Good Lord,' Strick gasped, 'you've gone completely off your head.' He stood up and went to the window. Below him the Main flowed, filled with the drainage of the whole region. A sewer along whose edges wine grew. Was all of history a stream fed by millions of toilets? That could not be?

He turned round and looked Tannert square in the face. Tannert's eyes were on him, glowing with friendly mockery. The lines at the corners of his mouth were curved round a smile he was holding in. Then, to Strick's immense relief, Tannert burst into laughter. Strick took a deep breath.

'We ought,' Tannert said, 'to have a frank discussion of what our "group" can do to help.'

CHAPTER TWELVE

THE air-raid command post was in the cellar of the headquarters building. It was a dungeon with whitewashed walls, dusty and rubbed, and with telephones, aerial situation maps, a command table, and a transmitter-receiver for radio communication with flak units. There were a number of plain benches along the walls, a few chairs, and a wooden arm-chair in sham Gothic style. Running across the long wall in heavy black letters was the sentence (placed there by Strick): 'Cowards die many times before their deaths.'

In the large wooden arm-chair Vogel loafed. He had his booted feet on the table, in the centre of the map. At the moment he was on air-raid warning duty. That meant sitting in a dimly lit cellar in broad daylight and snoozing by the telephone until some bomber flew into this area. Then he informed the air-raid officer – who was also relaxing in his booth – and then he invited the entire garrison down to the cellar. Alarm sirens – and they came fluttering in like a flock of pigeons. The job of air-raid officer was rotated. The air-raid officer for today was Lieutenant Strick.

A telephone rang. Again, damn it all! Vogel angrily lifted the receiver. 'Aid-raid command post. Vogel speaking. . . . How are things? Too slow for me too. German air supremacy uncontested – at least for the next twenty minutes. No occasion for "slight damage to property". I'm completely alone here, like the die-hard Teuton with his faith in Final Victory. . . . Of course, come on down. No other son of a bitch will disturb us, not to speak of any good Nazis.'

Vogel replaced the telephone and switched on the radio receiver. Since it was battery-powered, the receiver at once began bellowing in a monotone: 'Dora seven all clear. No enemy planes expected. Dora seven all clear. No enemy planes expected. Dora seven—' Vogel switched it off, grumbling. 'You can't depend on anything any more. We should never have started this war the enemy forced on us.'

He again stretched his legs over the map. Doors banged, hasty footsteps approached. The last door squealed open. Without changing his position Vogel called out to Strick: 'Everything under control, your grace. No heroic deaths in prospect for the next half-hour.'

Strick looked round. 'Are we alone?'

'We are that, Lieutenant. Always alone. We have our Fuehrer to thank for that. The enemy is always listening, but that need not bother us. The doors and the hatch to the control room are closed tight.'

The control room was adjacent to the command post, and there was a small hatchway connecting the two rooms. Anyone sitting in the control room could hear clearly every word spoken in the command post as long as the hatch was open. When the hatch was closed nothing at all could be heard; the command post was acoustically well insulated, as it had to be for swift and sure transmission of information. Now, at any rate, the hatch was closed. They were alone and undisturbed.

'I paid a visit to Tannert's home last night, Vogel.'

'To see the father or the daughter?'

'Pig. The old fellow, of course.'

'Aha, you were trying to recruit him for the Party.'

'On the contrary, he recruited me for his party.'

Vogel whistled so sharply that it seemed the dust must trickle off the walls. 'And?'

'Everything is straightened out. We have now found one another.'

'You don't say – you've found one another. And is that all? I suppose you're preparing a grand beer-hall party with new songs, a new flag, brass band, and commemorative speeches. And then, after the fiftieth glass or so, you'll make a motion that the command be handed over to some one, probably the senior in rank; torches will be lighted, and then you'll march. For any old idea, against any old foe. And that will be a display of the undying spirit of the German people.'

Strick laughed. 'You're a bastard, Vogel, no respect for anything. But sometimes you hit it off. We always talk too much; we ought to act.'

'If you want action hand me a cigarette.'

Strick tossed him a packet and bent over the map. 'What's the date, anyhow?'

'July 19th, 1944,' Vogel said.

Strick opened the message book. 'What is the air situation?'

Vogel switched on the receiver again. It bellowed forth at

once in its monotone: 'Dora seven all clear. No enemy planes expected. Dora seven all clear. No—' Vogel switched it off again.

Strick looked down at the entry he had made. 'Too bad,' he said thoughtfully. 'I wouldn't mind having a few of my colleagues here in the cellar. I can break them down a lot quicker when they're scared stiff.'

Grinning with enjoyment, Vogel puffed out the smoke of his cigarette. 'Nothing to stop us from having an air-raid practice off our own bat. Just to keep headquarters on the mark, you know.'

'Each of your ideas is crazier than the last,' Strick said, toying with his pencil. 'Some day they'll lock you up. But don't think I intend to risk a palace revolution on your account.'

The sheet-metal doors boomed like struck gongs, but the footsteps were almost inaudible. Eri came in. 'Can I see you?' she asked Strick.

She was wearing a cotton dress, cut low at the neck. 'More light!' Vogel exclaimed.

'How did you know I was here?'

'Your office knew where you were.' She looked at Vogel as though he were a mud puddle she had to cross. 'Can I speak with you alone?'

'Go into the control room,' Strick said to Vogel. And as Vogel hesitated, looking questioningly at him, he added, 'Without the hatch.' Vogel moved off at once. 'All right – if that's the way you want it. German Greetings!'

'What does that mean – "without the hatch"?' Erika asked after Vogel had noisily tramped out.

'The control room is connected to this room by a hatch. Without the hatch means no communication.'

Erika sat down on the table facing him. 'I think I have everything you need,' she said. She took a document out of her briefcase. 'Here. Make a photostat of that.' She handed it to him. Strick looked at her, his eyes travelling from the rounded knee close to his, then up the firm, smooth thighs to waist and shoulders. 'What's in this thing?'

'Some stuff on the colonel,' Erika said lightly, passing the palm of her right hand over the back of her neck to make sure her hair was in order. 'If he should ever start any action against you I'll let you know in time. All you have to do is hint that you've seen this scrap of paper – and he'll behave himself.'

Strick paid no attention to the paper she had given him. 'Why are you doing all this?' he asked her, looking at the familiar face which could become so withdrawn, which so often stayed expressionless, or masked itself in a look of sarcasm. 'Sometimes I think, Eri, that, after all, you love me.'

Erika passed her hand over her forehead as though brushing away an annoying fly. He knew she hated high-sounding words, all-embracing promises. She had suffered too much from such things in her short life, and she would despise herself if she were ever again fool enough to believe in them. She had been deceived and lied to; she knew for certain now that lies and deceptions were basic to human nature. No idea could be trusted, no idea could be grasped by instinct, for that was how she had more than once gone astray. All that was left to go by was calculation. Life had to be treated like an example in arithmetic.

'Quite possibly I love you. I might even be sincere about it. At least, today. A man who is rising is always a lot more attractive than one who is holding on precariously to what he has. Besides, you're younger and stronger. All these are points to take into consideration.' She stretched a bit.

'And suppose I'm already on the wane, Eri? What then?'

'That's what I'm trying to prevent. So read what I've brought you.'

Strick moved the desk lamp so that the light fell on the paper. He began reading, stopped in amazement, and began again. He felt his way over the lines of writing gingerly, and for a moment he thought he could hear his blood roaring in his head like a heavy, monotonous rain. As he read he clenched his hands to conceal his excitement. His knuckles whitened as though the skin were being scraped off the bones. Finally he said, making an effort to keep his voice steady, 'The corrections on this page are unquestionably his handwriting, aren't they?'

Eri seemed to have discovered a tiny speck of soot on her leg. She licked the forefinger of her right hand, stretched out her leg, and rubbed her knee.

'This is really his handwriting, isn't it, Eri?'

Eri nodded. 'Which clearly proves that he has not only read the plan, but is the author of it,' she said, gazing with satisfaction at her outstretched leg.

'Did you type it yourself?'

'Yes, but without a carbon copy. He stood by me while I was doing it.'

Strick felt as if he had walked out of a dark room into a brutal blaze of light. On the table sat a girl swinging her legs, holding them out into the rays of light that poured from the lamp. And beside this woman lay a sheet of paper, a scrap of paper that seemed to be shouting at him. Strick stood up abruptly, moved away from the circle of lamplight, and retreated into the darkness for a moment, but he was attracted back to the sheet of paper like air steaming towards a fire.

'If anyone told me he had seen a rose growing out of the snow in the middle of winter – I would think it more credible than the existence of this document.'

'It's perfectly clear, isn't it?'

'It's simply incomprehensible,' Strick said, picking up the page and reading it again, as though to reassure himself that every word he had seen before was still there. It was. Nothing had been erased, nothing changed. 'Simply incomprehensible,' he exclaimed again. 'A plan for the resistance movement. For the resistance movement! Colonel Mueller in with the resistance movement! Bridges to be blown up, railways to be blocked, communications network seized, arrest of National Socialist personalities, including me. It's absurd. To think of Colonel Mueller as a renegade from Nazism. It's the final joke of the farce that history has become. If this is really true I'm a bitch with pups or a complete idiot.'

Erika calmly drew another sheet of paper from her brief-case. 'You can also make a photostat of this one while you're about it,' she said.

Strick looked suspiciously at the document. 'The same crazy business in green?' he asked.

'Exactly the same. Only turned upside down.'

He reached out for it hastily and read fast, running over the lines like a thirsty dog lapping water from a brook. Then the laughter erupted out of him. Erika looked at him with the raptness of a child watching a pony.

'Fuehrer, Folk, and Reich be thanked that such things still exist. So here we have a plan for crushing the resistance movement. Colonel Mueller defending the home front of National Socialism. Protection of bridges, railways, communications network, and important persons, this time even including me again. This is grotesque. It's the prime example of German Army humour.'

He shook with laughter. Vogel stuck his head in through the

hatch. 'What's the matter? Is He dead? I can't believe it.'

Strick stopped at once. 'Get your apparatus ready for photostats. Hurry up about it.' Vogel slammed the hatch shut with a dull thud.

'Is this man Vogel reliable?' Eri asked.

Strick nodded. 'He keeps his sound principles well hidden behind idiotic jabber. How long can I keep the originals?'

'Half an hour at most. Only while the colonel is busy talking with Dr. Friedrich.'

'That will be time enough.'

Strick looked at the two plans with an air of amazement and pleasure. 'I can still hardly believe it,' he said. 'The man has two totally different manifestos of principle lying on his desk. One for and one against the resistance movement. Later on you can testify for him in either eventuality. You can corroborate the fact that he made preparations to fight the evil, whichever one it is, and that he was burning to put his plan into action.'

'When you're finished photostating them,' Eri said, going to the door, 'please return the originals to me in my office. I must replace them in the safe immediately.'

'All right,' Strick said. And Eri left.

The documents grinned up at Strick. So this was another thing the resistance movement could mean! A business deal for those who did not want to miss a good chance for profit. A commodity for trading on the principles exchange. A market speculation in negotiable convictions.

After a considerable time Vogel returned. 'Hereby approaching in my capacity as soldier of the nation, sir. Apparatus ready. Further orders requested.'

The telephone jangled, Vogel lifted the receiver. 'Vogel, Corporal of the Fuehrer, speaking. Why so excited, my lady?' He handed the receiver to Strick. 'She's pining away for you.'

'Yes, Eri?' Strick listened a moment. Then he said, 'All right.' Slowly he replaced the receiver.

'Damn it all, Vogel, the colonel is due back any minute. We can't keep the papers any longer.'

Vogel looked up; he had been reading the two papers. 'Too bad, really too bad,' he said. 'They would have made a fine addition to our collection.'

Nervously Strick took up the documents. He considered. Then he asked slowly, 'What is the air situation?'

Vogel switched on the transmitter. It blared out in its monotone: 'Dora seven all clear. No enemy planes expected. Dora seven all clear—'

Strick made his decision. 'Give the air-raid alarm!'

Vogel could not believe his ears. 'What is it you want me to do?'

'Send out the air-raid alarm.'

Vogel glanced at Strick, glanced down at the papers in his hands, and said, 'Hurray!' He began at once calling on the special air-raid telephone network. To the alarm sirens: 'Air-raid command post speaking. Full alarm! What's that? Yes, you button pusher, full alarm. No time for preliminary warnings and such stuff.' To the anti-aircraft artillery: 'Air-raid command post speaking. Raid alarm. Fast formations from nine.'

Outside, the air-raid sirens began whining. Inside the command post it sounded like a long-drawn-out gurgling. Thirstily, Vogel drank in the sound. 'In a minute,' he said, 'the colonel will come rushing in here with all four cheeks quivering.'

'You make the photostats meanwhile,' Strick said. 'Take your time; do a good job of it. Do each one twice. We must be sure of these documents. As soon as you have them finished bring them down and pass them on to Eri.'

Vogel rolled the papers into a scroll and waved it like a marshal's baton. 'I'm expecting a medal for this. The Knight's Cross, *Pour le Mérite*. Or the order of *Pour le Sémite* – the one decoration Goering can't wear.'

Doors slammed, and footsteps approached. The first members of the garrison entered the air-raid shelter. Vogel squeezed his way through them to get to the stairs leading to his 'studio'. Strick sat down at the command table. He turned off the loudspeaker of the receiving set and switched to earphone reception. Now he was quiet and cold, opaque as frozen milk. He left his further course of action to his reflexes, as he always did when a skirmish began.

As usual Colonel Mueller was the first member of the headquarters staff to enter the air-raid shelter. In doing so he was demonstrating exemplary air-raid discipline, and giving an example of his preparedness for all eventualities. What was more, down below in the air-raid cellar he was able to indulge one of his truest passions – standing stooped over maps.

He loved maps. Maps dotted with tiny flags and coloured tacks, streaked by coloured pencils, cross hatched, bounded, marked, and rubbed out. A cross indicating a break-through; a circle as a symbol of an 88mm. gun; a parallelogram representing a tank. One pencil mark, one telephone call, and miles away there would be explosions. So that, when Mueller hurried into the air-raid room, he rushed directly to the large map. His step was elastic as he came in. Air-raid alarms had the effect of thinning his blood, and he walked as if he were on springs. 'Well?' he said tersely, and without waiting for a reply went directly to the large map spread out near the arm-chair.

Strick reported formally: 'Swift bomber formations from nine. Approaching directly.' He added, 'Sounds rather serious, Colonel.'

Mueller waved that aside. He did not care for private comments on an official report, and especially not comments that tended towards panic and prophecies of doom. He ran his finger carefully over the map tracing the presumptive course of the imaginary attackers. 'Any details on the precise direction of flight? Speed? Strength of formations?'

'None yet,' Strick reported.

The colonel was displeased. He required extensive information; he wanted to draw arrows on the map, make calculations on when the enemy might arrive, prepare himself inwardly. After all, it was quite possible that they might jettison their bombs over Rehhausen. Then things would begin to move here. Then he would show the men what real organization meant.

'I have switched the transmitter to earphone reception,' Strick reported. 'Direct loud-speaker reports always make the personnel nervous.'

'You're quite right, Strick,' the colonel approved. 'There are some here quite capable of wetting their pants in my presence. Psychologically that is understandable. The soldier at the front can defend himself; our duty confines us to the cellars. Sitting here often demands more courage than waiting in the trenches for the enemy. Keep that in mind, Strick. Four months in the cellar are often equivalent to four years at the front. I am speaking only of those holding responsible posts, of course. The others cannot even guess the weight of care upon us.'

He sat down in the chair, and listened to the sounds from the adjoining cellar rooms, which were quickly filling. The command room was reserved for the personnel of the headquarters staff. The others crawled off to hide, but here work went on, plans were forged, the enemy courageously waited for.

The new headquarters company commander, Captain Wolf's successor, trotted in. The colonel had personally chosen him with a connoisseur's eyes, and so well had he selected him that Vogel called the new man Captain Wolf II. Wolf II was carrying two handsome suit-cases and a stuffed brief-case with him. 'Situation very dangerous?' he speculated.

'Always, Captain, always,' Strick replied. 'Life is dangerous, but a marvellous discipline.'

Wolf II put away his suit-cases and sat down close to them, spreading himself on the bench and exulting in his temporary safety. The thick concrete walls were reassuring. And round him were his fellow-officers, among them some who would not scare easily. That gave him confidence, at least for the time being.

The colonel was on the telephone. 'Hello, flak artillery. Is this flak? Commandant speaking. What is the situation? . . . No enemy planes in sight? Not yet? Fine, give me your commander. . . . Hello, my dear Major. Everything all right out there? . . . That's good. I hope the Tommies have the nerve to come over here this time, so we can give them a good reception. Of course. Let your guns go for all they're worth. We could stand a little battle stimulation. Then at least there'll be front-line pay bonuses, jitters coffee, and special chow. Heil Hitler, Major.'

The colonel hung up and looked with some annoyance at his blank map. Then he turned to Wolf II. 'Well, Captain, how do you feel? I expect this is your first alarm in your new home?'

Wolf II slid his ample bottom a few inches towards the colonel, his fishlike stare passed concernedly over the map, where every bombing attack within a radius of seventy-five miles was marked with a red cross. 'The situation is really quite nasty, sir. When you look at the map and see what is left – it's clear that our turn will be coming soon.'

Eri entered the room, accompanied by Captain Geiger. Geiger was carrying a brief-case containing 'top-secret Government documents'. He was in high spirits, as though an evening of poetry recitation were about to begin. He was chatting with Eri, attempting to convey that he took bombing seriously, but was courageous in the face of it. 'You see,' he said, 'I have figured it out very carefully. If they drop their bombs from an altitude of ten thousand feet I can always reach the cellar in time, trotting at the double from the office.'

'But they might fly lower,' Wolf II objected worriedly.

'I've figured out each possibility,' Geiger said. 'That is why I always get here before it starts.' He went over to stand beside the colonel and help pore over the map.

'Take a look at that, Geiger. Fast bomber formations from this direction,' the colonel explained.

Wolf II came over to them. 'They're heading directly towards us.'

Captain Geiger turned to Wolf II. 'What of that? We all have to die some time.' Wolf seemed ill prepared for this eventuality. Quite taken back. Oh, well, Geiger thought, nothing surprising about that. What could you expect of the man? Probably never been in a dangerous situation yet. A greenhorn on the home front. Might as well have a little fun with the fellow, and amuse the audience. The colonel liked that sort of thing. 'By the way, Captain,' Geiger asked, 'are you insured? Made your will, ordered your grave-stone, chosen your last resting-place?'

The colonel turned to an intensive study of the map. Erika moved up to Strick and murmured, 'I met Vogel in the corridor. How much time will he need?'

'Ten minutes at most,' Strick answered, pitching his voice as low as hers. 'You'll have plenty of time to get the documents back in the safe.' He called loudly into the room, 'Situation unchanged. More fast formations approaching from nine.'

'No more details than that?' the colonel asked.

'None.'

Lieutenant Rabe appeared, followed by Magda and Old Tannert. Rabe announced in a voice audible throughout the cellar: 'There's not a thing in sight outside. We might just as well have gone on working.'

The colonel took offence at the implied reproach from this young whippersnapper. He said sharply, 'You are in no position to estimate correctly the extent of any danger, Lieutenant Rabe. I expect the officers of my staff to show exemplary air-raid discipline, and to avoid senseless sacrifice of lives. That is why I am always one of the first down here.'

'I am well aware of that, sir.'

'Then let that be a lesson to you.'

'It will be, sir,' Rabe said, sitting down near Strick and Magda.

There was an oppressive silence in the room now. The noise of conversations in the adjoining cellar had almost entirely died away. The air was stale, and produced a feeling of sluggishness.

Abruptly Wolf II emerged from deep meditations. 'I've heard that you die instantly from a direct hit, and that blockbusters flatten out the brain like a postage-stamp.'

'Can't you think of another subject for conversation?' the colonel reprimanded.

Wolf II would not be diverted. 'I always hear so much talk about limed corpses,' he said. 'Just what are they?'

The colonel turned away contemptuously and bent over the map. Geiger attempted a joke to relieve the prevailing gloom. 'Keep your trousers on, Captain,' he said. 'You've lost your chance to end up in a mass grave. This place is bomb-proof – ten feet of concrete. Will stand up to the heaviest-calibre bombs.'

'But suppose we're buried here?' Wolf II said staunchly.

'Then they'll dig us out, the way old Schliemann dug up the Trojans. That's your only chance to win immortality.'

'Kindly conduct less negative conversations, gentlemen,' the colonel said. He was still looking resentfully at his map. To his extreme frustration he had not been able to make the slightest mark upon it. 'Turn your minds to encouraging slogans. Let's have some endurance propaganda.'

Geiger fell in with the colonel at once. 'I formally recommend,' he said, 'the drawing up of a bulletin of psychological gymnastics in the cellar. Drill with anti-jitters slogans.'

'I beg your pardon, Captain!' Strick appeared to be gravely offended. 'After all, this is hardly a subject for cheap jokes.' Geiger looked stricken. Strick turned to Colonel Mueller. 'I will gladly draw up such a bulletin at the first opportunity, Colonel.'

Again silence settled over the cellar. The colonel stretched and glanced round at his colleagues. 'We really ought to ventilate this place,' he said emphatically.

Corporal Vogel entered the room, carrying some rolled-up papers discreetly in his right hand. He announced, 'Sound of motors from nine. Apparently strong formations.'

The colonel was at the telephone at once. 'Flak! Flak! Hello? Do you hear motor noises? . . . No? Nothing? Why not? . . . Connect me with your commander at once.'

While the colonel was telephoning, Vogel sat down beside Eri. He laid the papers on the bench. Eri picked them up and put them into a folder. Strick nodded almost imperceptibly, and Eri rose and went out with the folder.

The colonel at the telephone was shouting, 'Major! This is a hell of a mess. Your men are sleeping. No doubt about it, recognizable motor noises from . . . from . . .' Vogel obligingly helped him out. 'From nine, sir.' '. . . from nine. Your spotters seem to be wearing their ears on their arses, and sitting on them. After all, the defence of our city is in your hands.'

Meanwhile Vogel had relieved Lieutenant Strick. He sat down and pulled the earphones half-way down over his ears. Then, in a chanting monotone, he announced: 'Bomber formations have just veered off, Colonel.'

The colonel was still on the telephone. 'Your luck, Major. The bomber formations have just veered off. I'll speak to you again later.' He hung up angrily.

'The flak,' Wolf II said with conviction, 'has always been unreliable. When I think of all they have on their consciences . . .'

Geiger still felt the urge to tease Wolf II a little. 'Oh, come now,' he said. 'Those flak men have a healthy instinct. They know they might just as well be throwing stones at the planes – the result would be the same. Heroic struggle for German air supremacy, or dog barking behind a truck.'

Strick seized on the words. 'Don't you agree, Colonel,' Strick said with a good semblance of indignation, 'that such remarks are going too far?'

Yes, the colonel apparently agreed. He cleared his throat and murmured, 'Cut it, Geiger.' After a brief, deliberative pause he added, 'A small amount of jealousy between the Services is fine. Competition always acts as a stimulus to performance. But there are limits to everything. After all, all the Services are fighting for the same cause.'

A number of the officers nodded. Rabe was as alert as a pointer. Tannert blinked attentively; Magda sat leaning back. Strick let his eyes rest trustfully on the colonel. He appeared to be expecting more morale-building speeches. The colonel obliged.

'Gentlemen, we must never forget that we are in the middle of a decisive battle which we will presumably win because win we must. Because our nerves are sounder, our wills stronger, and our Fuehrer beyond comparison with any other in the world.'

'Very good,' Old Tannert exclaimed. "Fuehrer beyond comparison" is excellent.'

The colonel ignored this remark, and continued expatiating

upon his theme with greater and greater eloquence. 'Consider, gentlemen, the gifts of Providence for which we must be thankful. Conceive of our situation if we did not have the German people, the invincible Armed Forces, our reliable Party, and our glorious Fuehrer. Then what would you say?'

'Hurrah!' Vogel called out into the rapt silence. He removed his earphones.

The colonel was aghast. 'What's that you said?'

Vogel was unabashed. 'Hurrah! The bomber formations have veered off completely, and are now flying on towards eleven.'

Old Tannert had choked, and was coughing violently. Strick was pounding his back. Rabe and Magda were looking at one another with eyes more direct than they had been in the past. Wolf II was deliberating, trying to understand exactly what he had just heard. Geiger was fumbling for a joke which would lighten the tension, but could think of nothing. The colonel sat lowering in his chair, like a bulldog waiting for something to sink his teeth into. Eri, who had appeared at the door while the colonel was speech-making, called out, 'If the bombers have veered off we can go back upstairs.'

Every one agreed. The best solution was to get out of this cellar as fast as possible. But Strick remarked, 'I can scarcely believe the danger would be over so soon.' And instantly Vogel called out in his dry sing-song voice: 'More bomber formations approaching. Again straight from direction nine.'

The colonel hastened to switch the unfortunate conversation to a new track. 'Damn it all,' he exclaimed. 'More planes. Incredible the recklessness with which the enemy is throwing in his last resources.'

Geiger faithfully seconded this remark, although he went a bit too far. 'No sense of chivalry at all. Unscrupulous exploitation of crass material superiority, that's what it is.'

'It's easy to see you're no poker-player, Geiger,' the colonel chided him. 'The enemy is bluffing all the time.'

Some time back Strick had received some interesting data from Tannert. He thought that this was a first-class occasion for using it. 'May I,' he said politely, 'take advantage of this opportunity, Colonel, to bring up a few questions in regard to National Socialist troop leadership?'

'If time permits,' the colonel said slowly. And Vogel promptly called out, 'More strong formations continue approaching from nine.'

Strick mentally sorted his notes. 'According to approximate, very generous estimates, gentlemen, there are about one hundred and twenty thousand Party members in the Armed Forces. Taking the total number of the Armed Forces at about twelve million men, that would logically give one Party member to every hundred men in the services. Then how do you explain the fact that within our headquarters area, containing four hundred and fifty soldiers, there are not four and a half but fifty-two Party members? In other words, twelve times the statistical norm.'

The colonel slid round in his chair. 'What are you getting at?'

'I am putting the matter up for discussion,' Strick said.

'Interesting figures,' the colonel murmured uneasily.

Geiger spoke up manfully, acting as proxy for his superior. 'Are you suggesting making revisions in a headquarters staff where everybody knows his job thoroughly? Would lead to serious difficulties, you know.'

Strick's answer was in his smoothest and most apologetic tone. 'It seems a pity that those who really deserve it should be robbed of the privilege of experiencing front-line action.'

Lieutenant Rabe intervened. 'Aren't you forgetting something, Strick? Most of the Party members fought at the front in the first war.'

Strick picked up another figure out of his file. 'Of fifty-two Party members in our headquarters area seven participated in the First World War. Another sixteen took part in one or another of the blitz campaigns of the first months of this war. There still remain at least twenty-nine who must be fretting for a chance to testify to their convictions in battle.'

Wolf II felt that the reference was directed at him. 'I should like very much to fight, but can't,' he said. 'Varicose veins.'

In a voice that was slowly taking on edge, Strick said: 'In forty-one one of my men lost an eye. In forty-three he was back in my battery, passed fit for duty. He fell in battle a month later – for Fuehrer and Reich.'

'I have already volunteered for the front twice,' Geiger said testily. 'My application was blocked each time.'

'Then try it a third time.'

Wolf II, a great lump of flesh spread out over the bench, growled: 'Tell me what decorations you've earned that entitle you to talk like this?'

Strick threw him a long, challenging glance. Then he said icily. 'A few more than you.'

Colonel Mueller was stung into speech. 'This won't do at all, Strick. After all, you can't turn the whole headquarters upside down.'

'Why not, Colonel? The situation has become critical. Sabotage and espionage won't stop when they come to the borders of Rehhausen. There's a strong possibility, Kessler has hinted to me, that the Fuehrer's headquarters may be established near by. In that case it will become absolutely essential to clean up the district – overlooking nothing and nobody. I have the fullest authority to proceed. For the past three days I have had – assuming your approval, Colonel – a special group in constant readiness, equipped with machine-guns, hand-grenades, and full quotas of ammunition. We must allow for all possibilities.'

Colonel Mueller had been examining Strick's face while the latter spoke. Now he said deliberately, 'You are right. I admit it – the situation is grave.'

At this moment Vogel announced: 'All clear just came through. Enemy planes have again turned off.' He immediately busied himself telephoning in a loud voice: 'Air-raid command post. Air-raid alarm over. All clear. . . . Is this flak? Alarm over. All clear.'

Outside the sirens gave their high-pitched wail. The adjoining cellar emptied with a thunderous tramping of feet. Cheerful voices rang out, iron doors clanked. Wolf II picked up his suitcases. Magda, Eri, Old Tannert, Geiger, and Wolf II left immediately, obviously happy to escape the oppressive – in more than one sense – atmosphere of the shelter.

'Rabe,' Strick said. 'would you mind waiting for me in the next room?'

'Gladly,' Rabe replied.

'Vogel,' Strick said, 'you wait too.'

'Certainly,' Vogel said, winking. 'With the hatch, sir?'

'With Lieutenant Rabe and the hatch. Yes.'

Rabe and Vogel went out.

The colonel was sitting back in his arm-chair with an air of rather bleak satisfaction. 'I am slowly getting on to you, Strick,' he said in a low voice. 'At at any rate, you are not a National Socialist.'

Strick broke off his entries in the air-raid message book. He looked squarely at the colonel. 'What leads you to that conclusion, sir?'

'I wasn't born yesterday, Strick. I can see what is going on.

Everything has gone wrong – the situation is completely hopeless, so to speak. The Nazis' war is an outright fiasco, a losing proposition on a vast scale. That's your opinion too, isn't it?'

Strick revealed his teeth in a rigid smile. 'Your perspicuity is amazing,' he said.

Colonel Mueller stood up and posed ponderously. With the knowing, superior smile of a schoolmaster he said benevolently: 'I too am not unfamiliar with the word "resistance movement". Not at all. A few days ago I had a long talk with my friend General Huebner. And I have also made detailed inquiries into your life-history, Strick. Moreover, under close examination your methods can have only one meaning. Come along with me. We ought to have a thorough discussion on this matter.'

Lieutenant Rabe rushed into the deserted command-post room as though he had been shot from a catapult. Corporal Vogel clambered deliberately after him through the hatch, and watched Rabe's antics with delight. Rabe was as pale as a ghost, and his eyes had a frantic gleam. He rushed over to the transmitter and switched it on. It immediately resumed its monotone: 'Dora seven all clear. No enemy planes expected. Dora seven all clear. No en—'

Vogel obligingly handed him a telephone. 'The special air-raid line,' Rabe said. He listened. 'Is that central? Hello, central? This is command post seventy-four. When was the last hostile flight? ... Eight hours ago? ... Thank you.' He automatically laid down the receiver, and fell into a chair as though he could no longer stand.

'You never would have thought it, would you have, Lieutenant?' Vogel said, grinning. 'The things people are capable of.'

Rabe tried to get a grip on himself. He struggled to regain his normal footing. 'What will your dear friend Strick say when he finds out that we both overheard his conversation with the colonel?'

'Why, what should he say, Lieutenant? He'll say, "That's fine".'

'I take leave to doubt that, Vogel.'

'But he will. Didn't you hear Strick say to me, "With Lieutenant Rabe and the hatch." That was his code for saying: "With Lieutenant Rabe listening to the conversation." '

'Are you sure?'

'Do you doubt my word, Lieutenant? Suppose I swear by the Swastika and the Fuehrer?'

'I'd rather you didn't,' Rabe said bitterly.

'Why not?' Vogel said. 'I'm an old-time Nazi. I followed the swastika banner when there wasn't a swastika on it.'

Lieutenant Rabe looked at Vogel as if he were some fabulous beast. He had been willing to credit the man with almost anything, but not quite with this. 'What do you think of the colonel's affiliations with the resistance movement?' he asked.

Vogel shrugged that side. 'Have you ever seen cow-shit on a roof?'

'You don't believe he's sincere?'

'What do you mean, "believe"?' Vogel said. 'We know perfectly well what's going on here.'

'You think the honourable colonel is trimming his sails to either wind?'

'To either wind? Lieutenant Rabe, even a whirlwind wouldn't catch him napping. We have documentary proof of that in our camera. The good colonel is the Fuehrer's loyalest oppositionist, the jolliest character in the glorious third Reich. He can't lose. No matter who wins he'll be there to march in the ranks of the victors.'

Rabe thought he saw it clearly at last. The fronts were laid down, distinguishable; a fog-bank was lifting, and something glimmered before him. What would Strick's ultimate aims, ultimate conclusions be? 'Perhaps,' he said thoughtfully, 'prominent men such as the colonel ought to be used, exploited. No matter what side they are on.'

'Rot,' Vogel said stoutly. 'You won't decide either; you just think about things, like Strick. You like to speculate. You make molehills into mountains with your complicated brain-work. Do you mean to say that you too hope you can build the foundations of integrity out of such human trash? The time is ripe. Today or tomorrow or in three weeks or three months or a year, or almost any hour, the big resistance movement will start rolling. There's a tremendous opposition in Germany that has grown up quietly. Nobody knows anything for certain, none of us, at any rate. But any moment we may receive a telephone call or a message. Or else we will carry on here independently when something is started elsewhere. The time is more than ripe.'

Rabe's thoughts leaped days ahead. What could happen, how would it take place, what preparations were necessary? What precautions should be taken? Did Strick have the guts to push his work to its logical conclusion? How could he, Rabe, prepare for it?

'And you say all this is possible today or tomorrow? At any time?'

'Any time.'

'Then one ought to be prepared for it.'

'By all means.'

'How would it be,' Rabe said slowly, 'if I arrested you, Vogel?'

'Me? You've got the wrong address. I don't intend to be a practice case for you.'

'Arresting you, Vogel, under these circumstances would carry all sorts of advantages.'

'The only question is, for whom. Don't go off half cocked, Lieutenant. Eyes open, take a deep breath, count to fifty slowly, and then look far out over the next garden fence.'

'Hasn't your good friend Strick kept insisting that I ought to bestir myself a little more? All right, now I'm beginning. Consider yourself under arrest, my dear Vogel. But you can go on grinning; you have every reason to. We'll make it as pleasant as possible.'

Colonel Mueller had bored into Strick as though the N.S.G.O. were a ledge he was planning to blast. Afterwards he had used a medium-sized stick of dynamite. But the detonation had no effect whatsoever. They parted without having sounded each other's depths. Everything remained open, indefinite – but that could not go on much longer.

Strick strolled thoughtfully back to his office. If this place were blown sky-high, he thought, I should be relieved of a thousand problems in a tenth of a second.

When he entered his ante-room Magda Tannert told him that a visitor was there to see him.

'Who?'

'A lieutenant. A stranger here. He wanted to speak with you alone. He's waiting in your room.'

The man who rose to his feet as Strick entered was tall, slender, polished. He looked as though he had come direct from some party at an officers' club. He bowed and said, 'I have had a long drive here and must visit two more towns today, so permit me to be brief.' He held out a well-manicured hand to Strick, who shook it firmly. 'You are Lieutenant Strick, are you not?'

'Yes, and who are you?'

'The name is unimportant for the present. Call me Lieutenant von W.'

'You want to remain anonymous?'

The stranger sat down, and shook his head slightly. 'I don't want to, but I think it best for the present. If you insist I will gladly show you my papers. They happen to be genuine. But in certain eventualities it might be better for you not to know my name. Take your choice.'

Strick looked at the man's smooth, long face. The skull of a thoroughbred horse with human features. A living wax dummy with a sardonic twist at the corners of the mouth. And in that cool, matter-of-fact voice there was a great deal of stored-up energy. 'What do you want, Herr von W.?'

The man intoned his words with the flatness of a news-reader. 'You have been reported to us as reliable. We want to make contact with you. We sincerely hope that you share our views.'

Strick took a deep breath. 'Whom do you mean by "we"? What do you mean by "reliable"? Who informed you of my "reliability"? What kind of contact are you thinking of? What views do you stand for?'

Lieutenant von W. leaned back, reached into the side pocket of his tunic, and took out an elegant cigarette-case. 'Smoke?'

'No thanks.'

A match flared. 'Your caution is quite understandable, Herr Strick. Quite what I expected. Let me indicate the most essential points. We received your name from the British captain who owes his liberty to you. He sends his regards and wants you to know that he is safe. We got him comfortably across the border.'

'I think it is time you told me who "we" is.'

The lieutenant flicked the ashes from his cigarette with a long forefinger. 'You, Herr Strick, are an opponent of National Socialism. There are many like you; the best elements of the officers' corps are among them. But it is difficult, extraordinarily complicated, to find out who are our friends, who share our views. We – by that I mean a number of generals and Staff officers in the surrounding military districts – are members of a group. The leader of this group has already made contact with other groups. And so on. We are spreading out and increasing from day to day. We are gathering all the elements of the resistance into our ranks. We want to include you also. You and your group – for you must have allies in your area.'

'And what is the purpose of all this, Herr von W.?'

'To act together.'

'And when does this action take place?'

'Very shortly. We do not know the exact date, but we must hold ourselves in readiness.'

The man's thin lips tightened to a horizontal line above his sharp-hewn chin.

'Just how do you conceive it?' Strick said.

'You will operate here in your area in response to a cue. You must know what has to be done. Obstruction of all Nazi elements. A clear road for all resistance forces. Details must be determined by local conditions. You have a completely free hand. It is enough for us to know that in the Rehhausen district there is some one working for our principles.'

'For your principles!' Strick leaned to the left, and propped his elbow upon the arm of his chair. 'But suppose your principles don't fit in with mine?'

The other lieutenant's chin thrust forward. 'Details are totally unimportant. Motives may vary widely. It doesn't matter at all whether you are a Catholic, Communist, Socialist, Monarchist, Republican, or merely a pro-Army officer. The main thing is that you are opposed to National Socialism. That is all that counts at this time. I hope you understand me.'

'Your arguments make sense.'

Lieutenant von W. went on without the slightest change of tone or the slightest emphasis upon any one word or idea. He sounded like a recording-tape mechanically unrolling. 'The dissension or discussion that will come later is a matter for the future. All that is virtually insignificant compared with the one task that occupies us now – overthrow of the Nazis. That must be done first.'

'Very well,' Strick said. 'I'm with you.'

The lieutenant bowed politely. 'May I have paper and a pencil, please?' He took them, and again snapped a short bow. 'We work on the principle of simple direct contact. I am the only one of my group whom you will know. And you must remain the only one of your group whom I know. I will now write down three things which you will please learn by heart, so that I can burn this sheet of paper in your presence. The first, which I am writing here, is the cue word for the beginning of the organization uprising. I personally will transmit it to you. Therefore the second thing I am writing down is my name and full address. The third is the name of the officer who will take my place if I am unable to act, for any reason whatever.'

Strick took the sheet of paper and went to the window. He impressed the names upon his memory. He went over them, and then went over them again. The names were there to stay. At last he handed the paper to Lieutenant von W. A match flared, and fire ate into the paper, charring it. The lieutenant's hands rubbed it to a black powder that trickled to the floor. Lieutenant von W. carefully cleaned his hands with a handkerchief. 'I am very much obliged to you,' he said.

CHAPTER THIRTEEN

THE date was July 20th, 1944.

It was a day like any other. Nothing about it was unusual, and even the unusual was not considered so.

For example, Vogel's absence was not unusual. Strick missed him briefly, but not until he found his boots untouched and unpolished. They were standing where he had placed them the night before, dusty as ever, the leather as creased as the shrunken bellows of an accordion. But he knew he could expect anything of Vogel. Neglect of boot-polishing certainly came as no surprise. Since Rabe was taking his morning shower, Strick took hold of Rabe's bedspread and used a corner of it to wipe his boots over with.

This morning he had three hours of lectures. Then, round noon, he would check up on the kitchen's butter stocks. A rumour had reached him that the quartermaster had had cream puffs at home for the second time last Sunday. In the afternoon he would look into the library's list of borrowers.

One of these days he would have to have a talk with Vogel, and perhaps with Tannert too. Better with both of them together And with Rabe. He must see what was what for Lieutenant von W. It was high time for definite agreements to be sealed. He must challenge them all to a clear-cut decision. For – or against! Yes or no. Either you are with us, and then you accept all the possible consequences, or you are not, and keep your mouth shut. Or else you won't keep your mouth shut, in which case you'll have to be forced to.

That was the way it had to be done. But there was time – a day, three days, a week. The thing had to be allowed to mature slowly. No sense in rushing matters and acting prematurely.

'Do you happen to know where Vogel is?' Rabe asked while he was doing his fifty knee-bends.

'No,' Strick said. 'He must be knocking about somewhere around here.'

'You ought to be interested in his whereabouts, Strick.'

Strick paid no attention. He was packing up his papers and concentrating on the theme for the day, the advantages of delayed-action defence. He would explain the present military situation to the men. In 1939 and 1940, he would say, the enemy practised delaying action; now the enemy was on the attack, and we were fighting delaying actions; by and by it would again be our turn to attack. He would not add the proviso: even if it takes four or five years more. Since every moron sensed that the War could not go on much longer, the conclusion was obvious. Anyone who failed to understand was beyond help.

'Give Vogel my regards, Rabe,' Strick said as he left. 'If you see him tell him he's a lazy sonofabitch.'

'I think that is exactly his opinion of you,' Rabe said.

Strick started as if some one had pulled him back by a rope. He looked at Rabe critically, but only murmured, 'Well, well,' and went out.

That day Strick's thoughts would not let him alone. But this too was nothing unusual. He knew he had to keep away from the colonel. He would divert Vogel and duck out of any conversation with Tannert, as he had successfully avoided one with Rabe this morning. This was one of those many days when he regretted having undertaken anything, having got himself into this situation. It was too much for him. He had never wanted it this way. Half for fun he had pitched a pebble into a sluggish pond. The widening ripples had become waves. He had been washed into the water, and the current was carrying him along. But, as long as it was at all possible, he would try to preserve his independence of action.

The morning passed uneventfully. For a short time after noon mess Strick sat in the club garden. He was keeping away from Rabe, who had said he wanted to speak to him about Vogel. The sallow, bleached sky shone down upon him. Midsummer weather – the noonday heat lowered above the terrace and the garden. The smoke of his cigar moved upward languidly.

His head felt heavy, as though it were filled with liquid lead. Every time he moved or turned his head the weight shifted. He wanted to shed his coat and boots and sleep, but he could not go to his room for a nap. There Rabe would be lying in wait for him, and would insist on bringing up his supposedly important matters. The best thing to do would be to take a blanket somewhere and have a snooze at the farther end of the athletic field, in the tall grass. But that would not do either. In less than an hour they would be driving a mob of recruits out there for afternoon sports. Strick yawned.

He would go to his office and pretend urgent business, forbid visitors, and switch the telephone to his ante-room. The women there would guard his door like so many Cerberuses. Then he would open his collar, sweep aside the papers on his desk, drape his arms on the top of the desk and his head on his arms, and sleep.

Wearily he stood up. He avoided the way that led across the terraces and through the club. With long, slow steps he walked to the headquarters building. He climbed the steps, crossed the ante-room, gave Magda her instructions, and fell into his chair. In a moment he was sound asleep.

A harsh jangle attacked him, lungeing at his face like a big dog looking for some one to play with. He started up, ran his hands over his drowsy face and through his hair, and picked up the receiver. 'Didn't I say I wasn't to be disturbed?'

Madga Tannert's cool, fresh voice said, 'It's very urgent. Inspector Gareis wants to know whether you have received important news. If not you are to ask about it immediately. He is already on his way here.'

'What kind of news, Magda?'

'I don't know. He expressly said I must tell you: important news.'

'Very well.'

What was this all about? What did it mean? Important news? And Gareis was on his way here? Was this the inspector's usual bluff, or what? Could it be something else? Could this be IT? Nonsense. But Gareis was dangerous, a man to be taken seriously. Damned seriously.

Strick glanced automatically at his wrist-watch. It was shortly after three o'clock; he had slept for more than two hours. He went over to the casement window and opened one side of it against the wall, so that it acted as a mirror. The face it reflected was creased and red from resting on his arms, the skin was shiny – the face of a weary man, of a slack, strengthless, idiotic, drunken fool. He turned away, repelled, and dropped back into his chair. There he sat staring into space and tracing from floor to ceiling the angle where the walls met. His gaze lingered on the ceiling for a moment then slid aside down the smooth white surfaces of the walls, across the dusty books, and along the floor to the telephone in front of him. He picked up the receiver.

'General Headquarters.' He waited. The ink-well in front of him was soiled. Glass, dust, dried blue ink glistened metallically on the edges. Finally the operator replied:

'General Headquarters is accepting no calls. All lines are jammed.'

Strick became instantly wide awake, as though he were standing under an icy shower. 'The call is urgent.'

'Even so.' The operator apologized.

'Say I must telephone a report to General Headquarters at once. Party business.'

The operator promised to try her best. There was a succession of humming sounds, brief, hasty buzzes. Finally the General Headquarters answered.

'This is the Rehhausen N.S.G.O. Captain Kessler, please.'

'Kessler is not here.'

'Then his office.'

'I will connect you.'

Captain Kessler's office answered. An excited voice immediately barked into the telephone. 'Is Kessler with you in Rehhausen?'

'Kessler isn't here. What's wrong?'

The voice broke with excitement. 'Everything. Haven't you been informed yet? Attempted assassination of the Fuehrer. A resistance movement is trying to take over. Haven't you received instructions yet? No? Everything is topsy-turvy here. And just at this time Kessler would be running around God knows where. Watch your step. All necessary counter-measures should be taken at once, any possible mutiny of the troops nipped in the bud. You have full responsibility for your district. Are you still listening? If Kessler shows up there tell him to come back at once. Otherwise they'll kill us all here.'

The frenzied voice from Kessler's office was abruptly cut off. The connection was broken, and a succession of buzzes was all that came in on the line, with a low booming in the foreground. The Rehhausen operator broke in. 'You are no longer connected, Lieutenant.'

Strick slowly replaced the receiver on the hook. What now? What was going on, what should be done? He lifted the receiver again. 'Is there no longer any connection with Würzburg?'

'None.'

'With Nuremberg?'

'Also none. All lines except for those within the garrison area are blocked. Shall I call as soon as any one is cleared?'

'Certainly.'

And now what? He did not know, he did not want to know.

Inspector Gareis, bouncy as a rubber ball, with the sly, sad face of a rabbit, skipped cheerfully into the room. His little eyes twinkled at Strick. 'Well, my dear fellow! What do you say now? What have you started?'

Strick invited his lively visitor to sit down. 'Just why have you come here?'

'To watch, Strick. To see you at work.'

'You've certainly been in a hurry.'

'I have. Twenty-five minutes from Würzburg to this room. Not bad. And I have also informed the district leader already. He ought to be at headquarters here at any moment.' Gareis rubbed his hands vigorously as though they were cold. He blinked amiably at Strick. 'Well, what have you done so far?'

'Nothing.'

'You don't mean it!' Gareis froze as if in fright; his hands rested numbly upon one another. 'You can't afford the time. You know what has happned, don't you?'

There was a roaring in Strick's head. His brain laboured like a diesel motor. Do – what shall I do? What does he expect me to have done?

Again Gareis asked, somewhat amazed, 'You know what has happened, don't you?'

'Of course, Gareis. An attempt on the Fuehrer's life.'

'And?'

'Resistance movement at work.'

'Well, what about you?'

'What are you hinting?'

'Hinting? Don't pretend to be an out-and-out idiot, Strick. Things are happening fast everywhere. The first arrests have been made. Some are already hanging. And you sit here like a broody hen on her eggs.'

Strick did not know what attitude to take. 'I see no cause to take any measures here. It's quiet in Rehhausen.'

'Still, Strick. But for how long? Why don't you act? Unless you do you're likely to find yourself stood up against the wall.'

'By whom?'

'By one side or the other. Take your choice.'

'Just what do you want of me, Gareis?'

The little man shrank farther down into his chair. His eyes glinted at Strick, amiable and challenging at once. 'What do I want, you ask? I'll tell you quite frankly: I want to be arrested by you. That's something you always like to do. Kindly avail yourself of my person.'

Strick felt as though a swarm of insects were crawling over his skin. 'Just what have you in mind?' he brought out.

'Briefly, Strick, the following. For weeks I've known that an enormous mess of stew has been cooking. I saw it coming to the boil – all it took was a certain amount of inside information, which I have, and a bit of common sense. This assassination attempt is a risky business, but it may succeed. As soon as it became known things began to pop in Würzburg. My office has two doors – as you might have guessed. They came in after me through one while I popped out of the other. For days my car has been parked outside, ready to go. In other words, I fled. Now, where does a fugitive flee to? To his friends, of course. On the way I sent word to you, so that you could get ready. And here I am.'

Gareis grinned softly to himself.

'And now,' Strick said, without comprehending, 'I am supposed to arrest you?'

'I wish you would,' Gareis said politely. 'You see, Strick, I am pretty sure you are the organizer of the resistance here. I'm somewhat disappointed that you haven't done anything yet. You're wasting a great deal of time – and that augurs badly.'

'But why should I arrest you?'

'A small repayment for my services – that's all. You see, Strick, I personally cannot afford to be involved in any resistance movement – nor in any resistance to the resistance. The chances are fifty-fifty, and you know I always play for safety. So I'm cashing in my credit. You remember I deliberately overlooked the affair of the British captain. Now I'm presenting you with my bill. Lock me up. Take good care of me.'

'And suppose I haven't anything to do with this resistance movement?'

'Save your fairy-tales for somebody else.'

'And suppose I don't want to have anything to do with this resistance movement?'

'Are you ducking out of it?'

'I said suppose.'

Gareis shook his head slowly. He spoke in a low, astonishingly gentle voice. 'You have no choice, Strick. One way or the other today might very well be your last. I'll be completely frank with you. You *must* organize the resistance here. You've expected it – here it is, and now you can act. So go ahead. I won't know what is going on because you'll lock me up. If the resistance succeeds – very well. You'll be able to testify that I've played an essential part in it. If it fails you're done for in any case. You understand, I had to insure myself. There is a whole file on you in my desk, Strick. It contains so much on your anti-Nazi activities here in Rehhausen, including the affair of the British captain, that you would be court-martialled in a minute. So defend yourself, my friend. Get moving. For the moment the uprising fails I will eradicate its leaders – you need have no doubts about that.'

The little man's melancholy face had assumed an expression of utter vacuity. He looked like an idiot child, and was nevertheless one of the slickest eels on the face of the earth. Strick felt the blood rising to his head like water pumped through a fire-hose. His temples pounded, his pulse drummed inside his skull. Suddenly the sensation ebbed away; the blood dropped back as though a valve had been thrown open. He felt an enormous calm, and his brain began working clearly, coldly, with the precision of a fine watch.

'You're right, Gareis. I accept your suggestions. Where do you prefer to be locked up – in the cells of the headquarters guardhouse or in the local Army prison?'

Gareis snorted with satisfaction. 'Here at headquarters, under your personal protection. Keep me out of that Army prison. Anyone who falls into their machinery has a hard time getting out – I know our institutions.'

'You say the district leader is on his way here?'

'I sent for him so you could pick him up. He'll probably be in the colonel's office, so you can kill two birds with one stone. But please keep those two out of my cell. I intend to work. I'll be working out escape routes in the event of the resistance failing.'

Strick picked up the receiver. 'Operator? This is Lieutenant Strick. As the commandant's deputy I am issuing the following orders. All telephone communication is to be cut off immediately. From now on no more calls will be accepted, no more transmitted, through Rehhausen. Not a single one. I alone will authorize any exceptions. Nobody else. Nobody. Who is in charge at the exchange today? . . . Good – I am making you personally responsible for absolute obedience to these orders. Lieutenant Rabe, Corporal Vogel, and Herr Tannert are to report to my office at once – Herr Tannert is somewhere about the barracks putting up posters. At once.' He hung up the receiver.

'Now then,' Gareis remarked contentedly, 'you're beginning. Very good. The first measures are fine. Banning all communications creates helplessness. Nobody can get together with anyone else to oppose you. Splendid.' He rose. 'Incidentally, Strick, I did not hear the names you just mentioned. Keep one more thing in mind – the leadership principle is ideally suited for this situation. Barricade yourself behind a wall of opaque glass. Take the whole business into your hands alone. Simply send out your orders. But make sure your orders have a good foundation, even if you have to resort to some crude trick to make it sound logical that you're entitled to issue all orders.'

Strick greedily drank in Gareis's suggestions. 'Thanks very much, Gareis,' he said.

'If the affair goes amiss, Strick, it's always better for one or two to hang for it than two dozen. Right?'

That too was quite clear.

Gareis felt his collar and fingered his dark blue tie. 'One more thing: it's a tried-and-true principle to hide bloody work behind fine phrases. And remember the effect of shock. After all the splendid work you've been doing here every one thinks you're a model Nazi. If you suddenly set up as something else lengthy explanations will be needed. But is it absolutely necessary for you to appear as anything else? Pretend you want to defend National Socialism, and in doing it lock up all the Nazis.'

'Work with me, Gareis,' Strick offered impulsively.

Gareis waved the offer aside. 'I'd rather not, Strick. Show what you can do. But, if that isn't good enough, I'll get my chance to show my stuff. And then, you can take my word for it, no one will be safe who even so much as breathed the same air with an oppositionist.'

'Very well,' Strick said. 'As you like. I am in your debt.'

Gareis bowed ironically. 'May I request that I should be shown to my cell. While you're about it I suggest you have the barracks sealed off, the guard reinforced, of course, and placed under your personal orders.'

'Any other suggestions, Gareis?'

'Just one. Don't waste so much time blabbing. You've lost a good fifteen minutes on me. Just think of all you could have done in that time!'

The barracks was surrounded, the guard reinforced. The matter had been arranged without any difficulty at all. An order was given, and it was carried out. That was all there was to it. Orders and the execution of orders have been part and parcel of life in Germany for the past several centuries.

Three out of ten cells in the guardhouse were occupied. That would do for a start. And in one of these ten cells sat Inspector Gareis, drawing communications lines, curves, and circles on his excellent map. A pair of parallel arrowed lines ran in the direction of Switzerland. Beside him lay time-tables and special regional maps. Gareis was playing his favourite game: What would I do if—? His imagination coursed through all the possibilities. His brain worked like the minds of the prey whom he was accustomed to hunt. That was his method.

In front of the N.S.G.O.'s office waited the special armed group which had been set up days before and which was now to start functioning for the first time. The sergeant in charge was standing dreamily at a window. Two men were priming hand-grenades. One was testing the slide of a machine-gun. The other seven were sitting on a bench in the corridor or leaning against the walls. Their faces were expressionless, for they were on duty. They had been ordered to come here; they would be ordered to go somewhere else. Until that happened they waited. What their orders would be was a matter of indifference to them.

In the office Strick was making hasty notes on a writing-pad. He lifted the receiver. 'Hello? . . . Have you informed Lieutenant Rabe? . . . Coming? Good. . . . And Herr Tannert? Also coming? Fine. But where is Vogel? . . . You don't know. Search for Vogel everywhere.' He laid down the receiver and completed his notes.

Lieutenant Rabe came striding in. 'What's going on, Strick? Down at communications they're behaving as though the revolution has broken out.'

'That's just about the size of it. Sit down, Rabe – or stand if you like. I've just had a crucial message over the telephone.'

Rabe sat down slowly. 'Yes?'

Strick spoke carefully and distinctly. 'There has been an attempt to assassinate Hitler. The outcome is unknown. A resistance movement is trying to seize power.' And then, in even more measured and distinct tones, he said, 'This is the hour, and I do not wish to shirk it.'

Rabe straightened up, his youthful face radiating eagerness. He breathed deeply and gave Strick a long, challenging look.

'Then this is the decision,' he said.
'Yes.'
Resolutely Rabe snapped to his feet. 'What are we waiting for?' he declared forcefully. He pulled out a sheet of paper, unfolded it with quick, jerky movements, and laid it on the desk in front of Strick. 'Sign that.'
Strick read: order for arrest. It was the usual printed form which Rabe as provost officer customarily filled in. The colonel was the only one in the area who had the legal right to sign such forms. The colonel, and now Strick himself – by virtue of the special authority he had assigned to himself. Everything was therefore quite normal and in order. But in the space reserved for the name of the man to be arrested he saw: Corporal Vogel. And the reason given was: Sedition in the Armed Forces.
Strick's head hunched down between his shoulders, and he blinked up at Rabe. 'Where is Vogel?' he said menacingly.
'Locked up since yesterday.'
Strick stared into space, sagging suddenly with utter weariness. There was sorrow in his voice when he spoke. 'My God, Rabe, I always thought you were the one man here it was really worth trying to save. Men like you, I thought, would be clear-sighted where we had been muddled. I always imagined that some day, when the job was done, I could step aside and make room for your kind. I'm tired, Rabe, like so many others. There are thousands like me who have been worn down between the cog-wheels of these times. We're the expendables – all we're fit for is to settle accounts roughly. But I placed my hopes in men like you, Rabe. You're the way I was before this war began. You've kept your hands clean, and your mind clean. You've made mistakes, of course, mistakes are human, and the mistakes a decent person makes are always forgivable. It's on your kind of person that we ultimately depend. Don't stare at me with that innocent-lamb look, Rabe. I honestly tried to show you what a filthy mess this world is. If all that's happened here hasn't wakened you up yet – what ever will?'
He looked at Rabe reproachfully, with disappointment and a touch of anger. Rabe smiled faintly, almost modestly, as if he were apologizing for the misunderstanding. 'I think,' he said, 'we've been talking around the matter too much. What counts now is action. Why are you delaying? What shall I do?'
Strick took a deep breath, and expelled the air as though he were throwing down a burden. 'I'm an idiot,' he said. He looked

at Rabe, and Rabe looked at him. Both men smiled, and Strick nodded briefly. Then he looked down again at the paper on his desk. 'Why this order for Vogel's arrest?'

'A sudden inspiration. Vogel agreed to it. I've been trying all day to talk to you about it. I thought of it as a kind of insurance. After all, there's no knowing what is coming or how things will turn out. This way we classify Vogel as your opponent. If everything goes well we can wipe this arrest off the ledger. If things go wrong he might be the only one able to help us.'

'Agreed,' Strick said. 'Order for arrest issued as from the day before yesterday. Arrest took place yesterday. Good.' He signed the document. 'I hope Vogel is comfortable.'

'I've taken very good care of him,' Rabe said. 'He says he feels as though he's been pensioned off. As prearranged, he curses steadily at the N.S.G.O., and has already demanded the Bible and *Mein Kampf*. He keeps going to the toilet with one of them.'

'Excellent,' Strick said.

Rabe was afire with eagerness. 'All right – let's get going. We can divide up the work, Strick.'

'Divide it up? No. You've just called my attention to a possibility which we mustn't overlook. It can turn out badly. We have no way of knowing what will happen in the next few hours. All we know is that we must act. Therefore, the situation is this as far as you're concerned: I have received an order. I alone. What it says and from whom it comes nobody knows, neither you nor Vogel nor Tannert. No one else. I'll take responsibility for everything.'

For a moment Rabe's face softened with admiration and affection. 'Then what shall I do?' he asked.

Strick glanced over his notes. 'You will mobilize all available troops. Refer to special authority issued to me by the commanding general. The major of the training battalion is an obedient soldier; he will make no trouble. Place the barrack troops under his command. I'll prepare him by telephone beforehand. Then pick out a reliable officer and send him to me for instructions about the railway station. Every goods train passing through must be stopped. Any troops on them must be sent here. Turn over command of the flak to the major of the first division. Maybe the man is as steady as he looks.' Strick held out a sheet of paper. 'Here is a list of reliable private soldiers drawn up by Vogel.'

Rabe took the list of names, and read through it swiftly. 'Vogel gave me a larger list last night.'

'So much the better. All ammunition and other materials must be placed in the hands of these men.'

The telephone rang shrilly. Strick lifted the receiver. 'Yes – speaking. I'm coming at once, Colonel. Important news. Please wait for me with Dr. Friedrich.'

'Anything else?' Rabe asked.

'Not at the moment. I'll stay in this building. Keep me constantly informed.'

'Good. I'll be able to locate you.'

As soon as Rabe left the room Strick crossed out four of his notes. He opened the door of the ante-room. 'Please come in, Magda, and bring your typewriter. Ready. Write.'

Magda looked up at him. Strick paced the room, dictating. 'Heading: General Headquarters, and so on. Document number, series, top secret. Put in the heading: The Commanding General. Have you got that?'

The keys hammered against the ribbon, and came down on the platen.

'Now the title: Special Authority. Text: The – give my name, rank, and post – herewith receives, in view of the present emergency, all powers of command – underline "all" – within the garrison area of Headquarters forty-two. In the present emergency his orders take precedence over those of the Commandant. They are to be obeyed instantly and without question.'

Strick stopped pacing, and peered over Magda's shoulder. 'That looks fine. Now the date, from the beginning of this month. Leave plenty of space for a big signature with lots of flourishes. And then: Lieutenant-General. Do you have all that? Good.'

He took the paper, read it, and then signed it energetically. 'There.' He looked round. 'Now we need some kind of rubber stamp, put on so it's indecipherable.' He took the letter-stamp from his desk and banged it down on the paper, holding it at an angle. A wrinkled German eagle surrounded by illegible writing appeared on the sheet. 'That's fine. It always works.'

'Any more of the same?' Magda asked.

'Later, perhaps,' Strick said. 'Now call Geiger at once. Tell him I must speak to him – it's very urgent. Impress that on him. Is your father here yet?'

'He's waiting outside.'

'Then send him in.'

Old Tannert was wearing a broad smile as he came in. 'Looks like overtime today,' he said.

'Possibly until Judgment Day. I take it Magda has told you.'

'She has.'

'You're with us, of course, Herr Tannert. I expected nothing less from you.'

Tannert settled down in a chair. 'Another sign of the low opinion you have of people's intelligence. "I expected nothing less from you." That's endurance jargon, typical Goebbels propaganda. With luck that sort of talk might take in the nine-year-olds in the Hitler Youth. But I can do without it.'

'Talk, talk, all the time. Waste all your time talking. Never mind what happens to the resistance movement.'

'You don't say?' Tannert leaned back, wary and dour. 'So there's a resistance movement. Not started by the generals by any chance?'

'What's the difference who started it?' Strick snapped indignantly. 'Is any one of us a member of the General Staff?'

'You may not be one of the generals, but you're their hireling. You're working for the upholders of fame, honour, and patriotism. The worker works for the capitalists, the soldier for the generals. One group croaks, and the other profits. Herr Strick, I want a different society, but I don't particularly care about getting a new Commander-in-Chief.'

Strick drew back. 'Then you aren't with us?' he concluded coldly.

Tannert shook his head. 'I didn't say that. I merely stipulated that I have no illusions. What you have in mind may mean a step forward. It's still a long way from my goal, but if it brings that goal closer I won't oppose it.'

'But you have little confidence in it?'

Tannert ran his fingers through his hair. 'Practically no confidence at all. I admit that frankly. To my mind it isn't radical enough; there's too much dilettantism about it and too little preparation. The officers have been stewing for years. They've had about all they can stand, so they've blown up. But it's all improvised, all half-baked. This isn't a plan that has grown organically. This isn't a clash of principles – at most it means a shuffle of the men who give the orders.'

'And yet you'll go along with it anyhow?'

'Of course. Our officers' corps is an evil, but Hitler is a still greater evil. The choice between the two isn't hard for me. As I said, it's a step in the right direction.'

Strick stood up in front of Tannert. 'I don't like doing things by halves. I plan to act on the assumption that the entire future is at stake.'

'So long as you don't say the next thousand years. If you do I'll walk out.'

Strick went to his desk, and stooped over his notes. 'You, Herr Tannert, take over the headquarters communications exchange. Cut off all unessential conversations within the area, and give our calls precedence. Listen in on everything, and only let through the calls that help us. I myself will be either here or in the colonel's office. All right?'

'Have you your list of victims ready?'

Strick did not understand.

'I mean, do you know whom you have to liquidate? You need a clear field of operations. If there are any people in this area who can shoot back it will mean large-scale bloodshed. You know that.'

'Leave that to me, Herr Tannert. During the first few hours I will use whatever means are necessary. Any and all. Just one hour's time is all I need. If I have that, and if I use that to the full, I will have everything firmly in hand. Afterwards let them come; we will be able to stand a small private war. If it turns out badly – then I've just had bad luck. And I'll step down, quite alone, without any guard of honour. And the next time the occasion arises you will try it again. Again and again, until it finally works. Do you see all that clearly, Herr Tannert?'

Captain Geiger was the next visitor. He rolled in like a cannon-ball. 'Come along to the Old Man's office, Strick. He's cursing you up and down, sitting at his desk and ranting like a special edition of the *Voelkischer Beobachter*. Dr. Friedrich sits wagging his head and tail and repeating, "The honour of the Party." If you don't come soon they'll nail up your coffin. Theoretically they've already done it.'

Strick came straight to the point. Without preamble he presented the special authoritization that he and Magda had prepared a few minutes before. 'Would you kindly take note of this, Captain Geiger.'

Geiger dropped his head over the sheet of paper. He read it

carefully, then looked up with a frown of dismay. 'A palace revolution? Heroic attempt at self-slaughter? Or just a dress rehearsal?'

Strick folded his authorization carelessly. 'We don't have any definite information. There has been an attempted assassination of the Fuehrer. Nothing more is known. All I have to go by are the directives I have received.'

The telephone shrilled again. 'Yes? Tannert? A call for the district leader? Take it there. Say you will be able to relay it shortly. Give me the message.' He dropped the receiver back on the hook.

Geiger swelled like a sponge. 'Extensive shifts of personnel in all sectors, eh?' he asked premonitorily.

'Very extensive.' Strick spoke in his most formal tone. 'You understand, Captain, that it pains me extremely to transmit orders to you, since you are senior to me. But my action is based, as you know, upon specific instructions from the commanding general.'

Geiger responded with the suggestion of a bow. Then he almost snapped to attention, and in the brisk manner of the disciplined soldier replied, 'Don't mention it, Herr Strick.'

Strick intoned, as if he were merely transmitting orders from above: 'I am required to assemble the most reliable officers in the garrison and keep them in a state of constant preparedness. I am convinced that I can rely upon you.'

Captain Geiger clicked his heels, a brief, sharp tap. Geiger was ready.

'I am turning the barracks over to you, Captain. Mobilize your men at the guardroom. Equipment as provided for action against enemy parachute troops. Triple the barrack guards. Lieutenant Rabe is already alarming all the other troops within the garrison area. Here at the barracks let in anyone who wishes to enter, but let out no one without a special order from me. In addition you will be entrusted with arresting and guarding the men I order to be placed in protective custody. Inspector Gareis and Corporal Vogel are already in custody. We are going to add to the collection. Come along.'

Strick reached for his holster, took out his revolver, loaded it, and set the safety-catch. Then he placed the gun in his trousers pocket. He opened the door to the corridor. The sergeant in charge of the special squad looked up dutifully. 'One corporal and four men equipped with sub-machine-guns and rifles will accompany us,' Strick said. 'Load, keep at safe. The others will wait here for further orders.'

The sergeant relayed the instructions. In fifteen seconds a corporal and four men were ready to go. The rifle-breech mechanisms snapped, the safety-catches clicked. The men donned their steel helmets, thrust their chins through the chin-strap, and crammed their caps into their pockets.

Strick led the way, with Geiger at his side. The corporal with his tommy-gun followed, and behind came the four men with rifles clamped under their arms. Strick and Geiger stepped softly; the soldiers' hobnailed boots rasped over the paving of the corridor. A gun-barrel clanked against a steel helmet. 'Idiot,' an irritable voice said. Sidearms slapped against rifle butts in the rhythm of the march. With long strides they moved towards the Commandant's office.

CHAPTER FOURTEEN

THE action went through without a hitch. Lieutenant Rabe, tense as a strung bow throughout, encountered not the slightest obstacle. The headquarters company had been under the command of a sergeant, Captain Wolf II having gone out into the country to make purchases. Rabe had sounded the alarm, and gathered the men on the parade-ground. They had trotted up and stood together as indifferently as a herd of sheep while he addressed them. He said a few words about an emergency and the necessity for special measures. They stared dully at him; then they went to their barracks and put on their battle kit. Boots, steel helmets, cartridge-belts, bayonets, rifles. The order was given, the order was carried out.

They were to receive ammunition, thirty rounds each. They received it. They were to form action groups, a corporal and six men in each group. They formed them. They were to return to their rooms and remain in readiness to respond to the alarm. They remained in readiness. The order was carried out; that was all there was to it.

And that was really all. Orders are orders. If the order was given to fall in they fell in. If the order was: spread out, occupy the barrack fence at intervals of two yards, dig in – that order would be carried out precisely. If the order were to concentrate fire upon every approaching automobile they would pump every car as full of holes as an old tin can. And if they were marched up to face a number of men who stood with a wall behind them, and were ordered to fire – their guns would crash in unison, and the men who faced them would drop to the ground.

The evidence of how easy it was burned inside Rabe. Good God, what an apparatus for killing! Everything was possible. There was a good chance, for example, that the resistance movement in Würzburg would get nowhere. In that case Strick would only have to load three trucks with soldiers, machine-guns, and ammunition and give the order: Take General Headquarters in Würzburg. And the men would take it – because orders were orders.

Major Wittkopf, the commander of the training battalion, was already waiting for Lieutenant Rabe. Strick had got him on the telephone and prepared him. Wittkopf heard: 'The commanding general has ordered . . .' And Wittkopf poured himself a couple of glasses of brandy for a pick-me-up. His pink face breathed a faint fragrance of alcohol; he seemed galvanized into life.

'What's happened?' he demanded.

'Attempt on the Fuehrer's life,' Rabe snapped out. 'Immediate readiness for action. Await further orders.'

For a disciplined soldier of Major Wittkopf's calibre, further questions were superfluous. He would show this young lieutenant how things were done in his battalion. 'Alarm!' he called out. The major's adjutant pressed all the buttons on his desk. A wave of movement surged through the entire training-battalion area. 'I've rehearsed this many times,' the major declared proudly. 'Alarm drills are part of my training course. You'll see, in twenty minutes the entire battalion will be ready to march.'

The training battalion buildings were instantly transformed. Lectures and drills stopped. Recruits raced off at the double to their quarters. Even the clerks and the fatigue-squads put on speed.

The commander, Major Wittkopf, took his stand in the large square between his barracks to check on the general alacrity. He had taken out his watch, and was standing with an air of expectancy, his eye on the minute-hand of the watch. Ten minutes had already passed. In a moment the first squads would be lining up. He would give the very first squad an encouraging look and announce the time it had taken. And he would pounce upon the last with a public reproof.

Uniformed men burst out of the doors, trailing their rifles, buckling their belts or buttoning their uniforms as they ran. They lined up in a hollow square, the first company on the major's left, the second and third in front of him, the fourth on his right. Corporals and sergeants shouted, officers growled a single refrain: 'Hurry up, hurry up, hurry up!'

In sixteen minutes the major benevolently accepted the report of the third company. One minute later, to his gratification, the first company reported. The fourth company arrived a full three minutes later, and twenty-two minutes after the alarm had been given the major, swelling with pride, saw his entire battalion standing before him, awaiting his commands. He stood like a totem pole, expanding his chest at the expense of his paunch. His right leg, bearing his weight, was rigid, his left leg bent slightly forward to one side, in the posture once favoured by General Ludendorff. He smiled proudly at Lieutenant Rabe, and turned to his battalion.

'Men,' he announced, 'we are face to face with a great decision. It is possible that we may be called into action. I expect every man to do his duty, if necessary, to the last. Remember your oath of allegiance! Forty rounds of live ammunition are to be distributed to each man. Squad leaders stay with their squads. Platoon leaders post themselves in the corridors. Clerks to be on duty day and night. All officers report to me at once for orders. Companies fall out, and begin distribution of ammunition.'

The square emptied, the officers gathered round their commander. The major spoke a few more words about decision, readiness, and duty. Then he said to Rabe, 'Report that we are ready for action.'

Lieutenant Strick led the way up the steps to the Commandant's office. Over his shoulder he called, 'Corporal.'

The corporal came forward up the stairs to him.

'Corporal,' Strick said, 'I am relying completely upon you.'

'Of course,' the corporal said.

'What did you say?'

'Of course, sir.'

'Very well, Corporal. Captain Geiger here will inform you that any forthcoming action is being undertaken on written orders from the commanding general.'

'Yes, sir.'

'You will therefore promptly carry out my orders to the letter.'

'Yes, sir.'

The corporal radiated calm confidence. He was sure he would carry it off. He had no idea what was going to be asked of him, but he new what could be expected of him – tacit obedience to the order of the commanding general.

Strick and his companions strode through the outer office and through Sergeant Demuth's anteroom. Demuth sprang to his feet and opened the door to the adjutant's room. 'Take your pistol off safety,' Strick said to Geiger.

Geiger, his face the colour of cheese, could not control his trembling hands. He tried to master his agitation by taking deep, silent breaths. The soldiers with them watched expressionlessly;

they stood rigid as blocks of stone. The corporal was considerate enough to overlook Geiger's embarrassing condition.

'I hope you can stand above this situation,' Strick said to Geiger, in a low voice. 'This has to be done, Geiger. I'm sorry about it myself, but it can't be helped. I must obey the commanding general's orders. But don't worry. All the instructions I have received are quite clear, and I am in possession of evidence which makes this step completely logical.'

Geiger's lungs were working like a bellows.

'You wait here for the present, Corporal,' Strick said. 'Be prepared to make an arrest. And no ceremony afterwards: take 'em by the collar and down to the cell. I want to be able to report to the commanding general that I've done the job thoroughly.'

The corporal saluted, with a trace of a reassuring grin. The soldiers came to attention in imitation of their corporal. Strick gestured to them to stand at ease. Then he opened the door to the colonel's waiting-room. The room was quite deserted – Eri was probably with the colonel. With Geiger close at his heels Strick strode across the room and pushed open the door to the Commandant's private office.

The colonel looked up at him, his eyes wide with sternness, his lips tightly compressed. The district leader peered up out of his chair like a small rodent. Eri's eyes sparkled with excitement, and she shrank back against the wall to get a better view of the entire scene.

There was a faint veil of smoke in the room. A fair July afternoon blinked tiredly in through the window. A lazy sun shone down upon the river.

The colonel, unfurling to his full height, rose to his feet slowly. 'What does all this mean, Strick?' he demanded. 'There's an unusual stir throughout the garrison. Communications are blocked. Your office informs me you've received important messages. Inspector Gareis telephoned Dr. Friedrich and suggested he come to see me because of certain unusual events which he didn't specify. For the past twenty minutes I've been requesting you to come here in vain. Will you kindly explain just what is going on.'

From his seat the district leader lashed out at Strick. 'I suppose you're planning more changes in this district? My God, man, can't you ever relax? Must you do nothing but make fresh difficulties?'

'Unfortunately, yes, Doctor. This time enormous ones.'

Slowly the colonel's face began to flush. He opened his mouth. Before he could speak Strick said: 'There has been an attempt on the Fuehrer's life. A revolt is expected. I have received detailed orders from General Headquarters and full authority to carry out those orders by any and all means.'

The colonel slowly closed his mouth again, while his left hand groped for support. The district leader's face took on the doleful expression of a mule. Eri's red tongue licked swiftly over her red lips, and her eyes sparkled.

Colonel Mueller had at last found the arm of the chair, and was clinging desperately to it. 'What does that mean?' he said between his teeth.

Strick drew the revolver from his pocket as casually as if it were a house key. 'What it means you will now find out – Mueller.' The colonel twitched almost imperceptibly at the rudeness of 'Mueller'. Then he straightened up, and looked scornful. His mind was working like an adding-machine.

Fingering his gun, Strick explained dryly, 'I have evidence showing that you not only have supported criminal plans, Mueller, but have actually worked out some of your own.'

The colonel fought down a brief gust of amusement. In an almost toneless voice he said, 'You must be crazy, Strick. Put that gun away and be sensible. You've gone completely off your head.'

Dr. Friedrich sprang up as though a bayonet had been thrust through the seat of his chair. He pounded his knuckles on the colonel's desk, and declared in the resounding tones he used at public meetings: 'In my capacity of District Leader of the National Socialist Party I demand that you rescind this order at once.'

With gentle emphasis Strick informed him, 'You have no right to give me orders, Doctor.'

Dr. Friedrich roared as though he were shouting down an opponent on the platform: 'I protest. I shall appeal to the Gauleiter at once.'

'You have no time to do that,' Strick said. 'You are an intimate friend of this man.' He pointed the revolver at Colonel Mueller. 'I have every reason to suspect that you are an accomplice of his. Your present behaviour is additional evidence of that.'

'What the devil's the matter with you?' the colonel shouted. 'You don't know what you're doing.'

Strick turned to Geiger. 'Captain,' he said, 'take these two gentlemen to the detention cells at once. They are to be shown no favours, treated strictly according to regulations. No one to be admitted to see them without my express approval.'

The colonel was icy with rage. His hand clutched the arm of the chair convulsively, his knuckles showing white. His knees shook with nervousness; his thoughts spun round frantically. Strick said in a low, grim tone, 'Don't do anything foolish, Mueller. You ought to know me by now. If it were necessary I wouldn't hesitate for a moment to shoot you down like a dog.'

The safety-catch on his revolver flew back with a snap. The colonel felt drops of cold sweat on his forehead. It was too late now. He should have seen it coming, he should not have waited. He should have taken care of this fellow Strick earlier, ruthlessly, long ago.

Dr. Friedrich did not realize that the colonel had already made his decision, that he had yielded – for the present, at least. 'You'll pay for this, Strick,' the district leader stormed. 'This is an outright violation of the law.'

Strick laughed curtly, and stepped aside for Geiger. Geiger felt the approach of his great moment. Here was a classic German tragedy. Culture, his hobby! Shades of Schiller's Posa addressing Don Carlos. It was a noble part, and he would play it nobly. His face a mask of inexorability, he bowed briefly. 'Gentlemen,' he said, 'I must request you to follow me.'

Strick opened the door. 'Guard!' he called. The corporal came in carrying his sub-machine-gun. 'Take charge of these two prisoners and conduct them to the detention cells. Fire immediately if they attempt to escape.'

'Jawohl, Lieutenant,' the corporal said, struggling to conceal his grin of pleasure. The guards formed a square round the prisoners.

Geiger led the way, his elastic stride emphasizing his determination to sweep aside every obstacle. Then came Mueller and Friedrich, their faces so contorted that they scarcely looked human. The corporal followed them, his sub-machine-gun held ready, and behind him were the last two guards. Their footsteps thundered down the stairs, re-echoed from the walls and faded away in the corridors. Strick snapped his revolver back to safety, and slid it into his trousers pocket. A few hundred more men like himself, he thought, and the whole Army could be wrung out like a pair of socks that had just been washed.

Eri approached him. Her eyes searched his face. His own eyes were squinted tight together, as though he wished to see only a small segment of the world, and his face was expressionless. 'Have you considered everything carefully?' Eri asked.

'There isn't anything more to consider at this point,' Strick said.

The uprising coursed through Rehhausen like a river pouring with full force into a new bed that has been blasted open for it. The guards had been alarmed. The training battalion was ready for action. The prison-camp guards had been placed on emergency footing. In the Army prison men were being moved round to make room for new prisoners. But so far there were no new candidates for those empty cells.

Gareis was a jewel. His suggestion that Strick do everything in the name of Nazism had been invaluable. 'National Socialism' was taking over without the slightest trouble. The Party leaders in the town of Rehhausen had received a telephoned order, allegedly from the district leader, instructing them to refrain from all action. Within an hour detachments of soldiers from the garrison would take over the town; Rabe was already working out detailed orders. A thousand men, well equipped with arms and ammunition, were awaiting the word to go into action. The commander of those troops was in direct touch with headquarters – that is, with Strick. Their instructions were quite unequivocal; they were to carry out only those orders that emanated directly from headquarters – that is, Strick.

Strick was trying in vain to get through a call to Nuremberg, where Lieutenant von W. was posted. But he could not reach the lieutenant. Communication with Würzburg was still possible, but very hard to establish. The telephone lines to that city seemed to be covered with sticky pitch. Kessler's office did not respond to his call. Instead a major answered and wanted to know what was going on in Rehhausen. But Strick did not know who the major was, and therefore gave vague replies. The information he received in return was equally obscure. Tannert said that his own private grape-vine reported some pitched battles, but he had no details.

Down at the railway station a very young captain, the infantry officer of the training battalion, had the situation well in hand. He was certainly entering into the spirit of things. Within the span of an hour he had blocked three goods trains. Even before he began he had sent the station commandant to the Army prison, presumably for refusal to obey orders. In the course of the incident the station commandant had apparently had a few ribs smashed – all this on the strength of the authority given to Strick by the commanding general.

To Strick's mild dismay this captain had also already organized a kind of civilian auxiliary. These conscripted civilians were at the moment unloading a munitions train and reloading the boxes of ammunition into commandeered wagons and trucks. Of the thirty-man station detachment, the young captain reported with a certain pride, twelve were steadily employed rounding up more civilian auxiliaries. Another twelve were supervising the unloading of the train. The rest were ready for instant action. He wished to request reinforcements.

The second goods train, he informed Strick, had been sent to a siding. It contained spare parts which could not be used for the present action. But the third blocked train had been full of soldiers on leave. He had placed them under the command of the highest-ranking officer, and they would probably be at the barracks within twenty minutes. There, he thought, they ought to be formed into squads and ordered to stand ready for eventual action.

Strick ordered Major Wittkopf to assemble these soldiers at the gymnasium, sift them out, supply them with arms, and place them under the command of a suitable officer. Major Wittkopf was overjoyed and honoured at being entrusted with so important a task. He promised to do his best. He received the news of the colonel's arrest with regrets, but remarked that he had seen it coming. His private thoughts were spiteful. Arrogant bastard, that Mueller, capable of anything.

In short, the shutters were coming down fast. Rehhausen was well in hand.

Vogel was enjoying himself royally. He was reading *Mein Kampf* for the first time – and finding it wonderful entertainment. *Mein Kampf* was the official reading matter for men under detention, convicts, and the inmates of penitentiaries. Along with the Bible, of course – but Vogel had read that before.

Vogel also had a carton filled with food tucked away under his bed. Lieutenant Rabe had supplied him well. At first Rabe had tried to keep him down to the meagre regulation rations, but Vogel had made it clear that he was not sitting in this cell in order to practise a strict reducing diet. Whereupon Rabe had obligingly tripled the portion. Vogel was not far wrong in his assumption that he was now doing the eating for both Rabe and Strick; they were too busy to think about food.

Vogel had come to the point in his reading where the text spoke of 'the little gang leader Hitler' – so Adolf called himself before he became a big gang leader. The child's love of games had lived on in the moustached adult, at any rate. The only difference was that the marbles he had played with as a boy were now bombs.

The door to Vogel's cell – it was the largest cell in the building – opened. Vogel blinked at the heavily armed guard. A little afternoon sport, eh?

Through the door stepped Colonel Mueller and District Leader Friedrich. Well, well – very important persons! Was he going to be the object of an inspection? But the door slammed shut again behind the two men. A cloud of dust puffed into the air. Bolts rattled loudly. The colonel and the district leader still stood, embarrassed and ill at ease, near the cell door, like a pair of frightened rabbits which have wandered into a dance-hall.

'Damned mess,' the colonel spat. The district leader ran his snow-white handkerchief over his face, rubbing hard as though he wanted to take the skin off. Vogel had sat up, keeping his place in *Mein Kampf* with his forefinger, and was looking at his cell-mates with keen interest.

'I must sit down,' the district leader said wearily, as though he had just finished a five-mile run. Vogel readily made room for him.

'What are you doing in this hole, Vogel?' the colonel asked.

Vogel felt a strong impulse to counter with, 'What are you doing here, Mueller,' but he managed to get a grip on himself.

'Gaoled, sir,' he said humbly.

'So I see. Since when?'

'Since yesterday.'

'And who ordered it?'

'Lieutenant Strick, sir.'

'Aha,' the colonel said. And the district leader repeated, 'Aha!'

The colonel sat down on the bed beside Dr. Friedrich. He gazed at the faded floor, blinked at the greyish-white walls, and took snorting, regular breaths. Vogel was looking intensely respectful and ready to spring into action at command. But the colonel only examined the polish of his riding-boots, the cleanliness of his finger-nails, and murmured, 'Yes, yes.' After a while he looked up again and asked, 'For what reason have you been locked up?'

'Politics, sir.'

'Aha,' the district leader said again.

'Explain that more fully, Vogel,' Muller ordered, as if he were still sitting behind his desk.

'Explain it, sir?'

'Yes.'

Vogel appeared to be fumbling for the switch that would turn on his brain mechanism. After a pause he blurted out, 'I am a soldier of the Fuehrer, sir.'

The colonel nodded. That much he knew. 'Go on.'

'That's really all there is to it, sir. You see, Lieutenant Strick is no National Socialist.'

At this the district leader nodded emphatically several times; he had been convinced of that himself.

'What leads you to that conclusion?' the colonel asked.

Vogel radiated loyalty and integrity. 'It's easy to see that, sir. He gives himself away every time he lectures. And otherwise, too, he lays it on very thick. Makes all kinds of nasty remarks, and the things he has hinted in public – before the whole garrison, so to speak – are sheer treason. That kind of thing is an outrage to a good National Socialist, sir. Don't you agree, Dr. Friedrich? A man has to fight back against that sort of thing; you can't go on swallowing it. And so I said plainly what I thought of him. I wanted to write a detailed report on him. Lieutenant Rabe advised me to. Lieutenant Rabe saw through the man right away, he's always been against him. But before I could put a spoke in Strick's wheel somebody informed on me, so he put me behind bars.'

'He gets rid of his opponents,' the district leader said bitterly.

'A normal thing to do, after all,' the colonel remarked reflectively. 'We ourselves should have applied the same method – but we were far too slow.'

'I kept warning you, Colonel. If you had listened to me we shouldn't be sitting here now.'

'Don't talk rot, Friedrich. Whenever I hear the word "if" I want to retch.'

'If you want to go out to the latrine, sir,' Vogel said helpfully, 'you have to give two short rings.'

But the two others fell into an embittered silence. At last the district leader asked, 'How long do you think this will go on, Colonel?'

'I don't know, Friedrich. You'll have to ask Strick.'

'The error will soon be cleared up. After all, it's just a mistake, Colonel. Strick has only to ask the gauleiter, or Kessler, and they'll tell him that it's absurd to suspect us. The Gauleiter thinks a great deal of me. And I will vouch for you unconditionally, Colonel. That fellow Strick will pay for this abuse of his authority. Such men have no right to lay hands upon Party leaders.'

The colonel gaped. The district leader's persistent idiocy infuriated him. 'Good Lord,' he exploded, 'you mean to say you still don't realize what is going on here? An attempt on our Fuehrer's life! A resistance movement trying to take control. Do you really believe this man Strick is working against the resistance movement and for the Fuehrer? You certainly aren't very smart. He knows what he's doing when he has us arrested. He's getting the most forceful National Socialists – you and me – out of the way. Do you realize what that means? If his party wins we may well end with a rope round our necks.'

The district leader was stunned. His collar felt unbearably tight. Vogel looked at him with unconcealed concern.

'You mean this isn't a mistake on Strick's part?'

'Not a chance of it.'

'But then – if Kessler—'

'Don't mention Kessler to me again! Who knows where he is? Perhaps he's already stretched out in front of some wall in Würzburg with a dozen bullets through his head. If this whole resistance business doesn't collapse in time they'll manufacture soap out of our bodies.'

'That's the way it is,' Vogel said, in a solemn tone of deep conviction. 'But I fear the worst. Nobody listens to us at all.'

Strick still had no clear conception of what was going on in Würzburg. He could not get in touch with any of the other garrison headquarters. In the Rehhausen area itself there was an expectant hush. There was nothing he could do but wait – wait and be ready.

'What can possibly happen now?' Magda asked. She was sitting in Strick's office. Strick himself stood at the window, looking out. There were double guards at the barrack gate, patrols marching up and down along the fence. A machine-gun was posted on the roof of the guardroom, from where it commanded the street. Rehhausen, down below, looked as if it were taking an afternoon nap. The railway station was a hive of activity, but otherwise there was quiet. A quiet full of suspense.

'What now?' Strick pressed his palm against his forehead. 'We must wait, Magda. Just wait. We must anticipate difficulties, meet opposition, keep our ears sharpened to hear whether something is approaching us or withdrawing from us.'

'And then?'

'You mean later on, Magda?'

'Yes. When all this is over. What happens then?'

Strick was tired. He stared dully into space. The people and the landscape down below seemed to be hidden behind heavy veils. The whole world was a blinding, flickering brightness, a sudden, snow-white glowing, as though he were standing inside the core of an explosion. 'I don't know,' he said tonelessly. 'I don't dare to hope for anything any more.'

'And yet you're going ahead with it anyway?'

Strick shrugged. 'Why do you love one man and feel repelled by another? Why do you call one thing justice and another crime? Those are simply the things one does.'

'You make decisions very easy for yourself,' Magda said.

'What do you expect me to do? Am I to grind out profound thoughts, sit with puckered forehead in all the corners of life, meditate endlessly, and nod my hollow skull gravely and pretend I knew it all before, I saw it coming, and nothing in the world can possibly shock me any more? It's simply this, Magda: those brown-shirted and black-shirted scum sicken me. That's all there is to it. I have no other reason for acting the way I do. And, I assure you, this reason is enough for me.'

'What about your ideals? The better life, the finer life that must come after all this?'

'A life of beauty and dignity? In this sewer that the West has become? Is it enough to blow out a smoky, ill-smelling paraffin lamp for you to say, "Day has come"? There's no use talking about such things, Magda. Just because we extinguish what we have – that doesn't mean that the dawn is here already. And all I can do is destroy. That is what I've been taught, and now I'm showing them how well I've learned it. People like you must do the rest.'

'Why do you refuse to look beyond the moment?'

'For the past five years I have begun every day with the

thought that next day I might no longer be here, that I might be lying on some field, burned to a cinder or crushed to pulp – dead like a hero or otherwise, for reasons of State. That's the philosophy our enlightened twentieth century has to offer. I never realized that I wasn't alone in it, that since 1933 millions of human beings have had the same thought every day for four thousand days. Such an idea doesn't leave much room for life. You become spiteful, cold, heartless. You throw all ideals overboard, and no longer believe in yourself or in God. Even love is reduced to a simple function of the body. How can you expect me, Magda, to wish for anything beyond the opportunity to be the executioner of my own judges? Believe me, that alone is worth a man's life – to the last heart-beat.'

Footsteps moved hastily down the corridor. Old Tannert violently burst into Lieutenant Strick's office and stood, breathing heavily, in the doorway. Tense, agonized, he said: 'Kessler – is here.'

It took Strick several moments to grasp what that meant, or what it might mean. 'Where?' he asked coolly.

'At the guardroom,' Tannert reported. 'He's negotiating with Geiger, but through the gate. He doesn't want to come in; his car is standing out there with the engine running.'

'What does he want?'

'He wants to speak to you at once.'

'What is Geiger doing?'

'Squirming, referring to your special authorization.'

Magda said, 'I hope he doesn't say what special authorization he means. If he does Kessler will immediately guess what is going on here.'

'I have no real authority at all,' Strick explained to Tannert.

The telephone jangled. The piercing note suddenly filled the room and rebounded from the walls. Magda answered. 'Yes? . . . No, Lieutenant Strick is not here at the moment. . . . His secretary.'

'Who is calling?' Strick asked.

Magda covered the mouthpiece firmly with her hand. 'Kessler,' she said. Then she spoke into the telephone again. 'I expect him back any moment. . . . Yes, I hear you. . . . Yes, I will give him the message.'

She let the receiver slide slowly out of her hand and stood still in the posture of a frightened deer that has heard shots. 'Kessler has taken command of the garrison,' she said. 'Geiger has accepted his authority and turned the prisoners over to him. Kessler is interrogating them right now. As soon as you come back, he said, telephone him at once. He also requests you not to leave this room. He will look you up here as soon as he is through at the guardroom.'

Lieutenant Rabe rushed into the room, slamming the door behind him. Plaster trickled to the floor. 'You know Kessler is here, don't you? What do we do now?' The muscles in Rabe's face were hard and bunched. 'Well, what do we do now?'

Strick toyed somewhat nervously with a pencil, tapping it against the desk-top and letting his fingers slide down it. 'We might kill him. We might refashion the other's principles by force. We might also make a deal with the colonel. He had something in mind when he let himself be arrested without much of a fuss. Prussian honour can be turned both ways, you know, and the colonel is by no means unwilling to turn it.'

The telephone began ringing steadily. Magda lifted the receiver and listened. Then she said to Strick: 'The line to Würzburg is open again.'

'Get me Kessler's office at once.'

The telephone buzzed in his ear. Würzburg answered. 'Yes, this is Lieutenant Strick. . . . No, Kessler has not been here yet. . . . I see. He wanted to come out here? To see me? I understand. . . . Yes, I'll tell him.'

Strick hung up and said, 'The emergency measures are revoked. The uprising was a small, local affair. Hitler only slightly wounded. Mutiny nipped in the bud. Danger past. What they call the danger is past!'

He leaned against the table, as though for support, his hands dangling limply. Suddenly he recovered his self-control. He took a deep breath, reached into his trousers pocket, and pulled out his revolver. 'Might as well depart with a guard of honour,' he said harshly. 'One shot and a steady hand can produce a grand State funeral.'

Old Tannert gave him a smile that was slightly contemptuous and almost pitying. 'Put your gun away, Lieutenant Strick. Is shooting always the first thing you think of? That never makes an end of things, only an interruption. What worries me is who comes after you. It's well to keep a cool head, Strick, and not only in the firing-line. Courage calls for a lot more than that.' Tannert looked round at Rabe and Magda. 'Don't you think all of us are going to be needed? Or do you think we've saved ourselves up for this one day, for the others to have a cheap victory? Have we saved ourselves up for a ridiculous act of empty heroism? And to demonstrate how beautifully the Gestapo functions?'

'You wait and wait, Tannert, and we're getting older all the time.'

'And we,' Magda said, 'are growing up and learning to understand him.'

'What are you saying!' Old Tannert said. 'Funeral sermons don't wake up the dead. Act, Strick, but act sensibly. You're not alone in the world. You are responsible for the lives of several human beings. At least five. So what are you going to do?'

Strick dropped his revolver on the desk. It hit with a thud, slid along the dry wood a few inches, and lay still, a dead piece of iron. 'Very well,' Strick said. 'You, Rabe, offer your services to Kessler. I want no objections. Act as though you are my opponent. And rest assured that I shall never have loved an enemy as I did you.'

'I understand,' Rabe said. 'I'm supposed to convince Kessler that you alone are guilty. I will try to prove that all the others had nothing to do with the events of today. If they decide to hang you I will stand by passively, and if necessary carry out the sentence myself. That is what you expect of me, isn't it?'

'Exactly.'

'What else?' Tannert asked.

'You, Magda, go back to your office. You, Herr Tannert, for God's sake go on hanging posters. Both of you know nothing. You received orders and carried them out, that's all. You must go on working as if nothing has happened. Do you agree?'

'Strick, old man,' Tannert said, 'if you ever want membership in my group I'll vouch for you. But not without reservations. He has excellent possibilities, I'll say, we ought to try to make something of him. Well, I imagine we'll meet again at Mother Tikke's.'

They went out. Strick stood alone in the room, dwarfed as a rowing-boat on the high seas. A tiny figure in a sum of millions. Tomorrow, perhaps, he would be nothing but a document, a court-martial case. Charged with treason, no doubt. Or what, where would he be?

CHAPTER FIFTEEN

LIEUTENANT STRICK stood alone in his office, leaning forward as though he were listening to the gathering dusk. Round him was silence. From the barrack gate he heard scraps of barked orders. Far down in the valley a church bell rang.

He took a number of papers out of his brief-case and tore off the top sheet of his desk pad. Then he opened a desk drawer, searched briefly, and found a number of passport photographs and photostats. He crumpled them all in his hand and carried them to the window-sill. There he held a match to them. The flame ate crackling through the papers. The paint on the sill singed and formed blisters that swiftly broke. An evil-smelling smoke puffed up into his face.

Strick stood motionless by the fire, waves of heat from the burning papers rising in swift succession into his face. He did not shrink back. Even when he sensed a door being opened softly, cautiously, behind him he did not change his position. He stared into the flickering flame, now already going out. It had burned through all the paper, and was trying in vain to eat into the wood.

The door behind him was closed softly. The catch snapped home with a little click. No more footsteps could be heard, but there was some one else breathing in the room with him. He did not turn round. The fire before him flared up once more and then went out, smoking heavily.

He heard Eri's voice; he felt it in his spine. 'The end seems to be approaching,' she said. 'Who's the loser?'

'Suppose I am?' Strick spoke under his breath, as though he were addressing the still-blistering paint.

Eri did not come forward. She stood with her back against the door, looking at Strick's silhouette framed against the evening sky. His head was lowered, his shoulders hunched, and the window-frame was like a cross behind him. 'What do you expect me to do now?' Eri asked.

Strick took the charred bits of paper and rubbed them between his fingers. 'I have no right to expect anything of you except what you call "being sensible".' He held his hands out to the wind, and let the ashes trickle down into the garden. 'I wanted to make huge winnings with a small stake,' he said. 'The laws of arithmetic were against me.'

Erika's voice became a trifle harder; it rang out like plate glass. 'Whom did you count on? On the officers' corps? All they're good for is carrying out orders. They're not up to defeating National Socialism. They never were and never will be. I know a good cross-section of these officers, and I don't think much of them. I thought you were an exception. I thought you knew what your goal was. I thought you could think straight, and so were superior to all of them. But when it comes to the point you're nothing but an idealist and a visionary. And sooner or later you idealists always get shipwrecked. You dream too much; you're not hard-headed enough.'

Strick let his hands drop to his sides. They were dirty and smelled of smoke. He turned round very slowly, as though he were standing on a turn-table. Erika stood at the other end of the room, twenty feet away from him. Between them lay a dirty, trampled floor, the boards ripped and scratched by the nails of boots, greyed by the dust of the streets which had filtered in, and faded by water and sun.

'I want you to know,' Strick said softly, 'that I – liked you very much.'

Erika closed her eyes briefly. She sucked in her full lips, compressed them into a thin line. At last she said, 'I suppose that is one item in the account you are now going to settle.'

He looked squarely at her, as though to absorb her image fully. 'I am grateful to you for a great deal. It doesn't matter whether it was good or bad; it's there to stay, inside me. I'm almost beginning to recover my courage.'

Erika leaned her head back so that her shining hair touched the faded door-frame. 'What can I answer to that?' she said. 'Do you want me to make this parting easier for you? Do you want me to tell you: girls like myself don't bother our heads trying to understand you men, we take you as you come? If it's not you it will be the colonel. If he gets thrown out another man will come along. There's always some man who lives well, who has the best of it, and he will always want a woman like me. Is that what you want to hear?'

Strick's smile widened. 'It would be a good idea for you to forget me temporarily. I sincerely hope you succeed. You still have a great deal of life before you, and perhaps I've come to the end of the road. Perhaps. It's also possible that this is only a temporary stopping place. Everything is possible.'

'I'm sorry. I placed great hopes in you.'

'I didn't. But perhaps I'll be able to fulfil them some day.'

'And suppose I don't want to call it all off with you?'

He looked at her as though she were a picture, a poster flashing for a fraction of a second some priceless message of wisdom towards him. His gaze slid down Eri's body. The picture of her was as fleeting as though it were projected from a cine-camera. In a moment it was gone. He turned away abruptly, and stared into the gathering night. The evening mist was seething down below in the valley of the Main, swallowing up the houses, moving towards him with its long, clumsy arms. 'One life is enough for us,' he said roughly. 'Please go.'

'You're not forbidding me to come back?'

'Please go,' Strick said sharply.

He heard a footstep come towards him. Then she stopped, as though petrified. He heard a short, clipped, almost inaudible laugh, the suppressed laugh of a woman trying not to betray her joy. 'I think,' Erika said, 'that I have never really known myself. Not until this moment, at any rate.'

He heard the latch click behind him. The door opened, snapped shut, and then he heard her footsteps moving lightly away over the stone floor of the corridor. They faded away, seemed to be gone for ever – but possibly they were leaving only so that they might come back some day. Night was blurring the contours of the mountains, the broad, low, squat mountains. The lattice-work of the barrack fence condensed into an unbroken surface; the barbed wire crowning it grew hazy. Strick murmured under his breath, 'What alternatives we are given in life – to be blind men, martyrs, or murderers. It's been my fate to see things all too clearly, and up to now I've lacked the courage to choose between the other two alternatives. Up to now, up to now.'

Kessler opened the door that led from the guardroom into the square. He pushed it open violently, as if it were an obstacle he were shouldering down. Then for a moment he stood squarely, filling the doorway. He turned casually once more, looked past the colonel and Dr. Friedrich at Rabe, and remarked, 'You are absolutely right about that, Rabe. We'll have to make a clean sweep here.'

Kessler's cold eyes passed on to Vogel, and lingered for a moment on the corporal's sly, sanctimonious face. A cunning lad, Kessler thought; lucky he was on the right side. One of these smart young fellows was more valuable than half a dozen puffed-up heroes with empty heads. Kessler punched out a phrase with the distinctness and force of a steel press: 'You have sound instincts and a good head, Corporal. You manage to see a helluva lot more than certain idiots among your superiors.'

The colonel took a deep breath and restrained himself. The district leader, standing at his side, was nervous and embarrassed. During the past few hours he had endured the most trying difficulty of a life beset with troubles. And this last one was not over yet by any means. Kessler was not the man to make things easier for him.

Gareis, as though nothing at all had happened, was putting in order and numbering a sheaf of papers. Kessler went up to him. 'If a man like yourself lets himself get locked up here it's something I can understand. After all, you're a bloodhound, not' – he flung a quick glance at the colonel – 'not a hero by profession. But now, Gareis, I'm going to give you a trail to follow. You know what that means.'

'If the trail is warm,' Gareis said calmly, 'it means good hunting.'

'All right – let's go.' The words erupted from Kessler in the form of an order that would brook no contradiction. He set himself at the head of a procession that trotted obediently behind him. The colonel, in an attempt to recover face, moved up to Kessler's right side, so that Kessler, as custom prescribed, would be walking on his left. Dr. Friedrich eagerly did his part to restore the normal order of things. He hurried to the colonel's right side, so that the colonel now occupied the central position, as was only fit and proper.

Behind them came Rabe and Gareis, Rabe earnest and resolute, Gareis with an air of indifference that his sparkling slightly closed eyes belied. Vogel, his steel helmet tipped back on his head, a sub-machine-gun tucked like a cane under his arm, was leading the eight-man detachment of guards who, as ever, were ready to obey any command they received.

'I hope,' District Leader Dr. Friedrich said, not without dignity, 'that you will punish this incarceration in the severest manner, Herr Kessler.'

Kessler strode towards the headquarters building, his powerful body stooped slightly forward as though he were preparing to ram head-on any resistance that might arise. He answered spitefully, 'I'm not your governess, Friedrich. To think that you of all people permitted yourself to be locked up here! You, a district leader, a standard bearer of the Party, one of the first members of the Movement, and the devil knows what else – it's ridiculous.'

The colonel saw an opportunity to straighten things out. 'Don't forget, Herr Kessler,' he said, 'that this sort of thing could not have happened except for your own policy. You alone gave Strick the authority he has abused. If you look into the matter it's clear that what happened here could not have happened without your co-operation.'

Kessler stopped abruptly, as though he had run up against a wall. The entire procession behind him also halted precipitately, the marchers almost stumbling over one another. When he replied Kessler's voice had a metallic note. It was an old trick of his, one that he had often practised and that invariably worked well in interrogations.

'Your behaviour simply proved to me how correct were the measures I took. Both of you have acted like a pair of circus clowns. Any washerwoman with a little nerve can wipe the floor with the pair of you.'

The colonel was hurt, but a quarrel with Kessler at this time would be both unwise and undignified. And so he replied prudently. 'We will discuss this matter again some time, Herr Kessler.'

'Possibly before a court-martial,' Kessler answered icily. Then he turned away sharply, and took long strides towards headquarters. The little group trotted after him.

Footsteps rumbled in the corridor. A murmur of voices could be heard, and among them, rising distinctively above them, Kessler's sharp, brassy voice blaring like a bugle. The footsteps came closer, the voices grew louder. The distant rumble became the tramp of approaching feet. Kessler seemed to be entirely in control of the situation. He blared on loudly. Thrusting open the door, he turned to his entourage in the corridor and trumpeted, 'Everybody wait outside for further orders from me.' Then he moved massively into the room.

'So here you are, Strick.' He scrutinized the lieutenant as though he intended to nail him fast with his glance to the desk chair in which Strick was sitting. 'You've taken measures, Strick, which seem to be partly justified by circumstances. I recognize that. But on the other hand you've issued some orders which not only go too far, but seem actually – hm—' He squinted at Strick. Strick regarded him quietly, with an air of friendliness, his hands resting easily on the arms of his chair.

Kessler cleared his throat. 'To look at you sitting like that, Strick, one would almost think your conscience is clear as a babe's. But that's a lot of bunk. When a few crazy Staff officers in Würzburg started playing with their guns I ran over to see Gareis. I had to finish them off without his help, because Gareis was gone. But then I found in Gareis's desk a highly interesting file on you. That is something we'll have to discuss in greater detail.'

Strick's hands gripped the arms of the chair. Kessler threw him a grin of pleasure. He cleared his throat again, more loudly, and opened the door. 'Come in, gentlemen,' he blared into the corridor.

Inspector Gareis, Colonel Mueller, Dr. Friedrich, and Lieutenant Rabe crowded into the room. 'The guard will stay out in the corridor,' Kessler called. 'But you come in, Corporal.' Vogel stalked into the room wearing the expression of a destroying angel. He planted himself in front of the door, and stood there like a statue.

Kessler immediately plunged into his favourite occupation – getting people stirred in to action. 'Herr Rabe, will you please get my office on the phone.' Rabe went silently to the telephone. 'Sit down, Gareis, and start making plans. You too consider the immediate measures you are going to take, Colonel. And you too, Friedrich, if you feel up to it. Is that gun of yours ready for action, Corporal? We may want to shoot a few holes in people.'

Still in his chair, Strick said, 'People, Kessler? People might be you, too.'

Kessler was taken aback. Then he burst into laughter. 'You're not trying to threaten me, are you, Strick? You may be anything, but you're not an absolute idiot. You can see that you're outnumbered here. I don't imagine anyone in this room feels precisely friendly towards you.'

Kessler planted his broad backside on the desk. He fished a chair towards him, and placed his feet on it. 'For the present,' he said with a gentle, scornful intonation, 'I keep asking myself in amazement how the whole thing was possible at all.'

'Does that surprise you?' Strick said. 'The more surprising

thing is that these satellites you've brought in with you are still alive.'

'What do you mean by that?'

'That quite a few people are still alive who have no right to be.'

'Here's your call, Herr Kessler,' Rabe said from the telephone.

With a covert smile Gareis was turning the pages of the 'Slanderous and Trashy Literature', spread out on the table. He rubbed his nose briefly. Corporal Vogel did not bat an eyelash, but there was a faint glimmer in his eye. The colonel and the district leader were standing rigid with disapproval. Kessler went calmly to the telephone. 'This is Chief Storm Leader – er, I mean Captain – Kessler. . . . Yes, report. . . . Oh, I see. I'll come at once.'

He slammed the receiver down on the hook, and looked round with glowing satisfaction. His voice rumbled through the room. 'The boys want to make a *coup d'état* and don't know a damn thing about organization. A bunch of old Army mules behaving like dilettantes. All they know how to do is lose campaigns. *Coup d'état!* We'll make those petrified Prussians win the Final Victory in spite of themsleves.'

Kessler paused to contemplate with pleasure what he had just said. He wore a grin of delight. Sitting down again on the desk, he scrutinized each person in the room in turn. 'Anyone who tries to interfere with us,' he said in a menacingly quiet voice, 'will get kicked in the arse until he vomits up his brains.'

No one said anything. Everybody was looking at Kessler except Gareis, who went on looking through a book as though all this did not concern him at all. 'Isn't that so?' Kessler demanded. 'That's what we'll do, won't we, Corporal?'

'Jawohl,' Vogel responded smartly. 'That's the way it is. Anybody who opposes us is digging his own grave.'

Kessler nodded contentedly. A good man, this corporal – the voice of the people.

Then he snapped out his orders. 'You, Colonel, resume command of headquarters. Call off this whole business. If anyone suspected you I declare the suspicion unfounded. You, Dr. Friedrich, will no doubt find a few things to do. For the present, anyhow, don't let me disturb you in your valuable work. When I consider your behaviour as a Party functionary it becomes evident that you were once an excellent dentist.'

Kessler's broad behind slid off the desk. He straightened his powerful body and looked at Strick keenly. 'As for your behaviour, Lieutenant Strick, I find it – to put it mildly – suspicious.'

'I beg to differ,' Strick said evenly.

'My opinion alone counts here.'

'But for how long, Kessler? Do you really feel so secure?'

Kessler slowly stiffened. 'I thought all along, Strick, that you had only made a few mistakes. But you seem to be quite well aware of what you were doing here.'

'That ought to give you a thing or two to think about, Kessler.'

Kessler said slowly, 'You're crazy, Strick. You've gone off your head completely. You're an enemy of the State.'

Strick, unmoved, replied distinctly: 'But for how much longer, Kessler? Today you declare me an enemy of the State. Tomorrow you will be one. Today I'll hang, tomorrow you.'

'You're a fool,' Kessler said. 'You realize that you've lost, and now you're getting uppish. You think you're preserving your dignity, but it's only megalomania. We'll put you through the mangle like Monday's washing. I myself will conduct the trial against you as soon as I get back. Until I do our brilliantly informed police inspector Gareis will practise his medicine on you. And give him the full dose, Gareis. The fact that you were locked up hasn't done you any harm, Gareis. I imagine it will make you a little tougher. To say the least, I'm amazed that such a thing could happen to you.'

Gareis's small eyes looked dully at Kessler. No matter what he was thinking, Kessler mused, the man would always look like an imbecile. Oh, well. 'I must request you, Strick, to move into quarters where you kindly installed your Commandant and the district leader. Or do you disapprove, Colonel?'

'By no means,' the colonel roared with conviction.

'Moreover, Colonel since you now need a new N.S.G.O., I approve your suggestion and propose Lieutenant Rabe for the post. He was the one who sought out this corporal that Strick jailed. He was the only one, absolutely the only one here, who kept a clear head, who was able to appraise the whole situation, and who helped me a hundred times more than that credulous fool of a captain at the gate, who can't think of anything but how to obey the last orders that somebody gave him. If you're against Strick, which is understandable, you must be for Rabe. Agreed?'

'The Party would certainly endorse this choice,' Dr. Friedrich declared piously. And Colonel Mueller added, 'He has always been opposed to Strick. That certainly is in Rabe's favour.'

'Then you take over from here, Herr Rabe. See to security matters, and restore confidence in the Party leadership.'

Rabe nodded soberly.

'And you, Gareis, jump on our friend Strick. Take him apart and see what makes him tick. I imagine you'll find out a good many interesting things.'

Kessler strode towards the door. 'As for you two,' he said to the colonel and the district leader, 'I would advise you to interfere as little as possible with Lieutenant Rabe's work. Good evening, gentlemen. And Heil Hitler!'

He went out.

'Open the windows,' Gareis said. 'We need fresh air.'

Vogel obligingly opened them wide.

'Well,' the colonel said, rocking on his knees. 'Well.' He looked round at the silent, apparently indifferent, waiting faces of the others in the room. Finally he said, 'Do you still need me, Rabe?'

'Certainly not at the moment, sir.'

'I,' Dr. Friedrich declared benevolently, 'am very glad to see you taking over this important function, Lieutenant Rabe. The Party needs men like you. Difficulties must be overcome.'

'Exactly,' Colonel Mueller said, waving his hand vaguely. 'What always counts is who and what wins in the end. Integrity cannot easily be wiped off the face of the earth. Always remember, Rabe, that we are in Germany. That means that we are serving a nation whose principal virtue is honour.'

'I promise you, Colonel, that I will keep that in mind.'

'That is good, Rabe, my boy. If you need my help or advice in any way we'll be at the club. Come along, Dr. Friedrich.'

'Well,' Inspector Gareis said, shutting the book that he had been reading with interest. 'So there we are. Once more we know which is the side of justice and what we must do to serve it.' He placed his brief-case carefully and ceremoniously on a chair. 'Today I have no more time for any interrogations. We'll take care of that tomorrow, some time during the morning.' He relaxed his foolish-looking face, and rubbed his outspread fingers against his chin.

'Please see to it, Herr Rabe, that the – prisoner is delivered to me. It doesn't matter to me whether you bring him this evening or tonight or even tomorrow morning. I'll leave my brief-case here. I am sure you are the proper person to take care of it. There are some interesting documents in it – routes, time-tables, and suchlike. There's no need for me to lock it up. . . . Oh, yes, and please lend me this book, this one by Tucholsky. Very interesting reading.' He turned to Vogel, who gave him a friendly smile. 'I am also relying upon you, Corporal.'

'You certainly can, Inspector.'

'I'm sure of that,' Gareis said, smiling. He turned to Strick and whispered, 'If I don't see you again, you crook – good luck! Good-bye – you gallows-bird!'

'So we've come to the end,' Strick said.

'There's still a great deal to do,' Rabe pointed out. 'We have to prepare new paybooks, leave passes, and other papers. There isn't much time.'

'Let's get to Mother Tikke's first,' Vogel suggested. 'From there we follow Gareis's escape route towards Constance and on towards Switzerland. Let's hurry so that we can catch the first train. Strick and Vogel are retiring from service in the Armed Forces of Greater Germany. Since I am officially designated the most reliable non-commissioned officer in the garrison, Rabe, you will assign me to transport the prisoner Strick. And he will never arrive. We have decided to take a recuperation leave at the expense of the State. The wheels must roll for the Final Victory!'

'When the time comes we won't hesitate,' Strick said. 'And . . .'

'Long live Germany!' Rabe cried resolutely.

'Germany?' Strick murmured dreamily, as if he were suddenly overwhelmed by the hopelessness of it all. 'Germany?'

'Now, boys,' Vogel bleated, 'don't be sentimental.'

'Germany? Perhaps there'll be something left of her. Let us hope so.'

THE END

THE FAMILY 40p

Leslie Waller

Truly great novels about the Mafia are few and far between. *The Family* is not only the most recent but one of the very, very best. The *New York Times* called it "a jumbo entertainment, full of everything" and drew attention to the book's shattering combination of big business, violence, raw sex, protest and comment on the richest society in the history of the world. It is a dramatic and engrossing story that exposes a new breed of gangster less concerned with strong-arm tactics than with financial manipulation. Woods Palmer, chief executive of America's biggest banking empire, becomes the pawn in an operation of a naked ruthless power that only the Mafia's mighty, complex machine can wield with such effectiveness and shameless brutality.

THE MORNING OF THE MAGICIANS 50p

Louis Pauwels and Jacques Bergier

"Two theories were current in Nazi Germany: the theory of the *frozen world*, and the theory of the *hollow Earth*.

"These constitute two explanations of the world and humanity which link up with tradition: they even affected some of Hitler's military decisions, influenced the course of the war and doubtless contributed to the final catastrophe. It was through his enslavement to these theories, and especially the notion of the sacrificial deluge, that Hitler wished to condemn the entire German race to annihilation."

The incredible yet highly regarded theories of the frozen world and the hollow Earth have never before been expounded in this country. They are two amongst many such theories, including for example man's evolution towards some kind of mutant superman, that have remained secret and hidden in Britain while gaining strong popular support elsewhere. Now a new awareness is growing in our minds, and much of our new understanding we owe to this famous book and its two intrepid authors. Their interpretation of human affairs, very different from that put forward by ordinary historians and commentators on day-to-day events, is much nearer to the unexpressed instincts of the people.